THE TALES OF INSPECTOR LEGRASSE

THE TALES OF INSPECTOR LEGRASSE

BY

H. P. LOVECRAFT

&

C. J. HENDERSON

EDITED WITH AN INTRODUCTION BY

ROBERT M. PRICE

MYTHOS BOOKS LLC

POPLAR BLUFF

MISSOURI

2005

Mythos Books LLC
351 Lake Ridge Road
Poplar Bluff
MO 63901
U. S. A.

WWW.MYTHOSBOOKS.COM

Published by Mythos Books LLC 2005

FIRST EDITION

ISBN 0-9728545-1-7

Set in *Adobe Garamond Pro, Ashley Script* and *Eccentric*.

Adobe Garamond Pro by Adobe Systems Incorporated.
www.adobe.com

Ashley Script and *Eccentric* by Linotype Library.
www.linotype.com

Typesetting, layout and design by PAW.

A mezzotint rendering of John Raymond Legrasse, an Inspector of the New Orleans Police Department. It was taken from a portrait sketch made in 1908, at St. Louis, during an annual meeting of the American Archaeological Society. His attendance at that esteemed gathering caused a sensation. Inspector Legrasse put on view a curious statuette to Society Members in an effort to take advantage of their professional knowledge and get their help in identifying it or its possible origins in relation to an ongoing investigation.

DEDICATION

People come into our lives
Every day.
For a thousand reasons.

Some are worth knowing,
And some aren't.

And then there are those,
The knowing of whom,
Is an honor.

Thus, with that thought in mind
This book is dedicated to:

VINCE SNEED

—C. J. Henderson

CONTENTS

INTRODUCTION

NAME OF A PIG—LORD OF THE FLIES

Aperverse thought occurs to me. Perverse, as most of my thoughts may be judged, but perhaps true nonetheless: what if H. P. Lovecraft's Inspector Legrasse (in "The Call of Cthulhu"), a Malone-clone borrowed from his earlier tale "The Horror at Red Hook", was intended as a kind of homage to (or even a parody of, if you can parody a silly character by making him serious!) Jules de Grandin, phantom-fighter and offspring of Seabury Quinn, a fellow *Weird Tales* contributor? Both of them French investigators of the paranormal, see? I know, HPL was not fond of Quinn's work, despite (or rather more likely because of) the popularity of the latter's work among the WT readership. But we know from "The Lurking Fear" and even implicitly "The Haunter of the Dark" that Lovecraft had a fondness for the basic idea of an occult investigator. Legrasse = De Grandin? Maybe I will meet HPL in a dream and will have the opportunity to ask him. It has happened before.

At any rate, C. J. Henderson has certainly seen the implicit logic of the situation by expanding the role of Legrasse from what we see in "The Call of Cthulhu." As Lovecraft freely admitted, he made no attempt whatever to create believable characters. For him characters were mere plot devices, windows through which the reader may view the unfolding of the action. They are "narrative-men" (Tzvetan Todorov), incarnations of the narrative, as we can see from some of the names of Lovecraft's characters. The protagonist of "The Shadow over Innsmouth" is named (in the story notes) 'Olmstead,' i.e., 'old homestead,' to which he returns. The narrator of "The Call of the Cthulhu," Henry Wayland Thurston, is the man with the thirst for dangerous knowledge, like his uncle George Gammel Angel, now among the angels because of his own ill-starred delving. Thomas Malone stands alone in his opposition to evil. Even narrating characters like Akeley and Wilmarth are personifications of the setting of the story in which they appear since Lovecraft simply borrowed the names from local registers and gravestones in the regions he had visited and then set the stories in.

Though many, even among us sympathetic (okay, sycophantic) to Lovecraft, may think to bemoan this seeming failure, as if the stories, as great as they are, would have been better with solid characterization. But I beg to differ. I think Tom Ligotti has the same sound instinct as Lovecraft when the former refuses to attempt writing horror at novel length, fearing that the only way to do it is to pad the narrative with narrative ballast, filler between the moments of horrific revelation, like a script for a porn flick. What's the point?

Let's just get down to business, shall we? What Ligotti sees about mundane action, Lovecraft saw about (mundane) characterization. It's all just soap opera.

Unless you do what Chris Henderson does and set the weird and horrific action inside the character. As Peter Berger and Thomas Luckmann (*The Social Construction of Reality*) show, integral to our selfhood (our own living "characterization") is our 'cognitive universe,' the culture-derived map of reality we carry around inside our heads and which we use to navigate a course through life. It is our governing set of assumptions and beliefs. This is what is always threatened in Lovecraftian fiction. The impending destruction of the world at the hands of Cthulhu or Wilbur Whateley is symbolic for the destruction of one's worldview, as when Thurston's cherished rationalism has been irretrievably smashed, his anthropocentric cognitive universe debunked. Henderson sees that this is where the action is. Thus for him, Inspector Legrasse, having undergone a major inner revolution in the Louisiana bayou, has become a microcosm of cosmic horror. He capsulizes the Lovecraftian-Copernican revolution. The same is equally true of Henderson's own original occult sleuth Teddy London, and to a lesser degree in Henderson's stories of Anton Zarnak, a Lin Carter character.

"Beelzebub" means "Lord of the Flies," denoting a Philistine oracle god (demonized by later Jewish monotheism) who provided revelation by the insect-like buzzing (which is what the Arabic *al azif* means) of the desert jinn, whispered into the ear of the seer. (Hence also Brian McNaughton's cloud of revelatory flies, "the Host of Ekron," Ekron being one of the great Philistine cities.) In William Golding's great novel Lord of the Flies, the severed and staked pig's head, aswarm with flies, is the demonic totem of the castaway boys, anything but noble savages once the flimsy clothing of civilization is ripped away. It represents the new cognitive universe they are constructing from base instincts. Henderson, as I understand him, believes that all tidy worldviews are precariously poised on the verge of an abyss and so in imminent danger of annihilation. But that is not the only possibility. Horror and the dissolution of the protagonist's worldview (shared with the reader, probably) can equally challenge us to leap off that verge in the direction of transcendence. Henderson's heroes are evolving into supermen to match the terrors they face. They turn the horror against itself in a variety of Nietzscheanism: "Whatever does not kill us makes us stronger." The stories thus reflect a very real spiritual-ethical stance taken by their author, an old friend of mine. Reading them will not kill you, and I hope they will make you stronger.

—*Robert M. Price,*
May, 2005

THE CALL OF CTHULHU

FOUND AMONG THE PAPERS OF
THE LATE FRANCIS WAYLAND THURSTON, OF BOSTON

"Of such great powers or beings there may be conceivably a survival … a survival of a hugely remote period when … consciousness was manifested, perhaps in shapes and forms long since withdrawn before the tide of advancing humanity … forms of which poetry and legend alone have caught a flying memory and called them gods, monsters, mythical beings of all sorts and kinds … "

—Algernon Blackwood

I. THE HORROR IN CLAY

The most merciful thing in the world, I think is the inability of the human mind to correlate all its contents. We live on a placid island of ignorance in the midst of black seas of infinity, and it was not meant that we should voyage far. The sciences, each straining in its own directions, have hitherto harmed us little; but some day the piecing together of disassociated knowledge will open up such terrifying vistas of reality, and of our frightful position therein, that we shall either go mad from the revelation or flee from the deadly light into the peace and safety of a new dark age.

Theosophists have guessed at the awesome grandeur of the cosmic cycle wherein our world and human race form transient incidents. They have hinted at strange survivals in terms which would freeze the blood if not masked by bland optimism. But it is not from them that there came the single glimpse of forbidden aeons which chills me when I think of it and maddens me when I dream of it. That glimpse, like all dread glimpses of truth, flashed out from an accidental piecing together of separated things—in this case an old newspaper item and the notes of a dead professor. I hope that no one else will accomplish this piecing out; certainly, if I live, I shall never knowingly supply a link in so hideous a chain. I think that the professor, too, intended to keep silent regarding the part he knew, and that he would have destroyed his notes had not sudden death seized him.

My knowledge of the thing began in the winter of 1926—1927 with the death of my grand-uncle George Gammell Angell, Professor Emeritus of Semitic Languages in Brown University, Providence, Rhode Island. Professor Angell was widely known as an authority on ancient inscriptions, and had frequently been resorted to by the heads of prominent museums; so that his passing at the age of ninety-two may be recalled by many. Locally, interest was intensified by the obscurity of the cause of death. The professor had been stricken whilst returning from the Newburyport boat; falling suddenly, as witnesses said, after having been jostled by a nautical-looking Negro who had come from one of the queer dark courts on the precipitous hillside which formed a short cut from the waterfront to the deceased's home in Williams Street. Physicians were unable to find any visible disorder, but concluded after perplexed debate that some obscure lesion of the heart, induced by the brisk ascent of so steep a hill by so elderly a man, was responsible for the end. At the time I saw no reason to dissent from this dictum, but latterly I am inclined to wonder—and more than wonder.

As my grand-uncle's heir and executor, for he died a childless widower, I was expected to go over his papers with some thoroughness; and for that purpose moved his entire set of files and boxes to my quarters in Boston. Much of the material which I correlated will be later published by the American Archaeological Society, but there was one box which I found exceedingly puzzling, and which I felt much averse from shewing to other eyes. It had been locked, and I did not find the key till it occurred to me to examine the personal ring which the professor carried always in his pocket. Then indeed I succeeded in opening it, but when I did so seemed only to be confronted by a greater and more closely locked barrier. For what could be the meaning of the queer clay bas-relief and the disjointed jottings, ramblings, and cuttings which I found? Had my uncle, in his latter years, become credulous of the most superficial impostures? I resolved to search out the eccentric sculptor responsible for this apparent disturbance of an old man's peace of mind.

The bas-relief was a rough rectangle less than an inch thick and about five by six inches in area; obviously of modern origin. Its designs, however, were far from modern in atmosphere and suggestion; for although the vagaries of cubism and futurism are many and wild, they do not often reproduce that cryptic regularity which lurks in prehistoric writing. And writing of some kind the bulk of these designs seemed certainly to be; though my memory, despite much familiarity with the papers and collections of my uncle, failed in any way to identify this particular species, or even hint at its remotest affiliations.

Above these apparent hieroglyphics was a figure of evidently pictorial intent, though its impressionistic execution forbade a very clear idea of its nature. It seemed to be a sort of monster, or symbol representing a monster, of a form which only a diseased fancy could conceive. If I say that my somewhat extravagant imagination yielded simultaneous pictures of an octopus, a dragon, and a human caricature, I shall not be unfaithful to the spirit of the thing. A pulpy, tentacled head surmounted a grotesque and scaly body with rudimentary wings; but it was the *general outline* of the whole which made it most shockingly frightful. Behind the figure was a vague suggestion of a Cyclopean architectural background.

The writing accompanying this oddity was, aside from a stack of press cuttings, in Professor Angell's most recent hand; and made no pretense to literary style. What seemed to be the main document was head "CTHULHU CULT" in characters painstakingly printed to avoid the erroneous reading of a word so unheard-of. This manuscript was divided into two sections, the first of which was head "1925—Dream and Dream Work of H. A. Wilcox, 7 Thomas St., Providence, R. I.", and the second, "Narrative of Inspector John R. Legrasse, 121 Bienville St., New Orleans, La., at 1908 A.A.S. Mtg.—Notes on Same, & Prof. Webb's Acct." The other manuscript papers were all brief notes, some of them accounts of the queer dreams of different persons, some of them citations from theosophical books and magazines (notably W. Scott Elliot's *Atlantis and the Lost Lemuria*), and the rest comments on long-surviving secret societies and hidden cults, with references to passages in such mythological and anthropological source-books as Frazer's *Golden Bough* and Miss Murray's *Witch-Cult in Western Europe*. The cuttings largely alluded to outré mental illnesses and outbreaks of group folly or mania in the spring of 1925.

The first half of the principal manuscript told a very peculiar tale. It appears that on March 1st, 1925, a thin, dark young man of neurotic and excited aspect had called upon Professor Angell bearing the singular clay bas-relief, which was then exceedingly damp and fresh. His card bore the name Henry Anthony Wilcox, and my uncle had recognised him as the youngest son of an excellent family slightly known to him, who had latterly been studying sculpture at the Rhode Island School of Design and living alone at the Fleur-de-Lys Building near that institution. Wilcox was a precocious youth of known genius but great eccentricity, and had from childhood excited attention through the strange stories and odd dreams he was in the habit of relating. He called himself "psychically hypersensitive", but the staid folk of the ancient commercial city dismissed him as merely "queer". Never mingling much with his kind, he had dropped gradually from social visibility, and was now known only to a small group of aesthetes from other towns. Even the Providence Art Club, anxious to preserve its conservatism, had found him quite hopeless.

On the occasion of the visit, ran the professor's manuscript, the sculptor abruptly asked for the benefit of his host's archaeological knowledge in identifying the hieroglyphics on the bas-relief. He spoke in a dreamy, stilted manner which suggested pose and alienated sympathy; and my uncle shewed some sharpness in replying, for the conspicuous freshness of the tablet implied kinship with anything but archaeology. Young Wilcox's rejoinder, which impressed my uncle enough to make him recall and record it verbatim, was of a fantastically poetic cast which must have typified his whole conversation, and which I have since found highly characteristic of him. He said, "It is new, indeed, for I made it last night in a dream of strange cities; and dreams are older than brooding Tyre, or the contemplative Sphinx, or garden-girdled Babylon."

It was then that he began that rambling tale which suddenly played upon a sleeping memory and won the fevered interest of my uncle. There had been a slight earthquake tremor the night before, the most considerable felt in New England for some years; and Wilcox's imagination had been keenly affected. Upon retiring, he had had an unprecedented dream of great Cyclopean cities of titan blocks and sky-flung monoliths, all dripping with green ooze and sinister with latent horror. Hieroglyphics had covered the walls and pillars, and from some undetermined point below had come a voice that was not a voice; a chaotic sensation which only fancy could transmute into sound, but which he attempted to render by the almost unpronounceable jumble of letters, "*Cthulhu fhtagn.*"

This verbal jumble was the key to the recollection which excited and disturbed

Professor Angell. He questioned the sculptor with scientific minuteness; and studied with almost frantic intensity the bas-relief on which the youth had found himself working, chilled and clad only in his night-clothes, when waking had stolen bewilderingly over him. My uncle blamed his old age, Wilcox afterward said, for his slowness in recognising both hieroglyphics and pictorial design. Many of his questions seemed highly out-of-place to his visitor, especially those which tried to connect the latter with strange cults or societies; and Wilcox could not understand the repeated promises of silence which he was offered in exchange for an admission of membership in some widespread mystical or paganly religious body. When Professor Angell became convinced that the sculptor was indeed ignorant of any cult or system of cryptic lore, he besieged his visitor with demands for future reports of dreams. This bore regular fruit, for after the first interview the manuscript records daily calls of the young man, during which he related startling fragments of nocturnal imagery whose burden was always some terrible Cyclopean vista of dark and dripping stone, with a subterrene voice or intelligence shouting monotonously in enigmatical sense-impacts uninscribable save as gibberish. The two sounds most frequently repeated are those rendered by the letters "*Cthulhu*" and "*R'lyeh.*"

On March 23rd, the manuscript continued, Wilcox failed to appear; and inquiries at his quarters revealed that he had been stricken with an obscure sort of fever and taken to the home of his family in Waterman Street. He had cried out in the night, arousing several other artists in the building, and had manifested since then only alterations of unconsciousness and delirium. My uncle at once telephoned the family, and from that time forward kept close watch of the case; calling often at the Thayer Street office of Dr. Tobey, whom he learned to be in charge. The youth's febrile mind, apparently, was dwelling on strange things; and the Doctor shuddered now and then as he spoke of them. They included not only a repetition of what he had formerly dreamed, but touched wildly on a gigantic thing "miles high" which walked or lumbered about. He at no time fully described this object, but occasional frantic words, as repeated by Dr. Tobey, convinced the professor that it must be identical with the nameless monstrosity he had sought to depict in his dream-sculpture. Reference to this object, the doctor added, was invariably a prelude to the young man's subsidence into lethargy. His temperature, oddly enough, was not greatly above normal; but his whole condition was otherwise such as to suggest true fever rather than mental disorder.

On April 2nd at about 3 p. m. every trace of Wilcox's malady suddenly ceased. He sat upright in bed, astonished to find himself at home and completely ignorant of what had happened in dream or reality since the night of March 22nd. Pronounced well by his physician, he returned to his quarters in three days; but to Professor Angell he was of no further assistance. All traces of strange dreaming had vanished with his recovery, and my uncle kept no record of his night-thoughts after a week of pointless and irrelevant accounts of thoroughly usual visions.

Here the first part of the manuscript ended, but references to certain of the scattered notes gave me much material for thought—so much, in fact, that only the ingrained scepticism then forming my philosophy can account for my continued distrust of the artist. The notes in question were those descriptive of the dreams of various persons covering the same period as that in which young Wilcox had had his strange visitations. My uncle, it seems, had quickly instituted a prodigiously far-flung body of inquiries amongst nearly all the friends whom he could question without impertinence, asking for nightly reports of their dreams, and the dates of any notable visions for some time past. The reception of his request seems to have been varied; but he must, at the very least, have received more responses than any ordinary man could have handled without a secretary. This original correspondence was not preserved, but his notes formed a thorough and really significant digest. Average people in society and business—New England's traditional "salt of the earth"—gave an almost completely negative result, though scattered cases of uneasy but formless nocturnal impressions appear here and there, always between March 23rd and April 2nd—the period of young Wilcox's delirium. Scientific men were little more affected, though four cases of vague description suggest fugitive glimpses of strange landscapes, and in one case there is mentioned a dread of something abnormal.

It was from the artists and poets that the pertinent answers came, and I know that panic would have broken loose had they been able to compare notes. As it was, lacking their original letters, I half suspected the compiler of having asked leading questions, or of having edited the correspondence in corroboration of what he had latently resolved to see. That is why I continued to feel that Wilcox, somehow cognisant of the old data which my uncle had possessed, had been imposing on the veteran scientist. These responses from aesthetes told a disturbing tale. From February 28th to April 2nd a large proportion of them had dreamed very bizarre things, the intensity of the dreams being immeasurably the stronger during the period of the sculptor's delirium. Over a fourth of those who reported anything, reported scenes and half-sounds not unlike those which Wilcox had described; and some of the dreamers confessed acute fear of the gigantic nameless thing visible toward the last. One case, which the note describes with emphasis, was very sad. The subject, a widely known architect with leanings toward theosophy and occultism, went violently insane on the date of young Wilcox's seizure, and expired several months later after incessant screamings to be saved from some escaped denizen of hell. Had my uncle referred to these cases by name instead of merely by number, I should have attempted some corroboration and personal investigation; but as it was, I succeeded in tracing down only a few. All of these, however, bore out the notes in full. I have often wondered if all the objects of the professor's questioning felt as puzzled as did this fraction. It is well that no explanation shall ever reach them.

The press cuttings, as I have intimated, touched on cases of panic, mania, and eccentricity during the given period. Professor Angell must have employed a cutting bureau, for the number of extracts was tremendous and the sources scattered throughout the globe. Here was a nocturnal suicide in London, where a lone sleeper had leaped from a window after a shocking cry. Here likewise a rambling letter to the editor of a paper in South America, where a fanatic deduces a dire future from visions he has seen. A despatch from California describes a theosophist colony as donning white robes en masse for some "glorious fulfillment" which never arrives, whilst items from India speak guardedly of serious native unrest toward the end of March. Voodoo orgies multiply in Hayti, and African outposts report ominous mutterings. American officers in the Philippines find certain tribes bothersome at this time, and New York policemen are mobbed by hysterical Levantines on the night of March 22-23. The west of Ireland, too, is full of wild rumour and legendry, and a fantastic painter named Ardois-Bonnot hangs a blasphemous "Dream Landscape" in the Paris spring salon of 1926. And so numerous are the recorded troubles in insane asylums, that only a miracle can have stopped the medical fraternity from noting strange parallelisms and drawing mystified conclusions. A weird bunch of cuttings, all told; and I can at this date scarcely envisage the callous rationalism with which I set them aside. But I was then convinced that young Wilcox had known of the older matters mentioned by the professor.

II. THE TALE OF INSPECTOR LEGRASSE

The older matters which had made the sculptor's dream and bas-relief so significant to my uncle formed the subject of the second half of his long manuscript. Once before, it appears, Professor Angell had seen the hellish outlines of the nameless monstrosity, puzzled over the unknown hieroglyphics, and heard the ominous syllables which can be rendered only as "*Cthulhu*"; and all this in so stirring and horrible a connexion that it is small wonder he pursued young Wilcox with queries and demands for data.

This earlier experience had come in 1908, seventeen years before, when the American Archaeological Society held its annual meeting in St. Louis. Professor Angell, as befitted one of his authority and attainments, had had a prominent part in all the deliberations; and was one of the first to be approached by the several outsiders who took advantage of the convocation to offer questions for correct answering and problems for expert solution.

The chief among these outsiders, and in a short time the focus of interest for the entire meeting, was a commonplace-looking middle-aged man who had travelled all the way from New Orleans for certain special information unobtainable from any local source. His name was John Raymond Legrasse, and he was by profession an Inspector of Police. With him he bore the subject of his visit, a grotesque, repulsive, and apparently very ancient stone statuette whose origin he was at a loss to determine. It must not be fancied that Inspector Legrasse had the least interest in archaeology. On the contrary, his wish for enlightenment was prompted by purely professional considerations. The statuette, idol, fetish, or whatever it was had been captured some months before in the wooded swamps south of New Orleans during a raid on a supposed voodoo meeting; and so singular and hideous were the rites connected with it, that the police could not but realise that they had stumbled on a dark cult totally unknown to them, and infinitely more diabolic than even the blackest of the African voodoo circles. Of its origin, apart from the erratic and unbelievable tales extorted from the captured members, absolutely nothing was to be discovered; hence the anxiety of the police for any antiquarian lore which might help them to place the frightful symbol, and through it track down the cult to its fountain-head.

Inspector Legrasse was scarcely prepared for the sensation which his offering created. One sight of the thing had been enough to throw the assembled men of science into a state of tense excitement, and they lost no time in crowding around him to gaze at the diminutive figure whose utter strangeness and air of genuinely abysmal antiquity hinted so potently at unopened and archaic vistas. No recognised school of sculpture had animated this terrible object, yet centuries and even thousands of years seemed recorded in its dim and greenish surface of unplaceable stone.

The figure, which was finally passed slowly from man to man for close and careful study, was between seven and eight inches in height, and of exquisitely artistic workmanship. It represented a monster of vaguely anthropoid outline, but with an' octopus-like head whose face was a mass of feelers, a scaly, rubbery-looking body, prodigious claws on hind and fore feet, and long, narrow wings behind. This thing, which seemed instinct with a fearsome and unnatural malignancy, was of a somewhat bloated corpulence, and squatted evilly on a rectangular block or pedestal covered with undecipherable characters. The tips of the wings touched the back edge of the block, the seat occupied the centre, whilst the long, curved claws of the doubled-up, crouching hind legs gripped the bottom of the pedestal. The cephalopod head was bent forward, so that the ends of the facial feelers brushed the backs of huge fore paws which clasped the croucher's elevated knees. The aspect of the whole was abnormally life-like, and the more subtly fearful because its source was so totally unknown. Its vast, awesome, and incalculable age was unmistakable; yet not one link did it shew with any known type of art belonging to civilisation's youth—or indeed to any other time. Totally separate and apart, its very material was a mystery; for the soapy, greenish-black stone with its golden or iridescent flecks and striations resembled nothing familiar to geology or mineralogy. The characters along the base were equally baffling; and no member present, despite a representation of half the world's expert learning in this field, could form the least notion of even their remotest linguistic kinship. They, like the subject and material, belonged to something horribly remote and distinct from mankind as we know it; something frightfully suggestive of old and unhallowed cycles of life in which our world and our conceptions have no part.

And yet, as the members severally shook their heads and confessed defeat at the inspector's problem, there was one man in that gathering who suspected a touch of bizarre familiarity in the monstrous shape and writing, and who presently told with some diffidence of the odd trifle he knew. This person was the late William Channing Webb, Professor of Anthropology in Princeton University, and an explorer of no slight note. Professor Webb had been engaged, forty-eight years before, in a tour of Greenland and Iceland in search of some Runic inscriptions which he failed to unearth;

and whilst high up on the West Greenland coast had encountered a singular tribe or cult of degenerate Esquimaux whose religion, a curious form of devil-worship, chilled him with its deliberate bloodthirstiness and repulsiveness. It was a faith of which other Esquimaux knew little, and which they mentioned only with shudders, saying that it had come down from horribly ancient aeons before ever the world was made. Besides nameless rites and human sacrifices there were certain queer hereditary rituals addressed to a supreme elder devil or *tornasuk*; and of this Professor Webb had taken phonetic copy from an aged *angekok* or wizard-priest, expressing the sounds in Roman letters as best he knew how. But just now of prime significance was the fetish which this cult had cherished, and around which they danced when the aurora leaped high over the ice cliffs. It was, the professor stated, a very crude bas-relief of stone, comprising a hideous picture and some cryptic writing. And so far as he could tell, it was a rough parallel in all essential features of the bestial thing now lying before the meeting.

This data, received with suspense and astonishment by the assembled members, proved doubly exciting to Inspector Legrasse, and he began at once to ply his informant with questions. Having noted and copied an oral ritual among the swamp cult-worshippers his men had arrested, he besought the professor to remember as best he might the syllables taken down amongst the diabolist Esquimaux. There then followed an exhaustive comparison of details, and a moment of really awed silence when both detective and scientist agreed on the virtual identity of the phrase common to two hellish rituals so may worlds of distance apart. What, in substance, both the Esquimaux wizards and the Louisiana swamp-priests had chanted to their kindred idols was something very like this—the word-divisions being guessed at from traditional breaks in the phrase as chanted aloud:

"*Ph'nglui mglw'nafh Cthulhu R'lyeh wgah'nagl fhtagn.*"

Legrasse had one point in advance of Professor Webb, for several among his mongrel prisoners had repeated to him what older celebrants had told them the words meant. This text, as given, ran something like this:

"In his house at R'lyeh dead Cthulhu waits dreaming."

And now, in response to a general and urgent demand, Inspector Legrasse related as fully as possible his experience with the swamp worshippers; telling a story to which I could see my uncle attached profound significance. It savoured of the wildest dreams of mythmaker and theosophist, and disclosed an astonishing degree of cosmic imagination among such half-castes and pariahs as might be least expected to possess it.

On November 1ˢᵗ, 1907, there had come to the New Orleans police a frantic summons from the swamp and lagoon country to the south. The squatters there, mostly primitive but good-natured descendants of Lafitte's men, were in the grip of stark terror from an unknown thing which had stolen upon them in the night. It was voodoo, apparently, but voodoo of a more terrible sort than they had ever known; and some of their women and children had disappeared since the malevolent tom-tom had begun its incessant beating far within the black haunted woods where no dweller ventured. There were insane shouts and harrowing screams, soul-chilling chants and

10

dancing devil-flames; and, the frightened messenger added, the people could stand it no more.

So a body of twenty police, filling two carriages and an automobile, had set out in the late afternoon with the shivering squatter as a guide. At the end of the passable road they alighted, and for miles splashed on in silence through the terrible cypress woods where day never came. Ugly roots and malignant hanging nooses of Spanish moss beset them, and now and then a pile of dank stones or fragment of a rotting wall intensified by its hint of morbid habitation a depression which every malformed tree and every fungous islet combined to create. At length the squatter settlement, a miserable huddle of huts, hove in sight; and hysterical dwellers ran out to cluster around the group of bobbing lanterns. The muffled beat of tom-toms was now faintly audible far, far ahead; and a curdling shriek came at infrequent intervals when the wind shifted. A reddish glare, too, seemed to filter through pale undergrowth beyond the endless avenues of forest night. Reluctant even to be left alone again, each one of the cowed squatters refused point-blank to advance another inch toward the scene of unholy worship, so Inspector Legrasse and his nineteen colleagues plunged on unguided into black arcades of horror that none of them had ever trod before.

The region now entered by the police was one of traditionally evil repute, substantially unknown and untraversed by white men. There were legends of a hidden lake unglimpsed by mortal sight, in which dwelt a huge, formless white polypous thing with luminous eyes; and squatters whispered that bat-winged devils flew up out of caverns in inner earth to worship it at midnight. They said it had been there before d'Iberville, before La Salle, before the Indians, and before even the wholesome beasts and birds of the woods. It was nightmare itself, and to see it was to die. But it made men dream, and so they knew enough to keep away. The present voodoo orgy was, indeed, on the merest fringe of this abhorred area, but that location was bad enough; hence perhaps the very place of the worship had terrified the squatters more than the shocking sounds and incidents.

Only poetry or madness could do justice to the noises heard by Legrasse's men as they ploughed on through the black morass toward the red glare and muffled tom-toms. There are vocal qualities peculiar to men, and vocal qualities peculiar to beasts; and it is terrible to hear the one when the source should yield the other. Animal fury and orgiastic license here whipped themselves to daemoniac heights by howls and squawking ecstacies that tore and reverberated through those knighted woods like pestilential tempests from the gulfs of hell. Now and then the less organized ululation would cease, and from what seemed a well-drilled chorus of hoarse voices would rise in sing-song chant that hideous phrase or ritual: "*Ph'nglui mglw'nafh Cthulhu R'lyeh wgah'nagl fhtagn.*"

Then the men, having reached a spot where the trees were thinner, came suddenly in sight of the spectacle itself. Four of them reeled, one fainted, and two were shaken into a frantic cry which the mad cacophony of the orgy fortunately deadened. Legrasse dashed swamp water on the face of the fainting man, and all stood trembling and nearly hypnotised with horror.

In a natural glade of the swamp stood a grassy island of perhaps an acre's extent, clear of trees and tolerably dry. On this now leaped and twisted a more indescribable horde of human abnormality than any but a Sime or an Angarola could paint. Void of clothing, this hybrid spawn were braying, bellowing, and writhing about a monstrous ring-shaped bonfire; in the centre of which, revealed by occasional rifts in the curtain of flame, stood a great granite monolith some eight feet in height; on top of which, incongruous in its diminutiveness, rested the noxious carven statuette. From a wide circle of ten scaffolds set up at regular intervals with the flame-girt monolith as a centre hung, head downward, the oddly marred bodies of the helpless squatters who had disappeared. It was inside this circle that the ring of worshippers jumped and roared, the general direction of the mass motion being from left to right in endless Bacchanal between the ring of bodies and the ring of fire.

It may have been only imagination and it may have been only echoes which induced one of the men, an excitable Spaniard, to fancy he heard antiphonal responses to the ritual from some far and unillumined spot deeper within the wood of ancient legendry and horror. This man, Joseph D. Galvez, I later met and questioned; and he proved distractingly imaginative. He indeed went so far as to hint of the faint beating of great wings, and of a glimpse of shining eyes and a mountainous white bulk beyond the remotest trees—but I suppose he had been hearing too much native superstition.

Actually, the horrified pause of the men was of comparatively brief duration. Duty came first; and although there must have been nearly a hundred mongrel celebrants in the throng, the police relied on their firearms and plunged determinedly into the nauseous rout. For five minutes the resultant din and chaos were beyond description. Wild blows were struck, shots were fired, and escapes were made; but in the end Legrasse was able to count some forty-seven sullen prisoners, whom he forced to dress in haste and fall into line between two rows of policemen. Five of the worshippers lay dead, and two severely wounded ones were carried away on improvised stretchers by their fellow-prisoners. The image on the monolith, of course, was carefully removed and carried back by Legrasse.

Examined at headquarters after a trip of intense strain and weariness, the prisoners all proved to be men of a very low, mixed-blooded, and mentally aberrant type. Most were seamen, and a sprinkling of Negroes and mulattoes, largely West Indians or Brava Portuguese from the Cape Verde Islands, gave a colouring of voodooism to the heterogeneous cult. But before many questions were asked, it became manifest that something far deeper and older than Negro fetishism was involved. Degraded and ignorant as they were, the creatures held with surprising consistency to the central idea of their loathsome faith.

They worshipped, so they said, the Great Old Ones who lived ages before there were any men, and who came to the young world out of the sky. Those Old Ones were gone now, inside the earth and under the sea; but their dead bodies had told their secrets in dreams to the first men, who formed a cult which had never died. This was that cult, and the prisoners said it had always existed and always would exist, hidden in distant wastes and dark places all over the world until the time when the great priest Cthulhu, from his dark house in the mighty city of R'lyeh under the waters, should rise and bring the earth again beneath his sway. Some day he would call, when the stars were ready, and the secret cult would always be waiting to liberate him.

Meanwhile no more must be told. There was a secret which even torture could not extract. Mankind was not absolutely alone among the conscious things of earth, for shapes came out of the dark to visit the faithful few. But these were not the Great Old Ones. No man had ever seen the Old Ones. The carven idol was great Cthulhu, but none might say whether or not the others were precisely like him. No one could read the old writing now, but things were told by word of mouth. The chanted ritual was not the secret—that was never spoken aloud, only whispered. The chant meant only this: "In his house at R'lyeh dead Cthulhu waits dreaming."

Only two of the prisoners were found sane enough to be hanged, and the rest were committed to various institutions. All denied a part in the ritual murders, and averred that the killing had been done by Black Winged Ones which had come to them from their immemorial meeting-place in the haunted wood. But of those mysterious allies no coherent account could ever be gained. What the police did extract, came mainly from the immensely aged *mestizo* named Castro, who claimed to have sailed to strange ports and talked with undying leaders of the cult in the mountains of China.

Old Castro remembered bits of hideous legend that paled the speculations of theosophists and made man and the world seem recent and transient indeed. There had been aeons when other Things ruled on the earth, and They had had great cities. Remains of Them, he said the deathless Chinamen had told him, were still to be found as Cyclopean stones on islands in the Pacific. They all died vast epochs of time before men came, but there were arts which could revive Them when the stars had come round again to the right positions in the cycle of eternity. They had, indeed, come themselves from the stars, and brought Their images with Them.

These Great Old Ones, Castro continued, were not composed altogether of flesh and blood. They had shape—for did not this star-fashioned image prove it?—but that shape was not made of matter. When the stars were right, They could plunge from world to world through the sky; but when the stars were wrong, They could not live. But although They no longer lived, They would never really die. They all lay in stone houses in Their great city of R'lyeh, preserved by the spells of mighty Cthulhu for a glorious resurrection when the stars and the earth might once more be ready for Them. But at that time some force from outside must serve to liberate Their bodies. The spells that preserved Them intact likewise prevented Them from making an initial move, and They could only lie awake in the dark and think whilst uncounted millions of years rolled by. They knew all that was occurring in the universe, for Their mode of speech was transmitted thought. Even now They talked in Their tombs. When, after infinities of chaos, the first men came, the Great Old Ones spoke to the sensitive among them by moulding their dreams; for only thus could Their language reach the fleshy minds of mammals.

Then, whispered Castro, those first men formed the cult around small idols which the Great Old Ones showed them; idols brought in dim eras from dark stars. That cult would never die till the stars came right again, and the secret priests would take great Cthulhu from His tomb to revive His subjects and resume His rule of earth. The time would be easy to know, for then mankind would have become as the Great Old Ones; free and wild and beyond good and evil, with laws and morals thrown aside and all men shouting and killing and revelling in joy. Then the liberated Old Ones would teach them new ways to shout and kill and revel and enjoy themselves, and all the earth would flame with a holocaust of ecstasy and freedom. Meanwhile the cult, by appropriate rites, must keep alive the memory of those ancient ways and shadow forth the prophecy of Their return.

In the elder time chosen men had talked with the entombed Old Ones in dreams, but then something happened. The great stone city R'lyeh, with its monoliths and sepulchres, had sunk beneath the waves; and the deep waters, full of the one primal mystery through which not even thought can pass, had cut off the spectral intercourse. But memory never died, and the high-priests said that the city would rise again when the stars were right. Then came out of the earth the black spirits of earth, mouldy and shadowy, and full of dim rumours picked up in caverns beneath forgotten sea-bottoms. But of them Old Castro dared not speak much. He cut himself off hurriedly, and no amount of persuasion or subtlety could elicit more in this direction. The *size* of the Old Ones, too, he curiously declined to mention. Of the cult, he said that he thought the centre lay amid the pathless desert of Arabia, where Irem, the City of Pillars, dreams hidden and untouched. It was not allied to the European witch-cult, and was virtually unknown beyond its members. No book had ever really hinted of it, though the deathless Chinamen said that there were double meanings in the *Necronomicon* of the mad Arab Abdul Alhazred which the initiated might read as they chose, especially the much-discussed couplet:

> That is not dead which can eternal lie,
> And with strange aeons even death may die.

Legrasse, deeply impressed and not a little bewildered, had inquired in vain concerning the historic affiliations of the cult. Castro, apparently, had told the truth when he said that it was wholly secret. The authorities at Tulane University could shed no light upon either cult or image, and now the detective had come to the highest authorities in the country and met with no more than the Greenland tale of Professor Webb.

The feverish interest aroused at the meeting by Legrasse's tale, corroborated as it was by the statuette, is echoed in the subsequent correspondence of those who attended; although scant mention occurs in the formal publications of the society. Caution is the first care of those accustomed to face occasional charlatanry and imposture. Legrasse for some time lent the image to Professor Webb, but at the latter's death it was returned to him and remains in his possession, where I viewed it not long ago. It is truly a terrible thing, and unmistakably akin to the dream-sculpture of young Wilcox.

That my uncle was excited by the tale of the sculptor I did not wonder, for what thoughts must arise upon hearing, after a knowledge of what Legrasse had learned of the cult, of a sensitive young man who had *dreamed* not only the figure and exact hieroglyphics of the swamp-found image and the Greenland devil tablet, but had come *in his dreams* upon at least three of the precise words of the formula uttered alike by Esquimau diabolists and mongrel Louisianans? Professor Angell's instant start on an investigation of the utmost thoroughness was eminently natural; though privately I suspected young Wilcox of having heard of the cult in some indirect way, and of having invented a series of dreams to heighten and continue the mystery at my uncle's expense. The dream-narratives and cuttings collected by the professor were, of course, strong corroboration; but the rationalism of my mind and the extravagance of the whole subject led me to adopt what I thought the most sensible conclusions. So, after thoroughly studying the manuscript again and correlating the theosophical and anthropological notes with the cult narrative of Legrasse, I made a trip to Providence to see the sculptor and give him the rebuke I thought proper for so boldly imposing upon a learned and aged man.

Wilcox still lived alone in the Fleur-de-Lys Building in Thomas Street, a hideous Victorian imitation of seventeenth-century Breton architecture which flaunts its stuccoed front amidst the lovely colonial houses on the ancient hill, and under the very shadow of the finest Georgian steeple in America, I found him at work in his rooms, and at once conceded from the specimens scattered about that his genius is indeed profound and authentic. He will, I believe, some time be heard from as one of the great decadents; for he has crystallised in clay and will one day mirror in marble those nightmares and phantasies which Arthur Machen evokes in prose, and Clark Ashton Smith makes visible in verse and in painting.

Dark, frail, and somewhat unkempt in aspect, he turned languidly at my knock and asked me my business without rising. When I told him who I was, he displayed some interest; for my uncle had excited his curiosity in probing his strange dreams, yet had never explained the reason for the study. I did not enlarge his knowledge in this regard, but sought with some subtlety to draw him out. In a short time I became convinced of his absolute sincerity, for he spoke of the dreams in a manner none could mistake. They and their subconscious residuum had influenced his art profoundly, and he shewed me a morbid statue whose contours almost made me shake with the potency of its black suggestion. He could not recall having seen the original of this thing except in his own dream bas-relief, but the outlines had formed themselves insensibly under his hands. It was, no doubt, the giant shape he had raved of in delirium. That he really knew nothing of the hidden cult, save from what my uncle's relentless catechism had let fall, he soon made clear; and again I strove to think of some way in which he could possibly have received the weird impressions.

He talked of his dreams in a strangely poetic fashion; making me see with terrible vividness the damp Cyclopean city of slimy green stone—whose *geometry*, he oddly said, was *all wrong*—and hear with frightened expectancy the ceaseless, half-mental calling from underground: "*Cthulhu fhtagn*", "*Cthulhu fhtagn*." These words had formed part of that dread ritual which told of dead Cthulhu's dream-vigil in his stone vault at R'lyeh, and I felt deeply moved despite my rational beliefs. Wilcox, I was sure, had heard of the cult in some casual way, and had soon forgotten it amidst the mass of his equally weird reading and imagining. Later, by virtue of its sheer impressiveness, it had found subconscious expression in dreams, in the bas-relief, and in the terrible statue I now beheld; so that his imposture upon my uncle had been a very innocent one. The youth was of a type, at once slightly affected and slightly ill-mannered, which I could never like, but I was willing enough now to admit both his genius and his honesty. I took leave of him amicably, and wish him all the success his talent promises.

The matter of the cult still remained to fascinate me, and at times I had visions of personal fame from researches into its origin and connexions. I visited New Orleans, talked with Legrasse and others of that old-time raiding-party, saw the frightful image, and even questioned such of the mongrel prisoners as still survived. Old Castro, unfortunately, had been dead for some years. What I now heard so graphically at first-hand, though it was really no more than a detailed confirmation of what my uncle had written, excited me afresh; for I felt sure that I was on the track of a very real, very secret, and very ancient religion whose discovery would make me an anthropologist of note. My attitude was still one of absolute materialism, *as I wish it still were*, and I discounted with almost inexplicable perversity the coincidence of the dream notes and odd cuttings collected by Professor Angell.

One thing I began to suspect, and which I now fear I *know*, is that my uncle's death was far from natural. He fell on a narrow hill street leading up from an ancient waterfront swarming with foreign mongrels, after a careless push from a Negro sailor. I did not forget the mixed blood and marine pursuits of the cult-members in Louisiana, and would not be surprised to learn of secret methods and rites and beliefs. Legrasse and his men, it is true, have been let alone; but in Norway a certain seaman who saw things is dead. Might not the deeper inquiries of my uncle after encountering the sculptor's data have come to sinister ears? I think Professor Angell died because he knew too much, or because he was likely to learn too much. Whether I shall go as he did remains to be seen, for I have learned much now.

III. THE MADNESS FROM THE SEA

If heaven ever wishes to grant me a boon, it will be a total effacing of the results of a mere chance which fixed my eye on a certain stray piece of shelf-paper. It was nothing on which I would naturally have stumbled in the course of my daily round, for it was an old number of an Australian journal, the *Sydney Bulletin* for April 18, 1925. It had escaped even the cutting bureau which had at the time of its issuance been avidly collecting material for my uncle's research.

I had largely given over my inquiries into what Professor Angell called the "Cthulhu Cult", and was visiting a learned friend in Paterson, New Jersey; the curator of a local museum and a mineralogist of note. Examining one day the reserve specimens roughly set on the storage shelves in a rear room of the museum, my eye was caught by an odd picture in one of the old papers spread beneath the stones. It was the *Sydney Bulletin* I have mentioned, for my friend had wide affiliations in all conceivable foreign parts; and the picture was a half-tone cut of a hideous stone image almost identical with that which Legrasse had found in the swamp.

Eagerly clearing the sheet of its precious contents, I scanned the item in detail; and was disappointed to find it of only moderate length. What it suggested, however, was of portentous significance to my flagging quest; and I carefully tore it out for immediate action. It read as follows:

MYSTERY DERELICT FOUND AT SEA

Vigilant Arrives With Helpless Armed New Zealand Yacht in Tow.

One Survivor and Dead Man Found Aboard.
Tale of Desperate Battle and Deaths at Sea.

Rescued Seaman Refuses Particulars of Strange Experience.

Odd Idol Found in His Possession. Inquiry to Follow.

The Morrison Co.'s freighter, *Vigilant*, bound from Valparaiso, arrived this morning at its wharf in Darling Harbour, having in tow the battled and disabled but heavily armed steam yacht *Alert* of Dunedin, N.Z., which was sighted April 12th in S. Latitude 34°21', W. Longitude 152°17' with one living and one dead man aboard.

The *Vigilant* left Valparaiso March 25th, and on April 2nd was driven considerably south of her course by exceptionally heavy storms and monster waves. On April 12th the derelict was sighted; and though apparently deserted, was found upon boarding to contain one survivor in a half-delirious condition and one man who had evidently been dead for more than a week. The living man was clutching a horrible stone idol of unknown origin, about a foot in height, regarding whose nature authorities at Sydney University, the Royal Society, and the Museum in College Street all profess complete bafflement, and which the survivor says he found in the cabin of the yacht, in a small carved shrine of common pattern.

This man, after recovering his senses, told an exceedingly strange story of piracy and slaughter. He is Gustaf Johansen, a Norwegian of some intelligence, and had been Second Mate of the two-masted schooner *Emma* of Auckland, which sailed for Callao February 20th with a complement of eleven men. The *Emma*, he says, was delayed and thrown widely south of her course by the great storm of March 1st, and on March 22nd, in S. Latitude 49°51', W. Longitude 128°34', encountered the *Alert*, manned by a queer and evil-looking crew of Kanakas and half-castes. Being ordered peremptorily to turn back, Capt. Collins refused; whereupon the strange crew began to fire savagely and without warning upon the schooner with a peculiarly heavy battery of brass cannon forming part of the yacht's deck, and being forced to kill them all, the number being slightly superior, because of their particularly abhorrent and desperate though rather clumsy mode of fighting.

Three of the *Emma*'s men, including Capt. Collins and First Mate Green, were killed; and the remaining eight under Second Mate Johansen proceeded to navigate the captured yacht, going ahead in their original direction to see if any reason for their ordering back had existed. The next day, it appears, they raised and landed on a small island, although none is known to exist in that part of the ocean; and six of the men somehow died ashore, though Johansen is queerly reticent about this part of his story, and speaks only of their falling into a rock chasm. Later, it seems, he and one companion boarded the yacht and tried to manage her, but were beaten about by the storm of April 2nd. From that time till his rescue on the 12th the man remembers little, and he does not even recall when William Briden, his companion, died. Briden's death reveals no apparent cause, and was probably due to excitement or exposure. Cable advices from Dunedin report that the *Alert* was well known there as an island trader, and bore an evil reputation along the waterfront. It was owned by a curious group of half-castes whose frequent meetings and night trips to the woods attracted no little curiosity; and it had set sail in great haste just after the storm and earth tremors of March 1st. Our Auckland correspondent gives the *Emma* and her crew an excellent reputation, and Johansen is described as a sober and worthy man. The admiralty will institute an inquiry on the whole matter beginning tomorrow, at which every effort will be made to induce Johansen to speak more freely than he has done hitherto.

This was all, together with the picture of the hellish image; but what a train of ideas it started in my mind! Here were new treasuries of data on the Cthulhu Cult, and evidence that it had strange interests at sea as well as on land. What motive prompted the hybrid crew to order back the *Emma* as they sailed about with their hideous idol? What was the unknown island on which six of the *Emma*'s crew had died, and about which the mate Johansen was so secretive? What had the vice-admiralty's investigation brought out, and what was known of the noxious cult in Dunedin? And most marvellous of all, what deep and more than natural linkage of dates was this which gave a malign and now undeniable significance to the various turns of events so carefully noted by my uncle?

March 1st—our February 28th according to the International Date Line—the earthquake and storm had come. From Dunedin the *Alert* and her noisome crew had darted eagerly forth as if imperiously summoned, and on the other side of the earth poets and artists had begun to dream of a strange, dank Cyclopean city whilst a young sculptor had moulded in his sleep the form of the dreaded Cthulhu. March 23rd the crew of the *Emma* landed on an unknown island and left six men dead; and on that date the dreams of sensitive men assumed a heightened vividness and darkened with dread of a giant monster's malign pursuit, whilst an architect had gone mad and a sculptor had lapsed suddenly into delirium! And what of this storm of April 2nd—the date on which all dreams of the dank city ceased, and Wilcox emerged unharmed from the bondage of strange fever? What of all this—and of those hints of old Castro about the sunken, star-born Old Ones and their coming reign; their faithful cult *and their mastery of dreams?* Was I tottering on the brink of cosmic horrors beyond man's power to bear? If so, they must be horrors of the mind alone, for in some way the second of April had put a stop to whatever monstrous menace had begun its siege of mankind's soul.

That evening, after a day of hurried cabling and arranging, I bade my host adieu and took a train for San Francisco. In less than a month I was in Dunedin; where, however, I found that little was known of the strange cult-members who had lingered in the old sea-taverns. Waterfront scum was far too common for special mention; though there was vague talk about one inland trip these mongrels had made, during which faint drumming and red flame were noted on the distant hills. In Auckland I learned that Johansen had returned *with yellow hair turned white* after a perfunctory and inconclusive questioning at Sydney, and had thereafter sold his cottage in West Street and sailed with his wife to his old home in Oslo. Of his stirring experience he would tell his friends no more than he had told the admiralty officials, and all they could do was to give me his Oslo address.

After that I went to Sydney and talked profitlessly with seamen and members of the vice-admiralty court. I saw the *Alert*, now sold and in commercial use, at Circular Quay in Sydney Cove, but gained nothing from its non-committal bulk. The crouching image with its cuttlefish head, dragon body, scaly wings, and hieroglyphed pedestal, was preserved in the Museum at Hyde Park; and I studied it long and well, finding it a thing of balefully exquisite workmanship, and with the same utter mystery, terrible antiquity, and unearthly strangeness of material which I had noted in Legrasse's smaller specimen. Geologists, the curator told me, had found it a monstrous puzzle; for they vowed that the world held no rock like it. Then I thought with a shudder of what Old Castro had told Legrasse about the Great Ones; "They had come from the stars, and had brought Their images with Them."

Shaken with such a mental revolution as I had never before known, I now resolved to visit Mate Johansen in Oslo. Sailing for London, I re-embarked at once for the

Norwegian capital; and one autumn day landed at the trim wharves in the shadow of the Egeberg. Johansen's address, I discovered, lay in the Old Town of King Harold Haardrada, which kept alive the name of Oslo during all the centuries that the greater city masqueraded as "Christiana." I made the brief trip by taxicab, and knocked with palpitant heart at the door of a neat and ancient building with plastered front. A sad-faced woman in black answered my summons, and I was stung with disappointment when she told me in halting English that Gustaf Johansen was no more.

He had not long survived his return, said his wife, for the doings at sea in 1925 had broken him. He had told her no more than he had told the public, but had left a long manuscript—of "technical matters" as he said—written in English, evidently in order to safeguard her from the peril of casual perusal. During a walk through a narrow lane near the Gothenburg dock, a bundle of papers falling from an attic window had knocked him down. Two Lascar sailors at once helped him to his feet, but before the ambulance could reach him he was dead. Physicians found no adequate cause for the end, and laid it to heart trouble and a weakened constitution.

I now felt gnawing at my vitals that dark terror which will never leave me till I, too, am at rest; "accidentally" or otherwise. Persuading the widow that my connexion to with her husband's "technical matters" was sufficient to entitle me to his manuscript, I bore the document away and began to read it on the London boat. It was a simple, rambling thing—a naïve sailor's effort at post-facto diary—and strove to recall day by day that last awful voyage. I cannot attempt to transcribe it verbatim in all its cloudiness and redundance, but I will tell its gist enough to shew why the sound of the water against the vessel's sides became so unendurable to me that I stopped my ears with cotton.

Johansen, thank God, did not know quite all, even though he saw the city and the Thing, but I shall never sleep calmly again when I think of the horrors that lurk ceaselessly behind life in time and in space, and of those unhallowed blasphemies from elder stars which dream beneath the sea, known and favoured by a nightmare cult ready and eager to loose them on the world whenever another earthquake shall heave their monstrous stone city again to the sun and air.

Johansen's voyage had begun just as he told it to the vice-admiralty. The *Emma*, in ballast, had cleared Auckland on February 20th, and had felt the full force of that earthquake-born tempest which must have heaved up from the sea-bottom the horrors that filled men's dreams. Once more under control, the ship was making good progress when held up by the *Alert* on March 22nd, and I could feel the Mate's regret as he wrote of her bombardment and sinking. Of the swarthy cult-fiends on the *Alert* he speaks with significant horror. There was some peculiarly abominable quality about them which made their destruction seem almost a duty, and Johansen shews ingenious wonder at the charge of ruthlessness brought against his party during the proceedings of the court of inquiry. Then, driven ahead by curiosity in their captured yacht under Johansen's command, the men sight a great stone pillar sticking out of the sea, and in S. Latitude 47°9', W. Longitude 126°43' come upon a coast-line of mingled mud, ooze, and weedy Cyclopean masonry which can be nothing less than the tangible substance of earth's supreme terror—the nightmare corpse-city of R'lyeh, that was built in measureless aeons behind history by the vast, loathsome shapes that seeped down from the dark stars. There lay great Cthulhu and his hordes, hidden in green slimy vaults and sending out at last, after cycles incalculable, the thoughts that spread fear to the dreams of the sensitive and called imperiously to the faithful to come on a pilgrimage of liberation and restoration. All this Johansen did not suspect, but God knows he soon saw enough!

I suppose that only a single mountain-top, the hideous monolith-crowned citadel whereon great Cthulhu was buried, actually emerged from the waters. When I think of the *extent of* all that may be brooding down there I almost wish to kill myself forthwith. Johansen and his men were awed by the cosmic majesty of this dripping Babylon of elder daemons, and must have guessed without guidance that it was nothing of this or of any sane planet. Awe at the unbelievable size of the greenish stone blocks, at the dizzying height of the great carven monolith, and at the stupefying identity of the colossal statues and bas-reliefs with the queer image found in the shrine on the *Alert*, is poignantly visible in every line of the Mate's frightened description.

Without knowing what futurism is like, Johansen achieved something very close to it when he spoke of the city; for instead of describing any definite structure or building, he dwells only on broad impressions of vast angles and stone surfaces—surfaces too great to belong to any thing right or proper for this earth, and impious with horrible images and hieroglyphs. I mention his talk about *angles* because it suggests something Wilcox had told me of his awful dreams. He said that the *geometry* of the dream-place he saw was abnormal, non-Euclidean, and loathsomely redolent of spheres and dimensions apart from ours. Now an unlettered seaman felt the same thing whilst gazing at the terrible reality.

Johansen and his men landed at a sloping mud-bank on this monstrous Acropolis, and clambered slipperily up over titan oozy blocks which could have been no mortal staircase. The very sun of heaven seemed distorted when viewed through the polarising miasma welling out from this sea-soaked perversion, and twisted menace and suspense lurked leeringly in those crazily elusive angles of carven rock where a second glance shewed concavity after the first shewed convexity.

Something very like fright had come over all the explorers before anything more definite than rock and ooze and weed was seen. Each would have fled had he not feared the scorn of the others, and it was only half-heartedly that they searched—vainly, as it proved—for some portable souvenir to bear away.

It was Rodriguez the Portuguese who climbed up the foot of the monolith and shouted of what he had found. The rest followed him, and looked curiously at the immense carved door with the now familiar squid-dragon bas-relief. It was, Johansen said, like a great barn-door; and they all felt that it was a door because of the ornate lintel, threshold, and jambs around it, though they could not decide whether it lay flat like a trap-door or slantwise like an outside cellar-door. As Wilcox would have said, the geometry of the place was all wrong. One could not be sure that the sea and the ground were horizontal, hence the relative position of everything else seemed phantasmally variable.

Briden pushed at the stone in several places without result. Then Donovan felt over it delicately around the edge, pressing each point separately as he went. He climbed interminably along the grotesque stone moulding—that is, one would call it climbing if the thing was not after all horizontal—and the men wondered how any door in the universe could be so vast. Then, very softly and slowly, the acre-great panel began to give inward at the top; and they saw that it was balanced. Donovan slid or somehow propelled himself down or along the jamb and rejoined his fellows, and everyone watched the queer recession of the monstrously carven portal. In this phantasy of prismatic distortion it moved anomalously in a diagonal way, so that all the rules of matter and perspective seemed upset.

The aperture was black with a darkness almost material. That tenebrousness was indeed a *positive quality*; for it obscured such parts on the inner walls as ought to have been revealed, and actually burst forth like smoke from it aeon-long imprisonment, visibly darkening the sun as it slunk away into the shrunken and gibbous sky on flapping membraneous wings. The odour rising from the newly opened depths was intolerable, and at length the quick-eared Hawkins thought he heard a nasty, slopping sound down there. Everyone listened, and everyone was listening still when It lumbered slobberingly into sight and gropingly squeezed Its gelatinous green immensity through the black doorway into the tainted outside air of that poison city of madness.

Poor Johansen's handwriting almost gave out when he wrote of this. Of the six men who never reached the ship, he thinks two perished of pure fright in that accursed instant. The Thing cannot be described—there is no language for such abysms of shrieking and immemorial lunacy, such eldritch contradictions of all matter, force, and cosmic order. A mountain walked or stumbled. God! What wonder that across the earth a great architect went mad, and poor Wilcox raved with fever in that telepathic instant? The Thing of the idols, the green, sticky spawn of the stars, had awaked to claim his own. The stars were right again, and what an age-old cult had failed to do by design, a band of innocent sailors had done by accident. After vigintillions of years great Cthulhu was loose again, and ravening for delight.

Three men were swept up by the flabby claws before anybody turned. God rest them, if there be any rest in the universe. They were Donovan, Guerrera, and Angstrom. Parker slipped as the other three were plunging frenziedly over endless vistas of green-crusted rock to the boat, and Johansen swears he was swallowed up by an angle of masonry which shouldn't have been there; an angle which was acute, but behaved as if it were obtuse. So only Briden and Johansen reached the boat, and pulled desperately for the *Alert* as the mountainous monstrosity flopped down the slimy stones and hesitated floundering at the edge of the water.

Steam had not been suffered to go down entirely, despite the departure of all hands for the shore; and it was the work of only a few moments of feverish rushing up and down between wheel and engines to get the *Alert* under way. Slowly, amidst the distorted horrors of that indescribable scene, she began to churn the lethal waters; whilst on the masonry of that charnel shore that was not of earth the titan Thing from the stars slavered and gibbered like Polypheme cursing the fleeing ship of Odysseus. Then, bolder than the storied Cyclops, great Cthulhu slid greasily into the water and began to pursue with vast wave-raising strokes of cosmic potency. Briden looked back and went mad, laughing shrilly as he kept on laughing at intervals till death found him one night in the cabin whilst Johansen was wandering deliriously.

But Johansen had not given out yet. Knowing that the Thing could surely overtake the *Alert* until steam was fully up, he resolved on a desperate chance; and setting the engine for full speed, ran lightning-like on deck and reversed the wheel. There was a mighty eddying and foaming in the noisome brine, and as the steam mounted higher and higher the brave Norwegian drove his vessel head on against the pursuing jelly which rose above the unclean froth like the stern of a daemon galleon. The awful squid-head with writhing feelers came nearly up to the bowsprit of the sturdy yacht, but Johansen drove on relentlessly. There was a bursting as of an exploding bladder, a slushy nastiness as of a cloven sunfish, a stench as of a thousand opened graves, and a sound that the chronicler could not put on paper. For an instant the ship was befouled by an acrid and blinding green cloud, and then there was only a venomous seething astern; where—God in heaven!—the scattered plasticity of that nameless sky-spawn was nebulously *recombining* in its hateful original form, whilst its distance widened every second as the *Alert* gained impetus from its mounting steam.

That was all. After that Johansen only brooded over the idol in the cabin and attended to a few matters of food for himself and the laughing maniac by his side. He did not try to navigate after the first bold flight, for the reaction had taken something out of his soul. Then came the storm of April 2nd, and a gathering of the clouds about his consciousness. There is a sense of spectral whirling through liquid gulfs of infinity, of dizzying rides through reeling universes on a comet's tail, and of hysterical plunges from the pit to the moon and from the moon back again to the pit, all livened by a cachinnating chorus of the distorted, hilarious elder gods and the green, bat-winged mocking imps of Tartarus.

Out of that dream came rescue—the *Vigilant*, the vice-admiralty court, the streets of Dunedin, and the long voyage back home to the old house by the Egeberg. He could not tell—they would think him mad. He would write of what he knew before death came, but his wife must not guess. Death would be a boon if only it could blot out the memories.

That was the document I read, and now I have placed it in the tin box beside the bas-relief and the papers of Professor Angell. With it shall go this record of mine—this test of my own sanity, wherein is pieced together that which I hope may never be pieced together again. I have looked upon all that the universe has to hold of horror, and even the skies of spring and the flowers of summer must ever afterward be poison to me. But I do not think my life will be long. As my uncle went, as poor Johansen went, so I shall go. I know too much, and the cult still lives.

Cthulhu still lives, too, I suppose, again in that chasm of stone which has shielded him since the sun was young. His accursed city is sunken once more, for the *Vigilant* sailed over the spot after the April storm; but his ministers on earth still bellow and prance and slay around idol-capped monoliths in lonely places. He must have been trapped by the sinking whilst within his black abyss, or else the world would by now be screaming with fright and frenzy. Who knows the end? What has risen may sink, and what has sunk may rise. Loathsomeness waits and dreams in the deep, and decay spreads over the tottering cities of men. A time will come—but I must not and cannot think! Let me pray that, if I do not survive this manuscript, my executors may put caution before audacity and see that it meets no other eye.

PATIENTLY WAITING

*"The universe is full of magical things,
patiently waiting for our wits to grow sharper."*

—Eden Phillpotts

"Well, well," smirked the grinning lieutenant, his feet up on his desk, "look who's back!" Throwing himself out of his chair, he stood quickly and then bent low to make a sweeping, near-comical bow, ushering inside the man in the doorway.

"Sooooooo very good to have you back, el Grande."

Inspector John Raymond Legrasse scowled at the bowing figure. The tall, thick-boned man was weary from both his long train journey and then the carriage ride from the station, delayed as it was by the monsoon-like storm pelting the city. Cold, tired and wet, the inspector was not quite in the mood for the shenanigans of his second-in-command. Dropping his rain soaked travel bag, but not the package under his other arm, Legrasse stepped aside to allow the older man behind him entrance.

"Professor William Channing Webb," he said, stripping off his water-logged hat and gloves, "Lieutenant Joseph D. Galvez."

Recognizing the elderly professor's name from a wire his superior had sent ahead before leaving Missouri, Galvez's clowning came to an immediate end. He snapped to attention, his voice losing its comedic edge as he offered,

"Quite good to meet you, sir. Make I take your wrap, get you a hot beverage? Tea? Chicory coffee?"

"Oh, my," answered Webb, gratefully shucking off his drenched overcoat, "I've heard tell of your powerful Louisiana blends—that they simply grab a man's throat, pull it out of his body completely and then do a dance on it with pointed shoes before they stuff it back down his throat—usually wrong end first."

"Tea, then?"

"Oh, no," answered Webb, a twinkle in his eye indicating that he might be something of a jokester himself, "I've waited some twenty years since I first had the effects of Chicory described to me. At my age I don't believe it good to wait much longer. Please, sir, a large one. Black, with two generous dollops of sweetening, if you could."

Galvez smiled. He like the tall older man immensely. He did not know who the professor was beyond his title, but the inspector's wire had hinted at *why* the man had returned with Legrasse. And, if he was there for *that*, then taking care of his wrap and fetching him some coffee was short payment. Short payment, indeed.

As Galvez bustled off with the professor's coat, Webb asked,

"No coffee for you, Inspector?" Legrasse did not look up from his immediate chore. Still unwrapping the package under his arm, he answered,

"Galvez, fetch coffee for his inspector?" Switching his voice to a fair approximation of the short Spaniard's, he said indignantly, "I, sir, am a lieutenant. Not a waiter. What a suggestion ..."

"Let him get his own coffee."

The interruption had come from a returning Galvez. His bit of a joke raised the corners of Legrasse's mouth into something that actually resembled a smile. It was the first such moment the inspector had experienced in nearly six months. The muscles of his face, so unused to such treatment, stabbed him with mild discomfort as if to show their resentment. Legrasse merely rubbed at his cheeks, massaging the surprised muscles. An actual smile was too precious a thing to abandon merely because of an unexpected bit of discomfort.

The lieutenant handed Professor Webb his requested coffee. Deep, murky steam pushed its way through the rancid humidity hanging in the chilly air of the station house. The old man blew on the near boiling brew in his cup, then threw back a healthy slug. When the professor did not come away retching from the coffee's thickly pungent taste or crying from the scalding temperature, Galvez expressed his admiration for a novice who could down his dense blend so easily.

"My boy," answered Webb, "I've drunk brews made from tree bark moss, crushed wood grubs, and corn husks mixed with animal dung, to name only a few of the less revolting. In my field, you meet a lot of different people tucked away in all sorts of the world's far corners. Why, to some of them, this little delight of yours would be considered nothing more than a cherry frappe."

"Speaking of revolting," interrupted Legrasse, finally done unbinding the package he had so gingerly carried from Louisiana to Missouri and then back to New Orleans, "why don't we get down to business, eh?"

All eyes turned toward the inspector. There was not a person in the room who did not know what was in the package, who had not seen it before, who did not want to avoid seeing it again—and yet, they looked. They could not help themselves.

Pushing back the slick oil paper wrapping, Legrasse discarded the box's thin wooden top, drawing forth the wads of protective stuffing between him and the "revolting business" within. When finally the box's contents were laid bare the inspector pulled on one of his drenched travel gloves once more. Then, with only the slightest hesitation, he reached in and extracted the thing which had sent him to Missouri in the first place—which had pulled Professor Webb back to New Orleans with him.

It was a statue, a diminutive figure between seven and eight inches in height. It was a piece of exquisitely artistic workmanship. It was also a thing whose utter strangeness and air of genuinely abysmal antiquity had sent the collective world of archaeology into unbelieving spasms when the inspector had shown it days earlier at the annual meeting of the American Archaeological Society in St. Louis. Indeed, Webb had followed him back for the chance to examine the site of its discovery, forsaking all on his already overcrowded schedule. Legrasse was happy to have him.

Setting the figurine on the desktop before him, the horror of the familiar piece assaulted him again—a blow he simply could not grow used to no matter how many times it was struck. Of course, as a mere piece of art, the statuette was not so fearsome on its own.

There was no doubting that it was an odd subject for a sculpture. The piece represented a monster of vaguely anthropoid outline, but with an octopus-like head whose face was a mask of feelers, a scaly, rubbery-looking body, prodigious claws on hind and fore feet, and long, narrow wings behind. The thing, whatever it might be, was designed with a somewhat bloated corpulence. It squatted evilly on a rectangular block or pedestal covered with undecipherable characters. The tips of its wings touched the back edge of the block, its seat occupied the center, whilst the long, curved claws of its doubled-up, crouching hind legs gripped the front edge and extended a quarter of the way down toward the bottom of the pedestal. The figure's cephalopod head was bent forward so that the ends of its facial feelers brushed the backs of the huge fore paws which clasped the croucher's elevated knees.

But, it was not the unnatural design of the beast or any particular skill on the part of the artist toward the bizarre that gave the bit of stone its repellant aspect. It, itself—either the very stone of it, or some mark left upon it by some foul previous contact, like the breath of a drunk pulled up out of the gutter, or the hand prints of a muddy child on the linen suit of its father—it was simply a malignant *thing*. A sketch of it, or a photograph—even one of the Lumiere brother's moving pictures—would never be able to convey the monstrous horror one discovered through simple proximity. Merely staying in the same room with it for any amount of time was to invite nightmare. Handling it flirted with damnation.

"Didn't get any prettier," whispered Galvez. "Did it?"

"No," responded the inspector absently, "but then, neither did you."

Galvez grinned sourly. Several of the other men in the vicinity chuckled. For anyone else the excitable young Spaniard would have had a ready response. But, rank having its privileges, the lieutenant allowed the crack to stand, knowing he would get his chance at Legrasse later. In the meantime Professor Webb moved forward, more fascinated than repelled. He asked for the use of the inspector's chair. When it was granted the older man sat and then leaned forward, taking up once more the study of the figurine which he had begun in Missouri.

"What's with the genius, J. R.," asked Galvez under his breath. "He know something about this thing?"

"Maybe," answered Legrasse. "It seems the professor came across something like our bunch of crazies before. He won't really know for certain until we take him out to the swamp to inspect the site where we found the statue."

Galvez crossed himself involuntarily. On the first of November, the previous year, he, Legrasse, and nineteen other officers had filled two carriages and an automobile and headed down into the usually quiet lagoon country to the south of New Orleans to answer a frantic summons for help. When they had finished, it appeared the squad had easily handled the crime they had rushed off to investigate. On the surface, anyway.

The swamp squatters who had begged their assistance were of a breed that usually desired as little contact with the outside world as possible. But, their people had been disappearing in a mysterious and bloody fashion and all those left behind found themselves in the grip of an unknown malevolence none of them could withstand.

The police had gone in, pressing off into the swamp when their local guides refused to take them any further, finding the source of the disturbance on their own. A group of naked men had taken over a grassy island in the middle of a natural glade. There they—or some unknown group before them—had erected a great granite monolith. Using it as their central focus, the savage troupe had built a monstrous ring-shaped bonfire around its base, which they themselves circled, dancing wildly. And, around them stood a wider ring, one made up of ten scaffolds set out at regular intervals. From these hung, head down, the oddly marred bodies of the missing squatters.

Legrasse and his forces routed the near hundred celebrants without any losses to their own numbers. Although those captured did not—indeed, could not—give the police any useful information, the operation had been considered an unequivocal success by the inspector's superiors. Legrasse and his men had solved the disappearances, captured scores of those responsible, and all with no loss of life except for that of five worshippers slain during the melee. The officers had returned with forty-seven prisoners, the statue which was discovered atop the monolith, and an unsteady feeling that they had concluded their operation with far more luck than they actually deserved.

As the months went on, however, the supposed "open-and-shut case" proved to be an incredible baffle to Legrasse in particular and the law enforcement agencies of New Orleans in general. First, their prisoners turned out to be worse than useless. The men all proved to be of a low, mixed blood and mentally aberrant. Most were seamen, but there were enough Negroes and mulattoes—mostly West Indians or Brava Portuguese—to give a coloring or voodooism to the heterogeneous cult.

But, before many questions could be asked, it became manifest that something far deeper and older than mere African fetishism was involved.

Degraded and ignorant as they were, the prisoners held with surprising consistency to the central idea of their loathsome faith.

They worshipped, so they said, the Great Old Ones who lived ages before there were any men, and who came to the young world out of the sky. Those Old Ones were gone now, inside the Earth and under the sea; but their dead bodies had told secrets in dreams to the first men, who formed a cult which had never died. The cult had remained constant, and always would, its practitioners said, hidden in the distant wastes and dark places all over the world until the time when the great priest Cthulhu, from his dark house in the mighty city of R'lyeh under the waters, should rise and again bring the planet under his sway. Some day he would call, when the stars were ready, and the secret cult would be waiting to liberate him.

And that had been all the inspector, his men, or anyone else who made the attempt could wring out of any of the prisoners. Most of the miscreants had already been dealt with by the courts, routed on to the appropriate mental institutions or the hangman, whichever had been deemed the more appropriate. And, if the horrific crime had been in any way even one step closer to a thing of normalcy, that might have been the end to it. But too much of the strange had continued on since that night in the swamp for the police to simply mark the case satisfactorily complete.

Even though Legrasse's superiors considered it a job well done, the inspector, himself, had not been able to close the books on the incident in the swamp. He had made note of too many odd occurrences since its primary conclusion to simply let off his investigation. The most powerful of these observations had been the fact that none of the prisoners sentenced to execution protested the judgment. In truth, they almost seemed relieved at the prospect.

Legrasse and Galvez had attended the first, an action prompted more by empty curiosity than anything else. Sitting in the back courtyard where the sentence was to be executed, they watched as the condemned was led to the scaffold. Polite and acquiescent in his brutish way, he climbed the stairs eagerly, his eyes gleaming with the fierce triumph of a boxer who had just taken a great world prize, or an early Christian awaiting the release of the lions.

Having refused a last meal, and then either a smoke or a blindfold as well, the swarthy individual asked only to be permitted the opportunity to speak a few last words. Because of his genuinely calm nature which those in charge of the proceedings mistook for some form of repentance, the request was granted. His hands still tied behind his back, the noose around his neck, the man stood over the trap, smiling, nodding his gratitude. Then, throwing back his head, his wild hair whipping with sweat, he bellowed in a clacking tongue,

"Ph'nglui mglw'nafh Cthulhu R'lyeh wgah'nagl fhtagn."

There may have been more to his speech, but the small crowd was not to hear it. The hangman, a Godly man of a stern order of harsh Protestantism, released the trap pin sending the jabbering prisoner on to the next realm. He did so on his own initiative, without orders to do so. No one saw fit to reprimand the usurpation of authority, however.

Legrasse and Galvez had left a bit disturbed, as had most of the crowd. More than simple curiosity drew the two officers to the next execution. That time they waited with dread holding a constricting hand across their breath. Once more, a model prisoner was brought forth who had but one request, a few last words. Smiling, he went to his end spewing the same incomprehensible billage. When a third and fourth execution brought forth exactly the same results, Galvez suddenly decided he had seen enough hangings for one year.

But Legrasse had not. He went to them all, adding another layer to the horror building within him with each one witnessed. Why he thought of the cultists as horrific merely because they went cheerfully to their deaths, all shrieking the same line of nonsense, he could not explain. But, horrify him it did. What he later found in the asylums was worse.

Deciding to check the state of those prisoners found too unstable to stand trial, the inspector visited both of the hospitals in New Orleans to which the various cultists had been relegated by the courts. In the first, a bleak, cold series of buildings which confined its inmates to singular rooms of a tiny, claustrophobic nature, he found that the new patients had taken to the asylum routine quite gracefully once they had been assured that they were merely being held for execution. None of them had anything new to tell Legrasse. They simply thanked him for his visit, several asking, politely, if there might not be some way in which he might speed up the waiting process so that they might be taken to the gallows faster. The inspector demurred from comment.

In the second hospital, however, Legrasse found a different situation. The next facility was far more modern than the first—the methodology used within its walls quite advanced and experimental. It was a sunnier, healthier environment than practically any mental hospital in the country at that time. The hospital's progressive administrators along with the doctors and nurses at that institution had assured their new charges repeatedly that no one meant them any harm—that they were in no danger of execution there, and that they would be well cared for. Thus the staff could not understand why the patients had existed in a state of dread, obsessive terror since their arrival—a state that only grew more shrill and violent with each new battery of assurances.

Several of the cultists managed to commit suicide. One in particular stood out from the rest. The danger of his possible self-destruction visibly obvious to all in attendance, the man was kept in a straight jacket to thwart his desires. One morning he was found dead, smothered in a manner the staff would have thought previous to his success to be impossible.

The man had chewed through the thick mattress layering which covered his floor, straight down to the hardwood slats beneath. Then, he had continued onward, gnawing away at the boards below until finally he had reached a state where he could hook his teeth into the wood to the point where they would anchor him against the floor. After that, he had induced vomiting and choked himself to death in a pool of his own liquefying dinner.

It had only been after examining the hole chewed into the smooth oaken boards that Legrasse finally began to feel the same despair which had shaken his lieutenant so much earlier. Indeed, at that point the inspector began his search for anything or anyone outside the usual sphere of police influence that might shed some light on what had motivated the happenings in the swamps outside his city.

Finding nothing for several weeks, Legrasse's last hope had been the conference to which he had taken the idol. Meeting Professor Webb had given the inspector a bit of hope. The elder academic had found the same cult, even the same type of graven image as Legrasse had, across the world in the frozen mountains of Greenland. His eagerness to explore the site of another branch of the same lost religion inspired Legrasse to the point where he thought he might finally be able to close the books on the monstrous case once and for all.

As he continued to stare at the dark idol on his desk, the inspector ordered in a soft voice, "Galvez, gather all the men who were with us in the swamp into the announcements room, would you?"

The lieutenant went off to do what Legrasse had requested. As he did, the inspector and Professor Webb merely continued staring at the curiosity in the middle of the desk. Neither man touched the black stone—the dreams resultant from previous contact had taught them better—but stare they did.

For the moment, they could do nothing else.

*   * * *   *

"And that, gentlemen," concluded Legrasse, "is all the back history any of us needs." The inspector had taken nearly an hour's time to retell the entire story to Webb, Galvez, and the nineteen other officers who had gone into the swamp, making sure each man in the room was as aware of every detail as everyone else present—giving them all the chance to contradict and correct the official record as well.

"So now, let us begin to outline what must be done next." Throughout the room, his officers shuffled uneasily. Knowing what was in their minds, knowing also that none of the men of lesser rank would dare speak, Galvez asked for them,

"Sir, is there anything that says all the men from the first raid need go on the second?"

The quiet in the room stirred like the dust of an ancient tomb at the feet of the first to uncover it. The dry silence stirred soundlessly, moving against its will and then finally settling back to the ground. Feeling its weight, Legrasse answered,

"I never ask any man to set foot where he knows he can't walk. I ..." his voice faltered for a moment, his mind deciding exactly how much truth was good for his officers. He continued after a moment, admitting, "I understand what hesitations there might be in a man's mind over all of this."

"Ain't no man here what's scart too bad to follow *you*, Inspector," answered a street officer, Joel Carrinelle. He was a tall but thin man, with the bony hands and protruding Adam's apple common in those of lanky frame. Unconsciously brushing back his cropped hair, he swore, "God's oath, sir, if your gun's in hand, mine's at your back and you're covered right up to Satan's front door if need be. You strike the knocker, Inspector, I'll keep the neighbors busy."

"Thank you, Officer Carrinelle. I'll keep that in mind should we need to venture so far south." As some of the men chuckled, Legrasse invited Professor Webb to the front of the room. Loud enough for his men to hear him, the inspector said,

"I want these men to know just what I plan to drag them into. Please, professor, tell them what you told me in Missouri." As Legrasse took a seat, the professor began to address the assembled police officers before him.

"You are brave men," he said sincerely, "all of you. Of that there can be no question. Why do I say this, you ask? I will tell you. You men have looked upon the cult of Cthulhu and not only not gone insane, but apparently kept your wits as well. From what I know, *that* act, gentlemen, takes a brave heart, indeed." Coming from behind the podium Legrasse had used, Webb moved out in front of it, spreading his hands as he continued.

"These cultists are, I am certain, the most odious, faithless, monstrous representatives of humanity there are to be found anywhere in this world. As a group they claim to be everywhere, hidden from the eyes of mankind. I believe them. Those that I discovered years ago, those you have found—curious and degenerate? Unquestionably. They are a deliberately bloodthirsty and repulsive pack of things. The mere mention of them to peoples from outside their number who might still have knowledge of the cult causes even those possessing only the most rudimentary traces of civilization to shudder and turn away."

The officers listened intently. Webb told them what science could of the human sacrifice and queer rites practiced by the menace they were opposing. When he ran through his short bit of exact knowledge of the Cthulhu cult, he went on to tell of other, lesser sects he had studied. He told the officers of men who ate the hearts of their enemies to possess their souls, of slavers and exotic tortures and the secret prophecies of a score of religions, all twisted and foul— one more loathsome than the next. Then finally, he told them,

"For all we know, these practitioners you have stumbled upon could be capable of any of these cruelties, or things far worse that none of us could even imagine. But gentlemen, that is why I believe it is precisely you and only you twenty in all of New Orleans—perhaps in all the Americas—that are capable of standing against these beasts."

"Beggin' your pardon, Professor," ventured a flush faced Sergeant named Muller, "but what's so special about us?"

"A good question, officer," answered Webb. "And I shall answer it. You men have all faced these maniacs once. I am told that several of you froze for a moment, that one of you fainted. You won't again. I'll tell you why. When first you see ... oh what? A yapping dog, perhaps. It barks and howls and you pull back, not so much because it is so fierce, but because its presence came unexpectedly. Once you see what it is and gauge its ability to do you injury, your fear disappears. These things are no different."

Walking back toward the front of the room slowly, Webb threw his words over his shoulder.

"They are merely *men*. Nothing more. They might commit brutish, horrific crimes, but they are not more than flesh and blood. You proved that once. And that time they had the cloak of mystery and the unknown within which to hide their crude ordinariness. But you have stolen that wrap from their shoulders. They can not wear it to fool you again."

"But what about ..."

Webb turned. One of the officers blurted the few words only to be hushed by his fellows. When the professor could not draw the man out further, Legrasse demanded the speaker finish his question. Reluctantly, surround by a sea of curious but embarrassed faces, all listened as he asked,

"Professor, what if these bunch *be* more than just men? We ain't been eager to say much about little, but it could be you maybe don't know everything about this. I ain't meanin' no disrespect to you nor your learnin', sir, but we ..." The man hesitated again, flustered and uncomfortable. His pause evaporated, however, forcing him to blurt, "we, we saw things out there, *heard* things. Plenty of us saw those eyes—glowing eyes, off in the distance—and that mound, the white mound. It was alive. Alive! And that wasn't but all. There was giant things around us—flyin' things! *Flyin'!*"

"That's *enough*," snarled Legrasse, his tone curt and final. He understood his men's fears. He had been in the swamp with them, had felt the cold stare of unseen eyes following them throughout their raid. In truth, he had felt those eyes more than once since that night, even amongst the cultured and learned elite with whom he had met in Missouri. But, he would not have officers in his command chattering in frightened shrieks. As the man sat back down, Webb took over, telling everyone,

"There are many things in this world that none of us understand, my son. I won't bother debating with you whether or not there was something else unseen out there in the swamp with you. In all honesty, from some of the blasted texts and unpublished works I have read over the years, I feared there might have been even before your mention. But, I will ask, if there was, who else is there to stop it but yourselves?"

As the officers looked from one to another, the professor told them,

"Every religion awaits some sort of final outcome. Catholics, Jews, Protestants, Hindus, et cetera, all look toward the return of their messiah. Gentlemen, this cult of ours is no different. Those words shrieked by each of the executed cultists, as your inspector discovered during his interrogations, mean 'In his house at R'lyeh dead Cthulhu waits dreaming.'" Staring into the eyes of the officer who had been brave enough to give voice to his comrades fears, Webb said,

"This Cthulhu is their messiah, and they await his return as you do that of yours. If the sound of great wings here means otherworldly presences, all I can say is if the angels of some devil-worshiping cult's messiah have arrived on the scene, then it is all the more important for you to prepare for battle."

Legrasse was glad no one was present save the men who had actually been in the swamp. What they were saying would have seemed madness, perhaps even unintelligible, to anyone who had not stood in the fetid air of the dark bayou that night, listening to the foul snap of giant wings, feeling the cold taste of hungry eyes rubbing against their backs. As the inspector pushed the unnerving memories back to a safer compartment within his brain, Webb moved closer to the officer he had picked out from the others, telling him,

"Where others would be venturing into the unknown, *you* have been there. As frightening as the thought of returning might be, imagine what it would do others—others without your experience? Others who had not so seen and done all of what you twenty have seen and done. You men, you have a better chance than any force in the world."

"A better chance of what?" asked Galvez, the words popping out of his mouth before he could stop them.

"Of surviving, of course," answered Webb, matter-of-factly. When asked "surviving what?", he answered honestly, "I won't know that until I've inspected the site of the melee."

"And what if you don't survive?" asked yet another officer.

"Then I would suggest you kill all the cultists in your custody and every other one you can find, before they succeed in returning their God to this plane, which … if my calculations are correct, they will be attempting to do again ..." the professor reached into his jacket pocket and pulled forth a small note pad. Flipping it back several dozen leaves, he finally found the page he had been looking for. He scanned it for a moment then, one eye brow raising of its own volition, Webb answered,

"Some time next month."

* * * * *

Luckily for the quartet of boaters, the torrential storms which had been plaguing the area off and on for several months had stopped once more during the night. The next morning, despite the danger presented by the swamps treacherous bogs, Webb, Galvez, Carrinelle and Legrasse set off for Monolith Island, the colorful name given the site of the November 1st foray by the lieutenant. Unlike the first trip, however, this time several of the locals accompanied the investigators the entire way. Having the use of the swamp-dwellers' crafts along with that of their owners' services in getting them to the island made the trip a far easier thing to accomplish than it would have been on their own.

Thanking their guides with both words and a pair of silver dollars, Legrasse instructed the boatmen to return for them in four hours—a time far into the late April afternoon, but still enough in advance of sundown to keep everyone happy. The pair of squatters agreed, departing in one boat, leaving the other behind in case their passengers had some then unforeseen need for it. By the time their sleek, hand-carved bottom dragger had disappeared back into the moss-hung reeds, the inspector turned to find Webb hard at work, struggling to reach the top of the monolith.

With Carrinelle boosting him, the professor acquired the platform of the great stone, a smooth surface of some five to six square feet. Legrasse ordered Carrinelle to remain with Webb while he and Galvez scouted about. The officer acknowledged his orders, taking up his post at the foot of the monolith while the professor busied himself atop it. At the same time, Legrasse and his lieutenant moved off to the other side of the island.

"Inspector," Galvez asked as they walked, "what do you make of the Professor's talk yesterday, all that stuff about the things we thought we heard and saw? About heathen religions having their own gods and all?"

"Joseph," answered Legrasse, "what do you want from me? Should I say I think he's crazy and not be prepared? Should I say I think he's right and that we're surrounded by monsters from some savage's idea of Hell? I don't know what to think. None of us do. Maybe we were all letting things get to us last year. But then, maybe not. You have to remember, he needs facts just as much as we do. The more wild suppositions we give him for facts, the more wild the answers he has to give us back."

The inspector stopped for a second, staring out over the vast mud flat the relentless rains had made of the island. The unnatural chill of the past few days still hung in the air, made to seem all the more damp by the oppressive cover of hard gray clouds teeming from horizon to horizon. Legrasse fought the urge to snap at his lieutenant. The breakdown of his self-control had been inching forward for months, each new bizarre occurrence shaking him along just another small fraction toward the comforting embrace of madness and fear. Resisting their inviting lure, however, the inspector turned to Galvez, saying,

"We're policemen, Joseph. We have a job to do. No one ever said anything about winged monsters when we signed up—that's true. But then no one ever made you any assurances about anything. You swore to uphold the laws of the city of New Orleans and to act in good faith to protect its citizens." Legrasse shuddered slightly as a strange thought passed through his mind. Instantly he seized upon it as a way to make his point.

"Twenty-two years ago when I joined the force, no one said anything to me about monsters. But two years later, we all read the papers out of London as they rattled on about the ghoul there carving up women. Twenty years now and that one's never been captured. Flesh stripped from the bodies of the victims, organs removed, breasts cut away, hints of perverted sexual mutilation … whose to say that monster didn't have wings?"

Galvez tilted his head as if he had been slapped. His nostrils flared with distaste. It was not that the lieutenant did not like cases that made him think. He was a man of rare intelligence, skilled in moving his ability to reason down clear, deductive paths. But this case was beyond his ken. Galvez had long been known as a man who could anchor himself firmly and pull the facts of a situation to him, no matter how deep he might have to dredge the various mires in which they were hidden.

This time, however, he found he could not position himself. The case seemed too much like the swamp that had borne it. The lieutenant could find no ground solid enough to plant his feet so that he could begin dragging for the clues he needed to effect a solution. Every other moment, instead of helping to clear his vision, each new fact seemed to only obscure things further—leaving him groping for the shore of his consciousness, drowning in the darkness. Abandoning the front lines, he acquiesced to Legrasse instead.

"So then," he asked, "what do we do?"

"Whatever Professor Webb needs us to do. We two aren't going to get anywhere with this on our own. We've been over this island twice by daylight now and not found anything that meant much to us. Our only hope now is that somehow …" And then, before Legrasse could continue, Professor Webb's voice interrupted his line of reason.

"Inspector! I say … have you made note of that clearing over there?"

Legrasse and Galvez both looked off in the direction in which Webb was pointing. From their lesser vantage, neither man could even make out that a clearing existed behind the bank of intervening rushes and overhung festoons of Spanish moss. So eager to investigate that which only he could see, the older man nearly fell from his high perch. The inspector ordered Carrinelle to assist the professor's descent while sending Galvez back to bring the squatter's flat bottomer around so they might all be able to move across the swamp to whatever it was that Webb seemed to have discovered. The lieutenant turned to head back for the boat, but just before he did so, he reminded Legrasse,

"Inspector, over there—that grove—I think that's where, I mean, the men who saw the eyes ... and the big white shape ..."

"Get the boat," the inspector said quietly. Staring over at the remote ring of trees, he thought to himself that he needed no reminder as to where they were heading.

It took some time longer than Legrasse had anticipated for the quartet to make their way to the hidden clearing. Although the recent rains had brought up the water level of the swamp, allowing them to navigate past many of the bog's hidden traps—old logs, hidden sand shelves, grasping quick muds, and the like—that little traveled part of the swamp was dreadfully overgrown, forcing Galvez to hack their way clear several times while Carrinelle tried to hold their vessel steady with his pole.

Even climbing the bank leading to the clearing proved nearly fatal when Professor Webb slipped, slamming into Carrinelle, sending him sliding backward down into the bog. Galvez managed to catch hold of his sinking fellow officer and pull him back to safety. Webb, of course, offered his profoundest apologies, which the policeman accepted with extreme good grace, commenting that if the worse thing that happened to him while they were there was a dirty uniform then he would be well pleased.

Finally, however, the four men reached the clearing. Unfortunately, what they found there denied them any answers, instead inspiring far more additional questions than they would have thought possible. Descending the bank, the quartet moved cautiously, watching their step as best they could as they moved through the surrounding ring of trees and out into the open ... a strange and unnatural opening that should not have existed.

"I don't get it, Inspector," offered Carrinelle. "What could do something like this?" Not having an answer for the younger man, Legrasse deferred to Webb. The professor took a moment, then just as he was about to speak, he spotted something at his feet.

"I, I think maybe ... yes, maybe ... ?"

Bending down, Webb knelt to examine the strange matting beneath all their feet. The clearing was a circular space roughly thirty yards wide at its diameter. The longer the inspector stared at its circumferential edge, the more convinced he became that it was a true circle, geometrically perfect.

Getting closer to the ground, Legrasse studied the flooring of the area with an interest to match the professor's. He found the reeds and moss and other vegetation woven together into a type of matted carpeting. The sight stupefied the four, eventually dragging the others to their knees for a closer look as well. The inspector did not know what to think. He poked his hand vigorously against the pattern but could not force through so much as a single finger. Common horsetail and scouring rushes were webbed together with club moss and marsh ferns, all of it tightly interworked until it was virtually as solid as plate iron.

"Professor," asked Legrasse in a puzzled voice, "what could have done this? The storm, maybe?"

"This is simply fascinating," answered Webb, almost unaware he was doing so. Not looking up, crawling along the ground as if intent on inspecting every square inch of the puzzling phenomenon, he continued, saying, "Look at the workmanship. Not a stem broken, not a leaf or shoot torn away from its mother stem. No storm did this. This is even beyond the work of human hands."

When Carrinelle scoffed, the professor ignored his protests, saying instead, Look—look, will you? This work isn't recent, either. You can see this was done some time ago. Note how the new growth is all above the lines of intersection." Standing, the professor told the others,

"I'm no botanist, but I'd be comfortable guessing that we are seeing four to five months of winter growth here since this circle was woven."

"You're saying the cultist's did this?" asked Galvez.

"No," answered Webb noncommittally. "I'm merely implying that it was most likely done around the same time of their ritual."

"Well," asked Legrasse, disturbed to have discovered a completely new mystery instead of any new answers, "if the cult didn't do it—and I wouldn't suspect any of that lot being of a very artistic bent—who or what did?"

"I appreciate your curiosity, Inspector," answered the professor. "And I will tell you the only guess I have, although I'm afraid none of you will want to hear it."

The men around Webb all hesitated to varying degrees. Each had been wishing to turn the bizarre puzzle of the swamp into something easily processed and stored within the human mind. The professor's offer did not sound as if he would be providing such an answer. Having nothing of their own to add, however, each of the three nodded their willingness to hear what Webb had to say.

Understanding their apprehension—actually feeling some of it himself—the professor told them, "Again, gentlemen, I am not trying to mock you, nor am I saying that what I have to offer is the only answer. I am merely going to relate to you several stories I have heard."

All three policemen remained quiet, their eyes riveted to Webb. Nodding his head in tight-lipped acceptance of their attitude, the professor swallowed a breath of the gray swamp air, and then launched into his tale.

"Back a few years, what was it ... '83, I believe. A Mexican astronomer named José Bonilla photographed over one hundred circular objects that moved across the solar disc. Before the end of that same decade, a Texan farmer saw a large circular object flying overhead. He called it a saucer. Now, mayhap none of you heard of either of those cases, but I'm certain that you've all heard of the scores of sightings of like objects over the past ten years." The professor paused to swat at a large, blood-seeking insect. Sending the buzzing annoyance on its way, he wiped at his brow, then continued.

"All across the country, people have been seeing giant ... what would one call them? Airships, I suppose. Traveling much faster than any dirigible, capable of changing course at what appear to be frightfully high speeds, many have described them as seeming more alive than man-made."

"Very well and fine, Professor," interrupted Legrasse. Pointing downward with both hands, he spread them apart to indicate the entire clearing while he asked, "but what exactly does any of that have to do with *this?*"

Nodding with the understanding that he had failed to come to the point, Webb answered,

"Wherever in the world these 'saucers' have been seen in the sky, sooner or later, on the ground below, circles such as these have appeared ... almost without fail."

* *** *

Legrasse raised his glass to his lips, downing another healthy slug of bourbon. He was not usually one to drink with his men. In fact, he was not usually one to drink at all. "Usually" no longer applied, however.

After exiting from the swamp, Legrasse, Galvez and Carrinelle had taken Professor Webb to Jim Dandy's, a tavern of little repute on one of the darker back streets of the Quarter. Once properly hidden from public view in a dark, practically moldering corner, the four had set to work on a bottle of local bourbon. When that one was finished, they promptly started a second. Older than the others, Webb found the opening of the second bottle his cue to remove himself to the toilet for a moment's relief. He had reached a state of nervous agitation on the way back from the swamp, the edge of which hard drinking had not yet been able to remove. As the elder academic tottered off, Carrinelle made an announcement with a thickening tongue.

"Sir, I don't know what to think."

"About what, Joel?" answered Legrasse. The liquor bending him to a more familiar tone than usual, he explained, "I mean, I know 'what about,' but 'what about' in particular?"

"Oh, Hell, sir," admitted the more than slightly drunken officer. "Anything. Everything. I mean, I mean … I … I mean … what? What was that? That professor … sayin' he wasn't certain anymore about, about … what was that again?"

"About 'the timetable of arrival,'" quoted Galvez.

"Yeah? Lookin' in his little book, climbin' all over that damn hunka stone. What was he talking about? And the way he's been getting' since we left— spooky, crazy. I don't know. I don't know."   Carrinelle raised his glass to knock back another powerful slug. Suddenly, however, he simply set the glass back down and asked quietly, "What? What're we doin', sir? What?"

"I don't know, either, Joel," answered the inspector honestly. Staring over the rim of his glass, his eyes leveling off in a straight line made up of heavy hoods and broken blood vessels, Legrasse said slowly, "Who could know? Do you know, Joe?" When the lieutenant merely waggled his head back and forth, blowing a few foamy bubbles through his moist lips, Legrasse pointed toward the lieutenant as drunken proof of some sort, saying,

"See?" The inspector drained a third of his glass as if in triumph. Then, instead of refilling it immediately, as had been the quartet's wont throughout the evening, he set the tumbler back down. Closing his eyes, Legrasse held his neck rigid, then shook his head several times. He could feel the bones at the top of his spine crack, could trace a sluggish pain within his head—the beginning screams of mild alcohol poisoning. Ignoring them both, realizing Carrinelle deserved a better answer, he took a deep breath, then tried to find one.

"What are we supposed to do? I don't know. We put an end to some swamp voodoo. Kill a few of the sect, capture some, run the rest off. That's it—usually. But, no, not for us." The inspector waved his hands in frustration.

"No, we can't just have a group of entrail readers painting each others' faces in chicken blood," he started again. "Oh, no … not us. We're special. We have to have … have to have … what? Some kind of monumentally evil devil worshiping secret society from the beginning of time. A human-sacrificing illuminati that hides in frozen mountains and swamps and every other out of the way place in the world."

"It's our luck," said Galvez thickly, lifting his glass. Both the other officers lifted their own glasses as well. The trio brought their tumblers together, clinking them softly.

"Our luck," they all slurred, taking large sips immediately after. Then, as Carrinelle topped off all their glasses, Legrasse pushed his spine against the back of his chair, its rattan covered top curve pressing into his shoulders.

"It's all so odd," the inspector announced, more to himself than to the others. "These cultists ... murdering swamp squatters. Why? Monsters watching us, flying monsters, cultists happy to die. Why? And Webb's saucers in the sky, that clearing ... that horrible little statue ... I wonder ... I mean to say ..."

And then, Legrasse froze. The words he was trying to utter hung suspended in his throat, trapped behind the weight of the connections his brain had started to make. In a blinding moment of clarity, the inspector had suddenly made a jump in reason too frightening for him to accept without further consideration. Next to him, Galvez began to raise his glass once more. Legrasse stuck out his hand, though, grasping at the lieutenant's wrist.

"No," he ordered, desperately pushing at the fogging clouds settling within his brain. "No more for now." Understanding the tone in his superior's voice, Galvez asked,

"What is it, sir?"

"Webb ... he treats this all so, so ... serious. He's the only one who doesn't act as if he thinks we were children who scared ourselves out in the swamp. You tell me, Joe—*did* you see something out there last year or didn't you?"

"Well, I ..."

"Damnit, Lieutenant. Did you or didn't you?!"

"Yes, sir," answered the excitable Spaniard. Propelled by the liquid courage of many a deep sip, he pushed aside the cautious responses he had given months before and finally admitted, "Yes, I did. You can throw me off the force for saying it, but I swear on my grandmother's grave ... where we stood today, where the reeds and all were wove together like some damned devil basket ... I saw a pair of demon eyes—gigantic things—watching us through the trees ... shining yellow slits carved in a mountainous white bulk ... Madre Dios, it was there. I swear it, Inspector."

"Don't worry, Joseph," said Legrasse reassuringly. "I believe you." Before the inspector could say more, however, the owner of Jim Dandy's came to their table. Bending low, he whispered to Legrasse who merely nodded an assurance to the visibly disturbed man. As the owner left the table, the inspector told his men,

"It seems the professor is having some difficulty in the toilet. Joel, see to him."

The officer rose without speaking, heading straight off to see what the matter was and to deal with it as quietly as possible. Legrasse and Galvez did not speak while he was gone. It somehow did not seem proper to either man to discuss what was happening to them all with one of their number absent. Finally, after some ten long minutes, Carrinelle returned to the table with Webb in tow. As they took their seats again, Legrasse gave the newly returned officer a look which asked what the problem had been.

Carrinelle, knowing Legrasse did not want him to embarrass the professor, merely rolled his eyes and gave a shrug of his shoulders, moving his lips in a manner that indicated Webb was loosing his grip. The inspector took the hint and decided to ignore whatever troubles there had been, having a feeling he already understood anyway. Thus, instead of wasting time worrying about the professor's nerves, Legrasse grabbed up their bottle and topped off Webb's glass, asking him directly,

"So, is this all real or isn't it?" When the professor protested the unsubstantiated theoretical stand the inspector's question would force him to take, Legrasse brushed aside his complaints, adding, "Listen to me, Professor, you've been pushing us as if you want us to believe all this ... well, fine. Maybe we do. The question is—do *you* ... or don't you?"

"Inspector Legrasse, I don't want to argue with you now. You've had a great deal to drink and I ..."

"Goddamnit," roared Legrasse, "*do you or don't you?*" Heads turned throughout the tavern. Lowering his voice, the inspector continued. "You said their cult was a religion, that it had a god and angels. You said people have been seeing saucers in the skies and that wherever they see these saucers, circles appear on the ground ... just like that one out in the swamp."

"Well, yes, but what I ..."

"Listen—maybe the world's just changed too much for me. Maybe I can't keep up with it. When I was a boy men couldn't fly. Now they can. We have submarines, paint that comes out of guns, air conditioning, those, those ... vacuum tubes, and freeze dried blood." Legrasse jammed his teeth together, stopping the flow of words spilling out of him. Shaking his head again, trying to drive away some of the alcohol blurring his vision, he snapped,

"What I mean is, the cultists murdered the squatters. You said they were blood sacrifices. What if those sacrifices brought that thing my men saw—called to it? Or that damned statute—maybe that's their beacon." Not looking at any of the others at the table, the inspector found himself shaking his head, not so much consciously, but merely allowing it to twitch. Forcing the motion to stop, he slapped the table again, snarling,

"Who knows? Who even *Cares?!* What does it matter—how and why! *Where!* That's all that matters. If round things are flying down out of the sky and making those vegetation circles all around the world—then why not here? You said this damned Cthulhu cult was hidden in all the dark corners of the world. There's plenty that call New Orleans a dark corner. So, tell me, professor ... why not here?"

Legrasse grabbed hold of the edge of the table to calm himself. Instead, the shaking agitation raging through him caused him to set the table to bouncing nervously, startling both Webb and his own men. A terrible excitement pelted the inspector's consciousness with information, linking connections faster than he could vocalize them. Licking at the inside of his mouth, driving back the bourbon taste, he let go the table but continued on, asking questions in an excited tone.

"The cultists being executed—each one has said the same thing at the moment of their deaths. The same thing they were shouting when we broke up their ceremony. Is it a prayer? Are they priests?"

The professor turned away from Legrasse, his own hands trembling. Reaching across the table suddenly, the inspector captured Webb's lapels in his hands. Dragging the professor half across the table toward him, knocking over several of the glasses in the way as well as their new bottle, he shouted,

"Their god, whatever he is, this Cthulhu ... you said he was sleeping. Well, what if they've decided it's time to wake him up?! What if these flying things everyone's seen are the same things *we* saw, heard ... what if ..."

And then, Legrasse went calm. The building madness fled his eyes in an explosive moment of acceptance, replaced by a singularity of purpose. No longer questioning his beliefs, he asked Webb,

"When you examined the monolith, you said your calculations had been off. That you had been mistaken about when this god of theirs is supposed to arise. So tell me, if it's not to be in the next month, when is it to be?"

With a shudder, the shaking professor answered, "I didn't know then. It all seemed ... seemed so, so academic. So orderly. It was a great mystery to set into place. The pieces were fitting so nicely ... I never thought ..."

"When, Professor?" Asked the inspector again, giving Webb a harsh shake. Terrified, the old man yelped a single word.

"Tonight!"

Legrasse released the man, letting him fall back into his own chair. His eyes toward the table, hands clutching for his glass, the older man moaned,

"I never thought ... of course, it *could* have been real, but who knew? Who *could have* known? The concept of it ... all so, really, when you think of it— so, so ... outlandish, so terrifying, so, so ..."

Grasping at his overturned tumbler, the professor righted it and their bottle at the same time. Splashing the unspilled dregs of bourbon into his now-slippery glass, he let the bottle fall from his hands and then sucked down the several inches of liquor he had been able to salvage. At the same time, Legrasse ordered,

"Carrinelle, get back to the station house. Get all of our original investigation force together. Get anyone else you can. Break out all the weapons we have, and, and, send someone around to that construction in the north district up past Jordan Street, where they're taking down all those row houses. Commandeer all the explosives you can find."

"Yes, sir," answered the officer. Getting to his feet as best he could, he asked, "Where shall I take them, sir?"

"You take them wherever you like, Joel. I'll be headed out to the swamp."

A huge smile cracked open the lanky officer's face. Heading to the door, he answered, "Stay long enough to have another drink, sir, and I'll have 'em there before you."

As Carrinelle made his way to the door, Webb let out a moaning wail. He had drained his glass and had no more liquor. Seeing that his jacket sleeve was soaked with bourbon, he shoved it into his mouth and sucked hard, pulling a thin drizzle of linty alcohol down his throat. Paying him no mind, Legrasse turned to his lieutenant.

"Galvez," he said, "you're a dirty Spanish bastard and you can drink more than any man on the force and still come across as a bishop, agreed?"

"An old family talent," admitted the lieutenant with a sharp, clear-eyed smile that belied the amount of bourbon he had consumed that evening. "It is at your disposal, el Grande."

"Good. Is that old Navy destroyer still in dock?" When his man assured him it was, the inspector continued, ordering, "Then you get yourself down to the waterfront, find her captain, and put on a demeanor that will convince him to put to sea. Tell him we've got pirates, tell him anything you have to but get him out there lined up with the swamps."

"Yes, sir," answered Galvez, pulling himself to his feet. Turning to head for the door, he suddenly stopped and turned back, asking, "Why?"

"Why? So if any Goddamned monster falls out of the sky at us he can blow it to smithereens."

Galvez's eyes blinked wide for a moment, then relaxed. As the lieutenant pulled his thoughts together, he and Legrasse both rose from the table at the same time, smiling. Taking each others' hand, the two policemen stared for a moment into each others' eyes, both looking for the right words. Finally deciding that there were none, they let go their grip and then headed for the door. Behind them, Webb bent his head to the bourbon soaked table, tears streaming down his face as he chewed the tablecloth and licked at the wet boards beneath.

* **** *

This was much easier when someone else was doing all the work, decided the inspector. Making his way through the growing breeze and the dark swamp night in a borrowed squatter's boat, he allowed himself a grim chuckle, thinking, you'd better be right about this, Legrasse.

The inspector had been quieting the cautious voices in his brain ever since he left Jim Dandy's. He knew how things would look if he were wrong. Drunk, dragging a score of officers out into the swamp at night, confiscating explosives, commandeering a U.S. Navy warship ... and why? Oh, because some devil monster was about to descend on New Orleans.

If I have this one wrong, he thought, there won't be enough of my career left to feed a dog that's already had dinner. And yet …

Legrasse's mind turned to what he thought he knew. If he *were* right … a world filled with blood-sacrificing covens, monsters that flew down out of the sky—huge, barn-sized things—angels of some demon religion that sent its congregations out to find it blood and treasure …

"Oh, shut up," he whispered to himself. "After all, maybe the world will be lucky. Maybe I am the crazy one. Maybe this is all in my head, and the world is safe after all."

The paddle in his hand came up in a cool slow rhythm. As he passed it over the front of his skiff, drops fell in an arcing line, the natural flow of their descent giving the world enough normalcy for Legrasse to make a last wish.

"Maybe."

And then, cutting across the muddy green water of the swamp, the keening sound of a thin, reedy piping broke through the whipping trill of the hot, dry wind. Small and distant, it slammed against the inspector's ears, making him shudder.

"And then again …," he whispered, "maybe not."

He remembered the fluting noise from his first trip to the swamp. At almost the moment he and his men had become convinced they had lost their way, the distance sound of pipes and drums had drawn them to the monolith and the heathen insanity capering around it. Pulling his paddle inside his borrowed craft, Legrasse stopped all movement, sending his senses out into the marsh. Listening, he strained all his internal apparati, searching for any presence that might know he was about. Feeling that he was still secure, the inspector then pulled his pistol from beneath his jacket.

It was not common for officers, even high-ranking ones, to carry firearms. Legrasse had fallen into the habit after being caught in an alleyway by a trio of rum runners with a particular aversion to returning to prison. If not for the luck of a pair of passing beat prowlers, the inspector's career might have been ended far earlier.

Yes, he thought with sarcasm. What a pity if that had happened. I'd have missed all the joys I've found in this wonderful swamp.

The weapon was cold in his hand—cold and small and suddenly seeming far too light to be a engine of destruction. Legrasse's mind remembered the whispers of his men, of the gigantic white bulk so many of them had seen. Stroking the German-made automatic, he spoke to it quietly.

"Could you stop something so big, girl?" he asked it absently, his eyes staring ahead. "Can anything we do stop these things?"

And then, Legrasse suddenly jammed the gun back into his waistband. His cheeks burning, he wondered when he had become such a child. Whining, filled with self-pity ... pushing on into the unknown and yet sitting tight-kneed like some school girl. What was next, he wondered—the vapors? Was it the liquor, he wondered, grasping for an excuse? Was it Webb and his highbrow notions? Legrasse had known other men of science, confident and filled with advice and theories—until something went wrong.

Then it was always hand-wringing and frayed nerves and tears. Arrogance or hopeless fright—that's all you got from academics. Sliding his paddle into the water once more, the inspector pushed off toward the sound of the growing music. As his flat bottomer slid through the rushes, pushing aside those it could not crush over completely, Legrasse thought on Professor Webb.

He was grateful for the older man's assistance. Indeed, if the professor's theory was correct about the cult—and the crude tune filtering through the night was a strong indicator that he was—then his help would most likely prove invaluable. But, suggestions and clues and ideas, that's all his type—doctors and scientists—were good for. If Webb were there in the boat with him, he knew the man's horror would have already destroyed them.

Whereas, to be honest with himself, Legrasse was finding his true, inner self almost eager to reach the monolith. As a trace of light slashed through the cattails whipping back and forth in the mounting breeze before his boat, coaxing him on, he felt his pulse quickening. He was getting close.

"Good."

The single word was a whisper, barely louder than his heating breath, and yet it filled the inspector with a snaking thrill that churned his blood and made the juice run in his mouth. He had been away from the thick of things for too long. When promotion had raised him above the honest life of a patrolman, Legrasse had become a puppet of formality, an observer of human nature, a seeker of clues, a judge or some other form of civil marionette. But, still within him ached the heart of a man, one waiting for its moment—waiting for something worthy of his own self image against which he could test himself.

One silent stroke after another pushed the flat bottomer along, Legrasse having to almost forcefully hold himself in check. He wanted to charge forward, to take on the whole lot of them ... he could feel their bones breaking beneath his fists, taste their blood in his mouth, smell their fear as he tore at their eyes, hear the sounds of their tears mingled with his laughter ...

Stroke after stroke, the silent swamp boat glided through the marsh, Legrasse growing hotter and hotter for the moment of reckoning. His pulse racing, lungs filling to bursting, he knew he was as ready as a normal man could be for whatever lie ahead.

"Yes ..." he breathed, his nostrils flaring, eyes narrowing, smile growing cold and grim. And then, instinctively, the inspector stopped his bottom dragger. Reaching forward, he parted the rushes in front of the boat a fraction of an inch. There was no further to go. Legrasse had returned to Monolith Island. Returned to it as he had first seen it—returned to it as if through the gates of time themselves.

Once again, the massive bonfire had been built, naked dancers braying and writhing about its base ... and also, once again, the scaffolds had been erected. A score of bodies hung from the rough poles, each with at least one inverted corpse swinging from it, most with two, all of them running red from their feet to their heads. The inspector jammed his teeth together at the sight.

For a brief moment, he thought he had failed the squatters of the area. But then, carefully taking in their general appearance, Legrasse realized, the cultists had not made victims of the swamp dwellers again. This time, they had used their own brethren. From his vantage point, the inspector studied the area ahead, mapping his strategy. As the dancers rounded the monolith over and over, he counted in excess of a good forty foes. The numbers made sense. The inspector knew he and his men had swept up less than half the cultists during their previous raid. Counting the bodies hanging before him, he knew all of them had returned that night—one way or the other—to partake in their final ceremony. Which was to be ... what?

No matter which way he looked at his scant collection of facts, he could not put the puzzle straight. If the last sacrifice had been used to call a flying monster down out of the sky, then what had become of it? Where was it? And where had it been for nearly half a year?

As he watched the cavorting worshipers, trying to puzzle out his next move, Legrasse was forced to suddenly duck down. Catching him by surprise, the oddly heated wind, which so far that evening had been nothing more than a mild annoyance, now bent his cover of reeds and cattails back, nearly exposing him. The inspector was forced to lie in the flat of his boat, watching the vegetation before him slam back and forth in the mounting gale. And then, suddenly, as he watched the marsh weeds intertangling with each other, Legrasse exclaimed,

"Bloody God! That's it!"

Grabbing at his paddle, the inspector forced himself erect through the growing wind. He had been thinking of the monster as something substantial—a physical presence such as a dog or alligator. But Webb had hinted at godhood for the white mound. What if the older man had been right? What if they both had been right? What if the normal rules of science did not apply to this horror from beyond?

If the sacrifices *were* to summon their god, Legrasse reasoned, what if the cultists simply hadn't spilled *enough* blood by the time we arrived that first time? Perhaps it had just *begun* to appear when we arrived. Cutting off the flow of blood to it might have broken its link with this world ... and that was why only *some* of us saw it. It was here, but when we cut off the sacrifices, it disappeared back to the wherever from which it came.

Legrasse bent to work with his paddle. No longer concerned with stealth, he aimed his boat straight for the island, tacking against the fiercely growing wind as he thought,

What if they've been killing themselves all along to finish the job? Overjoyed to die one at a time, bit by bit ... using their lives as starvation rations for their god. Webb made noises about certain gravities needing to be right, stars positioned just so ... maybe, maybe these deaths since the raid have just been, been ... *snacks* for this thing of theirs. And now, as Webb said, if tonight *is* the night when they can bring their god back—fully back—to our world ... that would explain the abundance of death here tonight.

And then, a figure on shore pointed directly at Legrasse. For a moment, none of the cultist's fellows heard him over their own feverish musicians and the growling sounds of the ever increasing wind. But soon, drawn by his gestures if not his voice, others broke off from their dance, spotting the approaching inspector. Realizing he had no other choice, Legrasse pulled his Luger and pointed it toward the gesturing cultist.

"Very well," he growled, "you want to meet the devil tonight, you bastards ... let me help you."

The inspector squeezed his trigger. A great retort sounded across the marsh and the cultist's head burst open in a scarlet explosion. Before the dead man's knees could buckle, Legrasse fired again. The motion of his boat on the wind-churned swamp waters throwing off his aim, the inspector hit a second man in the chest instead of the head which had been his target. Falling to the ground, the severely wounded cultist croaked,

"*Ph'nglui mglw'nafh Cthulhu R'lyeh wgah'nagl fhtagn.*"

And then, a cheer went up from the dancers. Suddenly the force of the swirling winds cutting through the swamp doubled in speed and strength. Although the pipers and drummers kept up their sinister beat, the other cultists all rushed into the water toward Legrasse, chanting and laughing. The inspector used his bullets wisely, shooting down his best target each time, missing completely only once.

As the cultists worked their way through the bog and the fierce winds, Legrasse emptied his automatic. At the first "click," he coolly dropped out the magazine, pocketing the empty clip with one hand while fishing a new one out of his jacket pocket with the other. The nearest cultist was but ten feet from the inspector's boat when the policeman finished reloading and began firing once more.

His first shot tore through the head of the closest worshipper, blinding the man behind him with a spray of blood and gray matter as the back of the first man's head exploded open. Legrasse paid neither any heed. Shifting his aim over to the left, he fired again, dropping another.

By the time the jabbering pack reached his boat, the inspector had dispatched nearly a score of them, wounding several others. Bodies floated face down across the marsh, calling to the carnivores that lived throughout the swamp. Expending his last few shots recklessly, Legrasse dropped his weapon into the bottom of his boat and grabbed up his oar.

The first of the worshippers to reach the flat bottomer took the full force of the hard wood slat across his face. The blow spun the man around, sending him crashing into one of his fellows. The second to reach the boat, coming up on Legrasse's opposite side, received a slamming even harder than the first man—a blow so hard it shattered the paddle up the center.

Before the inspector could react to the destruction of his weapon, however, one of his attackers threw himself forward. The cultist hit Legrasse across the legs, but worse, he swamped the inspector's vessel. His arms flailed for but a second, then Legrasse fell backwards and disappeared beneath the dark, oily waters of the marsh, his gun lost, boat overturned. The inspector surfaced a moment later, however, coughing and gagging. As three of the cultists splashed forward toward him, Legrasse rose and spit out the last of the foul water he had swallowed and balled his fists.

Standing in some four feet of water, the inspector sent a driving blow into the face of the first to reach him, knocking the man off his feet. A second swing buried his left fist inches deep in one worshipper's abdomen. But sadly, his third swing missed, allowing two of the cultists to tackle him. The three men splashed about underwater, their struggle forcing them forward toward shore. The three wrestled briefly in the thin mud, crushing the centuries old stands of vegetation, tangling themselves in floating swamp creepers.

Legrasse finally managed to knock one of the cultists away, but the triumph was a small one. Two more men took their fallen brother's place, dragging the inspector to his feet with the help of the other man with whom Legrasse had first gone down. And then, the howling wind slamming all about them, the worshippers dragged the inspector to Monolith Island.

Legrasse struggled as best he could, but to no avail. He had swallowed too much swamp water, exerted himself too greatly to resist the dozen rough hands pulling him along. Dragging him up to the great block of granite in the center of the island, through the ring of bloodied corpses, the gibbering cultists shoved the inspector up against the massive slab. Lashing his left wrist tightly, they ran a stout ship's rope completely about the great monolith and then lashed his right as well.

Once they had completed their work, the cult members stepped back from their captive. As they did, the one acting as their leader, a large, glowering Negro with skin blacker than the surrounding night spoke to Legrasse.

"You one lucky white worm, piece shit boy, dat you be."

While the dancing began again, one sweating body after another passing before the inspector's eyes, the high priest came forward and caught Legrasse's chin with his hand. Holding the inspector's face firm, he laughed and said,

"You been try stop mighty Cthulhu. Foolish little white worm. You slide across the ground without feeling, you think you be the grand king of all, but you just a bag of air with no eyes. Blind and sad and fit for the grave."

Behind the high priest, Legrasse could see that the musicians had joined the dance, jumping and leaping with the rest of the worshippers as they circled the monolith again and again. Completing the circle, the wind joined them, revolving around the granite block in step with the cultists. Finally the inspector could see the whole picture. Blood and spells—whatever intricate pattern they wove—that called the wind. Twisting itself faster and faster, spinning the air around the monolith, the wind was what the cultists used to break the barriers of time and space to drag their foul gods to Earth.

"Yes!" answered the high priest as if he had read Legrasse's mind merely by looking into his eyes. "The worm understands! It *understands!*"

The storm was what wove the strange design in the plants they had found earlier, and it was what called forth the monsters from the sky. The high priest, delighted at the mad understanding he found in the inspector's eyes, unhitched the lead weighted club dangling from the girdle he wore, the only piece of clothing to be found on any of the cultists. Holding his weapon on high, an insane gleam in his eye, the black skin man shouted to be heard over the howling pain of wind and screams.

"You know—dat good. Good and good. Now you know why die must, to bring down the priests dat will rise up great R'lyeh, and thus free almighty Cthulhu!"

As a piercing whoop went up from the worshippers, the high priest aimed his club for Legrasse's head and intoned,

"*Ph'nglui mglw'nafh Cthulhu R'lyeh ... "*

The first bullet ripped through the side of the Negro's head, exploding out through his opposite ear, scattering an arc of blood through the growing wind. The second and third hit his body at different levels a split second apart, spinning his shattered frame first one way, then the other. Before Legrasse's brain could form the slightest prayer of thanks, suddenly two lines of police broke clear of the distant foliage where the inspector's boat had been swamped and came streaming toward the island.

The cultists raced to the water's edge to greet their attackers. None of them possessed weapons outside of teeth and nails, but they seemed oblivious to such concerns. Charging through the ever tightening circle of wind surrounding the island, they drove forward to the edge of the swamp and then off into its foaming waters, straight on at the attacking line of police.

Legrasse's men allowed them to gain no further vantage than had he. As soon as targets were clear, the officers opened fire, dropping one naked corpse after another into the churning marsh. The wind howling, spinning madly, the constant gunfire and the shrieks of those it cut down all conspired to fill the air with a masking cacophony, hiding what was truly transpiring. Still lashed to the monolith, however, Legrasse was not deceived.

"For our dear Lord's sake, *don't kill them!*"

But none could hear the inspector as he struggled against his bonds. One after another, he watched the cultists die, saw their smiling lips repeat the damning words ...

"*Ph'nglui mglw'nafh Cthulhu R'lyeh wgah'nagl fhtagn.*"

Carrinelle reached Legrasse's side just as the inspector had almost freed his left hand. Long strips of skin hung from his wrist and thumb, blood flowing freely, but Legrasse cared not. As his man cut through the last of the restraints, the inspector shouted,

"They can't kill them! That's what they want. Every death brings it a bit closer."

"What, Inspector?" asked Carrinelle. "Brings *what* closer?"

And then, a sudden dreadful knowledge gripping him, Legrasse looked upward through the horrible storm and pointed, screaming,

"*That!*"

Carrinelle looked up along the line of the inspector's arm. Shielding his eyes from the sand and other debris whipping through the cyclonic winds, the officer stared up into the sky. What he saw made him gasp. Descending slowly toward the island, some staggering distance overhead, a white shape spun wildly, hanging suspended due to the gale currents and its own great wings. Carrinelle jammed the fingers of one hand into his mouth. Words sputtered out around his drool-slicked fingers, meaningless and stupid. Grabbing him, Legrasse demanded,

"Get hold of yourself, man—that's an order!" When the officer continued to stare blankly, his pupils contracting to the merest pin points, the inspector slapped him, leaving a bloody outline on Carrinelle's cheek from his own dripping wounds. The man blinked, then began to beg Legrasse's pardon. The inspector silenced him, saying,

"No time, Joel. I understand. Forget it. Right now we've got to deal with that, that ... that *thing!*"

"But *how,* Inspector? What can we do?"

"Did you get the explosives?" When Carrinelle shakenly indicated that they had brought an entire boatload, Legrasse ordered, "Then get them up here—now!"

While the officer made his way to the beach, Legrasse turned to the monolith behind him. Heedless of his torn hand or his exhaustion, the inspector threw himself against the great granite slab, grappling for the hand and foot holds that would take him to the top. Blood smeared the rock from

53

his wounds as he made his way painfully up the great stone's side. The violently swirling winds threatened to knock him free several times, but he managed to hang on, leaving a flowing crimson trail behind as he finally pulled his head above the monolith's pinnacle.

Looking over the edge, there in the center of the small platform atop the monolith, Legrasse found another statue, exactly as he had the first time. His eye caught by the smooth dark carving, he fell into the spell of the hideous statue, lost to time until after he knew not how long, Carrinelle's voice came to him.

"Inspector! We've got the explosives!"

Grateful for the distraction, Legrasse grabbed the new statue with his unprotected hand and then released his hold on the monolith, sliding painfully down its side until he slammed against the ground. Staggering to his feet, he found that only some four of his men had managed to keep their wits besides Carrinelle. Where the rest had run off to—if they were even still alive—he did not know or care. He could not blame any man for cracking under what they had seen that night, he could only thank God for those that had not. Gathering those few, oh, so hearty souls together, the inspector pulled them close so as to be heard over the roar of the building storm.

"How you kept your wits, gentlemen," he bellowed, "I won't ask. We can all make thanks on Sunday come …"

"If we live that long," interrupted one officer, a wild, terrified look in his eye. Understanding, wishing he could give in to the madness eating at him, Legrasse nodded, saying,

"We'll live." Pointing upward, seeing that the ghastly white shape was half again closer than before, the inspector swore, "It's *that* thing that's going to Hell tonight. It's drawn by prayers and blood. Well, this is where the prayers were, and this is where the blood is, so let's fix it a dinner it will remember."

Understanding Legrasse, the men tore open the crates of explosives they had brought with them so gingerly through the marsh. As they worked to rig all the different boxes together to form one large bomb around the monolith, the inspector looked upward once more and whispered,

"So you and yours ruled the Earth a million years ago, eh? Well, we've got a few tricks now the cavemen didn't." Pulling one of the flaking tan sticks from the crate closest to him, Legrasse shook it at the sky. "This is one of them," he bellowed. "It's a German invention. They call it *dynamite!*"

"Sir," said Carrinelle, "we're ready."

"Then light the fuse," answered the inspector. Throwing the damnable figurine he had grabbed atop the monolith into one of the explosive boxes, he spat, hitting its tentacled face. Sneering, he added, "And let's get out of here."

The strike of a match and the smell of burning gunpowder sent the last six living human beings in the area charging through the massing tornado off into the swamp. Throwing themselves into the water, each man swam back to the general area of the boats. Above them, over the pitching howl of the storm, the grotesque sound of monstrous wings reached through the shattering din, calling to each of them. It was a plaintive, seductive sound, a buzzing song that promised all, a magnetic allure near impossible to resist.

Legrasse and Carrinelle reached one of the large flat bottomed skiffs. Dragging themselves inside, they looked about, trying to see how their fellow officers had managed. Two of the men they saw pulling themselves into one of the other boats. The other two, however, had not been so lucky.

Unable to fight the siren call of the monstrous thing descending from the sky, the pair had turned and begun staggering backward toward the island. Carrinelle made to leave the boat to try and restrain them, but Legrasse caught his arm and whispered,

"It's too late."

And, as if in response to the inspector's prediction, suddenly two cephlopodic appendages flew forward from the center of the grotesque bulk hovering over the swamp. One wrapped around each of the mesmerized officers, jerking them up out of the swamp, dragging them through the air and into the body of the nightmare in the sky.

"Damn you!" screamed Carrinelle. "Damn you to a thousand Hells!"

And then, flame touched powder, and the night seemed as dawn.

* * * * *

"Ah, look who's finally back amongst us."

Legrasse fought hard to stay awake—putting everything he had into opening his eyes completely. Turning his head slightly, he caught sight of the Chief of Police out of the corner of his eye. The man rose from his seat, admonishing the inspector.

"No, no, Legrasse. Don't try to move. The doctors' don't advise it. Rest. You rest and let me take a look at our hero of the hour."

It all came back to him. The explosion that tore apart Monolith Island, the shrieking of the horror in the sky as it was rocked by shock waves, pelted by massive chunks of granite. Its glimmering wings had caught fire, turning it into a torch seen, the reports would eventually confirm, in the skies of four different states.

"So, tell me ... whatever am I to do with you, Legrasse, eh?"

"I, I ..." the inspector was dismayed to hear how raw his voice was, to feel the weakness that had him so firmly in its grasp. "I don't know what you mean, sir."

"No, actually," acknowledged the Chief, "I'm certain you don't."

Legrasse could still see the burning horror, hanging in the sky, righting itself, healing before his very eyes. The inspector had stood in his boat, staring, pointing, laughing. Despite his best efforts, he had not beaten the monster. A simple explosion powerful enough to obliterate an island had not been enough to stop the cultist's god. Not nearly enough.

"But don't worry," the Chief of Police assured Legrasse. "I'll explain it all to you." Coming closer to the inspector's bed, the older man told him,

"You are in a hospital, Legrasse. You and most of your men survived. Thirteen of you made it back from the swamp. Word is six, perhaps seven of you will be fit for duty after a while. The question is, what kind of duty?"

"'Kind,' sir?"

As the winds grew even stronger, the thing had turned its attention to Legrasse and the others. Although they had not surrendered themselves to it as had the two officers drawn into its bulk, such trifles no longer seemed to matter. The inspector could feel inside his soul that the hovering white mass was coming for him. It was moving slowly, making certain of its energies. His plan had wounded it, slowed it down, but …

No good, he had thought, not enough. *Not enough!*

And then, the shelling had begun.

"Yes, what kind of duty can I give you now? I'll be frank, Legrasse. We've managed to keep a lid on this monster thing, but … well, this is New Orleans. The word of what went on out in the marshlands has run from one end of town to the other and back again—twice. And, of course, your legend grows with each new version."

Somehow, he had forgotten about Galvez. He had jumped up and down in the flat bottomer, laughing, shrieking. Two hundred pound shells rained from out of the night, splashing against the horror in the sky, crashing it down against the Earth. The force of the constant pounding flipped the already unstable boat, sending the inspector and his subordinate into the swamp just as its wind-dried surface was set ablaze. Legrasse and Carrinelle had surfaced and begun running for their lives.

That was the last thing the inspector remembered.

"That cyclone that started out there, after the Navy started their shelling … damn, how'd you live through that … it jumped up out of the swamp. Came back down upstate and dug a two and a half mile swath out of Louisiana and on into Mississippi. They say it killed over three hundred people."

Legrasse wondered at that. Perhaps the death of the flying thing, whatever it had been, had broken the spell the cultists had called forth. That energy released, maybe the storm could not simply be dissipated, and thus had come to ground far away, burning itself out in the simpler kind of mindless destruction people could take for granted. Before the inspector could dwell on the topic, though, the Chief of Police added,

"You know, there are people talking about running you for governor."

Legrasse's attention finally snapped to, focusing on the older man. Suddenly, a thousand different futures intersected within his brain, showing him how exactly the play of his destiny was depending on whatever course he set himself upon in the next few seconds.

While part of his mind reviewed the events of the past months within his head, another more immediate section weighed the worlds he had so recently discovered against the ones he had known all his life. Hero of the masses, chained to their petty antics by the cheap trinkets of cash and adoration, or a forgotten face, poking into all the dark corners of the world, searching for more of the reality he had only just begun to understand.

Signaling the Chief to bend closer, working his sore throat as best he could, the inspector whispered in a painfully thin voice,

"I think it best we downplay this story, sir."

"Really?" asked the Chief, equal portions of disbelief and relief obvious in his voice. Giving the older man no time to debate, Legrasse croaked,

"Yes, sir. I'm not much a one for public life. Besides, I would think one needs more credentials to run for the office of governor than the title of 'monster hunter.' Even in New Orleans."

The Chief of Police laughed. Just the reaction Legrasse had hoped for. The inspector was no fool. He knew how the world worked. The Chief had not come to visit an injured officer, waiting by his bed to be the first to see him when he awoke through some sense of noble duty. He had been sent by his political superiors to check out the threat of the city's new "hero" to their tiny, jaded futures. As if after what he had seen, after what he now understood, he could actually be interested in mere temporal gratification.

Picking up his hat, the obviously relieved Chief of Police said,

"You're a good man, Legrasse … a good man. Don't you worry, we'll downplay this ridiculous monster nonsense."

"Thank you," lied the inspector, suddenly impatient for the political stooge to leave. As the Chief closed the door on his way out, Legrasse turned toward the window. The sun was out, shining brightly. Was it the sun of the next morning, he wondered, or two days later—three?

Who knows? he thought. Who cares?

Smiling, he closed his eyes. Trapped as all men are trapped, fate had reached down and given him a chance to die foolishly side by side with an equal chance to rise above the snare of ordinary life. He had seen a slice of the world few men could observe and still keep their sanity.

Of course, he thought, who's to say you're still sane?

Legrasse chuckled, perhaps a bit too loudly. Insane or not, what did it matter? He knew what he would do next, regardless. Professor Webb had hinted that the world was filled with horrors and those men mad enough to keep truck with them.

He would not be able to set out immediately. He would have to regain his strength, put his affairs in order, and then one day just quietly slip away. He would put the idea to Galvez and Carrinelle. They deserved the chance to go with him. They had earned it.

Where they would go, what they might find, Legrasse had no way of knowing. Nor did he care to speculate.

One thing at a time, he told himself. One thing at a time. Whatever other horrors there be in this world, don't worry. They're out there. Patiently waiting. And we'll find them all.

Legrasse drifted toward sleep. His eyes heavy, tired, he blinked them several times, then closed them again. In seconds he was snoring lightly, a pleased, untroubled look settling over him.

From the window, the sun continued to flood his room, its rays warming the inspector, protecting him from harm.

TO CAST OUT FEAR

"There is no fear in love; but perfect love casteth out fear."

—Saint John

THE MEETING

Dr. Anton Zarnak slammed away at the nail, determined to move it to his will. Striking it and the wall around it several more times each, he grasped the nail and pulled at it to prove that it would hold solid. When the test concluded positively he smiled and dropped his hammer without regard, his attention firmly focused on reaching for the wooden mask waiting on his desk.

It was a leering thing, a gaudy horror painted in scarlet, black and gold. Its three eyes glared upward as the doctor's fingers ensnared it, the stylized flames pouring from its fanged mouth and flared nostrils cold to their touch. Hanging the mask against the tortured wall behind his desk, Zarnak stood back to survey his handiwork.

"There," he said with smug satisfaction. "Now it's *my* office."

"Indeed, this is so," replied a tall Hindu standing in the doorway. "But you are still soaking wet from your plunge into the harbor. You must change your clothing and take a meal."

The speaker was Akbar Ram Singh. Several score years earlier he had been charged by the monks of A'alshirie, a cold land hidden deep within the Himalayas, to stand as servant to whomever they sent to be master of their watchport on the other side of the world. The day previous, they had sent to him Dr. Anton Zarnak. Before the doctor could unpack his bag, however, he had been pulled into an investigation—one which had threatened to loosen a black and monstrous demon upon the world, plunging the entire galaxy into charred and burning ruin. The encounter had almost cost the doctor his life. He had survived, however, taking the mask of the horror's high priest as his souvenir—the first prize to be dragged by him back to Number Thirteen China Alley.

Cold and wet, tired, his clothing stuck to his skin, head still smarting fiercely from the effects of one of the fire devil's blasts, Zarnak stared at the captured mask with triumph. Although a part of his brain questioned whether or not he might survive another such confrontation to ever bring home a second trophy, all he said aloud was, "It really does looks good there, don't you think?"

"Yes, sahib," already sensing more about his new master than the doctor could have suspected, "you are a shrewd and insightful decorator. Now, if you might turn your attentions to the hot bath I have drawn and the dinner awaiting you, perhaps you might live to garner another such trophy."

And then it was that the knocking began. It was a politely discreet, uniform summons. But there was more to it—a feel of command, an understanding that the knocker expected immediate attention. Singh directed his master once more toward the joys of the steaming bath awaiting him. In A'alshirie, Zarnak had learned the secrets of speeding his heart rate to warm himself. He had also learned to ignore the cold, physical pain and hunger as well as techniques to dispel more esoteric cripplers such as depression, fear, anxiety and all of their sisters.

Even so, he mused, a hot bath did sound most wonderful. After all, considering what he had just been through, who deserved a spot of comfort more than himself? Zarnak was just stripping off his harbor-drenched shirt when the door to his office opened once more.

"I am sorry, master," said Ram Singh, "but it seems that perhaps an interruption is necessary, after all."

A man carrying a package no larger than a loaf of bread entered the room. He was tall and thick-boned, a hard man who held a dangerously cold fire burning within his dark eyes, eyes that were etching their estimation of Zarnak into some unknown ledger. As the master of 13 China Alley moved forward, the stranger said,

"I have been informed by your man-servant that you are not actually he whom I came seeking."

"I assume that means you came looking for Dr. Guicet," answered Zarnak. When the stranger nodded, his wet and tired host told him, "I'm sorry to have to inform you that the doctor has ... shall we say, left these premises. Abruptly, yes. But, anyway—an action which has necessitated his being replaced ... by myself. I am Anton Zarnak. May I be of some assistance to you?"

"I don't know," the stranger replied with abrupt honesty. "But if you can not, then a vast number of people—perhaps all the masses of the world—are in a great deal of danger."

"And you would know this because ... ?"

"Because for quite some time I have lived in nightmare, and now know the smell of it when it descends upon the land. I am John Raymond Legrasse, Dr. Zarnak—former Inspector of Police for the city of New Orleans—and I have learned what signs may be ignored and which must be acted upon. To be blunt, I have seen more than one such of these portents recently. One of them named your Dr. Guicet. And, if what killed him is that which I fear, perhaps I am already too late."

"Ah, my," answered Zarnak, finishing the peeling away of his still dripping shirt. "Well ... so much for my bath."

THE BLACK STATUE

After Singh brought him a thick cotton robe, Zarnak took the chair behind his desk. The mask of Yama watching all that transpired below, the doctor narrowed his eyes, studying the tall, thick-boned man before him. Quietly pulling a long breath into his lungs, Zarnak probed the air between himself and his visitor. He could sense immediately that Legrasse had not come to him with anything but business most urgent. There was more, however.

A dark, rank odor clouded the ether around his guest, a sinister presence clawing at the man's soul, a thing that so far Legrasse had managed to resist. But, Zarnak could see from the look swimming in the corners of the man's eyes that how much longer he could resist was anyone's guess. Fatigued to the depths of his own soul, the doctor nonetheless held out his hand and said, "All right, let's see it."

Somewhat surprised, but understanding, Legrasse reached into the package he had brought with him, instructing his host at the same time, "For your own safety, sir, until I have told you the rest of my story, please do not touch the artifact you are about to see."

Then, carefully keeping a thick rag between his hand and the contents of the box, Legrasse produced what he knew to be the "it" in question. "It" was a statue—a diminutive figure between seven and eight inches in height, a relic of exquisitely artistic workmanship. It was also a thing whose utter strangeness caused Zarnak's left eyebrow to lift dramatically. The horror of the piece lashed out at the doctor with its customary force. It did not frighten the man, however, a fact Legrasse noted with relieved satisfaction as he carefully set the piece down on Zarnak's desk so the doctor might view it more clearly.

The statue represented a monster of vaguely anthropoid outline, but with an octopus-like head whose face was a mask of feelers, a scaly, rubbery-looking body, prodigious claws on hind and fore feet, and long, narrow wings behind. The creature had been depicted with a round and bloated corpulence. It squatted firmly on a squarish stand etched with hieroglyphics so foreign that even Zarnak did not recognize the majority of them. The tips of the creature's wings stroked the furthest most edge of its stand while the long, curved claws of its doubled-up, crouching hind legs gripped the front edge and extended a quarter of the way down toward the bottom of the pedestal. None of that was what its viewers found so disturbing about the piece, however.

Slouching forward over a scaly and rubbery chest, the figure's cephalopod head was bent forward so that the ends of its facial feelers brushed the backs of the huge fore paws which clasped the croucher's elevated knees. The awkwardly formed cranium was tilted at an odd direction, an angle which forced its audiences to turn their own heads this way and that to get a clear view at the statue's eyes. Once accomplished, such a view left most individuals shaken and sweating.

Tiny they were, cold and silent, without depth or expression. Indeed, no great care had been taken by the figure's unknown sculptor in creating its eyes. They were, actually, mere circular gouges in the stone, neither uniform nor detailed. But still, somehow they had the power to command those who grew too near to it, to fill their minds with disquieting notions and sounds they had not heard since they were children—alone in the dark.

"Quite a find," said Zarnak finally. "But tell me, what connection has this thing with the horrors you mentioned earlier?"

The doctor kept his eyes riveted to the statue, motioning Legrasse to take a seat at the same time. The thick-boned man did so, gratefully, then began to speak once more, his eyes locking on the doctor.

"This is not the first of these statues I've come across. Some weeks ago, before I knew anything of the world beyond the one into which I had been born, this horror's twin came into my possession. At first, I thought it was a herald of something groping its way toward us. Recently, however, things have begun to happen that lead me to believe that whatever it is has actually gained purchase on our doorstep."

"The figure in the statue?"

"It, or one of its fellows," answered Legrasse. "My assumption is that either will be bad enough."

The doctor stared at the horrid length of ebony stone for a last, long moment. He did not have to decide as to whether or not his guest was correct in his assumptions. There was no doubt in Zarnak's mind that the paltry few inches of carved rock before him did not merely represent some terrible evil, but that the thing itself was a danger both loathsome and cruel.

"Let me assure you that I concur," said Zarnak finally. "I wish I didn't. Quite honestly, I've been most severely taxed of recent and would be much happier if I could brand you a lunatic and have my servant show you to the door. But, since such is not the case, it's obviously best we get down to business. Would you mind if I took my meal while we spoke? Are you hungry yourself?"

Legrasse declined Zarnak's offer, but insisted that the doctor have his own meal. In seconds Singh returned with a tray containing bok choi soup, chopped yellow bean sprouts with beef and pepper along with a main course of chicken wings and sliced potatoes in a thick curry gravy. As the servant departed, Legrasse explained that as police inspector he knew the value of a full stomach during an investigation.

"Especially one of these investigations."

"Oh, I agree," added Zarnak as he lifted his soup bowl, Chinese style, to drink directly from its lip. Finishing his sip, he added, "but then, I've always been one to look after my stomach. I studied with an order of monks for ... a number of years. They were always in agreement with Moliere, what was it he said … *'Il faut manger pour vivre et non pas vivre pour manger'* … 'one should, eat to live, not live to eat.' Alas, they were never quite able to win me over."

Legrasse smiled, offering, "Well, as Dr. Johnson said, 'A man seldom thinks with more earnestness of anything than he does of his dinner.'"

Delighted to be caught off-guard by his guest's unsuspected erudition, Zarnak thumped his desk top, laughing hard, spilling a few drops of soup, dribbling several more from his lips. His smile broadening into something warmer, he called out to Ram Singh. As the Hindu entered the room, the doctor told him,

"Mr. Legrasse will be joining me for dinner." When the inspector made to protest, Zarnak asked him, "Please, my friend, if we are to go rushing off to our deaths, whose advice shall be follow on the way, Moliere's or the good Dr. Johnson's?"

Smiling back at Zarnak, understanding him completely, Legrasse nodded to Singh, adding, "And if I might, sir, a double helping of those delicious smelling potatoes and chicken wings."

Ram Singh let it be known that performing no other task could please him more greatly. Then, as the Hindu left the room, Zarnak pulled a meat-free chicken bone from his mouth.

"Now, sir," he said, licking his fingers as he spoke, "while your plate is being warmed, tell me something of yourself, and about this horror that is racing toward us. And, if at all possible, could you try to make your story last long enough to take us through to coffee?"

THE INSPECTOR'S STORY

"So," said Zarnak, his brain struggling against the extra blood his stomach was pumping to it in an effort to slow his internal processes to the point where he might cease contemplating moving from his chair, "as Inspector of Police in New Orleans you came across a cult of devil worshipers who called down an insanity from the sky. You slaughtered most of the cult and called in the Navy to tackle the monster."

Pushing his plate away from himself, Zarnak stretched his arms out to his sides, pulling at the kinks forming in his shoulders. His left hand shooting back suddenly to cover a yawn, he stifled it, then added, "Quite a story."

"Yes," Legrasse agreed. "Since the whole affair began, I have witnessed a number of things I wish, quite honestly, I could convince myself were only constructs created by too liberal a dosing of bourbon and mash cherries."

"Why don't you?" asked Zarnak, his eyes narrowing slightly with cynical curiosity.

"Because, Doctor, as often as I have desired to return to the simple occupation of Police Inspector—to dealing with creatures that, while no matter how evil or pathetic or revolting, are still simple human flesh and blood—I can not ignore that which has happened to me. To that which I have been thrust toward head long."

Legrasse paused for a moment, his eyes darting about the Spartan walls of Zarnak's office. Not looking at the doctor—not actually focusing on anything, really—he continued, his voice low and filled with the sad knowledge that wishes were only the blankets children throw over their futures to try and hide their horrible inevitability.

"As I told you, after my first encounter with the dark beyond, a great number of the cultists perished. Many of them, yes. But not all."

"No? And what happened to the rest?"

Legrasse made a sour face. "Some were executed, still more committed suicide. But one, one had an incredible experience—a stroke of fortune I am ill-disposed to assigned to any agency other than Providence. The man was being transported from the asylum to the inevitable gallows that awaited him. Along the way, the vehicle—on a day as clear as the fate of the ignorant—was struck by lightning generated from a cloudless sky. Selective of its target, the bolt touched only the cultist, an itinerate seaman by the name of Maurizio."

At that moment, Ram Singh entered the room with a tray supporting a bottle of port and two glasses. Twisting away the last tendril of dusty cobwebbing still clinging to the neck of the bottle, the Hindu removed the cork, offering the crystal-encased affair to Zarnak. The doctor sniffed absently at the bouquet saying that he would pour later, thanking Singh, not needing to dismiss the servant as the man immediately took his leave. Nodding, Zarnak signaled Legrasse to continue.

"The officers with him were amazed—that they had not been struck, that Maurizio lived, that lightning could have been produced on such a day. But, the most surprising thing was the effect the mysterious bolt had on their prisoner."

"Yes?" asked Zarnak, leaning forward with the beginnings of curiosity.

"The man became a changed person. You see, sir, before that moment Maurizio had proved to be of a low, mixed blood, mentally aberrant—a degraded and ignorant man who worshipped, so he so sadly put it, 'the Great Old Ones who lived ages before there were any men, who ...'"

"Who came," interrupted Zarnak with a bored flourish, "to our world out of the sky when mankind was but undreamed of. Yes, forgive me, Legrasse, but I know all about the Old Ones and their sanctuaries inside the Earth and under the seas, where they wait to return to be masters of us all."

Taking up the bottle Singh had brought earlier, Zarnak held it over the glass closest to the ex-Inspector of Police. Legrasse nodded politely. As the doctor poured, he admitted, "I apologize for the show of nerves. My problem is that the cults of the Elder Gods never seem to die. They remain constant, hidden in the distant wastes and dark places all over the world. They imagine that someday great Cthulhu will rise from his dark house in R'lyeh under the waters, and again bring the planet under his sway. My particular edginess in this matter is that, like yourself, I have lived through one of these attempted liberations. The only difference is, mine ended perhaps an hour ago."

"And you're ready to charge forth once more …" Legrasse marveled. "Fire in the belly, eh? I was, I must admit, feeling somewhat the fool for thinking of challenging the darkness again, but with such an example …"

"Don't be too in awe of my recuperative powers," admitted Zarnak with surprising humility. "I was trained for this work, for far more years than you could guess. And, still I almost failed—would have failed, if not, in fact, for the intervention of a police lieutenant. So please … your story?"

"Yes, uh well, Maurizio. After his accident, he seemed a changed man. He wept freely, babbling about 'the veil being lifted from his eyes' and so forth. To draw to the point, let me say that the man was judged to be once more in possession of his faculties. He also immediately jumped at the chance to make up for his crimes which he claimed were all committed under a horrible fog."

"Fog?"

"He claimed he had acted as if under a spell—in a trance, as it were. Perhaps we who live in New Orleans take such things too much for granted, but …"

"No, no," answered the doctor. "Now, it actually isn't usual for the elder cults to work with such—there've always been enough volunteers to swell their fetid ranks—but still …" Zarnak contemplated what he had heard for a moment longer, then suddenly dismissed his doubts and instructed Legrasse to continue.

The inspector told him that Maurizio revealed many secrets of the cult. The seamen led the police to several warrens situated in the least reputable parts of New Orleans, odious centers of filth and depravity, all of them turning out to be connected to the city's sewer system. They were places that had obviously been in use until only a short time earlier, each offered up to the investigators all manner of clues to crimes committed on the premises—blood-soaked floors, furniture crafted from human bones, cushions and drapes fashioned from vulgar peels of human skin—barrels of revolting, sickening evidence of a hundred years' worth of monstrous depravities.

Legrasse, although no longer an inspector, was nonetheless invited along to lend whatever special expertise he might have to the investigation. After he and the police had rummaged through the debris of all the various lairs to which Maurizio could lead them, the seaman had taken them to one final site. Deep in the sewers, it was a large, even spacious, room that served as a main flow-way for the city's sewage. It was the last area known to him which had any relevance to the cultists. It was also to have been there that the blasphemous worshippers were to hold their next and, Maurizio had believed, final damnable ceremony.

"When I asked him what led him to believe that," Legrasse said, "he beckoned us forward toward the wall furthest from our position. We made our way carefully over the wet and treacherous stone flooring to find a breech in the wall, one disguised by an ingenious counterfeit section of brick."

Legrasse shifted uncomfortably in his seat, then said, "At this point Maurizio smiled. He told me that he could not explain what he was about to show me, but that I could find the answers I needed at Thirteen China Alley in New York City, from a Dr. Guicet. I made a note of the name and address. While I was busied writing, it happened."

Pointing toward the repellent figurine on Zarnak's desk, the inspector said, "Reaching inside the hidden chamber, Maurizio pulled forth … that."

At this point Legrasse stopped speaking. He held his lips tightly, one against the other for a brief moment, obviously pausing to arrange his next words carefully. Zarnak sat back patiently, still feeling the effects of their meal, just beginning to feel the effects of the port. After only a few seconds, however, Legrasse began again.

"I must admit, up until that moment I had held some reservations about Maurizio. Perhaps I was just hanging on to the normal paranoia of a policeman, but I had felt all along that the seaman was, although certainly transformed from his former self, still not dealing top deck—holding something back, as it were. What happened next changed my mind."

To the untrained eye, Zarnak's mood seemed to show no change. The inspector noted several small things, however, unconscious, practically imperceptible fluctuations in the doctor—in his breathing, the focus of his eyes, et cetera—that allowed Legrasse to know that his host's interest had suddenly intensified greatly. Having no desire to disappoint him, Legrasse continued his tale.

"The man started to hand the statue over to us, when suddenly he began shaking. Froth appeared upon his lips, his eyes bulged, his longish hair flailing wildly. He tried to throw the statue from his hand, but it had burned itself to his palm. The smell of searing flesh filling the chamber, overwhelming the putrid aroma of the place. Two of the other officers on the scene, suspecting a seizure of some kind, tried to wrestle the seaman to the ground. A good-hearted gesture, but a terrible mistake."

"Why, what occurred—exactly?"

"Maurizio began to scream—if 'scream' is even the proper word. What to use in its place … wail, perhaps? Shriek? Screech? I pause at this because, although the noises bursting forth from the man were certainly cries of pain, they were more than that. They were beyond the sounds a human throat can produce—beyond the shrill of birds, even. They were the vibrations of agony, and I will take their memory with me to the grave, as I will the sight of what happened next."

Stiffness assaulted Legrasse. He bowed his head slightly, not able to meet Zarnak's gaze, needing to cut himself off from even that slight human contact to be able to finish his story.

"The man's eyes exploded at that point. They had been bulging horribly, but then the expanded skin of them simply popped, blood and fluid shooting outward. His brain followed suit, boiling within his skull until a second later the room was filled with the burning shatter of blood and tissue. The two officers holding Maurizio down released him at that point, of course, but it was too late."

Zarnak sat silent, strong suspicions as to what came next shouting through his brain.

"A gaggle of thin, reed-like tendrils burst forth from the center of Maurizio's body. Lashing wildly, they adhered to whatever they came in contact with, slashing and choking. The rest of us, we retreated as far as possible in the confined space, as quickly as we could over the slippery stones ... the others were paralyzed, understandably panicked by the sight. Having more experience than the rest in such matters ... I was able to withdraw my revolver and begin firing. That ... that was all it took to snap the others out of their shock."

Legrasse went silent for a moment, his mind filled with the memory of himself and the officers with him blasting the transforming carcass—along with its two helpless captives. The inspector knew the pair stood no chance of surviving, that indeed they were dead already. Still he had wept as his finger closed again and again on his trigger. As he wept once more in Zarnak's office.

Tactfully ignoring the strength of Legrasse's emotion, the doctor nonetheless was somewhat startled by his guest's remorse. To Zarnak, Legrasse had acted properly. The men were lost. Any bullets that struck them not only assuredly had helped put them out of their misery, but may have actually been a blessing. The doctor wondered if he himself was even actually capable of experiencing such deep regrets over a situation in which he triumphed by doing the correct thing. Finally dismissing the question as a mere intellectual exercise, the doctor said,

"So ... with no other avenue open to you, you followed your only clue, which has led you here to me."

"Yes," agreed Legrasse. "And sir, now that I am here and you have heard my story, what do you think we should, or even *could* do next?"

"I would suppose," answered Zarnak, shifting his gaze once more to the statue in the middle of his desk, "considering what happened to the last person who touched this thing, that we should try to find someone who *can* put their hands on it."

THE EBONY HARLOT

"And that's all you want?"

The African woman sat in the chair next to Legrasse's, staring at the stone horror on Zarnak's desk. The doctor noted the woman's mocking tone, but he was not sure as to exactly what it was she was mocking. His other guest had no such uncertainties.

"Fear becomes your type, doesn't it?"

"You so big the ugly ol' beyond don't put the fright in your bones, you reach into its heart and pull out some answers."

"Madame Sarna La Raniella," Zarnak interrupted. "Let us not allow ourselves to be sidetracked. I would extend this suggestion to you as well, Inspector Legrasse."

"Legrasse, is it?" said the black woman with apprehensive surprise. "Legrasse." The word hung in the air like an accusation, or a prayer. Madame La Raniella's dark eyes narrowed sharply. Her nostrils flaring, she shifted in her seat, turning to face the one-time policeman.

"Legrasse … you far from home—'cept you got no home. You could root like a mushroom in de deep black shadows, but it wouldn't matter. You ain't got no place what will hold you to its breast now. No place that foolish. You a traveler, now. You walk de silver path. Dangerous for a stiff white man—your mind not flexible, can't bend really, can't stretch far enough."

"You listen to me, *Madame*," growled Legrasse. "You've heard of me— good. That means you know what I'll tolerate and what I'm capable of. As for your comments on my stiff, white man's mind, to date it's stretched admirably enough to keep me alive through everything your gruesome swamp friends and their Hellish playthings have been able to throw at me."

Pointing to the statue once more, he added, "And it's stretched far enough to bring me here with that horror tucked under my arm. Now, if you can help us determine what Dr. Zarnak's predecessor would have been able to tell us about it, then please, *Madame,* by all means, spin your own particular brand of voodoo. I promise to be most suitably impressed. But, if you have nothing more to offer than gibes and speeches, I assure you that we can acquire all we need of those on any corner from the soapbox socialists."

Madame La Raniella nodded her head, her full lips smiling in satisfaction. "They say you one tough patch of weeds, Legrasse. Maybe you won't get us all elected to de grave after all. Very well, let's review."

The woman dragged a small, but thick stone dish from her bag, as well as an opaque bottle. Pouring a thick dollop of a shimmering green syrup into the dish, she struck a match and lit the center of the resulting puddle. As it began to burn, she pulled back the light veil of her hat, then removed the wide brimmed affair altogether.

"You have seen de other side, both you two. Doctor, if you de good Guicet's replacement, that's enough for me. And Legrasse, as you say, the underworld is aswirl with tales of you amazing ability to alive remain. Meeting you now in person, I think this is maybe not being a fluke."

With a shrug bordering on the sensual, the woman knocked her shawl back from her shoulders. The colorfully embroidered black silk slid over the top of her chair, drifting to the floor, landing soundlessly. Waving her hand over the dish, she extinguished the growing flame, replacing it with a smoldering billow of exotically scented smoke. As its bluish tendrils drifted toward the statue next to it, La Raniella said softly,

"Legrasse, you had one o' dese before and blew it to Hell. Now another comes to you—looks the same, but de bite is different."

The woman stared at the statue as she rose from her seat. Stepping out of her shoes, she shoved them under her chair with small, casual movements, her eyes never leaving the nightmarish bit of stone.

"The first was a magnet … call things to it. But you, my ugly little child …" La Raniella's supple fingers reached out for the statue, turning only at the last second, drifting by mockingly as she whispered, "what kind o' thing be *you?*"

The belt holding the woman's skirt somehow came undone, allowing her to step out of it even as she bent her shoulders backward so that her jacket could slide to the floor as well. Her hands glided up the front of her blouse, undoing its buttons with a casual salaciousness that made Legrasse uncomfortable in particular. As she shrugged away that bit of cloth, her arms moving to some unheard rhythm, legs bending, hips swaying, the circle of her movement expanding with each rotation, the inspector bent his head toward Zarnak.

"Doctor, what in the name of Heaven …"

"A powerful place, my friend," answered Zarnak. "But one that has no answers here. I believe Madame La Raniella is attempting to, as the sophisticates might say, create an *atmosphere*."

"You right about that, Doctor," purred the black woman as she rocked from side to side. "De elder things … dey know many hungers … but *dis* hunger … dey don't know. Dey don't understand. But you do, don't you, Doctor?"

Before Zarnak could answer, La Raniella began to make her way around his over-sized desk. The mask of Yama leering down in approval, the woman released her undergarments one by one. Her motions were unlike anything either man expected, remarkably fluid, the silken scraps offering no resistance, falling to the floor like spring rain. Softly. Quietly. Their tender warmth unnoticed, the two men thought only on the storm to come.

"De elder things," whispered La Raniella from deep within her throat, "dey don't feel de lust for flesh, dey don't hear no blood pounding in der ears. Dey be cold things, swimming in blackness, their only interest in what dey can digest. Not like men ..."

The woman's toes dragged suggestively along Zarnak's thigh as she lifted her left foot over his right leg. In a husky whisper, she breathed steam into the doctor's ear.

"Not like you."

Legrasse pulled at his dampening collar, feeling the embarrassed moisture gathering within its fabric. As a police officer he had seen many and varied things in the dark underworld of New Orleans, but his badge had held power against them. Now, citizen Legrasse sat helplessly, watching the serpentine woman's limbs encircle Zarnak suggestively, listening to the overpowering beat of her bangles and bracelets as they rattled against each other. Listening to the growing throb of his own blood blasting through his veins. Smelling the growing passion within the office's ever shrinking boundaries.

"Can you feel me, Doctor?" moaned the woman as she slid her legs and buttocks across Zarnak's chest. "Do your fingers tingle, dying to touch? Is your tongue drowning? Does it ache, begging to be released from your mouth like a hungry viper?"

Zarnak nodded involuntarily. On one level he knew the woman was merely performing a ritual, setting forth a deceptive smoke screen under the cover of which she might handle the artifact upon his desk in safety. On a deeper, more personal level, however, his objectivity was clouding terribly. For all the control he had been taught in A'alshirie, the techniques availed him naught if he declined to use them. And, such was the case at that moment.

The feel of Madame La Raniella against his body—the smooth, frictionless sheen of her skin, the pulsating warmth that rippled outward from her muscles, the dripping, animal call of her mesmerizing voice—all of that coupled with the years he had spent apart from the female species in general had combined to infect him with an irresistible madness.

Nor could it have been any other way. The witch woman's potent smoke filling the doctor's office, her burning words spinning within his mind, each movement of her body, every clang of her carefully arranged jewelry was designed to arouse and enslave. Watching Zarnak slowly succumbing to Madame La Raniella's spell, Legrasse had to admit that if the gyrating woman were sitting on his lap, that he would be faring no better. And then, the wet smell of the room telling the witch that she had done all she could in the way of preparations, the woman reached out and took up the statue before her.

"Now ... what be you, eh, little child? What way mama got to stroke you to make you hers?"

Legrasse stared, his fingers nervously twitching, inching their way slowly toward his concealed pistol. If the same scene were to be replayed that he had witnessed in the sewer, if the same blinding speed were to follow, when he was still so close ...

The former inspector undid his jacket's buttons, fighting the part of his brain urging him to throw off all his clothes. His eyes, straining to stay on the horrid figurine, drifting ever upward toward the magnificent breasts, the wet lips, the dark, bottomless eyes ...

Zarnak noticed the shift first—long before Legrasse, even before Madame La Raniella who was in firm contact with the conduit. Banishing his fever as best he could, the doctor narrowed his eyes, then shook his head, catching his guest's attention. As Legrasse stared, wondering what Zarnak was up to, the melodic cadence of the woman's words suddenly shattered, replaced by a series of stumbling questions and observations.

"What's that? Who calls?" a fascinated horror tinged La Raniella's voice. "Cold the smell ... dark cold, old and wet ... green and great and wet and old ... what you want dis place? What you want Guicet?"

A vortex of sound filtered through the stone and wood and plaster of the walls, a dread pulse slapping at the tender flesh filling the room, organizing itself into words in the same fashion that grease formed puddles.

Guicet is no more

"We know that ..." answered Zarnak. "Are you responsible for his demise?"

We are responsible for all things

"What do you want here?" snarled Legrasse with a desperate relief at finally having something else to concentrate upon. As the inspector unlimbered his sidearm, the voice continued leaking into Zarnak's office.

Most interesting, it sniffed. *You have blocked us. We can see you, but cannot touch you ... for the moment. Intriguing*

"Answer the question," snapped Zarnak. "What do you want here? Name yourself."

"No, no," cried Madame La Raniella. Her voice small and frightened, she warned, "it's reach is shortened only by that which it does not understand— you can not confront such a power, you fools! Not here—not unprepared."

Too late, small thing. They already have

Before any of the three could react, a stygian length of force, a thing not muscle nor skin nor flesh of any kind, but a roping coil of self-conscious power exploded forth from the statue on Zarnak's desk. The indescribable essence slammed into the ceiling, driving a vast and wicked hole through to the next floor without injuring itself in any fashion.

Legrasse jerked free his pistol, jammed the barrel against the side of the frightening intensity and then pulled the trigger. One shot was all he got. The collision of separate universes exploded with a violence none of the humans present had ever before contemplated. Legrasse's weapon did not explode— there was no time for such a simple reaction. The device was instead transformed into a pure state of excited atoms, the interaction of which hurled the inspector across the room. Legrasse collided with the wall, hitting it hard enough to leave an impression detailing half his body.

At the same time Zarnak and Madame La Raniella scrambled away from the unleashed fury slashing out from the center of the desktop, even as its voice crackled through the room once more.

Guicet dead ... a good start. Soon you shall join him

Legrasse struggled to his hands and knees. Above him, the ceiling exploded in sparks and fire. A rainbow of unexplainable colors shattered the room's natural light, distorting not only the look of everything, but its feel as well. With a breath the pulsating maelstrom expanded, shattering the desk beneath, filling the air with splinters of wood and metal.

So few there are to stand against us. And so easily toppled You are the last

Crawling back to his feet, Legrasse grabbed up the over-turned chair he had been sitting in moments earlier. Hurling it at the ever-growing vortex, he shouted to Zarnak.

"The witch's spell! You have—"

Human sound was pulverized as the wood and leather touched the nether dank spinning in the center of the room. Once more Legrasse was thrown from his feet, once more hitting the wall as if flung from a speeding train. Slamming into the already shattered divider face first, the inspector's nose was broken, his forehead laid open, his jaw dislocated. From across a trillion miles of time, the unnamed presence stopped to laugh.

It was a cruel sound—mocking and pitiless—every syllable of its mind-wrenching trill steeped in a cold and passionless malevolence that struck all who heard it with an awesome terror. Outside Number Thirteen China Alley, those few people who braved the ancient street's greasy cobblestones fell to their knees in mindless horror, grasping their heads, retching their dinners, screaming as they felt the fabric of their souls being plucked and shredded.

Lying on the floor, panting, entangled limb to limb with Madame La Raniella, Zarnak tried to clear his throbbing head. The unknown force dragging its way into his dimension through the conduit opened by the now disintegrated statue had to be stopped. But, numbing his brain against the panic it wished to experience, calming his breathing, Zarnak could see no way to stem the tide. Maybe if he could get to his books, if he had hours to investigate the proper texts, there were people he could consult ...

The witch's spell ... you have ...

But no, he couldn't conduct a proper investigation—not the clever and swaggering Anton Zarnak. Several hours earlier his arrogance had gifted him with a lightning blast that left a jagged scar across the top of his head. Now, it seemed he had pushed himself and those with him into a plain and solid corner from which there was no escape ...

The witch's spell ... you have ...

Legrasse was moaning something across the room, but the doctor could not make out his words. The inspector's jaw was broken, and there was so much noise, so much confusion—La Raniella, filling the air with terror, her mind drained of hope, the atmosphere one of dread and frenzy ...

The witch's spell ... you have ...

And then, suddenly, Zarnak understood. Grasping the thrashing, terrified witch woman on the floor next to him, his hands gripping her head tightly, he forced her eyes to his. Locking his gaze on hers, the doctor caught her attention with a blinding flash of force. He pushed the radiant moment outward with desperate hope, plunging his heart into free fall as he blurted:

"I love you!"

Several of the colors flowing outward from the center of Zarnak's desk were suddenly stripped from the visible spectrum. The tendril of solidifying energy snapped sharply, its probing into the Earthly plane cut off as if it had run into a thick and daunting wall.

You will cease!

Lightning, black and pulsating, flashed from the blinded vortex, splashing cruelly against Zarnak's side, burning his arm and ribs, legs, head and shoulder. He did not feel it. Falling further and further into the dark fire that burned within Madame La Raniella's gaze, tears burst forth from his eyes as he cried out;

"I love you now and forever, with all my heart and all my being."

As he had been taught to slow his heart rate by the monks of A'alshirie, to maintain his breathing or to expel his fear, Anton Zarnak had been shown the secrets of controlling all human functions and sensitivities. Moving fearlessly into the depths of his emotional arsenal, he punched his way through La Raniella's spirits' protective doubts, imploring her with a truth that froze time and rationality.

"I love you, Sarna," he implored. "Now and forever—You are my universe, my focus. You are all that I have dreamed of, and every dream I shall ever have. You are my perfection."

Swimming through the madness all around them, Madame La Raniella strained to comprehend what was happening. Her eyes met Zarnak's even as the walls of the room began to snap and shatter. Plaster and ribbing board broke apart and began to swirl through the air, joining the splinters and nails and cracked shards of furniture spinning faster and faster around the exploding onslaught pouring into the room.

I will not be dismissed, ranted the assaulting storm of colors and decay. *I cannot be dismissed!*

"There is no one else for me," screamed Zarnak with passion. "Can not be anyone else for me. For now and all time, my beautiful Sarna ... you are my love!"

The chamber exploded, the shadows hissing, the air burning. Legrasse stared helplessly from the other side of the room. Crumpled in the corner, a pile of forgotten flesh, he could see that Zarnak had understood him. They had been so recklessly eager, allowing the witch woman to set up her veneer of temporary emotion to blind the thing clawing its way toward them, never stopping to consider in their careless rush that such a flimsy veil as desire was easily distracted and torn aside.

Zarnak had restored their fortification with love, however. Daring to reach into his heart with an honest hand, he had stolen the elder thing's glimpse of them by hiding them behind a shield the horror could not understand. He had had no previous feelings for the black woman, had never seen her before Ram Singh had summoned her through the use of Dr. Guicet's files. But that did not matter. Damning the consequences, Zarnak dared all, throwing himself headlong into passion.

But, thought Legrasse, although it can no longer see us, the invader is still secure in its purchase. To actually dislodge the beast is going to take something more ... but what?

Outside in China Alley, people crawled away from Number Thirteen, spilling out of their homes and the neighboring shops, screaming, bleeding, weeping. Above all of Chinatown, from the wharfs on upward toward the heart of the city, darkness filled the air, great purple and green shafts of burning light exploding from the sky, tearing free rooftops, blasting fire through the streets, melting brick and glass and pipe, filling the atmosphere with cinderized atoms.

Inside Number Thirteen, Zarnak pushed his lips against Madame La Raniella's face. He kissed her eyes, her nose, her mouth and neck. He kissed her cheeks, drying her tears with the heat of his ardor, then held his breath in cosmic joy as she whispered, "And I love you," before kissing him squarely back.

Again the barrier was reinforced, again the nightmare was denied. But still not repulsed. And then, Legrasse realized why. Staring at the naked black woman in the white man's arms, watching their souls meet in pure and happy joy, he found the chink in their armor against the elder horror clawing its way toward them.

"My God," he cried in shameful understanding, "it's me!"

Not simply shoving aside his distaste, but hurling it away, smashing it, denying it, Legrasse refused the power to judge, reaching for a higher power, instead. Crawling to his feet, pushing himself against the swirl of wind and hail blasting through the mangled room, the inspector held his hands before his face to turn aside the worst of the flying debris as he stared at Zarnak and La Raniella.

"What?" he asked himself aloud. "Tell me what is wrong in what you see."

In the honest depths of his heart, beneath his upbringing and the bigotry with which it had gifted him, Legrasse could find nothing wrong. Through new eyes he saw only two people, suddenly in love, oblivious to all else, with the power to shut out the world.

And, with Legrasse's blessing added to the mix, the veil became a river flowing beyond the clawing hunger's needs. With a rush of sound and color, the doorway faded, the vortex ceased, and three people screamed as the ceiling buckled and collapsed upon them.

EPILOGUE

Several hours later, Ram Singh had finally managed to clear a pathway from the hall into the battered office. He was amazed to find the trio within all still alive. His master's guest had fared the worst. The inspector had suffered a number of broken bones. His head and hands, back and legs and arms had all been torn and slashed in a thousand places. Splinters of wood and glass and metal all lay lodged beneath his skin.

Madame La Raniella and Zarnak had suffered far less physical damage. Ironically, the hard wood mask of the fire demon which the doctor had hung on the wall only hours earlier had fallen over them when the final explosions had slammed them up against the wall. It had leaned over Zarnak and the woman, just managing to support the ceiling beam that had toppled toward them. Even the mask survived nearly intact, only a few miscellaneous bits of its paint being chipped away.

Ignoring the shredded remnants of La Raniella's clothing, Singh instead gave the woman a set of his own pants plus a shift along with an overcoat so that she might make her way home. Zarnak grappled with the pain in his heart, bowing his head slightly as he struggled to return to the world of a few hours previous.

"I, I would like to thank you, Madame La Raniella, for … for all your assistance." Pointedly eyeing the gold band on the woman's left hand, he asked, "I assume …"

The woman nodded. Tears filled her eyes. Wiping at her face, lamenting the pain within her own heart, she whispered,

"I'm sorry … he's a good man … I couldn't … my son …"

And then she turned and fled China Alley, running not so much from the malignant, consuming horror she had witnessed, but from the tender sensuality she had been forced to accept. As real as any love ever felt since the beginning of time, the aching mark of it was carved forever within her heart as it was Zarnak's. A never-ending memory of what could not exist, but had to be.

Ram Singh left at the doctor's command, hurrying to escort Madame La Raniella to her home. She had been summoned to perform a service. The witch woman had risen to the challenge, responding to it with far more of herself than she had ever dreamed she would be called upon to give. At the least, he felt, they owed her safe escort back to the world they had ever destroyed for her.

Besides, thought Zarnak, with Legrasse mercifully unconscious for the moment, best to be alone just now.

Pulling a small set of tweezers from his medical bag, the doctor lay it alongside the scalpel he had already found and laid out. Then, taking a bottle of bourbon he had brought from the kitchen, he poured a healthy portion of alcohol over both instruments.

Legrasse lay on the table where Ram Singh had stretched him out. Still bleeding from a hundred wounds, Zarnak knew the ex-inspector was in for days of terrible pain. His skin had been flayed. Digging all of the splinters out of his body would take hours—every minute of it promising to be mind-numbing torture. Zarnak stared at the one-time policeman, the unlettered street fighter who had somehow thrown aside a life-time of prejudice in an instant for the good of the human race.

"We both gave up things today," muttered the doctor, staring at his patient. "And we were both injured in the process."

Feeling the longing in his heart for his Sarna, remembering her eyes, the curve of her hip, the way the left side of her upper lip bent when she smiled, the surprising softness of her hair, Zarnak felt his hard-learned controls slipping away. His cheeks moist, chest heaving, he grabbed up the bottle next to him once more and drank until he gagged.

Then, wishing he could take Legrasse's simple agony of a thousand wounds as his own, gifting the inspector with his broken heart instead, Anton Zarnak bent to the task before him. Propped against the wall in the far corner, the mask of Yama sneered at his efforts and laughed at his tears.

SO FREE WE SEEM

"So free we seem, so fettered fast we are!"

—Robert Browning

I t was the strangest thing the inspector had ever seen. The first thing he noticed, as had those few others who had peered into the old house out near the swamp, were the traps in the doorway. Immediately, there in the front foyer, surrounding the mail slot in the door, spread in a semi-circle, he had come across two lines of traps. Mouse traps. Rat traps.

"In here, el Grande ..."

Their positioning made them appear to be set for something their owner must have felt was going to come through the mail slot. A quick inspection showed the opening to be only one inch by three, covered by a springed hinge that had to be opened with a bit of effort.

"Come in and meet the former Hector Claro, and ..." the officer's voice shifted to a supercilious tone, "let me tell you right now, Inspector ..."

What, wondered former Inspector-of-Police John Raymond Legrasse, could the man have been expecting to come through such a tiny and hard to open aperture other than his mail?

"You're not going to believe this."

Legrasse hated to admit it, but his one time lieutenant was correct. Even after all he had seen in his time, he did not believe what he found in the next room. It was too odd. Too *despairing.*

"This isn't one of your pranks, is it?"

Too perplexed by the oddity of the inside of Hector Claro's home to make one of his usual wisecracks, Lieutenant Joseph D. Galvez shook his head gravely, admitting;

"I could but wish my sense of humor were this magnifico."

Legrasse nodded, understanding the smaller man without need for further explanation. The scene in the humble home's main room was one snatched from nightmare. The one-time Inspector of Police fell into old habits at once. In less than a minute his virgin notepad was bleeding its first page and a half—

Victim found sitting in a corner diagonally positioned as far from the front door as possible.

Victim appears to have been facing front door at time of death.

Found, foyer: on arrival: various spring traps set within the doorway. Immediately, three large traps—set but not baited—spread in triangle

81

formation before the mail slot in the door.

Further on, spread in semi-circle, two additional lines of traps. Mouse traps. Rat traps. Just in the foyer.

Inside: traps everywhere—scores? Hundreds? Set out ...

Patterns?

"Can you believe this guy," asked Galvez. The man's voice was indecisive, unable to pick a tone, to slide into either humor or concern. Or worse. "He surrounds himself with traps. He's scared of what? What? I dunno."

"You want to know why he did it?" asked Legrasse, half in humor, half seriously. "I'm still working on *how* he did it."

Galvez snorted, then sprang another trap with the cane in his hand, a handsome thing covered with graceful carvings which he had acquired from the umbrella stand in the foyer.

"Crazy," the Spaniard muttered, "set all these traps, but don't bait them. How you supposed to catch anything that way?"

It had been decided that, although they would, of course, need to leave as much of the insane landscape intact as possible to see if there was any clue as to what had happened in the old Backtown house out near the swamp-fronts, some would have to be sacrificed for both basic mobility as well as general safety.

"Smells wonderful," snapped the lieutenant, rubbing another wipe of preventive gel under his nose. Don't he?"

Legrasse merely flashed his eyes in response. Galvez went silent. Though his one time commander was now merely consulting, only a citizen, still he was Legrasse, who had lived through it all, and won against the devil himself. They had been through much together, and Galvez knew his old boss well. Already he could see the old instincts taking over, could sense his boss was closing in on what had happened within his mind. He watched Legrasse's hand moving across the page, knowing that somehow he would unravel the bizarre scenario before them.

Victim seems to have bolted all other doors behind him. All other rooms are cut off from the front room. Cracks around doors are stuffed with rags, old newspaper, slivers of cardboard cut to fit. Boards appear to have been nailed over all of this wherever possible.

Victim seems to have been afraid of something approaching him, something small enough to fit under a door, or through a mail slot, any small crack.

Victim does not seem to have been restrained in any manner. If this is the case, then the only conclusion one can have is that he remained in his corner, surrounded by his traps, until he starved to death, by choice.

Dying of thirst was preferable to him rather than …

Than what?

And then, Legrasse's eye caught a detail he had previously missed. Indeed, one that everyone had missed so far. Staring at the desiccated corpse in the corner, he asked Galvez;

"Do you see that bulge in Mr. Claro's breast pocket?"

The lieutenant indicated that he did. Legrasse asked him to fetch it if he could. Galvez stepped into the opening already made near the corpse and slid his hand gently inside the pungent cloth. His hand came out with its prize, a thin, leather-bound volume with a stub of pencil attached to it by a short length of string. The lieutenant paged through it quickly, then announced;

"It's a diary."

Legrasse accepted the black book and opened it to its first page. In a simple style made up of competent, but uncomplicated sentences of mostly one and two syllable words, Hector Claro introduced himself and his dilemma to the inspector.

Claro told his tale from the beginning. The first date showed that it had been some four weeks back, after a particularly violent storm which had rained lightning down on the swamps for an entire night and half the next day. Legrasse remembered the storm vividly. He had been caught outside in it and had been drenched in moments. The noise and electrical power of it had sent much of the city into a panic. Normally calm, well-mannered horses had gone wild in the streets, crashing carriages and trampling citizens. It had been one of those times Legrasse was glad he was no longer a public servant, and the memory of the violent night connected him to Claro in a personal way.

The man told of finding scores of dead fish and other swamp creatures the next day, floating on their sides in the muddy, boiled water behind his home. Great trees had fallen during the night, and the swamp had gone through such convulsions that Claro even noted a fresh spring bubbling up through the crayfish encrusted mud.

At first he had been pleased by the events. The shocked fish had provided him with a much needed windfall. He had quickly set to gathering and preserving as many of the still living, but insensate fish as he considered safe for the salting. The new spring was fresh, and looked as if it would be a constant rather than a fluke. All in all, the storm seemed to have been a blessing for Claro, unlike what it had proved to be for the rest of New Orleans. But then, the next night came, and his opinion of things took a different turn.

Claro's next episode told of a noise in the night, that of a rat trap being sprung. Due to his proximity to the swamp, the man had many such devices set about in the corners of his home and was not over concerned by hearing one go off in the middle of the night. But, instead of the squeals such a sound usually brought, if they brought any noise at all, he heard instead a series of strange, unfathomable sounds the curiousness of which forced him to leave his bed. Lighting his table lamp, he went out to examine his small home's main room where he found the most curious scene.

Claro described finding the trap dragged across the room from where it had been set all the way to the front door. He could tell this had happened easily enough because of the wet, sticky trail left from the trap's original position to where Claro discovered it, smashed and ruined beneath his mail slot. He could only think that he had snared quite a large rodent, one of sufficient size and strength to move the trap, although wounded unto the point where it was bleeding profusely. This line of thinking was diminished, however, when he realized that the smearing crossing his floor was not made up of blood.

Legrasse absently noted a faded line of coloration on the door, one leading from deep inside the large room into the foyer, indeed, directly up to the mail slot, which supported Claro's story. The dead man's words described the trail as a bluish-green, one with neither the smell nor taste of blood. He was confused by this, but with the simplicity of most swamp dwellers, soon forgot the incident, tired as he had been from the ordeal of collecting and salting down his windfall.

The next night, however, he was again visited after dark, and the night after that, and the one after that. He lay in his bed on all three occasions, the covers pulled up and over his head, frightened to the point where he questioned even the need to breathe. Every day he set out more traps, but each morning he found fewer of them sprung. On all three nights he listened intently as something, or some things, crawled and slithered throughout his simple home. Whether they were searching for something, or simply madly dancing, he had no idea, nor much inclination to find out.

Legrasse read on, fascinated. Galvez waited, balancing himself in various poses, using the cane from the umbrella stand to keep from toppling into the myriad traps. On the one hand he was impatient to find the answer to the riddle of the dead man and to close out the case. On the other, he was more than willing to wait to see what his former commander could determine. Together, the two had seen some horrific and terrible things in the bayou land outside their city. Indeed, in Galvez's mind, the mystery of Hector Claro could scarce compare to some of their previous exploits.

"Better safe than sorry," the lieutenant cautioned himself, and continued to play with the cane, twirling it in one hand, studying its odd carvings, amusing himself in any way he could think of while he waited for Legrasse's verdict.

The inspector had almost forgotten Galvez, however, his full attention falling to each successive page of Claro's diary. Legrasse had become engrossed with the man's description of the fourth night of his home's invasion and reread it simply to hear its words again within his head. That night, whatever had been searching about in the other rooms of his home, even under his own bed, found its way to what was on top of his bed.

Claro wrote of a weight passing over the blanket he kept tight across his face. Anything with eyes would have seen his form beneath the covers, he reckoned, but whatever this was, this probing, single length, it merely poked and prodded and rolled, intent in its search, but making no discovery. At first.

Claro's words dropped icicles down the back of Legrasse's shirt collar, making each vertebrae ache in turn as they uncomfortably made their way down his spine.

It were a horrible feeling, not being able to see, not being able to breathe, just scared and waiting for the damn thing to go away. Just holding my breath and waiting and praying and none of it doing no good. No good at all.

It just kept digging and scratching and tugging, like a big finger, but a stupid one. Like something that had never seen a bed or a blanket. I think how dumb it were was more frightening than anything else. Even a bear, or fox, or anything, anything that ever crawled up out of the swamp should have known what it had found. But this thing couldn't tell it had found a man under a blanket. So it just kept poking and digging at me.

And then, it found me. The crawling bastard thing finally found its way under the blanket and it slid under my leg and up over the other in a motion so fast I couldn't react. But, as it started to circle under my leg, like to grab it, or squeeze it, my fear left me, or it filled me, whatever, I don't know. I only know that was all I could stand.

It was a madness that took me then. I rolled out of my bed screaming. In the darkness, I grabbed at the thing coiling around my legs and I pulled it from me and smashed at it, beating it with my fists, beating it against the floor.

With a lightning speed it jerked free of my hold and retreated out of the room. I followed it, my hands grabbing for something to use as a weapon. They found a chair. I wasn't thinking, didn't care. I grabbed up the chair and ran to follow the thing, whatever it was, to break it, to kill it. Then, I got to the next room ... and I had to stop.

Legrasse read on, fascinated. Claro has stopped for he had found his home filled with vast lengths of roping flesh, something like the tentacles of a squid, but longer, thinner, and possessed of individual skills no cephalopod imaginable had ever displayed. He stood frozen, terror gripping his every muscle, as he watched the roaming tendrils poke and pull and slither in the moonlight. Then, the one he had just eluded found him again, and Claro beat at it with his chair until the seat had become splinters.

Racing about madly, the man had smashed the tentacles, beat them with his fists, even bitten into one of them. Although the tendrils retreated in seconds in the face of his attack, still Claro was left drenched in sweat from his encounter.

He spent the next day closing down the side of his home facing the swamp. It did no good. The next night the lengths returned, and again he was forced to do battle with the sucking, grasping coils. They came over the next two nights as well, and Claro began to take note of certain things. Each night the tentacles came earlier and stayed longer. They were beginning to be able to predict where he would be, what he would do. They were beginning to not fear him. Which is when he had decided to start setting the traps.

Legrasse gave the book over to Galvez, telling him to read some of it while he thought about things for a moment. The Spaniard nodded, handing the inspector the cane he had been toying with so that he could hold the book in two hands. While Galvez started, Legrasse thought on what he had read.

The book told of tentacles coming through the windows, slots, cracks, even his sink drain. Why the man stayed in his home, he did not explain. Nor did he explain why he did not at least leave at night, did not call the police, did not ask his neighbors for shelter, or assistance.

What could it have been, wondered Legrasse. *Why* was it? What did it want? Why did it come? Why?

Maybe Claro was just too stubborn to admit defeat. Maybe he simply went insane, bought the traps and spread them out, relying on the only thing that had truly worked for him. The last entry he had made, sitting in his corner, disturbed Legrasse the most.

free, free at last

The inspector studied the cane in his hand as he tried to piece the sad occurrence into a whole. Certainly the storm had unleashed whatever had found Claro. Perhaps it was some long lost horror, sealed away within the fresh spring so recently uncovered.

Legrasse stared at the corpse in the corner and wondered, did the dead man know something that some outré thing wanted to know, something it did not want anyone else to know? Or was Claro just the poor unfortunate bastard who happened to be the only thing nearby when the storm somehow opened a random portal that some bug just happened to accidentally poke its way through?

The inspector quietly checked Galvez's progress. He could see the man was barely halfway through the notebook. Looking about, Legrasse then took note of a section of the dead man's leg, where the pants were up far enough to reveal flesh above the sock line. Round red welts like sucker wounds appeared to circle the victim's leg.

Legrasse wondered at it all, at what the searchers could have been after. What was the point, he mused, of coming night after night, but never taking anything, never actually doing anything—*anything*. Why?

Absently smacking his hand with the butt-end of the cane, the inspector took a closer note of the carvings etched into its length. There was nothing remarkable about them, although he did notice they seemed somewhat fresh. Still, they seemed of no great importance. Indeed, his mind left them instantly as he noticed Galvez coming to the end of the notebook. Tossing the cane back to the Spaniard, Legrasse turned in his small clear space in the traps, studying.

Wondering.

"Hey, John," called Galvez, "anything you want me to do while you stare off into space at the taxpayer's expense?"

"It's your investigation," replied Legrasse absently. "Be creative."

The lieutenant nodded, looking for a direction in which to head. Legrasse looked down at the traps, wondering about them again.

He had been puzzled about them since he had arrived. So far all he had learned had only added to his puzzlement. He still could not believe Claro had set out all the traps. Their placement was so finely meshed, so intricate. And the patterns he had noticed, swirls and star-shapes, intersecting each other over and over throughout the main room—

Why, wondered Legrasse. Why would he do it?

The traps had not been working, the inspector remembered. Yet Claro had gotten more and more of them, ultimately painting himself into the corner, so to speak, with them.

Across the room, Galvez picked the next spot where he would knock a new hole in the traps so that he could move toward the back rooms. Sealed off as they were, none of them had been investigated yet. To the lieutenant's way of thinking, it was high time they were opened.

Ignoring Galvez's actions, Legrasse concentrated on the traps. There was something he was not seeing, something that was passing him by. He stared down at the floor again, trying to look at everything once more from the beginning, struggling to gain a new perspective.

The traps were everywhere. In tight, sophisticated patterns. Why? How could Claro have managed it, with only two hands? It did not seem possible. And, even if it were, why had he done so?

Galvez spotted the point where he could place his next footfall without disturbing too many of the traps.

Of course, he thought, the traps aren't so tight everywhere. Fairly sparse back by the door when you first come in. And where the patterns run up against one another. Indeed, that was where Galvez had been making his strikes, in the freer areas between the patterns.

Convenient, whispered a voice from the back of Legrasse's mind. He caught the tone, realizing instantly his subconscious was trying to tell him something.

The footfalls had been conveniently made, slivers of space left between each of the patterns, just right for a human of average height, spaced just so, placed directly where the average human eye would see them, would pride itself on being able to take advantage of them.

Galvez's arm stretched out, positioning the cane for its next strike. And, as it did so, the inspector's memory superimposed another image on the scene. He thought back to voodoo rituals he had witnessed, to the foul priest he and his men had stopped only months earlier, all of them, scratching patterns in the sand or the mud, making their magic gestures with their totem sticks—

"I'm going to take a look in the back rooms."

The lieutenant pulled his hand back, even as Legrasse's mind raced. What if Claro had not set the traps, or even if he had, if after his death, something else had moved them? Changed their positions, moved them into patterns …

Galvez's hand began to descend—

Into the same patterns it carved into Claro's cane, the cane left at the front door, where the traps were not so thickly spread, so that one could enter, and *pick up the cane!*

"No!"

Legrasse screamed at Galvez, even as he threw himself at the lieutenant. The lieutenant shouted as well, raising his free hand in response, trying to bring up the one wielding the cane, but it was too late. Both men went down painfully, rolling over and over in the flesh-tearing maze.

*   *   *   *   *

Most of their pains had long subsided, but Galvez was still not certain of Legrasse's reasons. Yes, he understood about the traps being laid out in the same patterns as those on the cane. He understood about the interconnected manner of most magics, and how, yes, perhaps he had been maneuvered into striking each of the patterns in turn with what could very well be thought of as a wand. And, yes again, considering the detail in which Claro had written in his journal, the fact he did not mention patterning the traps was an odd omission. Still …

"You could have just told me not to hit the traps again," he muttered, his dignity still as sore as his flesh.

Legrasse sighed. His hands and legs and arms and face had been snapped and gouged in just as many places as had Galvez. He had lost as much blood, had pulled one of the crushing things off his nose and one off an ear. He did not answer the lieutenant, however. There was no point.

As they stood on the edge of the swamp, watching the old house burn, he did not see where it mattered. When the conflagration was finished, the officers waiting nearby would dynamite the spring Claro had written of, the one they had found with so many sinister gouges roping up through the mud surrounding it. Afterward the entire area would be salted, then forgotten.

Holding the cane for a moment longer, Legrasse wondered if what he had seen in his mind were even possible. Could the blind lengths have carved the patterns, planted the wand, arranged the room to be discovered just so, waiting for some unsuspecting wretches to trigger the ritual?

And to what end?

"Just to take advantage of the fact that a storm somehow opened a random portal that some bug just happened to accidentally poke its way through?"

At that point, Legrasse did not care if he were right or not. Better sore ribs and a swollen ear than some foul horror flopping about loose. One poor dead bastard was enough.

But, maybe Claro was not the only one that had gotten too near the edge. The inspector wondered if, perhaps, he too might not have seen more than he could bear at this point. Maybe he was growing overly paranoid over the unspeakables he had encountered. Perhaps he was weakening, assigning them too much credit, too much ability. But then, how could one ascribe such beings with too much ability?

He might've been wrong, he snorted, but that didn't mean it wasn't possible.

Muttering a curse in Hector Claro's honor, Legrasse threw the cane as hard as he could into the blazing cremation before him. Then, he turned and walked back toward the police wagon parked well back from the swamp and the burning house. Like the snorting horses waiting there, he had grown tired of the smell.

LOCKED ROOM

"Philosophy is like trying to open a safe with a combination lock: each little adjustment of the dials seems to achieve nothing, only when everything is in place does the door open."

—Ludwig Wittgenstein

John Raymond Legrasse, a former Inspector of Police for the city of New Orleans, sat behind the desk of Dr. Anton Zarnak, his fingers moving a small steel ball back and forth across its well-kept surface. It was the work of four fingers only. The thumb could not be convinced to join the rhythm, and his other hand was firmly at work supporting its owner's head. Chin in palm, fingers moving his moustache about, masking the occasional yawn, his hands had found work for themselves and were quite busy, unlike the rest of him—save his eyes. John Legrasse's eyes were keenly at work.

They moved about within their sockets, taking in each and every item in the room one by one. They studied what they found from a distance, analyzing each piece, inspecting it, wondering if it might be a clue that could lead him to the next level. They moved from shelves to table tops, to corners filled to overflowing with stacks of books and other objects all crammed in one atop another. Indeed, there was so much clutter one scarcely knew where to begin.

Behind the former inspector, for instance, hung a mask which had arrested his attention for quite some time. It was a leering thing, a gaudy horror painted in scarlet, black and gold. Its three eyes glared upward, stylized flames pouring from its fanged mouth and flared nostrils. Legrasse remembered it from his previous visit. Zarnak had called it the visage of Yama.

Yes, well, he thought, his mind grim, chiding. Now, *that* fact's a help.

Is it?

Legrasse wondered for a moment, what if it was? Pushing his way past his sarcasm, he allowed himself to physically turn and stare at the mask. As he did he forced his mind to jump back, to remember all it had absorbed the last time it was in that room …

Is it?

Once more unlearning everything he had ever known.

It might be a clue, he knew. Anything within the room might be a help if what he suspected was true. In many ways Zarnak's office was a trash heap, a never-ending, always changing collection of the weird and strange objects of the universe. Legrasse had to force himself to remember that anything around him might also be some Pandora's box of poisonous trouble.

He stared at the things on the desk before him, the closed wooden chest adorned with a checkerboard pattern created from variously colored inlaid woods, the small stone figure of some South American deity, the copper bell with the double clappers, the small oval mirror in the silver frame, even the steel ball his fingers had been maneuvering—

Any piece of it, he reminded himself, could be death beyond reason if handled the wrong way. *After all I've seen these paths few years it would be fairly stupid to pack it in now from just barging into something.*

It was true. For some time now the one time inspector had been handed one lesson after another by the universe proving that there were, indeed, thinks not dreamt of in primitive philosophies. He had even begun hearing voices. He had never done such a thing before.

Are you me, he wondered at the words he heard in his head for the thousandth time. *Some subtle, deeper part of me? Are you?*

Yes, he thought, they had to be merely other parts of his brain posing questions to him; he was simply learning to think. Still, it was unsettling. Unnerving.

Are you?

Before his interior conversation could continue, a muffled knocking outside of Zarnak's office caught Legrasse's ear. In a moment the office door opened, and two men came forward. The one in the lead was a tall man, lean and rangy. A Hindu, he wore a pair of formless, baggy cotton pants topped by a well-worn sweater of red and blue. A spotless white turban wrapped with careful precision crowned him, if anything emphasizing his keen dark eyes. Though a completely deferential man on the surface, anyone who actually knew what made people tick could easily see he was a confident and dangerous individual. A fool would miss the obviousness of him, but then the world was filled with fools.

The second man, the one behind the Hindu, did not look like a fool. Or someone who missed the obvious.

"Hey, you Legrasse? Howdy—welcome to New York."

He was, like Legrasse, a big man. Balding, he wore his hair on the inside, crowning his shaved and polished dome with a black derby. It was a well known hat throughout much of the metropolitan area as one you did not want to see turning down your street. No matter what street you lived on.

"Lieutenant Mark Thorner, correct, sir?"

"Yeah, that's me." The man in the bowler eyed Legrasse with curiosity. As it had been explained to him, Legrasse had arrived to confer with Zarnak only to find the doctor not at home. This had been explained to the lieutenant whom the Hindu had then asked to come to the doctor's office at 13 China Alley as quickly as possible. That had been eighteen minutes earlier. That meant Legrasse had been on the scene for nearly a half-an-hour unsupervised. Thorner did not disclose his displeasure with that thought as he asked Zarnak's man servant;

"Ram Singh, so, tell me you didn't get us here for the reason I think?"

"I am sorry, Lieutenant," answered the rangy man, "but I have no one else to whom I can turn. The master of this house, Anton Zarnak, has disappeared."

"That's a mighty powerful word to be throwin' around, Singh," said Thorner. His tone was even, one filled with both questions and implications. "You want to narrow down exactly what 'disappeared' means in this instance?"

"He *disappeared,*" answered Zarnak's manservant." He was there and then he was gone. Is this not plain enough?"

"Not really," said Legrasse. "And I'd think you'd know that. What do you mean—did you turn around and he was gone? Did he just fade away before your eyes, has he merely been missing for a day or two? Did he go out for milk and not come back …"

The Hindu raised his hand in apology. Nodding further, showing he realized his mistake, Ram Singh showed detective Thorner to a chair and then explained himself.

"Earlier today," he said, starring at Legrasse, "Dr. Anton Zarnak walked into his office. This office. He called to me as I passed, and he asked me to shut and lock the door."

He's not staring at me, realized Legrasse, his eyes suddenly looking down, senses reeling—

"He had work to do, and he did not want to be disturbed until dinner time. It is a quite common request, and is usually quite helpful to all parties concerned. Much can be accomplished when one's superior is not about."

He's looking at the last place he saw Zarnak.

"So, if I get this," Thorner injected, holding his hands open roughly a half foot above his knees as if to encapsulate the moment, "Anton was sitting behind the desk, you locked the door; you opened it roughly six hours later and he was gone."

"It is all I know," responded the servant.

"Don't worry about it," answered the lieutenant. "Why don't you kick around in the kitchen and find some meat you can throw at some heat, or whatever, for our guest here and me, and we'll keep you posted if we find anything."

After Ram Singh left, Thorner settled himself in one of the large chairs on the visitor's side of Zarnak's desk as Legrasse asked him;

"You don't want to question the manservant further?"

"No need right now," came the lieutenant's reply. "I've been in on plenty of the weirdness that's passed by the windows of this dump. Believe me, if we can't trust Ram Singh, we are about as out of luck as two cops can get."

"Then where should we start?"

"Why don't you tell me what brought you here so conveniently on the day the Doc disappeared."

Legrasse thick eyebrows went up for a moment, then settled back into place. As bristling a question as Thorner's was, as a policeman Legrasse knew he was perfectly right in asking it. Unfortunately, the answer was of no help to them. The lieutenant had been hoping that the very reason which had brought the inspector northward might be a lead, but it was not to be. Legrasse had only come to return a number of rare books he had borrowed from the doctor, and to borrow some more.

"Sorry to disappoint," answered the Southerner, his accent thick with sarcasm.

"Let's not start this out with you bein' a wise guy, okay," snapped back Thorner, his own accent equally obvious. "You coulda been here to confer on somethin' that might have given us a lead is all."

"I'll tell you why we're snapping at each other," responded Legrasse. Getting up out of his chair, he pointed around the room, saying, "it's because we both know we're out of our league here. You, Lieutenant, do you actually know any magic?"

Thorner pushed his derby toward the back of his head with a single finger.

"Me, naw," he answered. "Me and the Doc were kind of a team ... New York's only recognized ghost grabbers."

"Recognized, you say?" The envy in Legrasse's voice was obvious.

"Well, sorta. The city, they know what the Doc does, got it? Before Zarnak, Doc Guicet ran things here. He disappeared, too, and Zarnak replaced him. I've always been the, ah, 'unofficial' liaison between the mayor's office and the chief of police and, ummm, what would you call it? The world beyond?"

"You say this Guicet predates Zarnak at this post? And he disappeared as well? Was that ever solved?"

"No," answered Thorner sourly. "And I'd hate to have to break in another replacement, so why don't we work on what happened to Zarnak, okay?"

Legrasse felt his confidence in Thorner's abilities instantly increase. The man was tough, as all New Yorkers were held to be, but it was a professional armor, a weapon he used against the world of evil against which it was his duty to stand watch.

"Have you seen much?"

Thorner let the question hang in the air like an annoying insect. The buzz of it tore through his memories; his earlier days with Guicet had been nothing—ghosts, walking dead, witch women—veritable carnival acts. Then Guicet had disappeared and Zarnak had come to town. The very next day the lieutenant found himself with his service revolver in hand, surrounded by scores of torture-mutilated bodies, facing down a fire demon capable of ravaging dimensions.

"Yeah," he said finally. "I've seen my share."

"I have as well," asserted Legrasse, not bragging, simply trying to give his ally cause to trust him. "Knowing how these types of evil never seem to wait, maybe we should start acting like policemen."

"My captain keeps tellin' me to try it for a change. Hey, why not?"

Finished probing each other, the two lawmen turned to the job of determining how the doctor had vanished from his locked office. Looking over Zarnak's desk, they first went through all his open papers. Every letter and piece of note scrap on its surface was scrutinized by them both as they searched for some clue as to what the doctor had been doing when he disappeared. Every box and chest and container was opened—some more carefully that others. Books were thumbed through to see if anything had been hidden within them, or even to see if the topic of the book itself might make it a subject for their further interest.

Long before the pair had finished, it became obvious to them that most everything they looked over might be the springboard to finding one such as Anton Zarnak. Ram Singh brought them a meal of greens in gravy with sliced abalone, peppers stuffed with shrimp meat and chopped nuts, spare ribs, broccoli heads in oyster sauce, as well as bowls of rice and shark fin soup. As they picked over the remains, Thorner complained;

"This is gettin' us nowhere."

"Maybe not," answered Legrasse. "I agree that no single object points us more strongly in any one direction that any other. But, what about combinations of them? I mean, perhaps this piece of correspondence prompted him to gather that notepad and this book of spells …"

"Ohhhh, I get it," said the lieutenant. Pushing his derby back on his head, he scratched his forehead absently, thinking over all they had just reviewed. Nothing came to mind.

For the next two hours the lawmen struggled to find a connection between the things on the doctor's desk—a letter asking for help and a reference book pertaining to the subject within the letter, a note about some sort of research and an indication that the day he disappeared he had been engaged in such, et cetera. The pair tried mightily, but to no avail. As their third hour of reading and researching began, they heard a noise outside of the office that sounded as if someone had come to the door. After a few moments, Ram Singh entered the office.

"Pardon me, sirs," he said apologetically, "but a gentlemen has come to the door saying that he is aware of Dr. Zarnak's disappearance, and that he wishes to help recover him."

Legrasse and Thorner eyed one another. Each could tell the other was curious, but cautious. Finally, Thorner said, "Hell, we ain't gettin' anywhere on our own …"

Legrasse nodded in agreement. Ram Singh bowed slightly and left for the front door. When he returned he ushered a thin, oddly shaped man with a sallow, leathery complexion into the office and then departed. The lawmen barely noticed his leaving as they looked over their visitor.

His white-grey hair had been combed sometime earlier in the day, but seemed to have suffered the effects of both the weather and the city's bustle. He wore a long jacket, not inappropriate for the climate, but shabby and patched in an odd fashion. The man's shoes, though expensive, were badly scuffed. His manicured hands were filthy, as if he had been digging in the mud.

All these facts and more the police officers noted instantly, almost absently. Consciously, they studied his face, looking for clues as to who he might be and what he might be about. Handing the man's business card to the lieutenant whose chair was closest to the door, Ram Singh said;

"Mr. Archibald Melgranir."

The name meant nothing to either of the lawmen. When offered a seat, Mr. Melgranir declared that he would rather stand. Taking no exception to his reply, Legrasse merely said;

"Very well, sir, as you like. I must admit I find your arrival now most fortuitous. If I can cut right to the heart of the matter—what can you tell us about Dr. Zarnak's disappearance?"

"He is missing. He must be found."

Off to the side of Melgranir, Thorner rolled his eyes, plastering an expression on his face for Legrasse to see, one warning that the lieutenant felt something was not right with their guest. The former inspector made a slight nod in Thorner's direction, one indicating agreement.

"Yes," answered Legrasse straight-faced. "We're trying to find him. Can you tell us anything about his disappearance?"

"He hides," replied Melgranir. "He has run to some hole and pulled the world in on top of himself. He hides. But he must be found."

The lawmen listened to the odd man's voice with a dreadful fascination. It was high, too highly pitched for the body from which it omitted. Also, it came in a disturbing monotone, one that made the backs of both men's necks itch.

"Yeah," barked Thorner. "We know he's hidin'. Like the Inspector here said, we're trying to find him. But you're not helpin' us any. Savvy?"

"You will reveal his hiding place."

"I don't think you understand," Legrasse pushed Zarnak's office chair back, giving himself room to maneuver. Still seated, but ready to move, he said, "we don't know where he is. We ourselves are looking for him as well. That's why I ask you again, *sir*, can you tell us anything about how or why he disappeared?"

"Where is Zarnak?"

"He's out waitin' for the Sunday edition of the funny papers," growled Thorner. His hand sliding underneath his jacket, he added, "He's a big fan of

The Yellow Kid, don't ya know? He's gotta read it as soon as it hits the streets. What about you? You read the funny papers? 'Cause, you know, you look like you *escaped* from the funny papers."

"You defy the questioner ..."

Melgranir began to shake then, not so much of his own volition, but as if he were in the grasp of some unseen force.

"You can not do so ..."

Thorner pushed his chair back with a powerful exertion of both feet, putting an extra yard between himself and the vibrating man, bounding out of the chair as it came to a stop.

"You must *not* defy the questioner ..."

Legrasse stood, the action shoving the desk chair back into a precariously stacked pile of papers. As he did, his eyes fixed on Melgranir's face. On one of his cheeks as well as his forehead, white spots appeared. They were frantic, wiggling things which, second by second began to grow, or more correctly, to elongate.

"You *must not resist* ..."

As the shrill voice chattered, the lawmen watched as the spots pushed forward, showing themselves to be some sort of lengths actually forcing their way outward through Melgranir's skin.

"My God!"

Legrasse went white as he realized what was happening. Not recognizing anything in the phenomenon, but having been witnessed enough similar events, Thorner leveled his service revolver, which he had already pulled, at Melgranir's head.

"Give it up, you snot, or your brains are wallpaper!"

"Shoot!" demanded Legrasse. "Do it—shoot! Shoot *now!*"

Thorner needed no coaxing. His trigger finger squeezed effortlessly twice, sending two .45 rounds through the vibrating man's head. Melgranir's skull burst, red and grey matter flecked with bone fragments flying everywhere throughout the office. His body did not fall, however. Nor did it take so much as a backward step from the attack. Instead, much to the shock of the lawmen, the headless body's arms tore at the buttons of its long coat. As Legrasse pulled out his own revolver, the automatic hands jerked the jacket back over Melgranir's shoulders to reveal his naked torso.

Here, as on his face, the same white lengths were seen to be protruding from the body's sallow skin. As the lawmen watched, the pencil-thick things continued to push their way out of their host until Legrasse shouted;

"Dear Lord, they're dholes! Or bholes, whatever they're called ..."

And then, the former inspector stopped talking and began to fire his weapon. Following suit, Thorner joined in, blasting away at the unmoving target before him. As Ram Singh stuck his head into the office, responding to the sudden increase in noise, Legrasse bellowed over the ringing vibrations set off by the gunfire.

"Fire! We need to *burn* this thing!"

Ram Singh retreated without question as Thorner grabbed up his chair and smashed it over what remained of Melgranir. The body splattered at the blow, blood splashing the lieutenant, bone fragments dancing across the floor, and more than a dozen worm-like creatures dropping everywhere about. Legrasse picked up a particularly heavy-looking jade statue from the shelves next to him and brought it down with all his might on one of the worms. Its body burst, releasing a sizzling purple ichor which instantly sank into the woodwork below, despite its multiple layers of varnish.

Thorner, a quite sizable man, leapt upward and came down on one of the horrid, wriggling things. As both worms died, they released a monstrous whining into the air which shocked the policemen's eardrums even more severely than their own gunfire. As they reeled from the impact of the noise, staggering to find another target apiece, Ram Singh returned.

Without waiting for permission or instructions, the Hindu splashed the human remains and the surrounding worms with the contents of several bottles. He went to strike a match, but the lieutenant was ahead of him, having his lighter ready, igniting it and throwing it into the slopping mess in the middle of the office floor. Instantly flames sparked and again the hideous whine filled the air, forcing all three men to hold their ears. Ram Singh retreated to the hall; Thorner fell to his knees, holding his head, screaming; Legrasse toppled sideways into the shelves from which he had taken the jade statue. His face hit one of the wooden panels badly, breaking open his upper lip and sending a cascade of blood spurting from both his nostrils.

In moments the horrible shrieks of the worms abated. Ram Singh returned to the office with a tub of soapy water which he dumped on the small but raging fire in the center of the office. The maneuver resulted in a thick, unpleasant smell and an offensive cloud of gray/green smoke, but it extinguished the fire before it could spread any further.

Checking the debris, the lawmen found Melgranir to be completely demolished. From what they could tell, none of the worms had escaped their attention. Picking his lighter up out of the smoldering mess on the floor, Thorner asked;

"So what the hell's a bhole, and why'd we need to set the damn place on fire to get rid of them?"

Legrasse dropped his old service revolver on the desk and himself into the desk's chair. As the lieutenant cleaned off his lighter, polishing it against the sleeve of his jacket, the former inspector gasped for a clean breath of air, then answered.

"Dholes, bholes, I can't remember the exact name, but they're terrible creatures. They can grow as large as a dozen whales lined up end to end. I believe I mentioned that I've been studying at Anton's direction. I read about them some months ago."

"What else ya know about 'em?"

"I know that if they'd started to grow, that they would have overwhelmed us in no time. Good work, cutting off their host brain like that. Nice shooting."

"Couldn't hardly miss at that range," answered Thorner modestly. As he carefully reloaded his revolver, he added, "but what'dya think it's all got to do with the Doc?"

"These things, I believe, serve some God or some such thing named Shub-Niggurath. It's been worshipped here on Earth for thousands of years, and supposedly on other planets as well."

Ram Singh came in at that moment with a chair from some other room and a bucket. Handing the chair to the lieutenant, the Hindu indicated that he would clean away the remains of their struggle. The lawmen nodded, Legrasse asking;

"By the way, just what was it you used to start the fire?"

"A combination of brandy and kerosene. The kerosene I keep for it is most excellent for removing stains. The brandy, that is most excellent for keeping Dr. Zarnak amused. As you might have put together from the bubbles in the water I brought in, I was doing the household laundry when I first heard your gunfire."

Thorner smiled. Reaching inside his jacket, he replaced his .45 and pulled out a thick cigar. Igniting it with his freshly cleaned lighter, he reached down and grabbed up the top of Melgranir's skull.

"Normally," he said, "I never smoke here in the office. But," he exhaled a large cloud, sighing as he did so, "in light of recent events, I find myself not givin' much of a damn for what's 'normal.'"

"Understood," replied Legrasse with a weary nod. "And the skull?"

"Hey," responded the lieutenant, "the place is messy enough. I need some place to dump the ashes."

"Yes," answered Legrasse absently. "And I think I know of something else we need."

* *** *

The African woman who entered the office was no stranger to any of the men. She had been summoned at Legrasse's suggestion. The one time he had actually battled those elder forces from beyond with Zarnak, she had been there. Indeed, she had been the deciding factor in their battle. A familiar assistant to Zarnak in his work over the years, she was well known to Ram

Singh and Thorner as well.

"Madame Sarna La Raniella," the lieutenant said with an obvious note in his voice. "The most beautiful hoodoo in all of New York City."

"You are looking well, Lieutenant." Thorner revolved his head in an exaggerated fashion, making a delighted lalala sound deep in his throat.

"Ahhhhhhh," he said, a playful tone is his voice. "It sounds to nice when she says it."

"The lady is married," reminded Legrasse.

"Ask me if I care."

Madame La Raniella's dark eyes narrowed as she used them to tell the lieutenant that play time was over.

"We are to be searching for the good Doctor, no?" she said in her normal throaty whisper. "Before you tell me all de wonderful things I already know about my deathless beauty, maybe you should be telling me what be happenin' here before it happen again, and all dat beauty becomes not so deathless."

Instantly the tone in the room shifted, the layers of societal protection ripped away. The veil of pleasantries pierced, the two policemen told Madame La Raniella everything that had transpired, from the moment of Zarnak instructing Ram Singh to lock his office door up until the decision was made to call her.

"After that, Ram Singh told us to go out to the kitchen. He had prepared a dessert for us, and it got us out of his way. By the time we came back from stuffin' ourselves he had the office fixed up."

The woman looked about quietly, her eyes taking in all beyond her veil. She could see the stained and scorched section of floor, took note of the missing office chair, could smell Legrasse's blood on the shelf, the gag of crimson aroma mixed with the dark poison of worm flesh and nightmare—

"*Mon Dieu,*" Madame La Raniella gasped. Having obtained a comprehensive enough picture of the events, she cut her senses off from the room with a sharpness that made her body quiver noticeably. "Anton, you … what have you done now?"

"You got some insight to somethin', Sarna?"

"The worms," she whispered. "I know dese things. Blind and old and bigger t'an pride, swallow up de whole world they could. You pennied de eyes of an entire nest. Lucky damn white men get all de world's good fortune."

"Luck is something you make," answered Legrasse.

"T'en you better start whipping up a very big batch, New Orleans," she told the former inspector, "because you playin' with fire so hot it ain't got no name."

Quickly, La Raniella explained that the creatures known as both the dhole and the bhole were indeed destroyers of worlds in the service of Shub-Niggurath, but that they were also indebted to other races as well.

"From what little I know," she told them, "t'ey are used by many of de powers beyond de shade for t'eir various purposes."

"So really," said Thorner, "you're telling us all we did was stop some out of town muscle—some mugs sent in to find the Doc. It doesn't tell us where he is, or who's after him, or why …"

"Then we must find out."

As the men watched, La Raniella pulled forth a small, but heavy stone dish and an opaque bottle from her bag. Pouring a thick, shimmering green syrup into the dish, she struck a match and lit the center of the resulting puddle. As it bubbled up into a thin, mostly blue flame, she pulled back the light veil of her hat, then set aside the pillbox affair and closed her eyes.

"What kind of mood you out to set, Sarna?"

With a careful motion, the woman pulled her shawl more tightly about her shoulders. The colorfully embroidered black silk gripped her tightly, ridging her flesh as every wrinkle dug into her arm. Waving her hand over the dish, she extinguished the growing flame, replacing it with a smoldering billow of exotically scented smoke. As its bluish tendrils curled toward the ceiling, La Raniella whispered;

"I'm spinnin' a web of memory. You boys, you sit still now, why don't you. De smoke, she goin' to move about the room, back in time until it find ol' Zarnak's trail. Den we gonna see somethin'. Den we know."

Legrasse and Thorner sat quietly, both watching the witch woman as she worked, eyes still shut tight, her body swaying, hands above her head, her supple fingers all moving, each to a different rhythm, all stirring the blue smoke, dragging it this way and that, animating it until finally it animated itself.

"Look," hissed Legrasse. Thorner's eyes followed the former inspector's stabbing finger, watching as the blue layers of haze compressed back into wisps, all of them reaching down toward Zarnak's desk. As the tendril crawled across the littered surface, the lieutenant let out a low whistle, answering;

"Yeah, there's somethin' you don't see every day."

Madame La Raniella let out a low sound as the bluish haze congealed on the desk, binding itself around the steel ball. A hum sounded in response, coming, as best the lawmen could tell, from the smoke itself.

"Oh, Zarnak boy, what have you done." As Thorner and Legrasse stared, La Raniella pointed at the steel ball. Her throat dry, voice shaky, she told them, "that's where he be."

"What?" Legrasse's confusion boiled his short temper. "What's that's supposed to mean?"

"T'ere," the woman pointed to the ball once more. Touching it with her finger, she rolled it across the desk toward the lawman, "In t'ere. Dat's where he is."

Legrasse began to fume, but Thorner held up a cautionary hand. The lieutenant understood the Southerner's instinctive distrust, but he also knew the witch woman far better than his temporary partner. Turning to Madame La Raniella, he asked;

"What'dya mean, Sarna? He's all shrunk up and buried in that thing?" His tone softer than normal, his question was a plea for understanding. Knowing what was at stake as well as the lieutenant, she soften.

"You both understand t'at t'is world is not t'e only world. You both know t'e elder beasts, know t'ey have t'eir own realms. Zarnak, he in one, and it," she paused, picking up the steel ball once more, "is inside here."

"Do you know what he's doin' in there," asked Thorner. "How we can get him out?"

"He can come out whenever he wants," La Raniella answered. "Unless he forgot how. He not dead. If he was, my smoke could not find him."

"Madame," interrupted Legrasse, his face far away and thoughtful, "if it were up to you, if it were your decision as to what we do next ... what would you do?"

"I would get in t'ere and find him, before it was too late."

"'Too late?'" Thorner repeated the words with more than a little alarm. "What'dya mean, 'too late?' When's it gonna be too late?"

"T'he longer you wait, t'ey sooner t'at time comes."

The two lawmen looked at each other, then at La Raniella. The officers knew the woman was speaking nothing but the truth. When they asked how one could reach Zarnak, she told them she could show them both the ways in and back out again. Though they said nothing, their faces told the witch woman they would both be going.

"It will take some time—t'ere are ... elements I must have to send you on your way."

"That's good," said Thorner, a sly look crossing his face. "Gives me time to make a phone call."

"Hummmph?" Legrasse gave the lieutenant a puzzled look, then asked, "who would you be calling now?"

"They say," he answered, heading across the room to the corner where Zarnak kept his telephone, "that before any long voyage you should look into gettin' some insurance." As he set to dialing the phone's heavy metal disk, he added;

"Well, I got some of the best insurance in the world in mind."

* *** *

Ram Singh escorted the two policemen into the large side room where Madame La Raniella was setting out the last of her preparations. When he offered them chairs, the officers nodded gratefully, staggered as they were by their loads. Thorner came in from Zarnak's office, rubbing his hands together.

"Okay, boys," he asked, his visage beaming like a child's at Christmas, "what were ya able to liberate?"

"We did the best we could, sir," answered the junior of the two patrolmen. He held out the box he had brought for inspection. Coming in behind Thorner, the printing on the side of the small crate was not lost on Legrasse.

"Police property," he asked. "Evidence room property, no less. What are you playing at, Lieutenant?"

"I'm playin' at bringin' Zarnak back out here where the rest of us are in one piece," answered Thorner indignantly. "We're talkin' about goin' to another world. Another *goddamned* world. You ever faced the kinda nightmares live in the kinds of places she's gonna send us?"

"Yes, actually," answered the former inspector, "I have."

"And you feel like takin' on that kinda shit with just your service pistol?" The Southerner's face went dark, but he did not reply. His tone only slightly sarcastic, Thorner said, "Yeah, that's what I thought." The lieutenant wrenched open the box in his hands and then pulled forth an oddly shaped rifle. Handing it to Legrasse, he said;

"Here, wrap yer mitts around this."

The lawman accepted the weapon, turning it over in his hands. For the most part it seemed a normal enough self-loader, save for the oddly wide-mouthed extension which had been fitted to its muzzle. As Legrasse stared, one of the patrolmen explained;

"It's French, sir, RSC Modèle 1917. It's a gas-operated. Takes 8mm shells—five to a magazine. It's already loaded with blanks."

"Blanks?" Legrasse stared absently, not understanding. The patrolman explained;

"Yes, sir. The blank propels the grenade." Quickly the younger man pulled an awkward-looking device out of a bag. Holding it up he finished, "Brit #36M, some call 'em a 'Mills Bomb'. Don't know why. Just know you load one, aim, shoot, and make sure you don't hit anything close by."

"Why not? Is the force of the explosion that powerful?"

"No, sir. It's not that. Too many people think grenades are bombs. They're not. They're shrapnel weapons. The explosive inside is minimal—just enough to blow the metal casing apart and drive the pieces into the enemy. That and whatever else is packed inside. Wire, nails, whatever."

Thorner slung a different weapon over his own shoulder, telling his men, "Good haul, guys." Then, turning to Legrasse, he added;

"Look, we did a raid on a guy who's connected all the way to Albany. He's gonna get off scot free. And if he buys the right judge, he's even gonna get his property back. Well, myself, I don't give the stink from the station house crapper about this mook's rights. If it was up to me, he'd get it all back used."

Legrasse admired the grenade rifle for a moment longer, then said quietly, "New York is certainly an exuberant town."

"You can bet mammy's grits on that one, brother." Smiling, the lieutenant turned to Madame La Raniella and asked, "Okay, what's it take to send us off to NeverNeverLand?"

"Excuse me, lieutenant," interrupted one of the patrolmen, "but me and Petey, ah … we was hopin' to volunteer for some extra duty."

Thorner stopped for a moment, his mouth unable to work. His immediate thought was that more hands were certainly welcome. Then he thought again. Remembering others who had frozen when confronted with the impossible kinds of things he had seen at Zarnak's side, seeing again officers torn apart by rampaging hell-things simply because their inability to understand what they were seeing dulled their senses, he said;

"This ain't no picnic, we're headed for, you know."

"We know that," answered the other patrolman. The shorter of the two street coppers, Petey pulled himself up to his full height and said, "but you promised me, you know you did—you said whenever Zarnak and you were heading into something that was going to be bad, you'd take me along."

Thorner scowled. He had made such a promise. And officer Peter Norton was as tough as they came. As the lieutenant struggled, Legrasse said;

"You had your first time seeing these elder monsters, and so did I. Men died all about me in a crazy swamp that bled with fire. It took the guns of a Navy ship to finally knock down what we were up against, and it killed three hundred people just in the falling back to Earth." Silence hung in the room for a moment, then the taller patrolman asked;

"Is that all true, sir?" When Legrasse assured the younger man it was, the officer shoved his partner, shouting, "Christ, this sounds even better than you said, Petey." The patrolman turned to Thorner then and saluted, saying;

"Patrolman Ernest Malloy reporting for duty, sir."

The lieutenant put his hand to his face and rubbed, both to show his extreme displeasure with his officers at putting him in such a situation, and also to hide the beaming smile of pride he could not contain. In control once more, he threw both his hands in the air and hollered;

"Okay, okay, every one has the right to pick the way they die if they want to. You laughin' boys bring enough armament for everyone?" When the two smiled sheepishly, Thorner pursed his lips, then shouted once more.

"All right, fine. But I'm tellin' you dingle heads, this ain't gonna be like nothin' you've ever even dreamed about before. You savvy?" When the men nodded, he added;

"Well, you heard what I told you I seen. If you think you can handle somethin' like that, or worse, let's do this."

As the four lawmen armed themselves, Madame La Raniella instructed them to move themselves and anything they wished to take with them inside a triangle she had laid out on the floor in the side room. The triangle had been painted on the floor with a thin yellow liquid after Ram Singh had both moved the few restraining pieces of furniture and rolled up the rug. Within the center of the triangle was a circle painted in the same thing yellow. The shape was roughly a foot in diameter, and in the center of it was the steel ball from Zarnak's desk. The witch woman cautioned the men to not step inside of the circle, and to not step outside the triangle.

"Just no step on t'e yellow, and you'll be a live fellow."

Once they were all safely inside the correct perimeters, the witch woman began to lay down a circle of powder around the triangle. As she worked carefully to position the purplish grains just so, Legrasse questioned what was in a large box the patrolmen had brought into the triangle with them.

"A bit of indigestion for these new friends we're to be makin'," answered Petey.

Legrasse was about to enquire further, but La Raniella snapped, "Quiet. You listen careful now. In a moment, I'm going to tell you to close your eyes. You do it. After that, I light the powder in the outer circle. As soon as I do, you gonna feel yourselves slippin' away. When the powder she all burned, you no more be here. As soon as you gone, I'll start to lay down another circle. When I light it, you gonna start fadin' back to t'is realm, t'is place. You gonna fade slow, and you gonna come back slow. You understand?"

"How long will we have in this other place?" asked Legrasse.

"Maybe one half hour."

"A half an hour? That's all," said Thorner. "You think that'll be long enough to check this whole place out?"

"Really," answered La Raniella. "You don't find him t'at amount of time—I don't t'ink you goin' find him at all." Several of the lawmen started to fidget, but the witch woman snapped her fingers and said;

"Shut your eyes—I'm lightin' t'e powder. I'll be chanting t'e whole time. You no more hear my voice, open you're eyes."

The four officers closed their eyes. In the darkness they could hear the crackling sizzle of the burning powder, the clear, scintillating voice of the witch woman, her hair scraping her shoulders, the soft rush of air as she took each new breath. They stood past the time they all developed itches, and they all stood past the time their eyelids screamed to open. Then, it began.

As their nostrils filled with the scent of the burning powder, they felt themselves becoming light headed, light all over. And then it hit them, all at practically the same split second. They were not growing lighter, but thinner, flatter. And then, as their stomachs churned, they realized the truth—they were becoming transparent.

They could feel the building smoke against their legs, their chests, touching them, moving through them. And then they felt it, heard it all in the same moment, the shrieking flight of their own world rushing away from them. With a silencing gurgle, they could feel the change through their nerve endings. It had worked. They were somewhere else.

Legrasse opened his eyes first. As he did he fell over, unable to stand. Before he could warn the others he could feel them toppling all about him. They had opened their eyes in a world of colored spheres.

"Where in all creation are we?"

"Malloy," answered Thorner, working hard to adjust his senses, "that's not a question worth worryin' about."

Light did not emanate in their new universe from either any kind of central natural point like the sun, or from any kind of mechanical devices. Instead it seemed that everything in the new dimension simply glowed—or nearly anything. The ground beneath the lawmen did not emit any illumination, nor did any come from the sky, outside of that coming from those spheres floating high above.

The spheres were of all sizes and all colors. They each shown with a different intensity, and all of them seemed to follow different natural rules. Some were as solid as rock, others floated in the air. Some moved slowly, some rapidly. Some floated higher and higher until they disappeared, others vanished by sinking into the ground. It was also possible for the heavy ones to float away and those lighter than feathers to fall down to the surface of their world and slide out of sight.

"Humpin' weird—eh, Ernie?"

"Don't worry about the landscape," snapped Thorner. "Let's get done what we came to do." The two patrolmen nodded sheepishly, working hard to get their nerves back under control. Looking for something stronger than his will power, Petey pulled a bottle from inside his jacket. Taking a liberal slug, he offered it to Thorner, asking;

"Care for a nip, sir? Good for what scares ya."

And then, before the lieutenant could answer, they heard it. A hideous baying came to them through the air, through the ground, vibrating everything in the swirling world. Bubbles blew apart, some falling from the sky to slit on the ground like rotten melons, other shattering as if made of concrete. Hundreds exploded into shimmering dust, much of that falling sideways and drifting away. Fingers tightened around their weapons. Sweat soaked collars which suddenly felt too tight.

"What the hell was that," asked Petey, his legs forgetting how to move forward.

"Just some new plaything, come to make friends."

Legrasse's voice was so calm, his words given so matter-of-factly, the patrolmen wondered if he might not be serious. Nudging them both into motion once more with the barrel of his weapon, Thorner whispered;

"Just some of that droll Southern humor you've heard so much about."

"I never heard nuthin' about Southern humor ..."

"Well, now you have. So shut up already and keep your eyes open."

"For what, Lieutenant?"

Yeah, thought Thorner, for what? What do I tell these poor mooks to do now?

Pray

The lieutenant frowned at the bothersome voice from the back of his head. He had tried prayer when dealing with such things. It did not seem to have much effect. Halting the party for a moment, the lieutenant told his men;

"Now listen up, you two. You knew what you were gettin' into. I warned ya, and you let me know what big damn tough guys you were. All right, you're here. Get yourselves together, or mark my words, there's gonna be some holes in the duty roster."

"Gentlemen," interrupted Legrasse, "time is short and we've no time except to be blunt." The horrible baying came again, the air turning sticky as if the breath propelling the noise were as large as the wind. Pulling open the knot in his tie, Legrasse went on.

"Feel the ground under you. It's solid. It's real. You can breath the air. You're good men, I'm certain. If you weren't, your Lieutenant would have sent you packing. All I'm going to tell you is to clear your minds and simply be ready to follow orders. Whatever either of us tells you, trust us. Do it, exactly as we say, and you might survive this."

The patrolmen muttered appropriate responses. The men were not surly, merely frightened, and working desperately to get past their fear. As the hideous howling sounded again, feeling as if its source was unbearably close, Petey stammered;

"S-Sounds like the c-captain, before he's had his coffee."

"You mean," answered Ernie, "before he's poured four fingers of Scotch in it."

All the men laughed. None of them gave out with anything like a hearty noise—they chuckled at best—but it was enough to unfreeze legs and shove hearts down out of throats. All four moved through the bizarre landscape once more, Legrasse and Thorner shoving aside the thinning spheres with their gun barrels, Petey struggling with the wooden box, Ernie walking backwards, watching behind them. The four covered nearly another forty yards, and then the howling sounded once more.

It was a shattering loud sound, a thing made of equal parts pain and nightmare. It was a warning and a plea, a murderous volume splashing its way over their bodies, infecting their nerves and clawing at their skin. None of the men spoke. There was no need. Each man knew the horror had found them.

As they watched, an awkward, almost crab-like paw pushed its way through a large mass of multi-colored spheres. The shapes exploded at the touch, revealing a terrifying sight. A bulbous snout, red and hard, masking a jaw possessed of multiple layers of needling teeth and fangs moved forward, attached to a creature roughly the size of a rhinoceros. A bluish pus dripped from the creature's sides, splattering and burning the ground wherever it landed. The thing was long of frame, like a racing hound, but it was thickly solid, and seemed to be covered with an armored shell. Black and yellow gases leaked out of the corners of its mouth as it regarded the men standing before it.

Sum dee tri hernil, Sum dee tri hernil ...

The horror regarded the quartet before it for a long moment, then finally spoke.

"None of you are Zarnak."

As the two patrolmen became animated at the mention of the doctor's name, Thorner cautioned them to silence. Slowing tightening his finger on his weapon's trigger, Legrasse answered;

"That's right. We're not."

"You will reveal his hiding place."

"We don't know where he is," said the former inspector. "We want him as well, though."

"You *can not* have him! He is mine. His blood is mine to spill. His soul mine to drink, to dance upon. You will answer me—where is Zarnak?"

"Catch on, gruesome," hollered Ernie with a voice a half note from cracking, "we wouldn't tell ya even if we *did* know!"

"You must *not* defy the questioner ..." Thorner waved his forefinger back and forth in front of the monstrosity's face, telling it;

"You know, I've got the same answer for you I gave the last guy who said that ..."

And then, before the lieutenant could continue, Legrasse tightened his trigger finger and launched the grenade in his weapon into the side of the slavering creature before them. The men leaped for cover as the projectile exploded, burying burning metal in the monster's hide. As the creature screamed, Legrasse fumbled to pull a second grenade from his pocket. The former inspector was successful, but at the last second one of the device's edges caught on a thread from his jacket and was jerked out of his grasp.

"Damn!"

As Legrasse dropped to his knees to retrieve the grenade, Ernie and Thorner stepped forward both firing their weapons. German submachine guns from the Great War, they were capable of firing four hundred rounds a minute. The policeman slammed the creature with lead, screaming as they did so, throwing their voices at the thing along with their bullets.

"Look out!"

Legrasse screamed to be heard over the thunderous firing. As the two policemen caught on to his intent and cleared out of his path, the lawman fired his second grenade. The dull-colored egg flew directly into one of the beast's eyes and exploded, sending shrapnel deep within the monster's head. Immediately the creature howled once more, arcs of a boiling purple slop jutting from the burned and ragged crack which had appeared in its face.

Sum dee tri hernil, Sum dee tri hernil …

Having exhausted his clip first, Thorner was in the process of replacing his spent magazine with a new one when Ernie's ran out. With no new force being thrown against it, the creature shook off the effects of the damage it had taken so far in an instant. Its eyes fixing on Ernie, smelling his fear as he realized he could not reload before the monstrosity could take him, the beast slammed one mighty clawed leg forward, hissing;

"You *defy* the questioner. You hide the Zarnak. You attack the unstoppable …"

His new clip in place, Thorner threw himself forward shouting;

"And you—you *fucking* talk too goddamned much!"

Ramming his weapon against the thing's skull he pulled his trigger and let fly with some seventy rounds before the horror could react.

Sum dee tri hernil, Sum dee tri hernil …

When it did, though, it flung one of its stout legs outward, smashing it into the lieutenant's weapon. The Bergmann MP18/1, one of the sturdiest armaments of one of the greatest weapon's manufacturer's of all time crumpled like a leaf in December. Thorner felt his wrist break upon the impact a split second before the force of the monster's attack truly reached him. On contact with the thing's appendage, the lieutenant was knocked off his feet, thrown head over heels so far back into the circling spheres that none of the others could see him.

"Eat shit, you bastard!"

As Legrasse and Ernie threw themselves to the ground, Petey flung forward three jam-tins, hand grenades also from the Great War. Two of the shredders landed under the creature, the third on his back. Instantly the air was filled with shrapnel. Petey took a large hit in the abdomen which spun him around, then knocked him from his feet, his bottle smashing open, the end of it grinding into his chest. Legrasse and Ernie felt metal tearing into their backs as well.

Sum dee tri hernil, Sum dee tri hernil …

Sitting up, Petey stared down at the blood oozing out around the twisted pieces of steel wedged in his abdomen. As he looked about, he saw that Thorner was still nowhere in sight, and that his partner and the Southerner were down. Reaching down into his box, he struggled to pull a heavy shape out of it, giggling as he did so. His mind gone, snapped like the slightest twig, he heaved a black sphere free from the confines of the wooden box, thick wads of cotton sticking to its rough surface.

"You want defiance, ya big slab'a beef," he asked with a laugh, staggering forward under the weight he carried. "I'll give ya some—Brooklyn style."

As the creature shook off the trifling pains which the lawmen's last attack had inflicted, officer Peter Norton broke into a run, despite the forty pounds of hollowed-out artillery shell in his arms. The old ball, left over from the Civil War, had been filled with nitroglycerine and fitted with a highly sensitive percussion cap. Called "land torpedoes," such infernal devices had been used to destroy all manner of heavy machines during the Great War. Moving at a run, his eyes wild, drool dribbling from his chin, Norton hurled himself at the creature, using his body as the final force to set off his bomb.

The resulting explosion shredded the patrolman. Much to those surviving him, the creature actually fell over from the attack, great gushing showers of its animating fluids arcing high into the sky. Pulling himself to his feet as quickly as he could, Legrasse fitted a third Mills into his Modèle 1917 and fired, blasting the horrid thing while it was down. Ernie followed suit, attacking once more with his Bergman, lashing the beast with non-stop fire while Legrasse fit another grenade into his weapon.

But then, before he could fire, the terrible beast reared up on its hind legs and then brought his forepaws down against the ground. The resultant shock waves knocked both lawmen off their feet, sending their weapons flying off into the spheres. Shaking its vicious head, clacking its rows of teeth together, grinding them, the creature screamed;

"You puny maggots thought to hurt me? *Me?*"

"Seemed … like a good idea … at the time," Legrasse sputtered, gasping for breath. Clawing the ground, trying to regain his feet, he looked in every direction for his weapon as the monster only yards away from him bellowed;

"Ridiculous, insignificant speck of nothing. You actually thought you could challenge the undying? You really thought to harm one such as me? You shall pay for your defiance."

"Oh, I don't think so."

All heads turned, staring up into the sky at the floating form of Dr. Anton Zarnak.

A demonic delight passed over the horror's face. Its good eye glistening, it laughed low in its throat.

"Now I have you," it snarled, its hideous claws tearing the ground, shattering spheres.

"Well then," answered Zarnak as he slowly descended from the sky, "if you have me you don't need them." Ignoring the beast, the doctor turned to

112

Legrasse, pointing behind himself as he did so.

"Thorner lies in that direction," he said. "Take this young man and head back to the circle." Legrasse's mouth opened to protest, but Zarnak snapped, "Do as you're told."

As the Southerner and the patrolman helped each other hobble away, the doctor's feet touched the ground. As the monstrosity continued to chuckle, preparing to charge, he told it;

"Do not excite yourself, Tind'losi. There is no triumph for you here. You shall be dead in moments." The great beast laughed all the harder, its stamping feet shaking the ground.

"I have owned you since I saw you spying on me through what you call time. I have chased you to this 'now,' and I shall end our contest here. There is nothing such as you can do to stop me. Your soul is *mine!*"

The creature stepped forward, arrogant in its power. It had good reason. Never had a hound of Tindalos failed to destroy a prey once it had taken to its trail. The creature's were susceptible to certain magicks and rituals, of course, but Zarnak had been given no time to do make such preparations. No matter how many tricks the doctor might possess, the beast knew it was now only a matter of time. Howling once more, it snapped;

"You have not drawn my essence, you have not spoken the words, you have not shown me darkness ... without these, you are just another pile of meat."

As the creature's breath poured over Zarnak, he raised a hand to stifle a yawn. Then, moving to the side so that he faced the horror's good eye, he said;

"Ah, but I have been speaking the words since you came together with my fellows here. And as for drawing your essence, Mr. Norton died when first he hit the ground. I animated him, gave him life long enough to do that which I could see in his mind. No, the words are spoken, and your blood is spilt. And ... as for darkness ..."

Zarnak stabbed forward suddenly, grinding the broken end of Petey's bottle into the monster's good eye. Anticipating the enraged monstrosity's attack, the doctor threw himself sideways, avoiding the thing's devastating charge. Running as fast as he could, the doctor disappeared through the spheres in the direction he had previously sent the others. Spotting the three after only a moment, he saw that they had reached Madame La Raniella's circle. Dashing for it, he screamed;

"Where are you, beast?!"

The Tindalos hound, hearing Zarnak's taunt, threw itself blindly forward through the spheres, desperate to catch the doctor. As he threw himself inside the triangle he could see within the circle on the ground, Zarnak observed the rate at which it was burning, put his ear to the wind, and then sighed with relief. Turning to the others, he instructed them;

"The beast is coming. Do not panic. Do not move. We want it to come—"

Thorner made to speak, but Zarnak cut him off, shouting, "*Trust me!*"

Putting a finger to his lips, the doctor cautioned the others to be silent as the monster knocked aside the last of the spheres between itself and them. As it nosed the ground, Zarnak studied the rate of burn once more, allowing the blinded thing to wander about, searching for them. Legrasse and the others watched as the seconds ticked by, and then suddenly, Zarnak shouted;

"Now!"

At the sound of Zarnak's voice the beast wheeled about and then leaped. At the same time, the doctor plucked the steel ball from the center of the smaller circle and threw it with all his might at the beast's forehead.

La Raniella's voice broke through the silence—
Steel smashed into bleeding flesh—
The powder burned down—
The spheres vanished—
And the world exploded.

* **** *

The three lawmen blinked, and suddenly they were back inside the walls of 13 China Alley. Though wounded, and somewhat mentally fractured, they were alive. Later Zarnak would explain how he had erred and allowed the Tindalos hound to see him as he spied on the ancient past through a crystal, how he had timed when the beast would reach their current century to the day, and had ensured that Legrasse would arrive on that day. Later he would give them explanations, For the moment, however, the ability to breathe, to know they would go on breathing, that was enough.

Thorner pounded on the floor, laughing, whooping with joy over still being alive. To the lieutenant, surviving yet another mad adventure with Zarnak was the greatest comedy in the world. When the doctor pointed to the steel ball, steaming in the center of the circle, letting them all know that because of them and their delaying tactics he had been able to trap the creature within its curves, Thorner only laughed all the harder.

Picking up the metal sphere, Legrasse turned it over in his fingers. As he stared at it, Zarnak thanked Madame La Raniella as well as Thorner and officer Malloy, then turned to Legrasse to apologize;

"Sorry to have used you so, but I had to do something quickly. I timed the thing's arrival to the day you were to come to New York, then removed myself from where it had seen me. There was no time for anything else."

"Why did you go where you did," asked the Southerner. "Why not just face the thing here?"

"I chose that dimension because spheres bother Tind'losi, curve trap them. I knew if you could find your way to me that you would be able to distract the thing long enough for me to ensnare it."

As the others stared at the steel ball Legrasse continued to move through his fingers like a stage magician's prop, Zarnak assured them the hound was imprisoned there forever. Then, as he apologized again for bringing them all into his struggle, Legrasse put up his other hand to cut the doctor off, telling him;

"It doesn't matter. Not really. Once you get a taste of this, you know, you either go mad, like poor Norton, or you just spend your days waiting for the next run in. Used up, spit out, wasted away, dead in some lonely place. It's the inevitable checklist of this occupation."

"Jeez," said Thorner. "Lighten up there, Johnny." As Legrasse turned to face him, the lieutenant said;

"Hey, we're cops, okay? What the hell's the difference between gettin' it tryin' to stop some two bit schnook from heistin' a payroll, or tryin' to stop some runaway god from destroyin' the world?"

"Saving the world is more important?"

All heads turned toward Malloy. Silence reigned for a long moment, then Legrasse nodded, saying;

"Yes—I guess that would be the difference."

The mood lightened then, and Zarnak instructed the policemen to sit so he could attend to their wounds. Madame La Raniella was provided with a sum equal to her highest fee and thanked profusely. Ram Singh was sent to the kitchen to prepare the largest feast 13 China Alley had ever seen.

While the Hindu busied himself, Zarnak set to work with hot water, blades and bandages, removing shrapnel from his rescuers' bodies. Malloy started drinking before the doctor made his first incision and continued throughout the night. Thorner smoked a pipeful of an unknown substance Zarnak offered him and found himself feeling good enough to sing while the doctor treated him. And all the while Legrasse sat waiting his turn, bleeding, wondering if it were even possible to save the world from the kinds of nightmares he had seen.

Then, he looked down at the monster in his hand.

And smiled.

WHERE SHADOW FALLS

*"Between the conception and the creation
Between the emotion and the response
Falls the Shadow."*

—T. S. Eliot

The man stared out over the side panel of his Ford motor car at the last fall leaves clinging to their branches, still not certain of his ability to carry out his plan. As an idea, sitting in the luxuriant comfort of his home, it had appeared logical, almost rational—a thing, considering the vastness of the stakes—easily accomplished by one such as himself. But now, hunkered in the open back seat of his vehicle, shadowed over by the foreboding skies that had hung like a leadened curtain above New Orleans for what had seemed weeks on end, doubt tore at him, its pin-prick claws digging into his pride, his fear of ridicule, into any part of his ego where it might gain a handhold and turn him from his current pursuit.

"Sir," repeated his young Negro driver without turning, "I said, we've arrived at the address you requested. 121 Bienville Street." Once again the man in the back seat ignored the information, lost behind the nagging battle raging within his breast until the driver added,

"The home of Inspector Legrasse. Will you be going up, sir, or shall I announce you?"

"Oh, Louis, no ... no," the older man answered from the back, the confused haze of his doubts clearing enough for him to pretend to take the reins of his life in hand once more. "This won't, I mean to say ... Legrasse would most likely ... ah, no. No. It has to be me."

The young Negro, sensing a firming of his employer's resolve to approach the white-painted, dilapidated wooden home at the end of the chipped and crumbling slate walkway, jumped up from his seat and strode quickly around the new model automobile. His hand firmly grasping the door release, before he could bring himself to open it, he leaned in toward his employer with obvious concern.

"Are you sure you'll be all right, sir," asked Louis quietly. "Alone ... I mean? With Legrasse?"

"All right? Safe, you mean?" The old man smiled sadly as he pulled his considerable bulk slowly across the seat. The driver snapped open the door smartly, allowing the passenger to lower himself carefully to the ground. As he disembarked, the old man added, "None of us are safe now, boy. None of us."

Achillie Giuseppe Buttacavala, feeling more than twice his fifty-six years, walked away from his shining car and pushed his way into Legrasse's small, overgrown yard. Stopping to catch his breath, the old man hung onto the rusting iron bars of the front gate as if gravity itself were attempting to refuse him entrance. Turning back to his driver, he gave his man several sharp orders.

"You wait with the car, Louis. I don't know how long I'll be. I don't even know if Legrasse will see me. I just know that I have to try. You know that. I *have* to."

His face tight with concern, the lanky driver stepped back to the small world of his automobile hoping to comfort his employer by assuring him, "I'll be right here, sir. Don't you worry none."

The old man smiled. His upper bridge biting down on his lower lip, he stifled the mad laughter he felt rising through his despair.

Don't worry none, he thought. What a wonderful idea. Why, there's an answer to all my problems. Don't worry none. Idiot—brainless, yammering idiot. Filthy, childish ...

Buttacavala cut off the torrent of self-pity and hate attempting to distract him away from what he had already convinced himself needed to be done.

Amazing—he thought, the notion popping unbidden into his brain in an almost frightening moment of clarity—how every petty sin can work against us.

Turning back to his driver one final time, the old man allowed what meager charity still dwelt within him to fill his eyes as he said,

"I'll try, Louis. I'll try."

And then, Achillie Giuseppe Buttacavala, tyrannical ruler of the largest criminal organization anywhere on the North American continent, once more began to make his way toward the tiny white home of his greatest enemy.

*   * * *   *

Buttacavala stood at the door, wondering precisely how long it would take someone to answer the knocker. Straightening his thick tie, brushing the crisp lines of his four button waist coat, the old man found his mind panicking—retreating to prayer, begging whatever God might still listen to such as him to bring Legrasse to the door.

Then, abandoning prayer with the impatience of a child, his hand grasped the simple, unstylized metal knocker once more. Up and down his desperation drew it, sending slamming echoes throughout the small house. His fingers crashed brass against brass a score of times, his face going flush from the fierceness of his exertions.

Legrasse *must* be home, he thought. They said he never goes out—not since that business in the swamp. That's why I've come—me, myself—*me!* He wouldn't dare not be here—he has to be here. Lord God, please—I cannot go away. I'd never have the nerve to return. Please ...

120

And then, the door opened. Buttacavala, taking sight of the man on the other side of the threshold, stepped back involuntarily, greatly disturbed by the silent figure who greeted him. The crime lord had never met Legrasse but, he knew the man's features, had seen his picture in the local papers more than once those many years earlier. The former Inspector of Police had broken up operations of the crime lord's that had sent hundreds of his people to prison—more than a few to the gallows. Legrasse had cost Buttacavala literally millions of dollars. Such a man's face the crime lord did not easily forget. But still, he did not recognize the man in the doorway before him.

It was an unkempt figure holding a dust-streaked, over-sized volume that greeted the crime lord. The shoes on its feet were old and worn, the laces of one broken and knotted over several times. The clothing covering it was baggy, frayed—unwashed for a period so long that the smell of them seemed less an aroma of honest work than it did the grave. Buttons hung by threads when they were even still intact. The one time highly starched collar slung carelessly about the figure's neck hung in tatters, the one-time blinding clean of it smeared over by the dirt of years. But, repulsive as it might be, it was not the figure's attire which gave the visitor such a start.

When Inspector John Raymond Legrasse had dropped out of sight, he would have best been described as middle-aged, commonplace-looking. Those were no words to paint a picture of the man before Buttacavala. The crime lord found himself staring into a long unshaved face, one that had not seen the sun for so many years, its whiteness approached the ghastly shade of a moldered egg, or that of certain deep-forest fungi. His mouth seemed to twitch—not when one was staring directly at it, but a moment after—giving the impression it was a conscious, mocking gesture rather than an involuntary one. His hair, ragged and wild—half across his face, half standing straight up—was shot through with careless white streaks. But, most disturbing of all were his eyes.

Buttacavala could put no name to the color he saw within them. It was a shifting shade—blue/black/brown/green—there was no telling for certain. The only thing the older man could be positive of was that the eyes were almost completely red where they should have been white, and that they were quite, quite mad.

"Yes?" the single word was a question, the speaker's tone somehow both conveying annoyance and curiosity at the same time. Buttacavala stammered, searching desperately for his voice. He was possibly the most powerful man in Louisiana—certainly in all of New Orleans—and yet he felt helpless, frightened, in the presence of the gaunt form in the doorway. Breaking eye contact with the disheveled figure, the crime lord lowered his head and then shook it, finally managing to choke out a sentence.

"I'm here in the hopes of seeing Inspector of Police Legrasse."

121

"I'm Legrasse," answered the ragged man. His head tilted at an awkward angle, he seemed to fade away for a moment, then focused once more, adding, "But, oh, well—I mean ... even though they allowed me to keep my title—formality, really—now, let me think—why, I haven't been with the police for almost ... what is it ... maybe fifteen years now."

Buttacavala raised his head again, confusion filling his face. The tales of Legrasse talked of an enormous powerhouse of a man, a skilled fighter, an excellent tactician, a daring and winning, born leader of men. The inspector would have had to have been an exceptional man to have brought so many of the crime lord's most profitable ventures to ruin. Despite his long absence, Legrasse was a name feared and respected still throughout the underworld of New Orleans. But the man before him—Buttacavala would not have trusted him to walk his wife's dog.

"Can I help you?"

"*Help* me? Help *me?*" stammered Buttacavala. Tears welling within his tired eyes, he started to laugh. The taste of salt in his mouth, he practically choked on his own bile as he cursed the man before him.

"Damn everything!" he screeched in a trembling note. "Damn all the Heavens! This is their revenge. This is how they taunt me—pushing me step by step into the mausoleum. I curse—"

Legrasse's hand shot up with lightning speed, his index finger gently coming to rest on the older man's lips, silencing him. As the stunned crime lord tried to step back in shock, his eyes wide with surprised anger, the object of his rage held him in place with an iron grip.

"We sometimes speak harshly in rash haste," cautioned Legrasse, "bringing down upon ourselves grievous punishments easily avoided by a moment's thought." As Buttacavala collected himself, more ill-at-ease than ever, the gaunt figure released his grip on his visitor's wrist then continued, asking, "Now, tell me, Calamari, what can I do for you?"

The crime lord's eyes narrowed, his nostrils flaring. Legrasse had called him by the nickname he had been known by over thirty-five years earlier when he was still a street mark, a shill-carper hustling the protection game and running penny-deuce games in the lowest basements of the old Quarter.

Two weeks earlier, any other man careless enough to identify Achillie Buttacavala by the hated old name would have soon found himself fighting for breath at the dark bottom of New Orleans harbor. But it was not two weeks earlier, and the man before him was—as far as the crime lord knew—the only person in the world who could help him gain the one thing he wanted. Closing off his anger, shaking as he fought the muscles in his face, willing them not to sneer, he growled, "You can help me avenge the death of my son."

Interest sparking in the corners of Legrasse's red eyes, he suddenly snapped shut the text book he had still been holding open. Shoving the volume under his arm, the inspector asked, "He was murdered?"

"Yes," answered Buttacavala, regaining his control.

"Huummmm ... and do you have any idea who killed him?"

"Yes, I know exactly who did it," answered the old crime lord. Pulling himself up to his full height, he stared once more into Legrasse's wild eyes and told him with defiant sorrow,

"I did."

* * * * *

The crime lord waited in the drawing room impatiently. While Legrasse busied himself in the kitchen, his guest stared about, trying to make sense of what he had seen so far. If Legrasse, the man, did not measure up to what Buttacavala knew of him, his home left the crime lord even more confused.

He had heard that his host was a fastidious man, orderly and organized, given to simple tastes. Although loyal and brave and fiercely proud of his ability to—in his time—keep his small corner of New Orleans reasonably civilized, Buttacavala had been led to believe that his old adversary was a man of few dimensions, pragmatic but dull, well-intentioned but ill-read and lacking in sophistication. These descriptions matched what he had seen no more than the face he had found at the doorway resembled the inspector's old newspaper photographs.

The first thing that had caught Buttacavala's eye was an over-sized wash tub on the floor toward the back of the room. It had been positioned to catch a steady dripping coming down from the ceiling. The water was a murky color, indicating that it was not leaking cleanly through from the roof, but passing through several layers first—floor and ceiling woods, plasterboard, rugs? Running down and leaching away the wallpaper, perhaps? The crime lord had no way of telling.

Drawn to the rusting bucket, he crossed the room, observing the metallic stain leeching into the soggy carpeting beneath it. There were footprints in the carpeting around the tub. Buttacavala could only suppose they were formed through the pressure of someone standing near it as they grappled the decaying bucket upward to empty it. He could see the spectacle in his mind's eye and it struck him as almost amusing, like something out of a burlesque skit. But then, as he moved closer, still trying to guess how many years the tub had sat there collecting the water coming in from its long unfixed hole, something caught his eye that forced his hand to his mouth, lest he should gag. In the shadow of the ancient bucket, in several of the soggy footprints between the tub and the wall grew a crop of pale tan mushrooms. Leeching their way up out of the carpeting, they were tall and spindly, swaying on their ill designed stems.

The crime lord backed away from the sight, returning to his seat. As he lowered himself into the chair, a small cloud of dust crushed out of its cushion. Smaller that the one exhaled when he had first sat down, there was still sufficient detritus within it to set him gagging. Buttacavala blessed himself with the sign of the cross, nervous fear forcing his brain to not draw connections between what he had just seen and what had brought him to Legrasse in the first place. The heavy-set man was rapidly being filled with a dread that he had made a mistake coming to the one-time inspector. The sight of the man had shaken his confidence, of that there had been no doubt. But that and the horrible tub were not the only things which did not match the description Buttacavala had brought with him.

Legrasse's home was filled with books, shelves and bookcases and massive stacks of every shape and size text imaginable. A number of piles stood around the room, growing wild, placed here and there with no apparent organization. They did not occupy the floor for want of not having been returned to their proper homes, however. It appeared there simply was no room left for them. The drawing room, for instance, was walled with floor-to-ceiling shelves, but they were each and every one wedged tight with as many volumes as they could handle. Some had even collapsed under their weight—the evidence to be found in scattered fragments of wood laying on the floor directly below spaces where shelves were obviously missing. From the look of the walls, his host's answer had been to pick the fallen books up and to simply replace them on top of those volumes on the shelf below their previous resting place.

It all made Buttacavala shake his head in sad misery. The crime lord had come looking for a man of action, someone who might understand what he was up against and do something about it where none so far had been able to prevail. Instead of a warrior, however, he seemed to have found some kind of scholar—a thin, pale academic more worried about where he had left his morning's post than he was over anything happening outside his small sphere of influence.

Buttacavala stared at the heavily draped windows, the dense purple curtains stained gray by ages of dust, thick streaks of powdery grit dribbling down from the ceiling of the room, covering everything in its creeping path. It lay in all directions, helping to identify the length of time different parts of the room had gone untouched. Here and there the crime lord spotted breaks in the sooty layers, spots where books had been pulled down and examined, areas with hand-shaped smears randomly breaking the uniform sheets of building decay. And, all the time the constant dripping in the back corner kept the thick silence from ever feeling anything like comforting. Sitting in the center of it all, for no reason he could name, the drawing room reminded Buttacavala of nothing more than the inside of a coffin.

This man cannot help me, thought the crime lord, a great sadness welling within him. He can barely help himself.

Thinking it best if he just left, leaving to spend his last days in mourning rather than grasping at the straws of revenge—for certainly if Legrasse were his only hope, then hope did not exist—the old man pulled at his hanging bulk and rose heavily from his chair. Turning on his heel, sadness draining even more of his energy, he began to move for the hall when suddenly he spotted a small statute, no more than seven inches tall.

It was a piece of exquisitely artistic workmanship. It was also a thing of horrific, monstrous terror that sent Buttacavala reeling backward as if physically shoved. Of course, as a mere piece of art, the statuette was not so fearsome on its own. In cold, analytical terms, it represented some monster of vaguely anthropoid outline, but with an octopus-like head whose face was a mask of feelers, a scaly, rubbery-looking body, prodigious claws on hind and fore feet, and long, narrow wings behind. The corpulent thing squatted evilly on a rectangular block covered with undecipherable characters.

There were more details one could see with further study, but Buttacavala had no wish to see any of them. Greatly disturbed, wishing to flee more than ever but now terrified of the idea, he fled back to his chair and fell into it as if having pulled an iron door shut behind him. A further cloud of dust was flushed from the seat's tattered cushion by the crime lord's great weight, sending him into a violent fit of tearful hacking. When the attack passed, cold silence flooded back into the room, broken only by the terrible, rhythmic dripping in the corner. Staring at the small statue on the other side of the room from him, tears staining his face, he remaining thus until Legrasse returned.

"What's the problem, Calamari?" asked the inspector, entering the room with a tray balancing two cups and a pot of hot tea. "You seem agitated."

"Where? Where did you get that—*that thing?*" croaked the crime lord, unconsciously pushing himself as far into his chair as he could. Pointing at the statue, he droned with fear throttling him, "My son, he had one in his room when we found him ... when he attacked his mother ... there was incense, blood ... he was praying to it—to *that!*"

"Like it?" asked the inspector. Putting down his tray, he crossed the room. Grabbing up the terrible image, he turned back to his guest, answering, "This one came into my hands on my last official case. Found it in the swamps when I went back out there to make certain that   things ... were calm. Should have been blown to bits at the time really. But, since it wasn't, I decided to keep it. Better in my hands where it will do less mischief."

Legrasse stared at the image for a long moment, studying it as if for the first time. His ruby-veined eyes remained locked on the blasphemous image, unblinking, as if there were some fabulous mystery to be solved if only he could concentrate on the graven stonework deeply enough. But then, suddenly losing interest, he shoved the statue head first into one of the few free spots on the book shelf closest to him and returned to his guest.

"Well, why don't you tell me what brings you here." Sitting down in another of the room's long unused chair, dust clouded up around the inspector as he adjust his form to its unyielding cushions. Picking up his tea, he took a sip, ignoring the grey film settling on it from out of the air. The, he fixed the stuttering Buttacavala with his stare.

"You said something about murdering your son?"

"I didn't murder him," barked the crime lord. His words twisted in his mouth, grief filling them with a painful sorrow that etched its way into the ear. "I *released* him."

"Ummmmmm, hummmm," mused the inspector absently, as if contemplating nothing more weighty than the latest boxing scores. Replacing his cup in its saucer, he asked, "Released him from what, exactly?"

The older man's head snapped as if struck. He stared at Legrasse with disbelief, his face a mask of confused intensity. The inspector studied his guest carefully, wondering at what the strange expression might mean. Finally, Buttacavala admitted,

"I don't know!"

"Well," mused Legrasse absently, "you must know something, or you wouldn't have come here. So, tell me what you do know."

The crime lord raised his head, regarding the inspector with not only suspicion, but also anger. Watching Legrasse calmly sip his tea, Buttacavala could not help but wonder whether or not the man was mocking him and his grief. Law officers were not known for their sympathy toward those of the criminal cast. One part of his brain urged Buttacavala toward the door, demanding that he speak his mind in snarling red fury and then depart.

But, a question whispered through his rage, to what end?

Unable to find an answer, the crime lord humbled himself further, whipping his frustration to the back recesses of his trouble consciousness. The fingers of his left hand digging into the fraying fabric of Legrasse's moldering chair, he began,

"Lake Pontchartrain, that's where it all started. My shipping concerns are all centered there. Easier to reach the open ocean from there than to follow the Mississippi down, or portage over to Cataouatche, work down through Salvador, Barataria, Bastian ..."

As Buttacavala trailed off, the inspector asked absently, "Easier to transverse, or easier to bribe one's way through?"

"You're a hateful man, Legrasse."

"Why, Calamari? Because I'm indelicate enough to remind you of the evil truth of your life? Or perhaps your years and the lost youth trailing behind them have begun to make that point more clearly all by themselves—showing you in bright lights how all paths do indeed lead to the grave but, that after that intersection has been obtained there are an equal number of paths leading outward. Could it be that you've finally begun to suspect what course you've set for yourself?"

Buttacavala struggled his sloppy girth back onto his feet, flinging his cup and saucer away from himself at the same time. Animal rage animating his limbs, he shook violently, his arm coming up, finger pointing at Legrasse.

"You, bastard! You miserable dog! Who do you think you are to judge me? How dare you talk this way to me?!"

"I do not *think* I am anyone," responded the inspector politely. "I *know* who I am. I am John Raymond Legrasse. And I dare to tell the truth because that it all any man actually possesses in this world. Your truth is that a life of murder and theft can somehow be justified by rationalizing that any honest, man is a fool who deserves to be butchered. Mine is that men such as yourselves are a draining threat to the integrity humanity needs to repel the growing horror lurking beyond the veil that hungers to swallow us all."

"Horror?" questioned Buttacavala. "What do you know of horror?" Setting his cup and saucer aside, Legrasse rose from his chair. Dust falling from his back and shoulders, he stepped forward out of the thin gray cloud surrounding him and said,

"*Ph'nglui mglw'nafh Cthulhu R'lyeh wgah'nagl fhtagn.*"

The elderly crime lord drew back, his eyes going wide, skin draining of color. He spun awkwardly around, face turned from Legrasse, his eyes straining wildly to find something on which they could focus. Grabbing at his collar to release the sudden rush of heat he felt flooding his body, he cursed loudly, wiped at the bitter tears streaking his face. Then he turned back toward the inspector shamefaced, croaking weakly,

"Where did you learn that phrase?"

"I went to witness the execution of a murderer. He was a model prisoner who had as a last request, nothing more than the chance to utter a final few last words. Smiling, he went to his end spewing that incomprehensible billage. So did one of his fellows, and a third and a fourth, and so on … but, before I bore you, let me ask … would those be the last words your son offered as you put him down?" When Buttacavala dropped his head in shameful silence, Legrasse nodded,

"Yes, I imagined such. Now, let me guess at the rest." The Inspector of Police moved toward his guest. He had never seen such as he was about to describe, but he had made numerous interviews and investigations since his first few run-ins with those things that crossed over from the beyond. Something about Buttacavala's manner suggested a different plague than the one he had personally faced. Playing his wild hunch, the inspector shifted to a softer tone as he spoke.

"Your boy began to change, didn't he?" asked Legrasse with a cold certainty. "His eyes went a watery blue—stopped blinking altogether after a while. His nose seemed flatter to you probably, lips thickened, pores gone coarse, cheeks grayed. His skin probably started peeling as well, growing patchy, scaly. Perhaps his manner of locomotion began to change as well, more of a lopping gait, I imagine."

"How?" asked Buttacavala in a whisper. "How could you know all this? We kept him hidden away. How could you know?" Turning his back on his guest, Legrasse walked toward one of his walls of shelves, careful to step over the puddle of tea surrounding the crime lord's cup and saucer. As he scanned the banks of volumes before him, he dredged through his brain for the appropriate bit of memory.

"I expect," he said finally, "that sometime before the transformations began that he became involved with some new customer of yours—unloading ships smuggling cargo into Orleans from either the far north, probably the Massachusetts area, Rhode Island, thereabouts from what I've heard, or, then again, perhaps it was from the South Seas. Did he oversee that kind of activity on any regular basis?"

"What is this? You think I'm stupid?" demanded Buttacavala angrily. "I'm supposed to be so grief stricken that I forget who I am and admit to things like that to you?"

Legrasse stopped for a moment, honestly puzzled. Then suddenly, as realization of what his guest meant finally struck him, he threw back his head and laughed. It was a brittle, gasping sound, tittering glee being forced through a throat and mouth so unused to such exercise that it only took a brief few seconds before the inspector found him face in actual pain. Inside his brain, competing voices shouted, ridiculing the crime lord's petty distress. In the face of the monumental knowledge Legrasse had gained since his first encounter with the beyond—a knowledge that Buttacavala now seemed to share to some extent—for the crime lord to still be concerned with concealing his dishonest livelihood struck the one-time official Inspector of Police as the very height of absurdity.

"Oh, Lord, how amusingly droll you are, Calamari," he finally managed to articulate. Holding his jaw, Legrasse lowered himself weakly into the nearest chair. Through a massive clamping down of his will he managed to continue speaking, although he could not help chuckling as he did so.

"It's been so long since I've actually found humor in anything. Thank you."

"Humor?" barked Buttacavala. "Humor? You find something in all this funny? You find me funny?"

"Oh, yes. Exaggeratedly so. But please, let us be serious." Using his open palm to indicate the room's only other chair, Legrasse instructed his guest,

"Now sit, and let us get to the bottom of this."

"No," answered Buttacavala. "I don't know what game you think you're playing with me, but I'll have no more of it." As the crime lord made to leave the room, Legrasse sneered,

"You are a fool and a coward, Calamari. You say you seek revenge for the death of your son, yet you haven't even given the cause of his death the slightest honest thought."

"You say this to me?! I know what happened to my boy is my fault," shouted the crime lord. "You think I cannot see the Hand of God in such punishment? I *know* where my life has taken me! I understand!"

"Pfah," spat the inspector. His face hard, the pale white of it seemingly intensifying, he roared, "Cretin. 'The Hand of God,' indeed. As if a supreme being has any interest in the likes of you. Your son dead at your own hand and still your overriding instinct is to protect the criminal activity that lead you to such an end in the first place. The sheer tininess to the parameters of your mind astound me."

The crime lord's face fell, his anger draining as his inability to comprehend what Legrasse was saying confused and frightened him. Until the night he had been forced to deal with his first born, Buttacavala had been a pillar of confidence, supremely assured that his will was all that mattered. Now …

"Legrasse," the crime lord begged, "I don't understand."

"You don't understand?" the inspector sneered, his voice a mincing parody of his guest's. "Well, allow me to explain. You are a thief. And thieves by nature are selfish, their arrogance that of a child who grabs food from a parent's plate because—from their ignorant viewpoint—there is nothing wrong in such an action for, after all, doesn't the world revolve around them?"

Buttacavala stared, unable to react. Within his brain, so many different responses demanded to be heard that the crime lord was frozen into immobility, unable to chose a path of action. Not caring what the elder criminal's response might be, however, Legrasse continued, drawing closer to the man with every sentence.

"That you can worry about something as meaningless as protecting your ill-gotten empire when the entire world is at stake is abominable. That you can think I would care more about prosecuting you for your petty crimes than trying to stave off the all too real horrors descending on mankind even as we speak is laughably insulting."

Turning away from Buttacavala then, the inspector crossed the room toward the shelf where he had previously buried his small statuette. Wrapping his hand around its base, Legrasse pulled it free violently, scattering several of the volumes that it had been jammed between with the force of his action. Then, he turned once more and shook the horrid image in the crime lord's face, shouting as he did so.

"You think yourself so important that I could turn my back on this—on *this*? Simply to give you the opportunity to bribe yet another judge into following you through the gates of Hell? *This* is what awaits us, Calamari. Right behind the door of darkness, this bloated fiend and ten dozen of its fellows—unspeakable creatures of such immense power that to try and create a scale by saying they are to us as we are to the ants is to insult both the ants and them by a hundred-fold."

"Why are you saying this?" screamed Buttacavala backing up step by step. His voice cracking, going disturbingly shrill once more, he fell to his knees almost overturning the slowly filling water tub behind him. Choking on his own fear, he bleated, "Why are you saying this?"

"Because," Legrasse answered, "it is the truth." Thrusting forward the menacing length of stone, the inspector forced the horrid statue into the crime lord's face, rubbing the smooth stone against him, grinding it against Buttacavala's forehead and the bridge of his nose as he shouted,

"This is what is coming for us—for all men, for all the Earth, and all the stars beyond. This is what is being drawn out of the shadow realm and solidly onto our plane of existence by the forces of evil piled up one bloody bone atop another by men such as you. This monstrosity is asleep, somewhere under the waters, its ears listening for the final note that will awaken it and bring it down on all of us—*us,* all the common ale it needs to quench the fire in its gullet."

"No, no!" Buttacavala swatted feebly at the statue. He did not manage to move it, only succeeding in knocking himself sideways, his massive body missing the water tub but knocking over several random stacks of books instead. The varied texts scattered across the floor as the crime lord caught hold of a small table and tried to pull himself upright.

As Legrasse stood waiting, Buttacavala dragging himself to his feet. Sweating, panting, the crime lord framed his host with a look of raging hate, then shoved his hand into the folds of his overcoat. Bringing it out once more, he revealed a pistol of moderate caliber which he thrust forward at the inspector's chest.

"Damn you, Legrasse," he swore. "*Damn* you!"

Standing his ground, the one time Inspector of Police answered the threat simply, "I'm not the one damned if that trigger is pulled."

And then, suddenly Achillie Giuseppe Buttacavala let the revolver fall from his fingers. His chest heaving, heart pumping wildly, pain smashing through his head and arms, the elder crime lord gasped, "Help me, Legrasse. Help me."

Crossing the room, the inspector put his arm around the crying man, helping him move back to his chair. Shoving him roughly down into the overstuffed seat, he told his guest, "There is no help for you, Calamari. But still, it really is time for me to get back to the world."

Looking down from the piece of stone in his hand to the sobbing form of the crime lord before him, noting the almost comic similarity between their poses, Legrasse offered,

"So, perhaps it would not be too great a waste of my time to allow you to help me."

*   * * *   *

Four men made their way up the tattered slate walkway to Legrasse's home. Three of them had worked with him in the offices of the New Orleans police department. The last the inspector had only known briefly before he had dropped out of sight. Though all approaching the house had tried to keep in contact with the one-time inspector, over the years Legrasse had grown more and more reclusive until finally he had cut off all contact with the outside world.

Thus, all in the quartet had been stunned to find that their former companion had suddenly returned to them from beyond his previously erected walls of solitude. Notes hand-delivered by a young Negro two of the officers recognized as the chauffeur for one of the local crime bosses, compelled the four to gather on a particular day and time at Legrasse's home. The invitations had been penned in a rushed scrawl. There seemed to be some attempt at the creation of legible script, but the impatience of the author won out, making the deciphering of the terse missives somewhat of a chore. Eventually, however, all had understood.

Contacting each other, the quartet arranged to gather as requested. On the way to 121 Bienville Street, the four men were absorbed with discussing their old friend and acquaintance. All knew of the arcane and blasphemous studies that had engrossed their one-time companion. None knew what to make of the situation, however.

Seeing the disrepair of his home, none of them knew what to make of that, either. The shortest of them, a Spanish-American by the name of Galvez reached for the door knocker when suddenly the front door was flung open with unexpected energy.

"Right on time, right on time—wonderful." A smiling Legrasse stepped away from the opening into his home and gestured emphatically, ordering, "Come in, come in. There is no time to waste, gentlemen. Not now. Not anymore."

Gone was the tattered, shambling figure that had greeted Achillie Buttacavala. The crime lord had sent several of his personal staff to reintroduce the inspector to the niceties of the outside world. They cleaned and aired out his home, then saw to it that Legrasse shaved and bathed, scrubbing his skin and hair until his tub had been littered with the dead remains of both. His long nails had been trimmed away, as had his wild mane. Brushed and combed and lacquered into place, John Legrasse looked much his former self—even his mad eyes had grown somewhat calmer, saner.

One by one, the four passed through the doorway, shaking hands with Legrasse, exchanging greetings, all of them noting that the man none of them had seen in the last ten years did not seem very interested in how they were doing, or what might have transpired in their lives. There was a single-minded force at work within him, pushing them along like the first crested wave of a flood-swollen river. Helpless, they surrendered to the human current sweeping them into the drawing room beyond, all of them wondering that if he did not want to know them again as people, what then was it that he did desire?

The clutter Achillie Buttacavala had found inside Legrasse's home had been as completely swept away as had his ragged appearance. The only oddity remaining was the rusting washtub, still squat in its corner, catching the rhythmic drippings which continued to fall from the cracked and ruined ceiling. Even it had been made more respectable, however, the area around it scraped and scrubbed until now it seemed only the stop-gap measure connected to some unfortunate accident instead of the signpost of decay it had seemed but days earlier. Sitting his four visitors down in his newly cleaned drawing room, the one-time inspector told them,

"I'm so pleased that all of you could make it today. Especially you, Professor Webb, considering the distance involved. I must tell you that a part of me would like nothing better than to try and turn back the clock, to give in to the temptation to simply chatter on over what has filled our recent pasts as if the last time we were all together were merely the blink of an eye. But, forgive me, I cannot."

The four men grew cold, the beginnings of a tiny dread creeping into all their souls. Years earlier when Legrasse had first glimpsed the dark mirror of the other side, they had all been a part of his effort to stem the tide against that which would have pushed its way free. The cost had been high. Hundreds had died, millions of dollars in property had been obliterated. Of the immediate forces the inspector had led, those now gathered were practically the only survivors. And, if one did not count those leading their lives behind the stone and bars of several New Orleans sanitariums, then they were, indeed, the only ones to have passed through the long gone night and emerged in any way whole on the other side.

"Inspector, I'm afraid to admit that I'm following you, for if I do, then something has come to pass which I greatly fear to be a part of." The speaker was Professor William Channing Webb, the eldest of the gathering. He was a tall man, thin, one who sported a finely cropped beard despite its having gone stark white decades earlier. He shrank in his chair as he spoke, however, his normal towering height melting away as he voiced his fears.

"Don't think that way," added the next oldest, a heavy-set man by the name of Randolf Muller. Flush-faced, sporting a thick, broken nose and brown eyes all run together too closely, he had been a sergeant the last time he had seen Legrasse. Since then he had been promoted twice and had finally retired from the force two years earlier. Pulling at his collar, he added, "This don't have to be about what we done in the swamp. Does it, Inspector?"

Before Legrasse could answer, however, Joel Carrinelle, a man seemingly all bone and skin, barked at the assembly, "Hey, leave off—what if it does? What's it matter? This is the Inspector here. If he needs us to go back to that, then we go. We strap it on and we button it up, and we go—all the way to Hell if we need to."

Carrinelle's outburst left everyone a bit nonplussed. Not wanting things to bog down in a foolish awkwardness for which they had no time, Legrasse turned to his old second-in-command, Joseph D. Galvez. The inspector had always considered the short Spaniard to be a man of rare intelligence—a rational, deductive thinker upon whom he could always count. Hoping he could count on him then, Legrasse asked,

"Joseph, you've not said anything yet. Could I ask your assessment of all this?"

"I'm always one to appreciate a good joke, el Grande," offered Galvez with a bit of a smile, using the nickname he had given the inspector decades earlier. "But something tells me we aren't here to be amused. I watched you slip away from the outside world, bit by bit over the years, losing yourself in studying what it was that happened to us in the swamp. I don't see you for almost a decade, then I get a letter from you asking for all of us to meet you—us, *us*— the only ones to survive with our limbs and minds reasonable intact …"

Galvez caught himself, pulling back on the rolling anger he felt building within his chest. Bypassing the belligerence, he dug down to the fear propelling it. Then, holding the growing wealth of terror in check, he swallowed a breath of air and continued.

"You want to know what I make of this? Sure, I'll tell you. You've finally found something, something big and evil and dangerous, and you expect us to follow you off to wherever it is and deal with it. No 'hello,' no curiosity as to whether or not any of us have families now. After all, it's only been ten years—*ten years*—since you've spoken to any of us. But, whatever, that's what you want. You want us to go monster-hunting with you. Again. And you won't be happy until we're all dead."

"Well," offered Legrasse, only a bit taken aback by Galvez's assessment of the situation, "although I might not have put it quite so strongly … I won't lie to you. Yes, you are correct—I have had something brought to my attention which I do not believe I can handle on my own. As to my concern for your well-being, however, please try to give me at least some of the credit you would have in the past."

Turning from Galvez back to Webb, the inspector offered, "Professor, I would only be asking your advise. Knowledge of one's enemy is a valuable weapon. That which you could tell us of what lies before us could mean the difference between our survival and our demise."

Arcing his neck slightly, Legrasse focused his eyes on Muller and Carrinelle, whose chairs were close together, and told them, "I know none of you have married. I don't have to look for wedding rings to know that—after what we experienced—none of us are headed in that particular direction. With where we went, what we witnessed—knowing that we had seen but the tip of the iceberg—were there any of us ready to attach ourselves to other people, to raise children? Children—brought into this world? A world but a thin fragile thought away from the terrors we have seen? How many of you have tried to win fare hand, knowing what is coming? How many of you can even sleep at night—even now?"

Silence ruled the room. A harsh and terrible quiet fell in the moment Legrasse took to catch his breath. It ate at the quartet's nerves, burrowing into their skin, making them itch and sweat. Finally, though, Legrasse turned back to his one-time lieutenant.

"Yes, Joseph," he admitted. "Something new is stirring. Many somethings. Most likely too many. And, yes again—I need you and Joel and Randolf at my side. A few days back, Achillie Buttacavala came to me ..."

"The Calamari?" asked Carrinelle. "The worst criminal bastard in Louisiana?"

"Yes, the same. His son had been contaminated by a type of horror I have so far only been told of, or read accounts of in antique volumes. What happened was a type of transformation—it came over the boy slowly at first, but in the end it molded and reshaped him into an amphibian-like hybrid of man and beast. Buttacavala was forced to shoot him when the boy turned on his own mother."

"But what brought the Calamari to you?"

"What happened to us in the swamp, of course. People still talk about it. They know. Even now, not a month can pass without some hoodoo man or witching crone showing up on my doorstep. Some of the swamp people still bring me gifts—fish, wild onions, cazmani ... the point is, we're the only one's who *know*."

Legrasse stopped for a moment, his breath coming in thin gasps. He had changed so much, he realized. Years of inactivity, years of nothing but quiet study had robbed him of much of what he had once been. Determined to overcome the effects of that robbery, however, he pulled in on himself and began again, slowly, pacing his meager energy.

"Professor Webb," he began, pointing to the older man, "you said it best years ago when you told us that we who had made first contact with the things we found in the swamp were best suited to return against them simply because we *had* seen them. Buttacavala has offered me unlimited resources. Anything—men, money, weapons—whatever I might require to wipe away the fungi that infested his son. The one thing he cannot furnish me, however, is the thing I need most … the experience you four have stored," Legrasse tapped his head, "in here."

The one-time inspector was just about to continue when Webb arose from his chair. His manner was tense and agitated. He turned his head in a circular, jerking motion, taking in the room as he did so, his hands trembling nervously.

"Mr. Legrasse," he stammered. "Please—allow me to make a few observations. This room … it appears that there has been a great deal of activity here. An anthropologist has to have a good eye for such things. This chamber—you, yourself—everything has been cleaned anew, hasn't it? Your face is smooth-shaved, but your chin shows the burn of skin no longer used to the razor's kiss. Your hair is smoothed out with grease because until recently it has not known soap or the comb. My suspicion is that since I was last in New Orleans, you have taken it upon yourself to make a study of that which we faced. A number of the books on the walls tell me that much. The pallor your skin has developed tells me that you have gone down this path with a single-minded ferocity, learning as much as you could, throwing your life away in the pursuit of this knowledge."

All eyes in the room remained transfixed on Legrasse. The inspector kept his place, merely listening and nodding as the professor spoke.

"Indeed, I do not believe you would have broken off at this point if this criminal you mention had not come to you. I know the pull. I have searched out clues to this and that for over fifty years. There is safety in the academic life—always one bit more knowledge to be unearthed, just one more fact before action can be undertaken." Webb lowered his head in a shameful pose, his white hair looking thin and sparse.

"That," he said, "was why I fell apart on you fifteen years ago, Mr. Legrasse. You came to me, a scholar safe in my ivory chamber and you dragged me down into the mud of reality and I could not handle it. Now, this Calamari has done the same for you, disrupting your sheltered life—forcing you to remember what existence is like away from the tomb of safety."

"It is true," admitted Legrasse. "I had forgotten there was an outside world. Sometimes I forgot to eat, sleep—I would pass out reading—worn out by reading!"

The inspector laughed at the memory with fond bitterness. Not allowing a pause, however, he started again immediately, saying, "Imagine—me, worn out by reading. And then I would awaken some time later and simply start again where I had left off. I know what I am asking of you all—better than you do, yourselves. I have read the legends and the warnings in a hundred ancient texts. I cannot begin to deceive any of you, nor would I care to. There can be no doubt that what I want to ask will lead us to death and madness—exactly as it did the last time."

Legrasse made to continue but, before he could, Galvez cut him off. The short man cursed himself inside as he stood. He had known for fifteen years that the day would come when the terrors he had faced would find him once more. He had spent years taming his fear, learning anew to sleep in a darkened room, training himself to not jump at every noise in the night, or to shake at the mention of swamps. Indeed, he had risen to the position of inspector himself. The official reasoning had been that he was an exceptional police officer, one always willing to lead the charge, to throw himself into the face of danger in the execution of his duties.

Galvez knew the truth, however. Certainly he had shown what had appeared outwardly to be bravery, challenging criminals more than twice his size, running headlong into hails of bullets, taking on two, even three brigands by his lonesome. But, it was not any kind of fearlessness that had made him do so. The simple fact was that deep down the man had hoped to earn some respectable, ordinary death before the fate he dreaded most caught up to him. Now that it had, however, he spat at his previous attempts to deny his fate and suddenly embraced it, extending his palm to Legrasse.

"Ask what you will, el Grande," he said with a rueful smirk. "You shall not stand alone."

Carrinelle leapt to his feet, closing his right hand around the clasped hands of the two men. As Muller moved forward also, the younger officer shouted,

"Legrasse? Alone? Never! We're both with you, to whatever and wherever you might lead!" And, as Muller's hand touched the others, Carrinelle added, "You see? Three are four. How many more could you need, Inspector?"

"I would think at least one more." All turned to see Professor Webb moving forward. Adding his hand to the tangle, he said, "Not for you particularly, Legrasse, but, if you can understand, for myself."

Legrasse nodded. Webb blinked.

"I will not fail you," he added, his voice almost trembling. "Not this time."

The inspector felt the heat flowing from hand to hand, not able to remember the last instance in which he had actually made contact with another human being. As the raw power of naked human energy transferred from man to man, doubling in effect as it passed from frame to frame, Legrasse lowered his head, biting at his lip, nearly unable to control the weight of emotion pressing down on him. After a moment, though, he raised his head again, a smile manufactured equally from confidence and anticipation stretching across his face.

"Gentlemen," he said to the others, praying he had not pulled them all together once more merely to unite them in damnation, "I think it best we begin."

* *** *

The meeting between Buttacavala and Legrasse and his people went as well as could be expected. Professor Webb, of course, bore the crime lord no ill-will. Indeed, as an academic, he was quite accustomed to seeing good and noble works funded by the most unscrupulous people for the basest of reasons on an extraordinarily routine basis. The others were not quite as reasonable as the good professor but, Legrasse was able to keep everyone in a pleasant enough humor to get them through the affair with a minimum of bad humor from all sides.

The two current and two former police officers questioned the crime lord and all of his people along lines that might possibly shed some light on what had happened to Carmine Buttacavala. The interrogations lasted for three days during which events were covered from every angle. The past history of the boy was detailed for years before the point where he could have possibly made contact with whatever agent of the beyond had affected him so. With Professor Webb directing the various angles of questioning from the sidelines, acting as coordinator and sometimes referee, the five men slowly began to narrow down their line of inquiry.

Inch by inch they moved forward until finally an ugly picture began to unfold. At the end of the third day, the quintet of investigators sat with Buttacavala in grim silence. None of the six were in anything resembling a good humor. They had all heard the same questions over and over, much the same answers given repeatedly from a hundred different mouths. They had interviewed everyone within the crime lord's domain who had had even the slightest connection with the man's son for the past year—grilling some of them unmercifully. Sadly, their efforts had garnered them precious little.

Sitting at a central table with the others, Legrasse stared into his coffee cup, watching the light from the warehouse ceiling play against the deep black within it. Without raising his head, he said, "I think it best we review what he have established so far, gentlemen."

"That won't take long," muttered Galvez. His head suspended backwards over his chair, sweat dripping from his forehead, running through his hair and down his neck, he groaned, "What've we learned? I can sum that up for you. We haven't learned anything."

"It's not that bad, Joe ..."

"What, Joel?" snapped Galvez. "What? What do we know now we didn't know three days ago—a hell of a lot about how Calamari here has greased his way through, that's for damn sure, but not much else."

"You said my people could talk freely," snapped the crime lord. Dragging his bulk up out of his chair, he leveled a finger at Legrasse, threatening, "If you go back on your word to me, so help me God, I'll ..."

"Please," answered Legrasse, his soft tone cutting through Buttacavala's bluster, "we are supposedly allies. Just because we cannot yet see a solution to our problem does not mean we have not found it." Everyone stared at the inspector. He did not notice, his eyes riveted to the black void inside his cup.

"So, as I said," he repeated, "let us review. The changes in Carmine Buttacavala began some eight months ago. Different people noticed different things first, but no one saw anything before then. Eight months ago is when he began to oversee you sea coast smuggling operations—correct?"

"You're going to keep these dogs of yours in line about this stuff—right?" asked the crime lord. "I don't care for myself, not anymore ... but my family, my people ..."

"Calamari," answered Legrasse in a low, dangerous voice, "I care not one fig for you or your people or what becomes of any of you. As for our pact, I myself have better things to do than worry about your petty activities." Shifting the direction of his voice, still staring into his cup, the inspector added, "Mr. Galvez, please remember that we are trying to investigate something bigger than common criminality here."

"Don't go hard on 'em, Inspector." Joel Carrinelle mopped at his drenched hair and neck with an already soaked rag. Wringing out the stale, salty cloth, he said, "the heat's just makin' us edgy. That's all."

Placing his cup down suddenly, Legrasse looked up. His eyes coming into focus, he said, "Yes ... the heat."

The sudden change in the inspector startled everyone in the stifling warehouse. Muller and Webb in particular leaned forward as if in anticipation of some sort of revelation. Catching his chin with the fingers of one hand, Legrasse pulled at the skin around his mouth, going back to his review of the facts they had gathered.

"It was eight months ago that Carmine first went to Massachusetts. He was supposed to move product coming in from England down the coast starting with Boston ... but he took it upon himself to move up the coast, did he not?"

"Yeah," confirmed Buttacavala, "to an old, played-out sea town name of Innsmouth. Worth it, though. He made a haul in this old antique gold jewelry. My wife was so happy. Opened a lot of society doors with that stuff. Lot of native crap, South Seas ..."

"Yes," responded Professor Webb. "We made note of that connection. The trade route he established was, of course, the beginning of his downfall. Tell me, Mr. Buttacavala, didn't anyone find it suspicious—West Indians and Brava Portuguese, Negroes and mulattoes, all wanting to be smuggled up to a New England sea town … paying their passage in gold tiaras and gem-encrusted statues of frogs?"

"Does it matter?" asked the crime lord in a sorrowful voice. Mopping at the rivers of sweat pouring out from under his greasy hair, he said, "I know what greed has cost me."

"No," answered Legrasse. "What we need here is clear vision, not morality. Tell me again, Calamari, how did your son come across the notion of arranging this extra bit of commerce?"

Throwing aside his drenched handkerchief, Buttacavala told the assembly, "Like I said, it was the scum themselves—mostly they were sailors anyway. They worked the docks, you know. Word gets around, questions get asked … you know how it is."

"Yes, but we don't know how it was *exactly,* do we? Which voice it was that set him on the tragic course to damnation—"

"Yes we do." All heads turned toward the flush-faced Muller. Redder than ever due to the heat of the warehouse, he puffed as he talked, answering the others' questioning looks by telling them, "It was that odd freak cripple what we talked to yesterday."

The others stared at Muller, moving their heads to look at each other, searching to see if anyone else had made the connection their companion had made. Only Legrasse kept his eyes directly on the old German.

"Well done, Muller." When the others turned to the inspector, he told them, "I remember him now—he was strange—hobbling and shuffling, and always scratching at himself … talking in that bleating tongue as if English were a third language to him. He sat his chair in this muggy hell box as if it were in the ice chest of a downtown restaurant. Wrapped up in coat and scarf, no less, and he mentioned bringing Carmine the notion. It was a slip, and he backed away from it as soon as he said it, spreading the responsibility for the idea out amongst a half dozen of his fellows—but it was him. Yes. It was him."

"Coat and scarf! *Coat and scarf!*" Galvez exploded. Cursing in a foul string of guttural Spanish, he suddenly resurfaced into the conversation, asking, "I know all the physical deformities Carmine went through, but what about the heat? Wasn't there something about him needing it to be warm?"

Achillie Buttacavala crossed himself as if Satan had climbed down into the room from the dark recesses of the warehouse ceiling. Shaking, he nodded his head violently.

"And, and I'll bet he wasn't just wearing a scarf to keep warm," guessed Carrinelle, "he was keeping' himself hid from us—so we couldn't see the changes. He's one of 'em, too."

Buttacavala's fist slammed against the table with a roaring violence, one that slashed its way through the old crime lord's growing internal doubts and terrors. As he had dwelt on what had happened to his son, slowly he had become immobilized, helpless to make the slightest decisions. Indeed, it had taken an enormous outlay of strength for him to even contact Legrasse in the first place. And later, as he had talked with the one-time inspector and his fellows, the old man's fall into numbness had proceeded at a rapid rate. The horrors they spoke of were too big, too monumental, too all encompassing for him to even contemplate, let alone understand. But this, this was something he could handle. Bellowing in a voice that shook the rafters, he called for his henchmen waiting in the next room. As his most trusted lieutenants gathered, he roared his instructions at them.

"That little gimp bastard, Thomton, Tommy Thomton," he asked. "You remember him?"

"The little bald creep?" asked one of the mobsters. "The one with the beard like torn-up wire?"

"Yes!" thundered Buttacavala, "the one who sailed the Boston route with Carmine ... you get him. Comb the streets, turn the docks upside down, but find him and drag him here to me. I'll pay ten thousand in gold to the man that finds him!"

"Don't cancel the reward," interrupted Legrasse, "but don't bring Thomton here. Find his home, and bring the information back to us. We'll handle it from there."

The men turned from the inspector to Buttacavala, looking for confirmation. Despite having been told they were to follow any orders Legrasse may give, their allegiance was to the crime lord and no one else. None questioned openly, but their eyes searched Buttacavala's nonetheless. To answer them, the old man thundered,

"You didn't hear the man? You need to be told twice?!" Raising his bunched fist, the crime lord roared, "Go—find that bastard son of a bitch. And do it like Legrasse said ... find him quiet. Once we've got him ... then we'll make some noise."

The henchmen withdrew, all anxious to spend the ten thousand each of them expected to collect. As they closed the door behind them, Buttacavala turned to Legrasse.

"They'll find him. Greedy sons of bitches. They won't leave a stone unturned in all of New Orleans." Staring at his hands, the crime lord made grasping motions with his fingers, watching them strangle an invisible victim the others were certain they could identify. As they listened, Buttacavala's voice trailed off into an almost gibbering whisper.

"They'll find him. Oh, they'll find him, all right. They'll find him."

With ten thousand dollars in gold at stake, no one in the room doubted the odious cripple would be found. When all was said and done, however, even Buttacavala was surprised with the speed with which the discovery was accomplished.

*   * * *   *

The quartet of cars traveled the back cobblestone roads at a slow pace. The pitted, collapsing old streets leading to the docks were not overly hospitable to motorized transport in dry weather. In the rain things only got worse.

"That's it up ahead," offered Louis. The driver nervously loosened one of his hands from the wheel to point out the building he meant. Cascades of rain slammed against the car carrying him, Legrasse, Webb and Muller, as well as the one following behind with Galvez, Carrinelle, and three of Buttacavala's thugs. The second set of vehicles carried more of the crime lord's people.

Half their number were men who had grown up with Carmine Buttacavala and wished to wreck appropriate vengeance on the person who had destroyed their friend. One of the others was the first to discover Thomton's most likely whereabouts. He had gone along mainly to make certain he was not somehow cheated out of his reward. The rest were mere soldiers, sent along as insurance. Galvez had watched them swagger and joke as they had made ready to leave. "Cannon fodder," he had called them.

Standing close by, Muller had nodded in agreement, adding, "Better them than us." The Spaniard had merely shrugged, wondering if such endings could be written in advance.

On the docks, a staggering shaft of lightning blasted the sky open, frying the rain and illuminating everything for a hundred blocks. The driver of the first car was so frightened he drove up over the curb and back down, having to slam on the brakes before he could regain control—more of himself than the vehicle. Understanding what was clawing at the chauffeur, Legrasse said, "Steady, boy, you'll do fine."

"Thank you, sir," answered Louis. Although the temperature had dropped considerably due to the advent of the rain and the basically instability of the late fall Orleans weather, the young man could not keep from perspiring. As he got the lead car underway again, thankful none of the drivers behind him had been forced to calamity by his nervous blunder, Legrasse instructed,

"Better pull over and let us go the last block on foot. Motor cars are still a novelty in a neighborhood like this. Four are practically a parade. Better to suffer a touch of dampness than to tip our hand to our Mr. Thomton."

"Yes, sir," answered Louis, grateful for the chance to stop fighting the storm. Pulling in next to the curb he cut the motor, receiving Legrasse's instructions on how long he should wait and what he and his fellow drivers should do if the former Inspector of Police and the others did not return with as much grace as he could muster. As those headed in after Thomton assembled on the rough sidewalk, Louis and his fellow chauffeurs gathered in the second vehicle, none of them able to even contemplate the thought of sitting alone in the dark and thundering storm.

The assembly of police officers and rogues made their way through the lashing storm, hats pulled low, hands in pockets, eyes reduced to slits to grant them the minimum visibility allowed. When they finally reached the doorway designated as leading to Thomton's vulgar pair of rooms, Legrasse positioned his people more through hand signals than verbal instructions. Looking over the layout of the area, the former inspector noted that Thomton had chosen to take his residence suspiciously near the open sea. Coming close to Galvez, Legrasse cupped his hands and spoke directly into the man's ear.

"If all we've been thinking is correct," he said, "I doubt we can snare this thing by going through the front door. Take Muller and a few of our new found friends and head around the back."

As the former lieutenant carried out his orders, Legrasse approached Carrinelle in the same fashion, telling him, "I've read too much about this Thomton's breed. Best we're ready on all fronts. You take those others Calamari supplied us and go over the side of the dock. Watch for anything like a trap door—Lord help us, you've covered New Orleans and its denizens long enough to spot out a smuggler's dodge without me having to draw you a map."

When the younger man grinned, Legrasse asked, "Do you have a lamp?"

Pulling a large pocket torch from his rain slicker, Carrinelle nodded, smiled again, and then took the remainder of the thugs in tow and headed over to the edge of the dock. Buttacavala's men proved to be well versed in clambering about the piers and the throng of toughs disappeared from sight in moments.

"Well, sir," said Legrasse, turning to Professor Webb, "it appears to be just you and me."

"Huuumm …" Webb raised his eyebrows, staring unblinking through the driving rain. He appeared to be looking at the inspector, but in reality his gaze was fixed on Thomton's door. His eyes finally closing for a split second, breaking the spell of the night and the rain, the elder sucked down a vast gulp of air, then said, "Perhaps we should be going then."

"Yes, I think so," agreed Legrasse. As they walked, the inspector told Webb, "I'll stay to the side while you try to bring him to the door." The professor agreed, the logic of the plan striking him as sound. He was, after all, by far the most inoffensive and innocent appearing of their group. If any might be able to lure the curious figure of Thomton to the door, it would be him.

Webb waited for Legrasse to secure himself far from sight of the door's obvious peephole, then knocked at the rough wood of the cracked and blistered door. The professor was struck by the barrier's spongy, nearly mushy quality. The older man fought the rising horror clawing at him as he felt his knuckles sinking a good fraction of an inch into the almost loose fibers of the slab. Grossly repelled by the noxious feel of the grainless panel, the professor shoved his unease aside, however, as his constant banging finally roused a response from within.

"What'da yer want?" came the muffled croaking through the door. Pulling together his courage, Webb answered the foul voice.

"Mr. Thomton? Is Mr. Thomton about?"

"Who wants to know?" asked the cracked, rough voice. "Go away. To hell with yer."

"Please, sir," responded Webb, trying to disarm the suspicions of whomever it was that had responded to his knocking, "I have his payment from Mr. Buttacavala."

"Payment?" Sudden interest flooded the horrid voice. The crudely crafted peephole was utilized, a watery, jaundiced eye staring out at the professor. Unable to escape the natural wariness of dock life, however, the still unseen party questioned, "For what?"

"For helping Mr. Buttacavala in some sort of questioning over the past few days." Webb had to draw deep breaths to be able to make himself heard over the storm. Pausing to let an unusually loud thunderclap die away, he continued, saying, "I don't know the particulars. I was only given a list and a wallet and instructed to pay off those marked. Mr. Thomton is on the list." When no answer was forthcoming, the professor added,

"Please, sir … I have an enormous amount of payments to make and I dislike traveling the docks with such a great quantity of cash …"

Legrasse's eyes sparked. He had not expected their quarry to allow them entry. Nor had he counted on Webb's ability to not only fabricate such a story, but to deliver it so plausibly. Much to the inspector's surprise, however, suddenly the sound of bolts being slid out of place rattled the other side of the door. Stepping forward, Legrasse motioned for Webb to move off to the side. Then, just as door began to be drawn inward, the one-time inspector threw his weight against it, sending it crashing inward.

Legrasse shoved his way into the darkened chamber. The room was thick with the aroma of heavy incense and rotting fish. Despite the darkness, however, the inspector could tell only one other figure was in the room—the one he had knocked to the floor when he had forced his way inside. Ignoring the overpowering, clawing stench thick in the air, Legrasse grabbed the form thrashing on the floor and dragged it to its feet, shouting,

"You're under arrest!"

No surrender was forthcoming, though. Instead the figure threw itself forward, sending Legrasse stumbling backward. Then, just as the one-time inspector made to cuff his prisoner, the figure gave out a horrid, amphibious croaking—a deep, gurgling noise which so startled Legrasse that despite his years of preparation for just such a moment, his hands opened involuntarily and his prisoner was free.

"Webb," bellowed the inspector, "look out—run for it!"

The professor threw himself out of the way, fleeing mindlessly for the supposed safety of the faraway automobiles as the thing Legrasse had accosted hurled itself through the door and out into the street beyond. The one-time inspector's hand was already within his rain slicker, pulling his old police whistle free. Somehow his feet managed to propel him toward the door without him giving them any conscious order. Finding his reactions slower than normal, however, he cursed himself, thinking,

Move, man—*move!* Blow the whistle. Call the others—run/dive/grab the thing/drag it down/don't let it escape! Do it, you fool/*do it!*

A piercing silver blast defied the pelting noise of the rain, alerting the others. The fleeing figure stopped for a moment, its head lashing from side to side. It knew the whistle had been a signal, but to who? Where? While it hesitated, not certain in which way to flee, Legrasse made his move.

Hurling himself through the rain, he slammed against the hunched figure, sending it flying. The heavily garbed form flopped badly forward, almost managing to keep its balance before it finally toppled, slamming face first against the rain soggy dock. Legrasse scrambled to his feet and then approached the downed form, his pistol drawn.

"Surrender yourself," he ordered harshly. "Do it, Thomton. Don't be a fool."

"Surrender?" The figure pushed itself upward through the staggering gale blowing across the docks, its ragged, unsecured scarf and coat torn away by the monsoon winds. The single word, croaked through a wide, white-lipped mouth running with thin blood, fell on Legrasse's ears like cold grease striking one's face on a humid day. Just hearing the thing's actual voice was a painful experience. And then, the one-time inspector experienced true pain.

A bolt of lightning split the sky, lighting the long pier for a single moment as brilliantly as if it were noon. While Legrasse stared, the exploding flash illuminated Thomton fully, revealing a sight almost more than the inspector could bear. The thing before him was predominantly a grayish green, though its belly was covered with a hard circle of grossly pale white. It skin was shiny and slippery, but was also possessed of hard, scaly ridges up its back and shoulders. Its eyes were bulging, unblinking. The sides of its neck sported palpitating gills.

"Damnation!" sputtered Legrasse.

"Damn me?" questioned the horrid thing, mercifully swathed in shadow once more. Taking a menacing step forward, it croaked, "Damn you, interloper. Damn you to the dark!"

The terrible blasphemy moved on, closing with Legrasse. The former inspector screamed at all the panicking voices within his brain, forcing something like order to settle within his mind. As the monstrous form neared him, he reminded himself of the things he had seen before, or the horrors he had faced, and beaten.

Big as a barn—and we killed it. Keep your grip, Legrasse, he sneered within his mind, you've stopped trouble ten times this before—you can stop *this*, too

And then, still a yard from the ex-inspector, the terror opened its yawning maw, letting its tongue dart forward. Horribly long and fast, the slimy pink length cracked against Legrasse's eyes, blinding him. The inspector staggered, falling to one knee. No longer content to merely escape, however, the thing sent forth its noxious length once more, this time using it to encircle Legrasse's neck!

Jerking its head, the creature pulled its snagged victim roughly toward it. Lashing out with one webbed paw, it slapped Legrasse across the face. Claws nicking his cheek, the blow stunned the former inspector, slamming him so violently that his feet slipped beneath him. The choking tongue released, Legrasse toppled backwards, splashing down against the dock.

"Don't move, Thornton!"

The creature turned, finding itself suddenly surrounded by Galvez and those he had taken with him to the back of the tenement. A half dozen firearms of various calibers were pointed at the crouching horror, all desperate to be discharged. Even as the monstrosity took in its current state, things worsened for it as Muller, Carrinelle and those that followed them below clambered back up over the dock. But then, before Legrasse could give any kind of warning to his gathering force, a frighteningly powerful bolt of lightning shattered the sky, illuminating the thing on the dock for all to see.

"Bloody God! What is it?"

The creature threw its arms upward as the night went electric, intentionally revealing itself for all to see. Its mouth dripping, bulging eyes staring madly, skin drawing the slashing rain to it with a hungry need, it belched up its defiance of all surrounding it, a rude, rumbling odorous note that sent several of the street toughs around it stumbling backwards in horror.

"Don't think about it," cautioned Legrasse in a desperate bellow. "Don't look at it directly. Don't panic."

But the one-time inspector's warning had come too late. Playing on the knowledge of what the sight of it would do to those around it, the creature leapt forward toward the nearest of the thugs, webbed claws extended. The monster had hoped to slice a path to the open sea through those packing in around it, using their momentary panic to its advantage. It did not succeed.

As Legrasse continued to shout out his warnings, the man directly before the bounding thing fired the shotgun in his hands, emptying both barrels at the horror. Although the tough's conscious mind had been frozen by his inability to fathom what he had seen in the split-second of illumination, his fingers had tightened in automatic reaction to the threat presented. And, his were not the only ones.

All around the creature men's nerves got the best of them. Nearly all the gangsters fired their weapons. Indeed, those that could, kept firing—some scores of times after all their ammunition had been expelled. More shotguns and several automatic weapons and a half dozen handguns cut loose, all aimed in the general direction of the leaping horror. Only a few hit their intended target. But many of them found targets nonetheless.

All around the pier, men fell screaming as they were gunned down by their panicking fellows. Blood slashed, brains exploded, and lungs coughed, gasping for air they could no longer find. Legrasse had seen the inevitable and thrown himself face down onto the water-logged pier. Now, pushing himself erect, he inspected the damage to those he had led to the site.

Webb and those others congregated at the vehicles were all shaken but fine. Muller and Carrinelle, both far back when the shooting had erupted had emerged unscathed. Galvez, however, had not been as fortunate. They found him clutching his arm, a bullet of low caliber having passed completely through it. He had heeded Legrasse's warning and ducked, the action most-likely having saved his life at the expense of his upper arm. His former commander was not the one to find him, however. Ignoring his men—indeed, ignoring everything else—Legrasse had headed straight for the monster flopping on the dock.

He found the creature still alive, dripping long strands of a green and purple bile that clung to the dock and its body in defiance of the saturating rain. Its left side was a gaping wound, its left leg completely sheered from its body. When the inspector knelt down beside it, however, the thing simply laughed

"Fool, Legrasse ...," it croaked. "Fool. Too late, this time. Too late. Nothing can halt the migration now. Nothing can stop the stars when right."

The pain-maddened thing was forced to silence as a great flow of dark fluid flushed forward from its mouth and gills. Then, in a far weaker voice, it began,

"*Ph'nglui mglw'nafh Cthulhu ...*"

The horrid death chant ceased as a bullet from Legrasse's Luger cut through the monster's brain. Kneeling on the dock, smoking gun in hand, rain pelting him, freezing him, the inspector cursed quietly against the thunder and the howls of the wounded all around him. Playing the words of the creature over in his head, a wave of madness filled Legrasse.

Too late, you heard it ... too late. Your life wasted, all the years ... all the years ... wasted.

Legrasse stood, staring at the body below him, the weight in his hand seeming to drag him down. Emotion raging through his system, another voice in his mind sneered at him—

Idiot ... all you could have done. Women ignored, wealth turned aside, power, happiness, success—idiot. All over now, all over. No chance for you now. Finish it, finish it.

His hand trembling, Legrasse brought the gun upward slowly. Staring at the dead eyes of the thing at his feet, the mindless well of self-pity thrashing within him pushed him toward the brink, imagining any horror it could to justify its bubbling fear as it spewed,

Do it, do it. Who needs this life? It's over, it's finished, it's time. End it. *End it!*

The one-time inspector's finger tightened. The folding slide of his automatic lifted then fell, sending a bolt of burning lead screaming into the night. And then another. And then another. And finally twice more, until the weapon was empty and the creature that had been Thomas Thomton was torn completely in twain.

"Who needs this life?" asked Legrasse, questioning the wind and the whipping rain. "I do. And all the powers of Hell shall not stop me now. This I *swear!*"

And then, John Raymond Legrasse turned and marched off through the dead and the dying, ignoring their howls and curses as he set himself to fulfilling the oath he had put off taking for fifteen years. Others could attend to something as simple as human misery. He had more important things to do.

* *** *

Carrinelle slammed his way into Legrasse's home, anger coursing through his frame. A great vein bulged in his forehead, seemingly threatening to erupt at any moment from some horrible pressure building within the man. At first the pair of Buttacavala's men who had been stationed at the door by the crime lord tried to restrain the officer, but their boss himself waved them off, allowing Carrinelle access to the house.

"What is it?" asked Buttacavala in a whisper. As the younger man began to rage, the crime lord made quieting motions with his arms, pleading, "Quietly, quietly ... we don't want to upset the Inspector."

"Upset the Inspector?" repeated Carrinelle. "Upset the Inspector? Who cares how upset the goddamned Inspector gets? Why should anyone care about that?!"

Buttacavala hovered about the officer, as if hoping his great bulk might muffle the man's shouting. The crime lord attempted to interrupt Carrinelle again, but the younger man cried out, "He leaves us behind—Inspector

Galvez wounded no less—to clean up the mess he created. He ransacks Thomton's apartment and then takes off with Webb. No worry or concern about the rest of us. Nothing. Like he could care less."

Jamming his finger harshly into Buttacavala's chest, he shouted, "We deserve better than that, do you hear me? *Do you?!*"

"Much of New Orleans has heard you by now, I'm certain."

Both men's heads turned as Professor Webb approached from beyond the drawing room. As Carrinelle's exaggerated Adam's apple bobbed up and down, the officer made to protest, but Webb's face frosted over as the older man snapped, "The Inspector is not to be judged by the likes of you. You were his greatest supporter—but now in the face of a single minor disillusionment you come snarling, bitter and resentful and needing your hand held like a child who's lost his penny candy."

Carrinelle went stiff, his face flushing red. Ignoring the officer's changing mood, the professor continued, telling him, "Well, find somewhere else if you need mollycoddling. Go dig up some street whore from whom you can buy a dollar's worth of cool fingers for your wounded heart. There is no time for childishness here—now or evermore."

And, so saying, the professor turned and started back up the stairs. With no further regard for the younger man, Buttacavala fell in place behind Webb. Before they could ascend more than a few steps, however, Carrinelle found his voice and called out to them, begging for some kind of explanation. Digging down into the spare well of patience he still possessed, the professor answered the younger man.

"Past faith buys you this one reprieve," he said. "John Legrasse is no longer like other men. He hasn't been for fifteen years but apparently it took until tonight for he himself to realize it. He has put the ordinary manners of this world behind him that he might be fit to deal with those from the next. Our world is dying, being strangled by its own hand by those who ... no ... not now, there is no time."

There was so much the professor wanted to say, so much he had just begun to put into perspective himself which he wished to theorize about, using Carrinelle as his sounding board, but he stopped himself. To do so was to follow the path of inaction—and that was what the enemy was counting on.

Yes, he thought, ruminate, contemplate, deliberate, reason it out, cogitate toward those rational conclusions, smugly reflect and study and speculate and analyze until they're here and we're not. That's how they win.

"You listen to me," the professor snapped. "Legrasse is no longer a man. He is a brain. Our brain. From this day forth he is the voice and you are but the obedient nerve that acquiesces to his desires for that may well be the only thing that stands in the way of the apocalypse. Do you *understand? Do you?!*"

Turning on his heel, Buttacavala following in near supplication, Webb called over his shoulder, "Come with us prepared to obey whatever orders Legrasse may have or crawl off and find yourself a liquor bottle to hide in. You've been taken out of the ranks of spectator and gifted with the privilege of choosing a role in Armageddon. Chose wisely, Joel, but do it quickly. There is no more time that can be wasted. Every second of continued existence is a millennium, and we shall need a billion of them if we are to keep our backs to the door and hold firm against the Devil's tide."

Joel Carrinelle watched the two retreating figures disappear up the stairway. Webb had said they were headed to the observatory, a term that did not register with the younger man. He had said much that had confused the officer, and more that had angered him. But, the professor had also intimated that Legrasse needed the young man.

In the end, that was all that mattered.

*   * * *   *

"So, Calamari, do you understand it all?" Looking over the mass of charts and notes spread out on the desk before him, the crime lord nodded.

"Hey," the heavy-set man answered with a sneer, "I told you before it was no problem. I only came by to let you know my people are already in place."

A smile crossed his face, a wicked, nasty line of hate that for a moment allowed the Achillie Buttacavala of old to show through. He caught his triumphant mood, however and strangled it, adding, "I'm sorry, I'm sorry, I'll go now."

But, before the crime lord could leave, Legrasse barked, "Damnit, Calamari, whatever am I to do with you?" Lips pressed firm together, head lowered, the inspector pulled in his anger and then said, "You must get past these ludicrous notions of good and evil. They will pull you down and destroy you if you cannot correct them."

"But, how can I make up for my past without ..."

"Without what?" interrupted Legrasse, "prayer and restitution? Listen to me—lighting candles and making novenas won't hold back that which is afoot in the world today. Renounce your criminal empire and you will be of no use to anyone. Don't you understand? There is a balance to be maintained here— yes. There are cosmic forces at work here which simple men such as we can scarce contemplate—yes, again. But to think that they can be described in any way adequately by terms such as 'good' and 'evil' is not understanding what is at stake."

Buttacavala made to insist that he would do whatever Legrasse wanted, but the inspector was adamant the man actually comprehend what they were up against. Moving past his telescope, feeling the breeze from the gaping hole through which it was aimed, he tried again.

"If God lets your sainted grandmother die in an ocean liner sinking," he

149

explained, "you do not assume your grandmother was evil simply because she died. Good and evil are not cleanly definable terms. Just because what we have set ourselves in opposition with is evil in our eyes, performing traditional acts of Christian goodness will not put credit in any Heavenly bank. I need you, Calamari—*you*—king of the Orleans underworld, master of her dark souls."

"You want me to maintain my organization?" asked Buttacavala as if questioning a second grade teacher over the possibility that he could have possibly given the right answer. With a firm voice, Legrasse answered his question.

"Maintain it?" thundered the one-time inspector. "No—I want you to expand it. I am just beginning to understand the magnitude of what we are undertaking. If we are to finish what we have begun, we will need massive amounts of capital. No, I am afraid I'm going to have to insist that you not only keep your organization intact, but that you put forth your best effort to strangle and consume those in as many other states as you might as well. By doing this I may be wishing a monstrous enemy upon the future generations to follow us, but if a stand is not taken here and now, there will not be any future generations to follow us."

And then, understanding dawned in Buttacavala's eyes. Suddenly he knew his place in the scheme of things, realizing in one blinding moment how fate had punished him for his sins, and then at the same time given him a chance to put them all to rights. Nodding his head, he allowed his sardonic smile to return, rubbing his hands together as he went forth to oversee his troops and to help them extract the revenge he had prayed for so dearly. At the same time, Carrinelle asked,

"Inspector, I got here too late. I don't understand—what is it you have Buttacavala doing?"

"Striking a blow for our side of the game." Legrasse was about to let the statement stand, but then suddenly reconsidered. His mind rebelled, insisting that if he could make the time to keep Buttacavala usefully within the fold simply because he felt the crime lord's money and power would be useful in the future, then he could make a similar amount of time for Carrinelle as well.

Instantly, however, a part of his mind rebelled, insisting that wasting time explaining himself to every strong back or gun-arm needed was intolerable. The voice within him that represented his former life silenced it, though. Placating his crusading persona with the reminder that as someone who had witnessed the types of horror they faced and passed through unscathed, Carrinelle was more than just another hired hand, Legrasse turned to the younger man and, at least for a moment, shoved aside the mantle of savior he had laid upon his own shoulders.

"I must appear insane to you," he said quietly. "Disappearing for so long, coming back to drag you into this new horror with no explanation or thanks

…" The officer protested but Legrasse smothered the objection, continuing on.

"I will state things bluntly. Fifteen years ago I lost my life—the role of Inspector Legrasse, guardian of one tiny section of a dirty city in a foul state, only a tiny part of one union of men on a minor, backwater world off to one corner of our universe. It was a small, uncomplicated life which I wish had never been interrupted. But, as you may have noticed, it was. I was shown a world beyond ours, and unlike our friends on the docks earlier tonight, I did not go mad from the viewing. Or at least, not mad enough to be comfortably locked away."

Legrasse's mind review his state of only a few days ago, the decay that had set in throughout his existence, wondering if he might not be overstating his case. Shoving the notion aside, he moved across the room back toward his telescope. His feet squished against the soggy floorboards, but after so many years he scarcely noticed the noise.

"Anyway, I tell you all of this to make a point." Grasping the end of his telescope, a fine instrument of German glass and British engineering, he spun it around, showing through example the range of its lens. As it continued to gyrate quietly on its smooth settled pivot, the inspector said,

"You cannot help but have noticed the hole I made in the ceiling here. Or the water dripping through the house, pooling in the drawing room. Years ago when it came to my attention that I would need to observe the stars, I sent for this telescope—the best I could afford—and then smashed free this opening for it. I could have had workmen create a proper opening, one that would not damage the interior of the house so, but there was no time. Such niceties were merely a waste of time—and I had none to spare."

Legrasse went quiet for a moment. His gaze fell to the floor, watching the remaining drops from the evening's earlier storm glisten as they tried to find entry through the drenched boards.

This is all you are to me, great Cthulhu, he thought with sarcasm. An alluring wet thing rotting all you touch. Well, try as you may, you haven't touched me—not yet, bastard.

"I think I understand, Inspector," said Carrinelle, breaking the silence in the attic. "I never quite got the big picture of it all before. But, could I ask, what is Buttacavala doing now? I mean, what was all this for?"

"A fair question. In Thomton's room, the professor and I found the last piece of the puzzle we've needed. Thomton was a man at one time, but he gave himself over to the other side. Pulled Carmine Buttacavala in behind him. They were mutated into monsters. You saw Thomton for yourself tonight."

Carrinelle pulled at his collar. Tommy Thomton was not the most horrible thing he had seen at Legrasse's side. But it had been many years, hard years filled with earnest attempts to forget. The inspector understood the officer's unease at the memories. Needing the younger man to be as familiar with their enemies as he was himself, however, Legrasse pointed to the papers before him.

"In Thomton's apartment," he said, "we found these charts—migration routes for these creatures. Over the years I have been studying the legends of these things; the only solid eye-witness accounts have come from the New England region. The thought of cold blooded creatures such as these surviving in the icy waters of a North Atlantic winter has never made much sense to me, however. Now I have the answer." Legrasse moved his hand to indicate the New England area.

"You see the route marked here," asked Legrasse, drawing his finger over the lines hand-scrawled lines along the coast. "The professor went through Thomton's papers. By consulting them, checking his notes against the stars, making a few calls to several of Buttacavala's operations along the coast, we have determined that Thomton's allies are on the move, coming to New Orleans for the winter. You might ask why Thomton would have notes and charts about all of this. Professor, if you could explain." Webb stepped forward, picking up where Legrasse had left off.

"True animals possess senses to aid them in migration. These deep fathom dwellers, though, are not natural, and thus to make their way from New England to our own ports, they need help. Thomton was to set a series of flaming rafts to guide his fellows in from the deep ocean."

"And now that Thomton is dead?" asked Carrinelle.

"Buttacavala and his ships will be there instead," answered Legrasse. "The Calamari came to tell us that his people had already intercepted several of Thomton's kind seeking to implement their plan. They were killed. And now, when the rafts are lit, instead of guiding these monsters safely into New Orleans harbor, they shall be directed instead into Buttacavala's fishing nets. The Calamari controls the docks … indeed …"

Legrasse allowed his voice to trail off as a sudden idea struck him. Aiming his telescope at the open sea, he waved his fellows forward as he spoke with excitement.

"Yes—it appears it has already begun."

The inspector stepped aside to allow Carrinelle a peek through the telescope. Peering through the eyepiece, the younger man could just make out a series of pin point lights on the water, surrounded by scores of dark ships. Making way for Professor Webb to take a look, the officer said,

"Inspector, you must forgive me. I …"

But then, whatever Carrinelle might have said, or Legrasse might have added, was interrupted by the a welter of frightful screams echoing upward throughout the old house.

* **** *

The first of Buttacavala's men to encounter the flopping horrors died almost instantly. He had not been present at the docks, had not witnessed as had so many of his fellows what nightmare they had all taken as their own. He stood in Legrasse's doorway, his mind reeling, fighting desperately to make some kind of sense of that which surged before his eyes. He could not. The wave of deep fathom dwellers rolled over him, each claw-tipped flipper tearing him anew before his struggles ceased altogether. His partner fared but little better.

Seeing his mate fall to the advancing horde, the second thug pulled both the revolvers he kept tucked within his belt and blasted at the malignant line approaching. Bullets ripped through the nearest bodies—heads exploded, slippery skin erupted in holes and bile, the air filling with the sharp bleats of inhuman voices. Bodies fell one after another, but more followed, hopping up over the corpses of their fellows.

Ten grotesqueries lay at the thug's feet, but still came the horde. His eyes wide with panicking anger, the man hurled his empty weapons into the face of the nearest of his attackers. One revolver missed completely, but the other tore open the left eye of the deep fathom spawn, spilling an explosion of yellow fluid down the front of the beast. The wound toppled the monster, but the horde shoved aside the cripple and pressed forward, their dripping limbs grasping for the defender.

"So, ya want the Crutch?" yelled the man insanely. Pulling eight inches of sharp steel from his boot, he screamed through the foam building in his mouth, "Come and get him, bastards!"

The thug hurled himself into the nearing insanities. His blade tore open the chest of one, stabbed through the guts of another, and then he was done. Dragged down by a score of glistening limbs, his blood-flecked screams were trampled under webbed-feet as the monsters poured into Legrasse's home unopposed.

"Which way?" One of the horrors stopped, looking about frantically as it shouted, "Where will we find Legrasse?"

"Legrasse, Legrasse," came a voice from above. "All anyone ever wants is Legrasse." The hordes' unblinking eyes turned to stare upward to the next landing. There they spotted Carrinelle, Bergmann MP in hand. Bracing its hard wood stock against his pelvis, he sneered at the inhuman assembly.

"You want to see the Inspector, make an appointment."

And then, he fired.

A score of bullets filled the air, grinding their way through the flopping nightmares below. The submachine gun's snail magazine feed it from the left, hammering down death on the now panicked attackers. When the first clip emptied, Carrinelle unlocked it and replaced it with another, but held his fire.

153

The beasts were disorganized, but not routed. The young officer knew he could not achieve victory. He did not have enough bullets for all the things swarming around the house. Of this he was certain. While still in the attic he and the others had looked down on the horde and seen its overpowering size from above as it had poured up out of the sewer from in front of Legrasse's home. But, Carrinelle also knew his job was not to defeat the monsters. His was a stalling operation. He had to keep the terrors busy as long as possible, buying time for those upstairs. Looking over the upper landing's railing through the gray haze of burnt gunpowder filling the air, noting that the deep fathomers were pulling themselves together, the officer spat,

"Oh, ready for some more? That's good—so am I."

In the attic, Legrasse and Webb heard the deadly weapon cut loose again. Ignoring the sound, the pair bent to their labors once more. While Carrinelle had gone out to hold the line, the two older men had worked quickly, turning the attic into an inferno. Dragging the inspector's old, weather beaten desk to a point under the observation hole he had cut years earlier, they pair stacked it high with crumpled papers and then lit it afire. Pulling the very roof apart, they threw anything combustible into the pile, encouraging the flames higher and higher.

"The gunshots will bring some kind of response," gasped Legrasse, staggering back from the building heat. "But how much, how quick, is hard to say. You want people to gather fast in New Orleans—fire! That's what brings out the crowds."

Flame leaped up from the desk, burning down into the wood, growling to reach the floor. Smoke billowed as the fire lapped across the water-logged floorboards, rotting steam gagging its creators. Down on their hands and knees, Legrasse and Webb made their way to the door, the professor dragging the telescope behind him. They had done all they could. Now they could only hope to outlive their rescue beacon.

The pair made the hallway, crawling out into it as sparks and ash rained down on their heads and shoulders from the burning roof. Choking on tar smoke and wood gases, Legrasse slammed the door shut behind him. He had seen enough house fires during his years on the force to know he needed to contain the blaze to whatever small extent he could. Already people had begun to approach the outside of his home; already the screams had started in the street. The legion of creatures had turned on the interlopers and chaos ruled Bienville Street. Police had begun to arrive, the noise of volunteer hosemen could be heard in the distance. But, Carrinelle's weapon had gone silent, and there was still a multitude of attackers coming onward.

And then, as the two men made their way down to the second floor of Legrasse's old home, the booming snap of the Bergmann rang out again. The inspector hurried toward the commotion, shouting, "Hold them, Joel—hold them. I'm on you!"

Of course Legrasse knew that the officer could not hear his cries over the cannonade echoing of his weapon, but he threw the words out nonetheless, breathing encouragement into the air as he raced to his comrade's aide. Wiping at his smoke stung eyes, still coughing out the bitter fumes he had swallowed, the inspector reached his one-time subordinate just as the man emptied his last clip.

The younger man stepped back into Legrasse, spun around with a start, and then smiled upon seeing the inspector behind him instead of one of the nightmares he had been keeping back. Far away, the pair heard brief whispers of the screams flooding the world outside, human and inhuman noises mixed with the sound of more gunfire. Madness tore through the streets, concentric rings of terror exploding out from the burning epicenter of Legrasse's home. A glance over the landing, however, left Carrinelle and the inspector wondering if rescue were possible. Below them scores of the croaking monstrosities still jumbled toward the stairs, all madly working to bring an end to Legrasse and his fellows.

How the monsters could know of the inspector's involvement he could only wonder. Perhaps more of Buttacavala's organization was infected with the horrors than they thought. Or, thought Legrasse as the boring heat roasted him from above, perhaps it was an instinct beyond the simple science of the streets. Mayhap the will of their foe could be focused on its enemies as a magnet could be to metal filings—an invisible death grip motivated by a force unseen and unstoppable.

"No." Coolly, Legrasse moved past Carrinelle, stepping to the top of the stairs. "Unseen, maybe ..." he growled, pulling his Luger. "But not unstoppable." Aiming the automatic at the first of the horrors nearing the top of the stairs, he added,

"Nothing is unstoppable."

And then he fired.

His first bullet splattered the head of the monster, sending its body reeling backward into those behind it. More of the horrors charged the stair—more died. Legrasse fired and waited, fired and waited, urging on his foemen and slaughtering them as they came. All too quickly, however, the inspector's bullets were used up. His finger closed on the trigger, but only an empty click was forthcoming. None could hear it, of course—man and monster alike were all deafened by the continual fusillade the defenders had set up—but there was no mistaking the hollow gesture Legrasse had made. The weapons were all empty. The defense had ended.

Their inhuman confidence thus bolstered, the deep fathom dwellers rushed the stairs again, fighting with each other to be the first to climb over the bodies of their brothers.

Legrasse was the focus ... Legrasse had been driven away but had returned ... he had been made harmless, but had returned ... he had not remained comfortable in madness, feeding great Cthulhu rich dreams ... he had returned ...

"Return is not allowed, Legrasse," croaked the monster that had taken the lead. "Presumption ... too great a crime. Punished you will be."

"Really?" asked the inspector, not backing away from the top of the stairs. Sweat pouring off his scalp from the terrific heat bearing down on him, his clothes plastered to his body, Legrasse stared forward, his heart straining, eyes unblinking. And then, when the monster was but a heartbeat away, the inspector reached out, grabbing his telescope away from Webb which such ferocity that he knocked the older man over.

Spinning around, the one-time Inspector of Police brought the instrument crashing against the deep fathom dweller's head, knocking it completely through the hand rail. The monster fell into the crushing melee below, only to be replaced by the thing behind it. Legrasse dealt with it as well, though, drawing the viewing end back and then ramming it forward, slamming it into the second attacker. The telescope erupted through the creature's back, sending a sluicing flow of blood and fluids splashing onto those behind. The thing's hands grabbed the metal length stuck in its body, however, holding onto it, denying Legrasse further use of his weapon. Blood bubbling up over its amphibian lips, it gurgled foully,

"Now what, Legrasse?"

And then, the roof fell in, raining fire and timbers on man and beast.

* *** *

When the morning sun finally found Bienville Street, there were still more than a hundred bodies—human and inhuman—waiting to be taken away. The police and other officials had worked to remove the remains of the creatures first, not wanting the public to see that which it could not comprehend. Still, even working throughout the night, they had not reached half their goal before the sun broke in to start the rumors of Legrasse flying from one end of New Orleans to the other once more. Many explanations of the evening were given, but the true facts were actually much simpler than the stories which eventually took root throughout the voodoo quarters of the ancient town.

When the desk from the attic had crashed through into Legrasse's drawing room, bringing down the floors weakened by years of neglect, the tide had finally turned for the defenders. The entire eastern end of the house began to crumble, fiery timbers smashing downward, crushing all in their path.

Outside, the deep fathomers had found their exit cut off as more and more people arrived on the scene. Confused, caught unawares, scores of human fodder died ignorant that a war had been declared. The curious and the Samaritan, all perished as the flailing clawed limbs sought their necks and hearts. The front of Legrasse's home toppled outward onto the main mass of the monsters, however, smashing the fight out of them.

At the first distraction, Legrasse had pushed forward on the telescope, shoving the creature impaled upon it back into those horrors packing the stairs. The monstrosities had gone down in a tangle, still seeking to unravel themselves when another massive section of the house had come screaming down from above, putting an end to their immediate menace. That the inspector, Webb and Carrinelle were able to escape without worse injury than smarting eyes and lungs and various patches of cooked flesh proved to be the most amazing surprise of the evening.

Later, when the trio had met with Buttacavala, the gangster had told them a fearsome but satisfying tale of his people and their encounter with the migrating horde. Thousands had died in the nets, strangled, shot, stabbed, killed in whatever manners the crime lord's people could devise. Dynamite had been utilized to bring the deep swimmers to the surface. Then, once netted, the seamen had poured the waters thick with oil and gasoline, setting it ablaze once they felt they had enmeshed the majority of their foes. The harbor air was thick with the wretched odor of burnt skin, the water covered with unholy colors for weeks before the rain and tides cleansed the area.

Buttacavala thanked Legrasse deeply for helping him to avenge him son. The inspector avowed that it was nothing—that if it had not been for the crime lord, the city would have found itself home to a vast army that, once it had joined with its fellows already living within the Orleans' sewers, might have wrecked incalculable damage on all.

Visiting Galvez at his home the next day, Legrasse told the Spaniard all that had happened, suggesting that a minor wound was a small price to pay to be able to avoid the nightmare he and the others had lived through the night before. Galvez thought to curse the inspector, or to make some manner of joke, but he surprised himself by merely agreeing, instead. The two men sat quietly on Galvez's back porch in the mild, late fall breeze, watching the last brown leaves struggle to hang onto their branches.

Setting down his mug of Chicory coffee, the Spaniard suddenly asked, "What will you do now, though, el Grande? Your home's burned—gone. All the books you assembled, your studies ... what will you do?"

Legrasse shook his head slightly, chuckling to himself. Turning to his old second-in-command, he said, "I used that place as a refuge from the battle to come—the battle all around us. Library, observatory, all of it, chains I used to justify my inaction while calling myself free. Hesitation almost did us all in. Best I'm rid of it all."

"But still, J. R., the menace is past. What will you do now?"

His gaze once more centered on the last cluster of leaves defiantly holding onto their place on the cold-beaten limb of Galvez's tree, Legrasse offered the best answer he had to give.

"The menace is never passed," he told his one-time subordinate. "We thought that once, and it took the deaths of how many of our own to prove we were wrong? We thought it again, and fifteen years later we find ourselves knee deep in corpses. No—we've stumbled across the toes of a savage god twice now, and have somehow luckily saved ourselves from ruin each time. Something tells me we'll not be afforded a third chance to stumble to safety."

The wind whipped up suddenly, tearing at the leaves, straining at the thin fibers holding them in place. His interest grimly frozen on the tiny tableau before him, the inspector said, "Next time we will have to take the fight to the enemy. There *is* an ending coming, Joseph, my friend, but if we are to survive it, it will have to be one of our own design."

The two men sat in silence, sipping their coffee, staring at the single tree at the end of the yard. Finally, though, Galvez asked,

"But, each time we've stood against these ... these ... *nightmares* ... the cost in life, the escalation ... next time ... do we dare risk ..."

Legrasse raised his hand, shaking it in denial of his old second-in-command's fears. Still watching the leaves battle to retain their hold, he whispered,

"He who hesitates, Joseph. A pair of English clerics, Julius and Augustus Hare, they put it best ... 'half the failures of this world arise from pulling in one's horse as he is leaping.' No doubts, Joseph. No doubts."

And then, the wind died away, and the leaves were left—triumphant—shining in the sun.

NOTHING TO FEAR BUT DUST

"Nothing in life is to be feared. It is only to be understood."

—Marie Curie

"I will show you fear in a handful of dust."

—T. S. Elliot

I.

The *Emma*'s great bow rose completely out of the water. All the way to her forefoot, a perilous forty feet of the two-masted schooner was once more forced skyward by a fiercely rolling sea that seemed malevolently intent on smashing the helpless ship. Once again black waves slammed across the deck and more men slid to their deaths.

"Johansen!" bellowed Captain Collins, "for the love of God, man, crowd in the jibtop!"

The second mate screamed a reply, hanging onto the staysail boom as best he could, praying for even a moment's footing wherein he could try to gather the massive billow before the raging winds tore it through as they already had the mainsail. The pitch-dark storm stirring the sea was a wild thing of intense lightning and growling, hail-spitting clouds. The blackened swirl had struck out of nowhere, churning the previously calm South Seas into a boiling madness the likes of which none aboard the *Emma* had ever dreamed of, let alone witnessed in all their collective years. The devil clouds had simply swirled up out of nowhere, sending down sleet that froze the riggings and coated the deck with ice some three inches deep.

"Billy, man," cried the second mate in desperation, "give us a hand here, damn you. Or we're headed to the bottom for sure!"

William Briden, first mate of the *Emma*, struggled his way across the icy deck to aid his fellow crewmen before more of their precious sails were lost. Another wave crashed across the *Emma*'s frozen deck. The water warmed the' battered sailors, but the effect was only temporary as it then instantly began freezing within their clothing. Hanging on, struggling to make his aching fingers bunch the sogging cloth of the sail, Briden's mind reeled at the chaos all around him.

Ice, he thought. Ice on our decks—a half day off the coast of Northern Australia! What kind of madness is this?

Another torrent of hail splattered against the ship. Minute pellets the size of grape shot rained down from the Heavens by the hundreds of thousands, frozen needles that tore relentlessly at the crew's exposed arms and faces.

161

Larger chunks followed—awful bricks of gray and purple ice, shot through with veins of a black-flecked green. They fell from the sky at angles opposed to the wind, smashing against the valiantly struggling *Emma* with the violence of cannon fire.

The captain grappled with the wheel, throwing both his arms against it, straining his blocky muscles until his tendons screamed and his bowels shriveled. Fear choked the elder seaman's brain, fear of things far worse than simple matters such as shipwreck or drowning. He was the only one of the crew old enough to have heard the stories he had—decades ago in the last century—words ignored during his ignorant youth. They were bizarre, unfathomable tales whispered by the native mariners of certain signs and times—and the horrors that would follow. He had seen the stars they had named, had watched other portents falling into place.

But—damnit, he cursed himself—I never thought, never believed ... they warned me, told me—and now, now this hellish storm—and *ice!* For the love of God, lightning and ice mixin' this far south—it's almost like ...

And then, straight ahead of the *Emma's* captain, racing toward the ship out of a boiling dark sea, came a shattering madness of black rock and the very beginnings of the end of the world.

II.

John Raymond Legrasse sat bolt right up out of bed. He did not gasp or scream or mutter any of the usual inanities spewed by those just escaping the dreamworld. His emotions catching hold of themselves neatly, the one-time New Orleans Inspector of Police—now holding the title only as an honorary—shook his head sharply. He blinked his eyes several times with a hard, purposeful rhythm, as if anything so simple could dispel the visions that had been scrawling through his sleeping brain an instant earlier.

Well, Legrasse, he thought with resignation. At long last ... it's time.

The thick-boned man sighed, a weary noise filled with a fearful honesty. Shoving aside the sad and clinging weariness hoping to claim him, the inspector swung his legs over the edge of his bed, allowing them to mechanically find his slippers. Once inside, his toes pushed upward against their worn vamps, rubbing back and forth against the thin and fading fur lining inside. Even though Legrasse lived in the southern most part of Louisiana, still it was early February and his room was sharp with a moist chill.

Besides, he thought, suddenly feeling older and more tired than ever he had before, any little reason to put off doing what must be done, eh?

Part of his mind cursing his determination, another part thanking God for it, the inspector pulled himself up off his bed with a Herculean effort, then crossed the room to his dresser. Despite the small chamber's utter darkness he dressed himself easily, not making enough noise to alert anyone else in the house to the fact that he was either awake or about. He picked casual, rough clothing—stiff work pants and a thick sweater. Without referring to a mirror, he brushed his thick, but neatly cropped hair straight back over his head.

After this he removed his valise from the closet and began packing his few belongings. Once a man known for his natty attire, he allowed himself a bit of a smile at the simple few articles of clothing he now owned. After that, the rest of his life's accumulation entered the bag. There were his shaving mug and razor, his moustache scissor, his brushes and a few other toiletries. After that he dug out the Luger he had carried for so long and several containers of ammunition. He held the weapon for a moment, rubbing his right thumb over its barrel gently.

One last time, old girl, he swore to the handsome piece, then thrust it and its cartridges into his valise. These were followed along by his notebook and some pens, several pencils, his pipe and then a few last other odds and ends that made up the entirety of his Spartan life's possessions. His closet and the one drawer he had used during his stay now empty, Legrasse turned to stare at his nightstand. Or, more specifically, at the statue standing on it. Even in the near pitch-blackness he could make it out. But then, even in the utter darkness of dream, he always knew exactly what every facet of it looked like.

The piece was a diminutive figure, exquisitely crafted, a thing whose utter strangeness and air of genuinely horrid antiquity gave most who had seen the thing over the years shuddering fits, if not episodes of unexplainable dread. The slightest brushing of fingers against the terrible old statue brought monstrous dreams and epileptic-like fits to those who came in contact with it—wild, rambling episodes of dark nonsense that soaked their beds with sweat, if not other fluids.

Not Legrasse, however. He had lived with the cold, hateful thing for too long, had kept it close to him for far too many years to be in any way taken aback by it at that point. He was simply familiar with the black thing past contempt and onward to boredom.

Scowl on, you ugly bastard, he thought. You've no power over me.

The inspector's eyes could make out hints of the terrible thing in the tiny light available. He could see the upper curve of its octopus-like head, hints of its mask of feelers, small glimmers reflecting off its prodigious claws and long, narrow wings. It was a miserable thing, of this Legrasse had no doubt. He had seen great evil done in its name, but that was not what convinced him of its true nature.

The indecipherable characters etched oddly into its sides might have given some clue to the sinister forces connected to the terrible thing, but Legrasse was beyond assessments made through humble mechanics such as sight. He had found a trust in deeper senses, and it was these that told him of the unnatural, malignant bend to the foul, inhuman thing depicted in stone sitting coldly before him.

Staring at the grotesque horror through the chill morning air, he whispered, "Yes, go on, smile—our day of reckoning is finally at hand. And I'll admit, I'm as tired of awaiting its arrival as you are."

Breaking eye contact with the horrid image, Legrasse stepped forward, grabbed up the cold stonework, then turned and exited his room. He meant to make straight away from his temporary abode, but paused outside the room next to his. Unable to completely turn his back on all who lived within the structure, he set the fingertips of his left hand against the door across the hall from his own, gently nudging it open. The room was scarcely larger than a closet, but it was perfect for its current resident.

Sticking his head through the slight aperture, Legrasse gazed at the child asleep in the crib within. The door to the adjoining room was open, as always, the babe's parents but several feet away. All three slept on without noting the inspector's interest. The old policeman smiled warmly in the direction of the slumbering child, thinking to himself.

All for you, little one, and those who shall come after. May you never have to know what we do in your name.

Then, he pulled the door back into place and turned away to silently make his way down the stairs. He did not feel any great amount of triumph at having been able to traverse the squeaking hallway or to descent the creaking staircase without arousing the household. Most of the Galvez clan were light sleepers, but the Inspector of Police had grown subtle in his ability to move freely without being detected. Turning when he reached the front door, he looked back into the dark reaches of the house, his eyes traveling up the stairs with only the slightest feeling of regret.

"Goodbye, old friend," he whispered. "I'll do my best."

His hand on the doorknob, Legrasse moved quietly out of the house. He pulled the door shut softly behind him, and then walked out of the small yard and off into the darkness. He would have liked to have slept longer, to have rested and left in the morning with the sun warming his way. But, he could not afford such luxuries. Not, that is, if he were going to be able to reach the moment of his death on time.

III.

"Good sir," announced the turbaned man, allowing surprise to enter his normally well-controlled voice, "this is a very quite surprising happening."

"I take it then that no one expected to see me here today?" asked Legrasse as he remained standing on the stoop to 13 China Alley, an address found in the lower reaches of Manhattan Island.

"Good gracious, no sir," added the servant. His instinctive manners shoving aside his shock, the tall Hindu stepped away from the door to allow Legrasse entry. "Please to come inside while I alert master Zarnak to your arrival."

"No need," announced a voice from down the building's long entrance hallway. "Our friend the Inspector is more prescient than we might have believed."

Akbar Ram Singh nodded curtly toward his master as Legrasse stepped inside with his over-sized valise and a small canvas sack. The Hindu took Legrasse's larger bag and disappeared off into one of the house's myriad rooms. His master immediately assumed the role of host, shutting the door on the outside world while guiding his visitor inside.

"My word," exclaimed Dr. Anton Zarnak, "it's been a long time. What is it, twenty years now since we've seen each other?"

"Close enough. You're certainly looking well enough, Doctor."

Zarnak nodded, taking the compliment with false modesty. In truth, he looked nearly exactly the same as when Legrasse had last seen him. Only his hair had changed, a jagged white streak now shattering the otherwise solid black of his mane, a lightning path that began at his temple, traveling all the way over his head back to the nape of his neck. The doctor was kind in his assessment of the changes he noted in Legrasse.

Although the inspector had maintained himself reasonably well for a man his age, Zarnak could see that Legrasse had gone through many changes over the years. Once a robust man, it was obvious to the doctor that his visitor had spent far too long confined indoors, doing nothing more strenuous than lifting books and flipping pages. It seemed to him that only in the last few years had Legrasse curbed his decay, getting out of doors and rebuilding his constitution to where it was somewhat returned to that of the man whom Zarnak had first met. Indeed, the doctor might not have noticed these minor changes in his guest at all if it were not for the unusual aspect that had come over Legrasse's eyes.

Zarnak could put no name to the color he saw within them. Once a solid, stable shade, they were now composed of several wildly shifting hues—blue/black/brown/green—all layering one over the other at a moment's notice. It was a condition the doctor had seen rarely, and only in those who had come up against the greatest oddities the world beyond had to offer. Still, for a person with none of Zarnak's extensive training—who had been forced to face the spawn of the nether dimensions on his own, with nothing but a Christian God to rely upon for supernatural support—the doctor had to admit with a grudging admiration that Legrasse seemed remarkably sane and in control.

As he was lead into the building's interior, the inspector noted that there had been a number of changes made since last he was there. An unadorned place years previous, now every corner of the residence was packed with some sort of exotic bric-a-brac. The small foyer itself was now crowded by an immense bronze incense burner resting on a teakwood stand. Tibetan scroll paintings rich with colorful, intricate silk brocade hung on the walls. Lush Persian carpets quieted their movements as they walked.

"You've been decorating," Legrasse commented.

"After your last visit," answered Zarnak with a hint of a smile, "if I remember correctly, there was a great need for—shall we say—some sprucing up?"

Legrasse grinned, something his jaws muscles did not resist as strenuously as they had in the past. As memories crowded through the inspector's mind, Zarnak asked him a question that brought both their moods crashing into blackness.

"You're thinking recent associations have made you soft." When Legrasse bristled somewhat, the doctor motioned the ex-policeman to a seat in his office while he explained, "please, it was a loud thought, one you would have made public soon enough."

"Am I that easily read?"

Zarnak seated himself behind his desk, an antique thing of carved and inlaid teak, one covered with a jumble of papers, notebooks and cracking, leather-bound volumes. Behind him, a leering devil mask painted scarlet, black and gold snarled down from the wall, symbolic golden flames coiling from its fanged mouth and disproportionately large nostrils. Almost hidden from his guest by the wealth of clutter all around him, the doctor answered,

"Only to those of us well versed in the language. If I might offer—since you left here years ago, you have prepared yourself for the battle to come with scholarship. You cut yourself off from the world, learned much, but allowed your health to suffer. Some time recently you reversed this. You undertook the building of yourself anew. Since I am feeling certain that the 'why' of it all will explain your visit, I shall ask ... *why* are you here?"

At that point Zarnak's Hindu manservant returned with an over-sized tray laden with food. Besides a large, ornate clay tea pot trimmed with cut jade and silver and a pair of brightly painted porcelain cups, there were a dozen bowls of various finger foods—lotus candies and almond cookies, ginger pastries, warmed nuts, crunchy fried peas, oil roasted noodles and other snacks that could be consumed without thought or formality. In the center of it all were a ring of bowls containing sweet and hot sauces as well as flavored powders and salts.

Unfolding a clever wicker stand with the snap of his free hand, the manservant had the tray set up next to his master's desk in but a moment. exiting the room with a silent bow. Zarnak indicated the tray in a manner than obliged Legrasse to help himself, then immediately popped a half dozen cashews into his own mouth. As the doctor poured two cups of tea, his guest finally answered his question.

"Years ago, even before I first came here, I knew something big was coming. I didn't know when, or why—what have you—but I could feel it, *knew* it. After meeting you, seeing how much education it takes to stand up to these things," Legrasse waved his hand toward the bookshelves filled with hundreds of scholarly-looking texts surrounding the room, "I realized I was going to have to start learning about what I'd gotten myself into."

A weary look flashed through the inspector's raging eyes. Zarnak understood the forlorn wistfulness that inspired the fatigue, but he also knew Legrasse was not asking for pity. The man had merely stumbled under his burden for a moment and been unable to hide his need of it. Like any true gentleman, Zarnak refrained from comment, the way one would not mention some minor defect in the countenance of an otherwise beautiful woman.

"Eventually there was another break through from the other side that entangled me. Lucky thing, actually. It woke me up, reminded me these things are not bested by knowledge alone. So, yes, for the last two years I've been taking the air and building myself back awaiting the day when that something I've been watching for finally returned."

"And, it's here?" asked Zarnak innocently, knowing the truth.

"Not yet, but it will be soon."

"And how do you know this?" questioned the doctor with sincere interest. Reaching into the small bag he had carried since he entered 13 China Alley, Legrasse pulled forth the macabre statue he had kept with him for so many years and placed it on the desk before him.

"An old friend told me."

Zarnak stared at the statue with alarmed surprise. True horror crinkled in the corners of his eyes, revealing to just what level he understood the statue's significance. Legrasse smiled, pleased to have been able to startle the usually unflappable doctor. To celebrate his triumph, the inspector ran a handful of fried noodles through the hottest-looking sauce on the tray and then popped the entire gob in his mouth with satisfaction. While he followed that with several lotus sweets, Zarnak surmised with surprising admiration,

"You've been using this as a dream monitor, haven't you?"

Legrasse nodded, pleased to see that his host was still every bit as sharp as he had remembered. Then, their meeting began in earnest.

IV.

"But, mistress Angela, you don't understand. It be John Legrasse out there."

The young woman turned stiffly from the crystal bowl of long stemmed, bearded irises she was arranging, her face a frozen mesh of dark, unforgiving lines. The black man at her drawing room door shrank back a step. He knew he was never to disturb his employer while she was working with her flowers, but he had had no choice. When her father had been master of the house, Louis Washington had known that any contact with the voodoo man was not to be taken lightly. Legrasse's any wish was to be fulfilled immediately. The Negro servant did not know, however, if his mistress understood her father's previous arrangement with the inspector. But, he knew in his heart that being fired from his position was in no way as bad a thing as angering Legrasse.

"Louis," snapped the ebony-haired woman, "I don't care if it's the Pope himself. This is the one time of day I allow myself complete solitude, and—"

"And so, miss," interrupted Legrasse's voice from behind the chauffeur, "it would seem best then that you hear me out so you can quickly return to shutting yourself off from humanity."

The woman's head snapped backward slightly, her shock at being so addressed paralyzing her momentarily. Her eyes froze, anger and intellectual curiosity struggling with each other for the right to dictate her next statements. As her mouth came open, Legrasse cut her off once more.

"Miss Buttacavala, I won't say that I'm sorry to see your father gone—he was a murderer and worse and the world is well rid of him. But, while I extend my sympathies at your loss, I must be blunt—your father and I had an arrangement. As the inheritor of his properties, his rackets and all his evil world, do you plan to make good his debt to me—or shall I leave you to play with your posies?"

The inspector studied the woman before him. He knew from the public records that she was well past thirty, but standing there she appeared no more than perhaps twenty-three or four. She stood straight and proud, her carriage erect and surprisingly well-muscled. Her loose wool suit hid such things from the casual viewer, but Legrasse could see that the Calamari's daughter was no stranger to the physical side of life, despite the wealthy surroundings in which she had been raised, or the millions at her command.

He found himself noting that her face was as well-chiseled as the rest of her—proud, high cheek-bones, rich brown eyes draped by long lashes and framed by thick black eyebrows. Noticing Legrasse's attentive look helped Angela Buttacavala find not only her voice but a direction for its response.

"You have no claim here, you bastard!"

"I have every claim here," responded the inspector quietly. "I helped your father achieve the blood revenge he wanted over the death of your brother, Carmine. Beyond that, you father understood what had happened to Carmine, and what would happen to you and all the world if he did not work with me to prevent the terrible turn of events which are just around the corner."

"And what would that be?"

Legrasse paused for a moment, his head tilting to one side as he considered his response. He stared at the woman intently, taking in more than just the surface look of her. As he would have decades earlier, he studied her as he would have a suspect, tearing apart her soul with his eyes, looking over each of the pieces thoroughly before putting it back. Finally, after a scant delay of only several seconds, he reached into the canvas bag under his arm.

"This is what is coming, Miss Buttacavala," he answered, crossing the room. Placing the demonic statue he had shown Zarnak in New York on the table in the midst of the woman's cut flowers, he said, "it is evil beyond measure. It is what consumed your brother and what is coming to destroy all this world."

Angela Buttacavala bent to inspect the horrid object, curiosity pulling her forward even as much of her will and mind was repulsed. As her hand reached out to touch it, Legrasse gave her a word of caution.

"I would warn you against making contact with the statue."

"Why?" she asked, her already ample suspicion growing further. "You handled it."

"I've had the time to grow used to it. Touching it by those not prepared for the results can be most disturbing."

"I'll tell you what I find disturbing," answered the indignant woman. "Your condescending attitude. You think I know nothing of you and my father—I know all of it. I know what my father was, Inspector. Every part of how he paid for this house, my education, every bite of food I ever swallowed ... I know how much blood and human misery was involved. And I know how at the end, when his fear of going to Hell for his sins made him crazy, he imagined my brother to be possessed by Satan and so he killed him. And that was when you came into his life, Legrasse—just another corrupt official with his hand out."

The inspector shook his head sadly. He did not mind Angela Buttacavala's indignation or even her erroneous assumptions about his relationship with her father. What others thought of him meant less than nothing compared with what he had to accomplish. But, if she were to refuse him the funds he needed, that would pose a near insurmountable problem. Thinking against that disastrous contingency, Legrasse was too slow of thought to stop what happened next.

"Let me tell you something," she said coldly. "There are no more Buttacavala rackets. My father explained everything to me on his death bed, and I've gotten rid of all of it. Do you hear me—if someone else is controlling his empire now, I don't know about it, and I don't care to, either. I couldn't stand the thought of anything remaining here that would remind me of those days. And that, my dear Inspector, includes you as well."

Her hand reaching for the terrible statue to hurl at Legrasse, the woman shouted, "Now get out of here—*get out!*"

And then, her hand closed around the graven image. Her eyes rolling upward into her head, Angela gave out a tiny, gurgling gasp and then fell forward onto the table before her, shattering the great crystal vase and sending her flowers scattering across the floor.

* **** *

Angela opened her eyes slowly. There was a wild discordance swirling within them, a raging animation that belied the utter weakness assailing her every limb. Louis, as well as her personal maid, an older, somewhat frantic woman by the name of Anna Lee, were kneeling next to her. Relief flushed their faces as they saw her eyelids part.

"Honey, you's alive."

"Yes," answered Angela slowly—weakly. "The ... the Inspector ... is he—"

"I'm here, Miss Buttacavala," came Legrasse's voice from across the room. Walking into view, he tapped the maid on the shoulder. "You—fetch your mistress a good tumbler of strong spirits—bourbon or rye—something with some punch to it. And bring her something to eat as well. Meat, cheese, bread—no fruit or vegetables. No sweets. Something solid."

The maid nodded and hurried to her feet, careful to keep her eyes from meeting the inspector's. The woman knew no good came from crossing the fabled Legrasse. As she hustled out of the room, the inspector bade Louis to crack open several windows. The chauffeur set off with the same quiet speed as the maid. The help occupied, Legrasse bent close to Angela. He did not bother to ask her how she felt—he knew the answer to that question. Instead, he asked her what she had experienced. She told him.

"I was in a strange place—an island, or a mountain top—I don't know. They seemed one and the same, yet not. Oh, I sound mad."

"True," agreed Legrasse quietly, "but not incorrect. Go on."

"I, I don't know how to describe what I saw," she told him. Her voice raw and slight, tears forming in the corners of her eyes, she whispered, "Everywhere I looked, I saw things ... out of place. Wrong—stone slabs of monstrous proportion ... all running at impossible angles. The geometry was backward—inside out. It didn't make any sense, not real sense—human sense. But there was something there that understood it, that owned it, created it ... a horrible thing, big and vast, like an ocean, or the sky—it was a squid, or a dragon, but it wasn't. It was more. Terrible ..."

Legrasse took the woman's hand as she shut her eyes and began sobbing. Comforting her as best he could, the inspector suggested softly that she not concentrate on that which she had seen. She had related all he needed to hear. If she wanted to recover, however, she was going to have to forget the vision that had flooded her brain—put it behind her.

"I can't," she told him, her delicate voice cracking. Then, suddenly stronger, she corrected herself. "I mean, I can't allow this to happen."

"What do you mean?"

"Inspector," the woman said sharply, he eyes suddenly drying. "You came here for financing, didn't you? You're going to the place I saw in my vision—correct?"

"I imagine if not that exact place, then certainly something alike to it."

"You can have the money you need," she told him. "No matter what the cost. On one condition." Legrasse stared unblinking, waiting. Angela gave him what he was waiting for. "You must allow me to accompany you on your journey."

The inspector pursed his lips. His mind dashed over a list of what he imagined her reasons might be for making such a demand. Then, realizing in only a fraction of a second that whatever her reason for doing such was really of no consequence to him, he answered her with a question.

"You do realize the possibility of not surviving this expedition is quite high?" The woman nodded her head weakly. Still looking into Legrasse's eyes, she asked her own question.

"If I understand the things I saw when I touched your statute, if this trip is not made, the possibility of everyone in the world not surviving is higher—correct?" The inspector nodded. "Good enough. The Buttacavalas have a great deal to make up for. This sounds like a good way to start."

"I'm goin', too." Legrasse turned in Louis' direction. "You heard me. When you went down to the docks for Master Buttacavala, I was there. But I didn't do nuthin'. I froze up. And when I wasn't froze up I was runnin' away. I gots things to make up for, too. You goin' do more like yous done before, you ain't gonna get dems many wants ta go along. I'm goin'."

As Anna Lee entered with a tray containing the exact meal Legrasse had prescribed, the inspector rose to his feet. Standing aside so the maid could approach her mistress, he told the others simply, "I'll contact you as to the when and where of it all."

With that, Legrasse gathered up his canvas bag and headed for the door. As he turned the knob, Louis called out to him.

"Dat's it? No argument? Yous gonna take us—no lie?"

"Why not?" he said simply. "Every war needs cannon fodder."

V.

Jim Dandy's was a tavern of little repute, situated on one of the darker side streets of the Quarter, its clientele made up almost exclusively of the worst elements of New Orleans and the police. Both enjoyed its rough, private atmosphere, and an easy truce had grown up between the two sides over the years which allowed both to share the common watering hole. However, in all the tavern's years, it had never seen a gathering quite like the one assembled there after Legrasse's meeting with Angela Buttacavala.

The inspector was there, along with his old comrades—Randolf Muller, a flush-faced, heavy set policeman, now retired, and the younger, still active officer, Joel Carrinelle, a tall, thin man with a protruding Adam's apple and large, bony hands. Representing New Orleans' criminal element were the Calamari's daughter, Angela, her chauffeur, Louis, and one Ernesto Nardi, one of the late crime lord's ranking lieutenants. The only outsider to both the armies of law and order and the underworld was the former chair of Anthropology of Princeton University, Professor William Channing Webb.

"So, we're going to ride in a dirigible?"

"Some problem with that, Randolf?" asked Legrasse. When the older man responded with only excitement at the thought of flying, the inspector continued his orientation. Referring those assembled to the U. S. Army map of the world he had spread on the table, he drew imaginary lines with his finger as he outlined their upcoming journey.

"As I was saying, the airship Miss Buttacavala and I have arranged for will be here within two days. It will take us non-stop across the Pacific to Bombay, in India. From there we will take a series of trains northeast to Calcutta, and from there further north to Bhatgaon in Nepal."

"That's around the world, Inspector," exclaimed Carrinelle, just beginning to grasp the enormity of what they were planning. Legrasse nodded. Sensing a moment where he could interrupt, Nardi shoved his way into the conversation.

"That's right," he insisted, his gaze focused on his employer. "Your papa, Angela, he wouldn't want this. Not you goin' for this, I mean. Let me take care of dis. I'll watch Legrasse here's back. I done it on the docks when we went after Thomton before. I can do it again. There ain't no need for you to do this."

"Paying others to do our dirty work is what forces me to do this now, Ernesto," answered the woman. Taking the older man's hand, she asked him, "What does the name Buttacavala stand for, can you tell me? Anything decent? Anything worthy or good in any way?"

"Ahh, now—you shouldn't oughta talk that way."

"I have to, Ernesto," Angela told him quietly. "My father, in his last years, he tried to make his peace with God by assisting Mr. Legrasse. I shall, as well. All my fortune is his."

"But you, Miss Angela, you don't have ta—"

"*Yes,*" the woman snapped suddenly. Her voice instantly lowering, she repeated, "Yes. I do. If you had seen what was coming, what I saw, you would … You'd understand."

"I seen it," the thick-necked criminal assured the woman. "Back when we worked with Legrasse the last time. Ugly, flopping, fish bastards. I seem 'em. I know. I ..." And then, the pug-faced man turned and stared into his employer's eyes. Suddenly, the dreams that had plagued him for the last two years spilled anew through his brain. Seeing the same dark whirl of mad terror reflected in the beautiful, but now transformed eyes before her, he broke off his gaze, nodding jerkily.

"Aw'right, aw'right ... maybe I do understand."

Legrasse remained quiet for a moment, assessing his team. Old men and a woman—too many of them out to prove something—trying to prove something to someone else, to themselves, to society, to God Almighty—

And you, Legrasse, asked a mocking voice within his mind, what are you trying to prove? And to whom?

The inspector pursed his lips at the thought, admitting that no matter what reasons might had brought those around the table there that night, they were the best he could hope for. He had seen the reactions of the uninitiated to the horrors those assembled had witnessed. Most could not stand against such things, their minds crumbling in frighten retreat, most often scrambling for the safe haven of madness. Angela's response had impressed him most of all. He knew from the look in the woman's eyes when she had regained consciousness that she had seen far more than most, and somehow had fought her way back to lucidity.

No, he told himself, no matter what I might wish, these are the best I can hope for.

He was about to tell them that when suddenly an angry figure stormed into the tavern through the badly hung front doors. Making none of the customary greetings to the owner or bartender, the man plowed directly for the inspector's table.

"You're a goddamned bastard, Legrasse!"

The inspector looked up from his drink, as did everyone else seated around the table.

"Joseph," answered Legrasse, "you're upset about something?"

Joseph D. Galvez, once a lieutenant under Legrasse's direction, now an Inspector of Police in his own right, stared harshly at those assembled. He ignored the others, however, choosing to continue his tirade against his one-time commander.

"You're going out again—against the cult. Deny it."

"Why would I insult your intelligence, Joseph?"

"Why would you go without me?" snarled the shorter man. "I'm too old now? Too excitable? Too florid for your tastes of a sudden? What is it, J. R.—what makes you think you can do without me this time? I look around this table and I don't see anything special." With a contemptuous wave of his hand, he added harshly, "What do any of these have that I don't have?"

"It's what you have that they don't, my friend—Maria. And little Lisa."

Galvez froze for a moment, his anger dissipated like steam in a gale, his tongue seeming to swell within his mouth. A war raged in his mind, his pride and desires overwhelmed by his responsibilities. Understanding—envying—the reasons behind his old friend's discomfort, the inspector indicated one of the empty rattan-covered chairs at the large table. Galvez sat down.

"After our last encounter with the beyond," Legrasse explained quietly, "you went out and found that which most of us dared not even dream of. You married. But more, in the face of all that we know, you went ahead and created life. You have a child, Joseph. A child—a beautiful girl most at this table know and love."

"She is a pretty one," interjected Muller. With a twinkle in his eye, he added, "Maybe that's why he come tonight—she's too pretty to be his."

Galvez's eyes flashed hot, his fingers snapping into fists. Just as quickly, however, he released his grips. An irreverent jokester himself, he knew what his old friend meant. Feeling the need to explain himself, however, he nodded toward Muller to acknowledge that he understood the jest—and that it would be paid back—then he turned once more to Legrasse.

"El Grande, you stay with us for so long, and then you slip away in the middle of the night—no word, no explanation. You leave me behind like a dog not fit for the hunt ..."

The inspector cut his old friend off at that point, telling him of the maddening dream that had come to him the night he had packed his bags and left Galvez's home. He told him of understanding its meaning that the end to all their efforts was about to come to a close, and of his need to act immediately.

"There was no time to argue with you, to make you think of your new responsibilities. And certainly I could not discuss such things with you in your own home, with Maria and Lisa present. You needed time to think, and I had to get myself to New York."

"You went to see that magician?" Galvez had been one of the few to hear of the inspector's previous trip to New York City. Legrasse had told him all he had known of Dr. Zarnak in case the time had ever come when his second-in-command had needed to pick up and carry on in Legrasse's absence. "Is he coming with us?"

"No," came the inspector's answer with a curious detachment. "The Doctor is heavily engaged with cosmic matters of his own connected to this very problem against which we ourselves have banded together. But he has promised assistance which should arrive here some time today or tomorrow."

Carrinelle pushed a bottle of aged Scotch across the table toward his commander as one of Jim Dandy's waiters brought a fresh glass to the table. Ordering a Chicory coffee as a chaser, the fierce Spaniard accepted both offerings, then poured himself a healthy libation. Knocking back half the amount in one swallow, he again turned to Legrasse.

"I have to go with you, el Grande. And it's because of Lisa." As the others stared at him, Galvez took another swallow from his glass, finishing his drink. As Nardi poured him another, he continued.

"None of you has children, do you? I never thought I would. Never thought I would care. But after that last time, when I met Maria, somehow, everything changed. I wanted something more—I wanted something to ... how can I say it, to follow me. Did I help save the world just to die out from it—was I so stupid?"

Another vast swig followed the two previous. Galvez drained the entire glass in one pull, a feat putting a hush over the rest at the table. His hand coming down harshly, the policeman answered his own question loudly.

"No—I wasn't. I became a father. Oh, but I was smug. The hero poppi, that was me. I could see it all. I would raise my beautiful girl, and I would tell her tales of how important I was. How the world keeps spinning on its axis all because her brave poppi had the courage to fight alongside John Raymond Legrasse."

Galvez sucked down a huge breath of air. Already his speech was growing quieter and somewhat slurred. Not ready to surrender the floor to anyone, however, he continued, telling the others, "I was going to tell my grandchildren, too. And my great-grandchildren. More of them, if my line was so blessed."

Suddenly tired, the officer pushed his empty glass toward Nardi who emptied the last of their bottle into the demanding vessel.

"But now, now everything has changed. It isn't over. We didn't beat them. The world isn't saved. The end was just postponed long enough for my precious Lisa to be born. Just long enough for them to have their revenge on me."

As the dregs of their Scotch dripped into Galvez's glass, pushing air out of a mere third of its depth, the officer stared at the inch and a half of amber fluid, whispering sadly.

"They can't have her, el Grande. And if I must die to keep them from her, then I die. At least such a death will be rewarded by God. But you tell me, what is the reward of a man who sees the future hurling toward his loved ones, and does nothing to stop it?"

"You burn in Hell."

Everyone, even Galvez, turned toward the source of the interruption. A man sitting one table over, ponderous in size, his wild, unkempt hair so long it hid his ears, raised his own glass to the next table in salute. When the others merely stared at him, he shrugged, laughed a short bitter note in their direction, and then downed his drink. Legrasse realized of a sudden that the man had been sitting close to them all evening, and yet none of them had actually seen him, so quiet and preoccupied with his own thoughts had he been. Now, however, their conversation had stirred something within him and he seemed determined to have his say.

Clutching his own bottle by the neck, he rose from his table and then, grabbing his high-backed chair roughly, he spun it around and shoved it toward a bit of an opening between Nardi and Louis. As several at the table protested his intrusion, something in the man's demeanor made Legrasse signal them to allow him to continue. Bowing with a clumsy grace in the inspector's direction, the man toppled into his seat, and then offered his bottle to the others. Legrasse gave Carrinelle a slight nod, signaling that he should accept the stranger's offer. Then, as the junior officer began pouring everyone a fresh drink, the inspector asked,

"So, friend, what is it you know about Hell?"

"I know the smell of it better than any of you. I heard you all night, talking of monsters and pain and galaxies of nightmare ... posh, I've known worse than any of you. You're all of you out of the average—policemen and professors and criminals. Even you—" the man said, pointing at Louis, "you drove around a millionaire outlaw. Not me. Nothing of interest for Billy."

"Why?" asked Louis, suddenly feeling a great affinity for the large man. "What did you do?"

"I sweat," came the harsh response. "Humped over a desk for years on end, I scribbled and scrawled and battled my ledger as if my life depended on it— which it did, 'cause men can starve." His bottle returned to him, the big man finally downed the drink in his hand, refilling his glass as he continued.

"And then one day I killed a man ... for no good reason. Oh, I thought I had one. Thought I was defending fair womanhood, standing up for all I held dear. What I was actually doing was proving just how large a horse's ass I'd been making out of myself for years, worshipping a empty vision. It was no one's fault but my own. I married an affected piece of bloodless porcelain, thinking I'd captured an angel. Full of myself one day, desperate to prove myself worthy of her, I snuffed out a life and threw it at her unworthy feet, as if I had the right to make such decisions."

The man took a surprisingly restrained sip from his glass, then completed his rambling speech. "After that I just ran away. I'd just gotten my pay check that day, so I cashed it and traveled from tavern to tavern until the money ran out. This," he said, holding up his glass for all to see, "represents the last of that princely sum, so vast it took all of a thousand miles of travel and some eight bottles of bargain-priced rye to go through it."

The man took another, almost dainty sip, then said, "So let Mr. Galvez accompany you to the other side of the world, for as they say, a man has to do what a man has to do."

"And what is it you have to do?" asked Legrasse.

The large man stopped, frozen by the inspector's question. Legrasse studied the huge figure, his mind of a sudden caught up with wondering at how such a person could come to be in the same place as all of them at such a time. Was it all an absurd coincidence—meaning the universe had no order—meaning that monstrosities such as the one he and the others meant to face were the supreme forces they considered themselves? Or had a higher fate brought him to them, delivering his wretched, elephantine former clerk to them to be taken along as an act of faith?

The inspector's mind reeled. Was he simply drunk to entertain such an absurd notion, or was he being tested by powers allied to his cause, forces as mysteriously alien to him as the things he would destroy? Suddenly, it seemed to Legrasse that the outcome of all he was planning depended upon whatever decision he made concerning the large man.

Well, he thought cynically, of course it does. Whether destiny sent him or not, if you bring him along and he fumbles everything …

Legrasse closed his eyes for a moment, fear quaking through his body. The reading of signs and portents was not his line. He had studied his foes for a decade and a half, but in the end he had never changed his essential nature. He was a man of action, pure and simple. He could not recite incantations with any confidence, read tea leaves or perform any of the wizard's tricks he had hoped to master.

Are you saying, Legrasse, his mind snickered at him, that you wasted years of your life, slaving under a false notion? Are you saying that while there were monsters to slay, that you made a clerk of yourself?

The inspector smiled. Extending his reach far enough to clink his glass against the large man's own, he asked the fellow his name.

"Bill Clutts," came the response.

"Well, Mr. Clutts," answered Legrasse, "if you didn't have any plans beyond perishing in the gutter, I was wondering if you might want to tag along and die with the rest of us?"

The large man's face broke into a broad smile that was a sobering mix of despair and rapture. Striking the cheaply-made glass in his hand hard enough against the inspector's to ring an almost crystalline note from it, he answered,

"Why, I thought you'd never ask."

VI.

Legrasse and Professor Webb arrived at the state sanitarium located outside of the city proper early the next morning. Under Angela's direction, the others were searching the city for the supplies they would need on their journey. Heavy winter clothing, something not found in great abundance in New

Orleans, had to be obtained for all of them, as well as an extensive checklist of camping and mountain climbing equipment, food stuffs, trade goods and all manner of defensive and offensive weapons. All of it needed to be found, purchased and then transported to the dock area where the dirigible expected the next day was to be met.

Important as these details were, however, Legrasse and Webb had another chore to attend to, one even more critical than those being handled by the others. Entering the bleak, cold lobby of a hospital the inspector had not seen for over fifteen years, he found his way to the administrator's office with practiced efficiency, demanding to see a checklist of those prisoners still remaining within the sanitarium's walls whom he had brought there so long ago. Save for those who had died—most by their own hand—he found that all the prisoners he had taken during his efforts expended against the cult of Cthulhu were still being held. Picking a familiar name, he requested the inmate be brought to him at once.

The administrator complied—half out of curiosity as to what interest Legrasse could have in the elderly patient after all those years, half out of dread of discovering the same. Eventually, the man was brought to an interview room and left in the care of the inspector and his companion. The administrator was not asked if he would like to remain. As the door to the room was shut, cutting him off from the three men inside, the official decided he would rather not know anything more after all.

"So, Castro," asked Legrasse, "how are they treating you?"

The now elderly *mestizo* smiled at the inspector, staring hard into his eyes. Moving his head slowly, he turned toward Webb, staring at him as well. After a moment, the immensely aged patient said, "You both be real, don't you?"

Legrasse nodded, understanding the unfocused look in the old half-breed's eyes. Despite the string of ghastly murders the inspector could ascribe to the wizened bag of brittle bones before him, he felt a strange sympathy for the cultist he could not begin to explain.

Mercy for the damned, Legrasse, the snide voice within his head questioned. Or do you see yourself jibbering in a corner someday?

I should live so long, the inspector thought, then turned his attention exclusively to old Castro.

"So, how's the noggin' these days?"

"You? You talk Castro? Castro talk you? You want Castro talk you?"

"That was the general idea, old fellow," added Webb. "We were wondering if you could answer a few questions for us."

Legrasse and the professor worked for almost an hour with the aged cultist, working their patience carefully against the senile elder's declining ability to respond to any human contact. As the time dragged on, however, the pair began to wonder if they would ever be able to get anything of use out of the patient. Castro had been old when first captured in the swamps by Legrasse and his men during the initial raid which had led the inspector into his never-ending war with the Cthulhu cult. Now, after an additional two decades of isolation, it was beginning to appear that he might be totally incapable of assisting them, even if he wanted to. And, of course, there was the fact that the two men were the enemy of Castro's gods.

"I'm beginning to wonder if there's any good we can do at all here," said Webb with a heavy sigh laden with defeat. Legrasse was just about to agree with him when one of the facility's attendants came in asking if they were expecting another member of their party. Curious, the inspector requested the newcomer be allowed entry. Moments later, a lean, tall man was admitted to the interview room. His face, strongly marked and gaunt, was smooth with the touch of youth, although there were already hints of gray in his hair, especially in the thick brows which overhung his keen grey eyes.

"Hello," he said, his hand extended toward the inspector, "You must be John Legrasse. I was sent by Dr. Zarnak."

The inspector took the younger man's hand at once, shaking it with warm enthusiasm. Upon asking how he found his way to the sanitarium, he explained that he had followed the directions of a young woman who seemed to be in charge of things at the address where he had been instructed to go by Dr. Zarnak. The young man proved to be a student Zarnak was mentoring. As he presented Legrasse with a letter of introduction, he inquired as to their progress with old Castro.

Webb brought him up to date, an endeavor which took little time as they had made wretchedly little progress. The professor explained, "The poor old boy's brain seems to have jellied. We've been trying to get an idea of the exact location of the cult's main lair out of him, but it's no good. He's got little juice left in him, it seems."

"Exact location, you say?"

"Yes," answered Legrasse. "Years ago, I questioned this man when he was far more lucid. He told us of a ceremony that would be invoked to release this thing Cthulhu from its slumber and ..."

The inspector trailed off as he noticed a blip of horror flash through the younger man's eyes. No longer concerned with questioning Castro, he asked what the matter was. After a moment taken to gulp down several deep breaths of air, he explained.

"You said ... Cthulhu. That we were ... Cthulhu. Ha. Ha—Cthulhu." The young man put a finger to his lips, trying to calm himself. Short bites of laughter escaped him in between his words, cackled segments of terrible noise interrupting his fragmented speech. "The Doctor ... heh ... he didn't, didn't—ha ha—didn't say anything, anything—heh—anything about ... about Cthulhu."

Legrasse held his tongue, giving the younger man a moment to gather his nerves from below the cliff over which they had so suddenly been thrown. Neither the inspector nor Webb thought ill of the apprentice. They knew exactly what such knowledge could do to a person. They could wait.

Luckily, they did not have to wait long. With a slow, purposeful blink of his eyes and a short, violent shaking of his head, suddenly the young man was in possession of himself once more. After a brief apology which Webb and the inspector turned aside immediately, lavish in their understanding, the apprentice reached into his bag and began rummaging around for something as he spoke.

"Let me take a crack at our patient here, eh? Perhaps I have something that might help. You were saying you had a partial location? Where—Arabia, perhaps? Is it Irem—major passageway, that, I hear—City of a Thousand Pillars—nasty business—"

"No, no—much further East, somewhere in Asia."

"Hummm," mused the young man, still bent over his bag. "Plateau of Leng, perhaps—Sung, maybe. Tsang—all nasty destinations. But, let's see what our friend thinks … ah, here we go."

Standing erect, the apprentice brought forth a number of pendants, all of them being of differing shapes and sizes. Each consisted of a simple silver chain attached to a small piece of gray-blue stone. Each of the stones, although varying in size, was stamped with an identical image consisting of a star with an eye in its center, that image altered by having what appeared to be a pillar of flame where the pupil should have been located. Handing one each to Legrasse and Webb, he instructed them to put them on at once. He informed them that he had been given a great supply of them by Dr. Zarnak for the expedition's use. Then, after slipping his own on, he turned toward Castro, holding one up so that the elderly patient could see it clearly.

"Look here, old fellow," said the apprentice, "Here's a toy your friends don't want you to have."

The aged *mestizo* stared unblinking at the chunk of grayly-blue rock dangling at the end of the chain before his face, the image engraved within its surface not registering within his aged brain. After a moment, however, the yellow moisture glazing his aged eyes hardened. The film snapped as he blinked, shattering outward and falling away from his face. His hair, suddenly alive as if his body had been filled with electricity, began to dance wildly, straining as if trying to fly away from his head.

"Take that out of here."

Both Legrasse and Webb were taken aback by the sound of Castro's voice. Gone were the infirmities of age and madness. The old half-breed's wandering, muttering tone had been replaced by an oily, gurgling bark filled with resentment and power.

"We want some information from you Castro."

Rising to his feet, his cage erect, his musculature seemingly expanding with every breath, "I said—take that out of here!"

With that, Castro leaped forward toward the apprentice. Legrasse's hand jerked his Luger from its holster beneath his jacket, but the younger man held up his free hand in caution.

"Don't worry—Mr. Castro here isn't going to trouble us? Are you, old fellow?"

"Die, human maggot."

Grabbing hold of the corner of the heavy interview table, the old man broke the inch thick triangle away and then hurled it straight for the apprentice. The block caught him neatly in the chest, sending the young man toppling backwards. Pulling on his own pendant, Legrasse broke the chain and held the charm out before him, snapping orders at old Castro.

"Back, you vile bastard"

Again Castro grabbed at the table, but the inspector used his pendant as a whip, slapping it against the aging half-breed's extended arm. A sparking explosion of thick, purplish light roiled out of the old man, blasting with vicious speed toward every corner of the room. It passed around the three investigators, coming within millimeters of their bodies, kept from touching them by the mystic protections they wore or held. A choking fetor remained behind for a brief instant, but even it was dispelled by the curious amulets.

At the same time, old Castro fell back against the wall, all life draining quickly out of him. Instinctively holstering his weapon, Legrasse crossed the room to the aged patient and cradled his head. A jumbled mess of words scattered from the old man's mouth like marbles spilling across a schoolyard. Phrases of praise and gratitude were mixed with sorrowful confusion. The inspector tried to cut through it all, but could not get Castro's attention. Kneeling beside the pair, the apprentice placed his hand on the old cultist's forehead. He kept it placed there firmly for several long moments, then told Legrasse he could release his grip on the patient. When the inspector asked why, the younger man told him,

"Because he's dead."

"Damn," spat Legrasse in disgust. Holding up his pendant in angry curiosity, he demanded, "Just what the devil are these things?"

"They go by many names," responded the apprentice as he stood back up. "Star stones, elder signs, signs of Kish—they're magical symbols that protect one from the minions of the Great Old Ones. Castro here seems to have been invaded at some point by a Bla'raff."

"What?"

"Sort of a watchdog. Some time in the past, Castro was felled by a fever. It would have been just a few degrees higher than normal, but while he had it he would have experienced a visionary delirium. That was the Bla'raff invading his body, well, his mind, actually. You see ..."

"Forget all that for now," snapped Legrasse. "We've still come up empty. Castro is gone and now so is any hope of finding the cult."

"Oh, not at all," answered the apprentice. "When I touched his head, holding the star stone in my hand, I was reading his mind. That's how I knew it was a Bla'raff. And that's how I know the cult will be holding the ceremony you're looking for on the Plateau of Tsang." As Legrasse and Webb stared for a moment, the younger man told them, "I saw it all within his mind as it was closing. I now know the entire way, as if I'd traveled the road a hundred times myself."

With a smile, Webb turned to Legrasse. "Now what do you think of that?"

"I guess," the inspector responded, "we'll have to make certain we keep this youngster alive." Then, as an afterthought, Legrasse apologized.

"Sorry, lad, but in all the haste, introductions seem to have fallen by the wayside. This is Professor William Channing Webb of Princeton. I, as you correctly surmised, am John Legrasse. And you, my boy... ?"

"Leigh," responded the apprentice, "Michael Leigh. And, despite my unforgivable initial apprehension, I'm pleased to meet you both and to be a part of this all."

Legrasse and Webb took turns shaking the younger man's hand. Turning to look about the room, though, the professor indicated the ebony stains etched in the walls from the flight of the Bla'raff, as well as the crazed look of terrible fear twisted across old Castro features.

"If you say so, Michael," he answered, a small shudder vibrating his shoulders. "If you say so."

*   * * *   *

Some time later, Legrasse found himself sharing a late supper with Angela Buttacavala. While the others were either tidying up their affairs or attempting to acquire some long needed rest, the inspector and Angela reviewed what both teams had accomplished during the day. Angela's report greatly pleased Legrasse as it seemed she and the others managed to secure everything needed for their journey.

"Funny how money just opens any door you can think of," joked Angela. Questioning the sour look on her dinner companion's face, Legrasse responded with the details of their session at the sanitarium. When she responded that it seemed things had worked out for the best, the inspector relayed to her the conversation he had had with Zarnak's apprentice on the ride back to New Orleans proper.

"As Michael explains it, these Bla'raff are like ... how did he describe them

… ah, psychic viruses. When these Great Old Ones, the beings that live in the worlds you saw in your vision, when they want to know something on this plane, they send these things out like germs. These deliriums people fall into, they're actually rather like infections. People don't remember what happened to them if they shake the germs, and if they don't shake them, they can't tell, because they're no longer in control of themselves."

"Like old Castro?"

"Yes," agreed Legrasse. Taking the moment to slide another tender chunk of egg-battered veal into his mouth, he chewed quickly, continuing his explanation as rapidly as he could. "Anyway, these Bla'raff control people for their masters, but there's more to it."

Angela stared at Legrasse, her face tightening as she waited for the words she could easily tell he did not wish to say. After a moment, his eyes finding hers, he explained, "These things are like radio receivers. Once inside a person, that person becomes a part of one of the Old Ones. It's a way for them to extend their eyes and ears."

"So," said Angela, feeling her way forward with caution, "what you're saying is, something out there knows everything this Castro knew—which means something knows we're coming now."

"That's not the worst part," answered Legrasse. His face heavy with pain, he told her, "from what Michael could read in Castro's mind … it seems they've known that for quite some time."

"How?" asked Angela, her eyes going wide in fearful surprise.

"I don't know. Neither did Michael. Castro just had in his mind that terrible fact—that some one of us has already been sending information back to its inhuman master."

"But who? That man, Clutts—he attached himself to us out of nowhere. Or your man, Galvez. He forced himself upon us. Or—"

"Or you, my dear," interrupted Legrasse with cold honesty. "Or me. You fell into a delirium trance when you touched the stone idol. I've lived with the dreams sent by the thing for years. There's no way for us to know exactly whom it might be until they give themselves away."

"And how will that be accomplished, I wonder?" snapped the young woman. "When they light a torch and send our dirigible to the bottom of the ocean? When they slit our throats one by one? Or maybe when they set off a bomb in the mountains? Why not?"

Standing from her chair, Angela suddenly grabbed her dinner plate and flung it across the room. The piece of French China collided with an eighteenth century marble bowl, one held in a gilt bronze mount decorated with both trumpeting angelic figures and stern griffins. As the pair of antiques shattered one against the other, she sobbed in a despair not tied to the loss of possessions, but instead tangled in her ill-concealed fear that there was no escaping the terror she saw before her.

"Why not?" she whispered, her arms outstretched toward Legrasse. To the inspector's credit, he was already in motion, coming around the table to comfort the younger woman. Although a career man and then a reclusive scholar for most of his adult life, still was he a man, and the compassion that Angela's animal terror sparked within him drew his arms about her shoulders in a tender manner.

"There's no way to know, dear lady," he told her softly. Angela collapsed against his breast, her wet cheek smearing her make-up into his starched white shirt. His left hand patting her back in a comforting motion, he told her, "Michael performed some kind of ritual he believes will block the thing's influence."

"Meaning we're safe?" asked Angela.

"Meaning we won't know anything for certain until it does or doesn't happen." Legrasse continued to hold the younger woman, her forlorn sobs filling him with distress. Seeking to comfort her, he added softly, "Of course, there's no actual reason for you to be there when we discover the truth."

"What do you mean?" she asked in a small and quiet voice.

"You have done all your father's pact with me requires. There is no need for you to die alongside all the rest of us."

"And," she asked, her eyes upturned and locked with his, "are you so certain death is all that awaits us?"

"I've been resigned to such a fate for a number of years now," he admitted to her. Swallowing hard, the back of his mind laughing at him for the thoughts he was entertaining, still he dared her ridicule by admitting, "although, to be honest, recently I have been of a notion that surviving might not be such a terrible thing."

Angela continued to stare into the inspector's eyes, neither dismissing nor encouraging the feelings he hinted at. Her sobbing folding in on itself, her body no longer heaving against his, but still she held herself close, waiting for him to say more.

"After all, if a banty rooster like Galvez could settle down … I mean …"

With a hint of a smile betraying the giddy lightness in her heart, Angela Buttacavala raised one of her hands and gently pressed her fingers to Legrasse's lips. Then, she closed her eyes and pressed against him all the harder, hoping that the delirium she was experiencing at that moment might last longer than the one she felt when first they met.

VII.

Few members of the Western party did not find the streets of Bombay in some way distressing. Mostly it was the feeling of utter alienation—the distant strangeness of the crowded, winding streets, filled with curious shops and even more curious peoples. A thousand thick and heady scents filled the air, jasmine and lotus and a hundred different curries alone mingled with the smell of the casual animals roaming the city's byways, honored and revered as most of the people around them could never imagine being.

Legrasse and those with him moved through the alien jumble of unintelligible babble and hostility as surreptitiously as possible, ignoring equally the furtive glances and outright cold and curious stares covering them like frost on a November field in Vermont. Even across the country, on the train out of Calcutta headed for Nepal, the travelers found no relief. Despite the rigid enforcement of British parliamentary order by the current ruling class, the subcontinent was not a place hospitable to any additional foreigners—especially those not blessed with English backgrounds and papers. As the members of the invasion force—as Carrinelle had taken to calling the expedition—sat together in their private, but sweltering travel coach, Legrasse outlined their progress to date.

"We're on schedule, but just barely. It isn't going to take much of an interruption to throw everything out the door."

"How much time do we have?" asked Leigh.

"Leaving New Orleans on the fifth of March, our journey to Bombay took us to the thirteenth. We made good time getting everything off the dirigible and onto our first train, which put us in Calcutta on the fifteenth."

"Seems long to me," interrupted Clutts. "I crossed just as much territory back in the States and it didn't take me two days."

"Then thank God you were traveling on an American train," snapped Galvez, "where everyone works on a standard time and the trains get where they're going when they're supposed to get there. From what I can see, we're lucky we didn't have to spend a month just getting from Bombay to here."

"Indeed," added the inspector, "for which I think again we can thank Miss Buttacavala."

"I'd like to thank her for securing this private coach for us," said Professor Webb. "Certainly makes things convenient. Let alone more private."

"I'll second that," added Galvez. Stretched out across several seats, the officer pushed his body deeper into their worn, but still firm wicker. "I find it simply amazing how money seems to make things happen even faster here than at home."

"And less of it, too," said Muller in an almost patronizing tone. Whether Legrasse noted anything in his old compatriot's voice he chose to ignore it, instead turning to the itinerary ahead. He informed the others that the next morning should bring them to Bhatgaon, where once more they would trade their mode of transportation. He confirmed that arrangements had been secured with the McClellen House Trading Company which had guaranteed enough heavy trucks to move them to the mountains. There, at the point where vehicular traffic could progress no further, two score mules would be waiting to transport them to their final destination.

"We will take the mules along this route," the inspector traced his finger across the map he had spread out on the car's central table, "to roughly here— approximately halfway between these prominent peaks, Kanchenjunja and Everest."

"And when we get there?" asked Louis. As the black man stared at Legrasse, the inspector turned to Leigh.

"What do you say, Michael? How best should we proceed against those we hope to find in this lunatic meeting place?"

"In all honesty, Inspector," answered the apprentice, "I think it best we simply kill as many of them as possible while we can."

Clutts hefted his right arm up off the table, giving Leigh a demonstrative thumbs up. Nardi nodded, a bent smile crossing his worn, hard face. Carrinelle and Muller indicated that their feelings were much the same. Galvez, however, stared at the younger man.

"Excuse me," he said, "but what does 'while we can' mean?"

"I can't imagine we'll get too far into their stronghold before we're detected," answered Leigh matter-of-factly. "Once they realize invaders are about, there are all manner of creatures they'll be able to summon to dispatch us."

"What're you sayin', man?" asked Louis.

"I'm saying that once we begin to fall it will happen rather quickly. With the proper amount of good fortune, however, we may be able to thin their ranks sufficiently that they will lack enough bodies to affect the dimensional displacement they're hoping to achieve."

"In English," growled Clutts. "Would ya?"

"If we're lucky," Leigh translated, "we'll kill enough of them to stop the ceremony before they've killed all of us."

"Good Heavens," added Webb. "It sounds as if you mean to say you don't think any of us will survive."

Leigh turned to the professor. The apprentice said nothing, simply staring at Webb with calm resignation. The older man looked deep into the young mystic's eyes, probing them for any sense of jest. After only a few seconds, the professor shuddered deeply, then rose from his seat.

"In my bag," he announced, "I have a bottle of bourbon I had thought to save for our return. For those interested, I am no longer of a mood to preserve it."

With that, the professor waited a moment, testing his legs both against the sinister rolling of the train car as well as his fear they might have become useless from fright. Finding he could move well enough, he launched himself in the direction of the party's luggage. He was not surprised to find many of their group following him.

* *** *

The dark figures worked their way across the top of the train with practiced stealth. As the rambling cars continued along their preordained route through the near-unbroken darkness of the mountain night, the silent, bare-foot crew inched along car after car, seeking the train's private coach. The gang of thugs numbered over thirty—all men tough of limb and cold of heart. Each carried a blade securely in their belt or sash. Some few had even managed to procure a firearm for that night's mission.

With expansive hand gestures calculated to be easily understood even when illuminated only by the occasional burst of starlight that managed to break through the surrounding forest, the leader of the group signaled to his fellows that they had reached the correct car. Forming two rows, the raiders lined up on opposite sides of the car—one man perched above each window. The remainder of the group then split into two parties, one each preparing to enter the private car through the doors found at either end.

The leader was just about to signal for the attack when the train began to lean into an especially long curve. The change in pitch threw the man off balance for only a moment, but it was long enough for disaster to strike his cause. As he threw out his arms to catch his balance, he was forced to grab at the car's roof to steady himself. His fingers struck the heavily lacquered wood only a glancing blow, but it was enough to make the man wonder if he had given away their presence.

Inside the darkened car, surrounded by his sleeping fellows, Bill Clutts stared intently toward a spot on the ceiling somewhat left of the center. He had stayed awake later than the rest—'sitting watch,' as he called it—a shotgun across his lap and a drink in his hand. As he scratched his head, he bit at his upper lip, wondering if he were imagining things. He laughed inside his mind at the notion.

Imagining things, the back of his mind whispered mockingly. No, never anything like that. Never any delusions for us.

Clutts glanced at the ceiling once more, then tossed off the last his drink. Grabbing up his shotgun, he set the empty glass on the table in the center of the car as a sneer crossed his face.

"I don't imagine shit anymore," he snapped. Aiming his weapon at the roof directly over the window before him, he roared, "I know what I know!"

His finger pulled back on the first trigger, releasing the shell in the right-hand barrel of his shotgun. Thousands of pounds of concentrated pressure and a handful of lead smashed their way through the ceiling, splintering the leg of the swarthy thug poised to come in through the window below. The man's surprised screams of pain as he fell away into the darkness alongside the speeding train were matched by the shatter of voices both inside and atop the car. Legrasse and Galvez came awake with weapons in their hands. Clutts pointed through the darkness at the windows, shouting;

"They're comin' in!"

Both officers fired without caution, each sending bullets through the window nearest them. Galvez's slug knocked the man before him completely clean of the train, his fate unknown. Legrasse's bullet tore through the neck of his target. The man floundered awkwardly in the window, grasping at the scarlet arcs spilling out of him.

"Jesus Sweet Savior God Almighty," shouted Nardi. The mobster came up out of the chair in which he had been sleeping, pulling a blunt, heavy .44 Hi-Power from under each arm. In his first sleepy seconds of consciousness he blinked away his fatigue, focusing on the action around him. Following Galvez and Legrasse's examples, he turned toward the windows across from him. Firing instinctively, he set off four precise shots, sending two more of the raiders screaming into the night. Then, as he turned for more targets, the doors at each end of the car burst open and the room filled with screams.

Webb pulled Angela to the floor, the pair huddling behind one of the car's lounge benches along with the mystic apprentice, Leigh. Muller and Louis, both armed with but a pocket knife and an empty bottle between them, stood back to back in the dark car, simply trying to stay alive.

Carrinelle grabbed for his valise, fumbling for it under the bench upon which he had been sleeping. His hand brushed against it, but only knocked it further away. The officer lunged after it, desperate to reach the Colt he had wedged in the bag's open top. His hand made contact with it once more, then his eyes rolled wildly upward into his head as a curved blade was drawn across his neck. Blood splashed the floor and wall, bulging from Carrinelle's throat and his murderer's head as Clutts fired a shotgun blast that cut the invader to meat from the shoulders up.

More men swelled into the car. Voices screamed on both sides of the conflict, but none could hear a thing anymore—everyone in the private coach had gone temporarily deaf from the violent noise of the repeated gun shots. Legrasse and Galvez ignored the commotion as a matter of course, working together as they had years earlier in the fetid back streets of New Orleans. Side by side, one would fire upon the enemy while the other reloaded his weapon. Over the course of some thirty, terribly long seconds they went through twenty-two shells working their way across the car to where so many of their crew were massed. Unfortunately, Nardi had no such system worked out.

Moving away from the others, the mobster had gone single-handedly against the dark figures coming through the back door of the coach. He emptied his .44s with careful calculation, wasting as little ammunition as possible. Of the eight who came through the door, six went down permanently. The other two rushed forward, their long sickle-like blades silent in the dark. One's weapon cut through Nardi's chest, slicing his heart one-third to two-thirds. The other's cut away the side of his head, taking out a scoop holding one eye, one ear and his nose.

"Bastard!"

Louis threw himself forward, clubbing one of the two men with his bottle. The man fell into his companion, but the blow was only casual to the second invader. Side-stepping, he came around his stunned fellow and with a quick move he knocked Louis' bottle away with his Kukri knife, shattering it in the air. Then, Clutts' shotgun emptied once more—two barrels fired simultaneously—and suddenly the battle was ended.

* * * * *

"Well, that could have gone better."

Legrasse ignored his one-time lieutenant's remark, waiting to see what could be learned from the attack. Of the score of men and ten who had tried to kill the group in their sleep, all had been dispatched. One only still clung onto life, but his grip was failing rapidly.

The sole survivor of the attack had been fallen upon immediately by the surviving lawmen. They question the gurgling, dying man in a frenzy, but with no luck. He spoke not English, French, Spanish or German, the only languages open to the three officers. At that point, Webb and Leigh volunteered their services.

The professor needed to listen to the man speak but a few phrases before determining which of the various local dialects he was hearing. After only a minute's questioning, trying out different variations of the man's native tongue, the professor was able to communicate with him directly. At the same time, Leigh sat close to the dying man, quietly holding the fellow's blood soaked hand.

"Ask him where he's from," demanded Legrasse. "Who sent him, why they wanted us dead. Were they just highwaymen—or what we assume them to be?"

Webb chattered at the man in his own odd dialect, the professor's tone sympathetic yet demanding. The man answered in turn, foaming bubbles of scarlet mucus continually growing from his nostrils, breaking with ugly popping sounds ever time he took a breath. The inspector and Galvez both fed the man questions all the while Webb worked with him until finally the professor turned to them, a sorrowful look stretched across his face.

"Forget it, gentlemen—it's over."

"What did he tell you?"

"Not much I'm afraid," responded Webb in a weary voice. "No matter what I asked him, he simply kept repeating the same things."

"Such as?" asked Legrasse.

"Most of the time, he was simply praying ..."

"There's some bullshit," spat Galvez with red anger. "I've heard these scum pray. Where were the references to Cthulhu ... or R'lyeh? Where was the whole ph'nglui mglw'nafh wgah'nagl fhtagn line of crap?"

"I'm afraid you don't understand me," responded the professor. Taking his glasses from his face, the older man indicated the body before him as he answered curtly, "this man was not praying to Cthulhu ... he was praying to God."

Heads turned throughout the car. Angela, who had been tending to the various cuts and scrapes members of their group had sustained, blurted out a question.

"Prayers? Christian prayers?" Her face distorted in the flicker of the coach's oil lamps, Angela snapped in confusion, "But that isn't possible. Is it?"

"They were Hindu prayers," answered Webb. "But they were aimed at saving his soul from damnation."

"Damnation he expected from our demon hands," added Leigh. "I remained in physical contact with our subject during his interrogation. I employed an old technique, which frankly I will admit to not yet having fully mastered. It is usually used to make contact with departed spirits, however, it takes only a tiny stretch to use it to reach the soul of one still alive."

"Forget the mumbo," said Louis. "Is you sayin' yous read his thinking'?"

"In a manner of speaking. But, as I was saying, I believe those impressions I picked up were genuine for it is very difficult for the dying to shield their thoughts."

"And what thoughts did you pick up?" asked Muller.

"This man and his fellows attacked us because they did not want us to reach the Cthulhu cult."

"Well, of course not," snapped Galvez. "I'd say it's fairly obvious the evil bastards don't want anything going wrong with their little plan to destroy the world."

"No, you misunderstand me," answered Leigh. "These people came after us because they believed we were here to help the cult ... that we were in some way the key to everything happening on schedule. As far as our attackers were concerned, *they* were the 'good guys' out to protect the world. *We* were the ones affecting to bring about its end."

Legrasse stared at the apprentice, but the young man merely shrugged his shoulders, spreading his hands wide, palms turned upward, trying to convey his own confused lack of understanding. The inspector sent his senses out as far as he could, trying in his limited, human way to see if he could smell any dishonesty in Leigh, perhaps something of which not even the apprentice himself was aware.

After only a moment, however, Legrasse simply nodded to the younger man and turned away. All his instincts—honed from years of police work in one of humanity's great Meccas of all the worst the species had to offer—told him Leigh was telling the truth.

What now, inspector? the back of his mind purred.

Not knowing how to answer himself, Legrasse went back to his previous task of clearing the last of the bodies from the coach. The others bent to their own chores, cleaning away broken glass and wood, wiping up pools of blood, trying to reassemble their belongings for the next day when they would disembark and head into the mountains.

Despite all of the screams and gunfire, their train had not stopped, or even slowed, in its headlong rush to reach Nepal. The conductor, a heavy man who had maintained his Londonderry accent despite not having seen Irish soil in nearly a score of years, had come to check on the disturbance. He had seemed not surprised at the bodies and blood, allowing that bandits attacking the trains was not in any way unheard of, even under British rule. Shaking his head at the damage to the coach, after a discreet amount of cash had changed hands, he advised they simply toss the bodies and say nothing when they reached Bhatgaon the next morning.

Taking the last body to the rear door of the coach, Legrasse and Clutts took up positions on the opposing cars' coupling platforms and then, on the count of three, pushed the corpse out into the darkness. The left side of the man's body was clipped by the edge of the train as it fell free, the action spinning the broken sack of flesh awkwardly off into the night. The grotesque dance lasted only a split-second before the train moved beyond where the two men could see. Clutts headed back inside to look for more liquor. Legrasse stayed outside.

From his spot between the cars, the inspector could see a wide range of the nighttime sky. Gazing into the black curtain beyond, he stared intently at the shimmering multitude of stars, watching them break the ebony strangle darkening the world.

Which ones? he wondered. Where is this cosmic alignment I keep hearing about?

In his scholarly days, the inspector had maintained a small, private observatory from which he charted the movements of the Heavens. Coldly, rationally, he knew which bodies had to be at what longitudes and latitudes for their celestial gravities to begin their horrible game. He knew the facts of it all to the point where he could have drawn a grid on clear paper, held it to the sky and matched up the points of light one for one without mistake. But his question had nothing to do with science.

"Heaven," he sneered, "where all good things come from."

Snorting a short grunt of dissatisfaction, the inspector pulled together the loose spittle in his mouth and then spat it out into the night.

"And all the demons of Hell, as well."

Then, Clutts' thick, guttural laugh bellowed out through the doorway, shattering Legrasse's contemplation. Looking up into the sky once more, the inspector shook his head sadly, then turned and went back into the coach.

VIII.

Three days more found the travelers deep within the mountains of Nepal. The morning previous they had abandoned their rented trucks, transferring all their provisions, weapons and the such to their waiting mules. Four locals accompanied them as guides, each man checked out by Leigh through the use of his "psychomanic" abilities. All of the quartet seemed to him hardworking and earnest—concerned only with getting their charges to their destination and earning the extravagant wages promised.

As the procession of mules wound its way through the never-ending procession of mountain passes, Legrasse spotted a long stretch of trail where two or even more of the beasts might maneuver side by side. Taking the opportunity offered, he guided his beast forward and alongside the one carrying Angela. Tipping his hat in almost a comical fashion, he smiled, asking;

"Enjoying the view, madame?"

"Being of a mind to give you an honest answer, Mr. Inspector, I would have to say 'yes.'"

With her left hand the woman made a sweeping gesture across the exceedingly wide view afforded the crew at that moment. The panoramic landscape below and beyond was a wild shuffle of rounded peaks—green, shaggy points blending softly one against another. A somber atmosphere hung over the area, still and cool. As the man and woman watched quietly, large black patches rolled across the ground below, shadows cast from the clouds seemingly now only yards above the traveler's heads.

"It is peaceful," admitted Legrasse, breaking the silence. "I'll give it that."

"But you aren't at peace, are you?" The inspector did not answer. Nodding her head slightly, Angela said softly, "There are so many things that could be tearing away at your soul at this moment I scarce know where to begin guessing."

"It is all of them, sweet lady," answered Legrasse. His hollow voice rang with sorrow as he told her, "It is having to throw the body of my friend from the train as if he were just so much garbage. Your man, Nardi, as well.

Whatever his background or his past sins, he was brave and he died nobly. Yet he too we hurled into the darkness like so much trash."

Angela stared at Legrasse, her heart heavy with the pain she could feel pouring off him—a cold shimmer of agony bleeding away from his skin almost scalding to the touch. Fearing not, the woman reached out and touched his exposed hand.

"I know," she whispered. "I also know there is far more troubling you. Tell me what it is."

"I haven't been able to shake what Webb and Leigh were able to wring from that thug we questioned. What if what he said wasn't nonsense? What if there was something to it?" Legrasse's eyes filled with a pain Angela would have thought beyond the hardened police officer. Before she could comment, though, he said something else she would had imagined beyond him. "More than that, what if I've brought you halfway around the world only to get you killed?"

"I remind you, Mr. Inspector," she answered coyly, "it was actually I who brought you here."

"Don't jest, Angela," he said with a soft anger. "When we're finally in the midst of whatever is to come, death will be on all hands, in all forms. Unimaginable forms. It could be when we're put against the darkness to come, the simple, decent ends Carrinelle and Nardi met may be things we'll be praying for."

Legrasse turned full to the woman next to him. Reaching across the way, he took up her hand as he said, "This is the Devil's own we go up against here. There is no imagining what these things might do to us, to our bodies—our minds, our souls. We are facing nightmare beyond all known human experience. I've read about what we're headed into, seen some of it … invisible monsters that tear people limb from limb, bodies turned inside out, used to spawn terrible things, beasts all claw and tentacle   and … things that live within your mind, drooling madness for all of your days followed by an eternity of damnation. Chaos …"

And then, Legrasse squeezed the woman's hand tenderly as he whispered, "A chaos into which I wish you would not enter."

"You make it sound very properly terrible," Angela admitted. "Even Biblical. But then, tell me, if this is to all be so terrible … why are you here?"

"What?" Legrasse turned toward the woman in mild confusion. Still holding her hand, he sputtered, "W—What do you mean?"

"I mean to ask of you exactly what I did—knowing all these terrible things … why are you here?"

"I, I have to be," the inspector stumbled in a nervous, trapped voice. "I don't have a choice. Not to cloak myself in grandiosity, but this is my destiny."

"Why?" asked Angela in all seriousness. "Who appointed you St. George to slaughter this particular dragon? Your domain was one small and wretched quarter of New Orleans. When were you promoted to policing the universe?"

Legrasse opened his mouth, but found no words waiting within. As he struggled to assemble an answer, Angela told him, "I am very pleased you have grown so concerned over my welfare, good sir. Indeed, it makes the staying so much more bearable. But stay I must, for the same reasons as yourself."

Gently stroking the inspector's captured hand with her free one, she told him, "You feel a natural duty to protect the innocent against all evil. I have a duty as well, to make up for the sins of my family. You hid from your responsibility as long as you could, but when the face of what was coming was presented, you rose to the challenge. Like Galvez, leaving his family to be with you. Like Carrinelle and Muller, following you as they always have."

Legrasse made to speak, but Angela flooded the air between them with a torrent of words.

"Even as Louis and poor Ernesto followed me. As Leigh does his master's bidding. Just as the professor follows his duty to science and knowledge. Even Mr. Clutts, he seeks the death he earned for himself, but his duty to, to what—himself? God? Destiny? Whatever, it makes him seek something grander than a firing squad or the end of a rope. He could have ignored us in New Orleans. Or he could have abandoned us once we got him out of the country. He didn't, though. He's still here. As are we all."

Legrasse's eyes filled with a thankful sorrow. As he again searched for words, Angela smiled.

"We know what's ahead. But we also know that if we do nothing, the world dies. You are too much of a true warrior to settle back and allow all to perish without at least trying to stop it."

"And you, sweet lady?" asked Legrasse.

"At first, I admit, I joined into this for the chance at mere self-respect, at putting my father's name to the side of the angels."

"Yes …" questioned the inspector, not vain enough to suspect the rest of her answer. "And now?"

"And now," she told him, her smile demure, yet sparkling, "now I ride willingly into damnation itself, as long as I can do it at your side."

Legrasse's head shot upward slightly, sharply—eyes wide—his shock revealed by the rapid wave of tension that flashed through his body. Sensing his sudden discomfort, Angela jerked her hand away with pained sorrow. She began a flustered comment, but Legrasse reached past her words, his hand tenderly cupping her chin. Quieting her protests with a gentle look, he told her;

"Forgive an old warhorse, my dear, but your words were only rejected by my disbelief that you could be serious." Taking her hand again, he asked, only half-joking, "I mean, if I understood you correctly, you were referring to you and I ... as if there could be something ... a woman such as yourself, young, intelligent, beautiful ... and me. Well ..."

Taking her turn, Angela silenced her partner with a finger touched briefly to his lips. Stroking the sides of his moustache in turn, she answered,

"Say not a word against yourself, John Raymond. You are respected, noble, courageous—an honest man and a hero both beloved and feared. You're every woman's dream." And then, after a wicked giggle, she added, "besides, while I will admit to being both intelligent and beautiful, I'm not nearly as young as your gentlemanly eyes see me."

The two looked at each other for a long moment, their smiles warm and hopeful, their minds blessed with the marvelous human ability to forget for a moment where they were and why they were there. Riding silently as their mules lumbered over the broken mountain terrain, whether miles were traveled, or mere yards, neither knew. Eventually, however, reality came crashing back into their midst, the two suddenly remembering to what point their lives had come. Balancing the horrors ahead against the expansive joy he felt growing within himself, the inspector said;

"Bless you, sweet lady, for such grand foolishness. If I can somehow survive this nightmare I will move every remaining Heaven in my path, and any Hells there might be there as well, to find your side. And, once there, I shall stay all of my days as content as a big dog on a warm porch."

Angela smiled. How emotion could have grown between the two of them—between any two people in such circumstances—neither could fathom. But, that they were happy with the knowledge of that which had passed between them there was no doubting. Feeling a boldness beyond measure, the inspector leaned far over in his thin, blanket saddle and pecked a small kiss on Angela's cheek.

He laughed as she blushed, then begged her leave and began slowing his mount so as to fall back in line once more. Reaching the end of their column, he pulled alongside Clutts. Suddenly, a great many things had fallen in place within his mind, and the hulking loner seemed just the person to whom he needed to talk.

* * * * *

Already far enough above sea level to have begun feeling the cold quite keenly, despite their proximity to the equator, the travelers huddled close together around their evening campfire. Their quartet of Sherpas sat at their own fire, smoking a mixture of herbs and leaves in their long, hand carved pipes. The men were old experienced hands at guiding foreigners through the surrounding mountains.

They did find the destination of this group odd, however, situated as it was between the two most common points of interest to outsiders. It was true that the plateau toward which they were headed did see a certain amount of traffic, but it was normally conducted by locals—and unsavory folk at that. The spot had various dark stories told about it, but they meant little to the guides. All the men had heard wild and terrible stories about almost every spot of any interest throughout the Himalayas—had made some of the tales up themselves.

Still, they found the group from America different than any other they had seen before. That a woman traveled with them was certainly novel. But there was far more. The party was obviously not composed of climbers. The one man was so fat the Sherpas had continually switched his mule so as not to tire any one animal out unto its death. The group was also far too heavily armed to be interested in mere sport, in chasing animals or challenging themselves against the elements. Most of those who had come through the area over the years were such laughable simpletons, spending kings' ransoms to risk their lives. Not these people, though. This group, thought the four guides, they were after something. Something valuable—something for which they were obviously willing to kill a great many people. A goal like that, the Sherpas all agreed, they could respect.

Around their own fire, Legrasse and the others worked out their upcoming schedule. From what maps they had available to them, it seemed that they should be able to reach their objective before the date of the ceremony which they sought to stop. They would simply have to keep pushing on, using every bit of strength and every ounce of daylight which they had available to them.

"As long as we keep breaking camp in the dark so that we're ready to get underway as soon as dawn arrives," said Legrasse, "and then keep moving all day, we should be able to make it."

"Yes," added Leigh. The only one who could speak to the guides in their own tongue outside of Professor Webb, he said, "the Sherpas are fairly impressed with our speed. They could, of course, go much faster without us, but for gua'lo—"

"What?" asked Muller.

"Oh, ah—Chinese word, means outsiders, foreign devils, ghosts ..."

"Ghosts?" snapped Galvez. "We're not dead yet, you know."

"Oh—no, no," Leigh corrected himself in embarrassment. "I'm sorry. You see, our guides are Mongolians. They share many common concepts with the Chinese. One such is the notion that they are a chosen people, a central people to the existence of the world, and that all outsiders are only pale imitations of them—ghosts, not true people—to them we're basically soulless creatures."

"I get it," laughed Clutts. "We're their niggers."

"Heh," snickered Louis. "Now maybe you'all can get an idea o'what it feels like."

Legrasse smiled wryly. Instantly Galvez began making jokes. Webb knew what Leigh had really meant, of course, but he allowed the group their fun. The apprentice made to correct the erroneous assumption, but his educated attempts to do so only spurred the rest of the group on to greater heights of hilarity. The eight laughed over a score of different topics after that, for once their evening passing with the enormous weight of what they were doing lifted from their shoulders. Each of them knew what the morrow would bring, of course. And each of them ignored it with deliberate ease.

* * * * *

Finally the merriment left the crew and they separated to assemble their bed rolls and get some sleep. Legrasse and Angela, designated as the first watch, took their positions around the dwindling campfire. Checking his pocket watch, the inspector assured Webb and Muller that he would rouse them in two hours to take their place. The added strain of their extended session after dinner joking around the fire, coupled with the thinner atmosphere of the mountains, worked to quickly put the others to sleep. Indeed, Clutts' snoring was echoing throughout the mountains before some of the others had even pulled their blankets about themselves.

At the fire, Angela clutched her own wrap in front of her, pulling it tight across her shoulders. Checking the shotgun he had chosen for that evening's sentry duty, Legrasse made certain it was loaded and ready. Putting it aside, he turned to his companion.

"It was a quite brazen thing you did today," she said to him. "Kissing me for all the world to see."

"My apologizes, sweet lady," answered Legrasse. "Although it excuses nothing, I can but plead that I was helpless before the impulse of the moment."

Leaning toward the inspector, Angela smiled, saying, "Hummmm, well, I suppose I could call that as good an excuse as any."

Her eyes wide open, the woman paid Legrasse back in kind. Ignoring the possibilities for disaster that might be all about, the inspector concentrated on the reality before him. Shoving death and horror from his mind, he thought for once not of the future, or the past, or even the present. Killing thought, banishing it from his world, Legrasse lived through a series of shattered seconds, jagged but indeterminable lengths of time which flooded his barren life with waves of passionate joy. All around the pair the mountains remained dark and still, taking no notice of the last happy moment the two hopelessly desperate people would ever share.

IX.

Some days later the small group found itself climbing. Their mules and two of the Sherpas left behind in a small encampment, the others had thrown themselves forward into forcing their way upward into the mountains. Snow and ice hampered them at every turn. Their guides picked the most expedient routes possible, but even with the pair of experienced hands forging their way, carving out easily-reached handholds and stretching knotted ropes down the sheer cliff walls, the group struggled slowly.

The younger and more fit members of the party did not have too much difficulty. Legrasse, Leigh and Angela made fairly good time while Galvez surprised everyone by possessing a natural ability no one, including the Spaniard himself, would have suspected. Louis, however, who simply hated the cold, found the going tougher with every yard conquered, as did the older Muller. Webb, familiar with mountain climbing, but older by far than any of the others in the party, began to have a terrible amount of difficulty as the altitude grew higher.

Far more than the professor, however, Clutts had an increasing amount of trouble. Falling further and further behind, the large man rejected all offers of extra help, extolling the others to make as much distance as possible. Clutts steadfastly refused to be the cause of the team losing ground. In the end, that nobility led to what seemed later to be inevitable disaster.

At one particularly steep cliff face, the group was spread out over a distance of some twelve hundred feet. Legrasse and one of the Sherpas at the head of the party were followed by Muller, the strategy being that while they secured and protected each new gain, this slower member of the party would set the group pace. Galvez followed behind the older officer to lend a hand when needed to his former comrade-in-arms. Louis and Angela helped each other along in the next slot, followed by the second Sherpa whose duty it was to shepherd Webb along safely. Leigh held the spot behind them, helping with Webb, but keeping an eye on Clutts who demanded the last position.

"Hey," he had chuckled, "if I fall everyone at my back is goin' with me, so I think I'd better be the one takin' the last seat on this bus."

Leigh had reported the day before that Clutts seemed to be having greater and greater difficulty in maintaining the same pace as the rest of the group, even with Muller and Webb slowing things as they were. Ironically, because of the relatively moderate pace being set, what happened that day caught almost all members of the party off guard.

The lead Sherpa had called a halt to the climb as he scouted ahead for another solid spot from which to launch their next—possibly their final—

assault. The group heartily welcomed the pause. All of them knew that the plateau they sought was only a few hundred yards above. Even though there was still a glacier field to cross once they reached the summit, they knew the worst of things was almost over. Pushing their backs into the mountainside so as to rest their aching arms and legs, most everyone gulped down large draughts of the thin but pure air. And then, when the climbers above were all at their most relaxed, disaster struck. From somewhere below Leigh's position, Clutts bellowed wildly, his voice tinged with rage and fear.

"Jesus Mother a'God! The ledge—the ledge!!"

At the same time, Leigh was slammed forward onto the ground, the rope knotted around his waist pulling him forward at disastrous speed. His face slashed by the ice, eyes filled with snow, he found himself being dragged rapidly toward the edge of the icy outcropping upon which he had stopped. Digging his heels and fingers in against the terrible weight pulling him toward oblivion, he screamed to Clutts.

"What's happened down there? Are you all right?!"

"The damn ledge," Clutts screamed. "It broke away—just fell out from under me. I'm hanging here—oh, God, I'm just hanging!"

Leigh tried to see over the edge, tried to drag himself to a safer position, tried to dig his fingers and toes in deeper. He found he could do nothing. Clutts' weight had him trapped. There was nothing the apprentice could do except wait to see if Clutts managed to grab hold of the mountainside again, or if he would fall to his death along with Clutts if the larger man failed to regain his perch.

"I'm gonna try to swing myself back," screamed Clutts, some of the panic washed from his voice. "Can you hold me?"

"I'll do it," shouted Leigh. "I can do it. Just get yourself back to us."

Long tense moments dragged by as Leigh strained desperately to hold his position, the rope around his waist cutting him cruelly. Up and down the line, members of the party shouted back and forth, letting each other know what was happening. Both Galvez and the second Sherpa started working their way back down the mountain once they realized what the problem was below. Leigh could see them, far above, moving slowly down the cliff face. Shutting his eyes against the pain of Clutts' weight pulling at him—seemingly threatening to slice his body in two—the apprentice shouted encouragement.

"Hang on, Clutts. Even if you can't make it back. Help is coming."

But then, Leigh lost his hold and slid a terrible two and a half feet further toward the edge of his perch. He cursed himself for screaming, but for a split second he had thought the inability of his frozen fingers and failing muscles had doomed both himself and Clutts. Swift desperation lending him a moment of incredible strength, the apprentice slammed his fist against the icy ledge and shattered enough of it to create a handhold. His index finger dislocated from the impact, but he ignored the pain. Digging his gloved fingers down into the crack, he hung on as tightly as possible, waiting for the moment when Clutts' weight would tear at him once more. The moment never arrived.

After several seconds, Leigh realized that something was terribly wrong. He screamed Clutts' name, but gained no response. Logic battering down fear, he chased the panic from his brain. After only a second of thought, he realized that no great jerk was coming. Clutts' weight had ceased pulling on him. The rope holding them together was now slack and limp.

Realizing suddenly the terrible truth, Leigh sat up and began to pull on the rope. He gathered it in a yard at a time with incredible ease, meeting no resistance whatsoever. After a few moments, the split and ragged end of the rope snapped up over the rock edge and the notion he had tried so desperately to push away came crashing in on him.

Clutts was gone.

* **** *

"There was no more you could have done," concluded Legrasse. Putting his gloved hand softly on Leigh's shoulder, he worked to console the younger man, telling him, "Don't torture yourself over this, lad. After all, it's not like any of us are really expecting to go home again."

"Stop saying that!"

Leigh shot up from his crouching position, knocking the inspector's hand away. With sudden violence he swung his balled fist at Legrasse's head. His wild blow missed, however, the force of the swing sending the apprentice sliding madly across the ice. As everyone stared, Leigh picked himself up and limped back to that night's meager campfire. The blaze was small, having been made with the last of the wood carried up the cliff faces on the Sherpa's backs. Sitting close to it, his hands wrapped about his knees, the apprentice trembled violently, his mournful eyes crusting with tears. When the inspector inquired as to why he was so much more upset over Clutts' death than he had been those who died in the attack on the train, the younger man told him.

"How can you be so calm? About dying? You talk as if you're looking forward to it."

"Not really," responded Legrasse in a faraway voice. "Not anymore. I suppose I've simply become resigned to it."

"Naw—da man's right, Inspector," added Louis. Looking up, his eyes cold and unblinking, the chauffeur said, "The way you go on likes dat—it's creepy. Likes we got no chance. I means, if we got no chance—then what the Hell we doin' here—freezing', dyin' one by one? What—what's da point?"

Galvez stood then, staring at Louis. Holding up his left hand, he extended a single finger in the chauffeur's direction. Wagging it back and forth, he said softly, "Now, now, let's not get excited, friend. After all, what better do you think you'd be doing back home tonight anyway?"

"Playin' cards, gettin' drunk—how do I know? Don't even know what damn day it is anymore. Just knows I'd be warm and I wouldn't be talking' 'bout dyin' all the time."

"Listen to me," snapped Legrasse. "All of you. Mr. Clutts is gone and that is unfortunate. Mr. Nardi and Mr. Carrinelle have perished as well. Tomorrow it could be any one of us. When we reach our destination it could be us all. Most likely will be."

Stepping close to the fire, staring down at Leigh and Louis whom coincidence had placed side by side, the inspector pointed toward them as he continued, saying, "So you had better get it out of your heads that this is anything but what it is. The fate of the world is on the scales and in our hands. Do you understand that? *Do you?!*"

Louis crawled backward several paces, his fear of Legrasse far greater than any terror their destination held for him or his desire to stay near the meager warmth of their fire. Leigh simply stared, ashen and shaking.

"We came here to stop these madmen from turning our world over to devils. Leigh, Zarnak must have taught you something by now—remind these rest of what lies ahead." When the apprentice hesitated, Legrasse reached down and smacked him a stinging open-hand blow across the face. "Tell them!"

"Tell them what?" demanded Leigh, his voice shatter by the timbre of tears.

"Tell them of Cthulhu. Tell them of the millions who will die in never-ending slaughter. Tell them of the oceans of blood that lie ahead. Of the centuries of mad darkness. Tell them about the twisted, fantastic shapes that will rule human destiny, that will consider the very planets of our solar system their playthings. Tell them!"

Legrasse reached down again and, grabbing hold of the younger man's coat, jerked him upward onto his feet. As Leigh looked forward into the inspector's face, he saw a strained mask of unblinking violence. Fresh tears burst forth from the younger man's eyes. His nerves shattered, his courage evaporated like warm water droplets sliding across a heated skillet.

"El Grande," said Galvez quietly, touching Legrasse's elbow with apprehension. "I think you've made your point."

The inspector's fingers snapped open. As Leigh fell backwards, Legrasse whirled toward his former lieutenant.

"Do you think I want to die?" he demanded.

"No, J. R.," answered the Spaniard honestly. "No more so than I. It's just the cards we've drawn. And it's a crummy hand, there's no denying that. But, what else were we to do?"

Stepping away from Legrasse, Galvez reached down and caught Leigh's arm.

Helping the younger man to his feet, he brushed some of the crusted snow fragments from his back, saying, "You're the only one here I feel sorry for. We came because we had to. You came because someone told you to."

"No," answered Leigh, still somewhat shaken. "Dr. Zarnak didn't force me to come." When Galvez arched one eyebrow at his response, the apprentice continued. "He was going to come himself, but I begged to take his place."

"Listen to this, El Grande," said Galvez with an astonished smile spread across his face. Laughter filling his throat, he added, "This one's crazier than us."

"The Doctor's work was too important for him to leave it for so long. Someone else had to be here for the moment of transference. You agreed, Inspector," Leigh said, pointing at Legrasse. Tears still falling from his eyes, freezing on his hairless cheeks, he blubbered, "you said it was the best way. But neither one of you said I was going to *die!*"

"Sorry I didn't mention it."

The anger flooding out of Legrasse, he reached out his arms and took the younger man by the shoulders. Suddenly speaking without passion, the terror drained from him, he said, "And I'm sorry I let my temper spill out over you. It was bound to happen, I suppose—you just happened to be closest when it did." Releasing his hold, Legrasse nodded to the younger man, holding his eye even as he spoke to all assembled.

"But," he said, "still, we all need to be ready. This is no penny dreadful. The plain and awful truth is that we stand but little chance to succeed, and even if we do manage to stop the ceremony ahead, surviving beyond that is most likely a near impossible thing. We all must be ready to go into this as if there is no chance for survival."

"But why?" asked Webb. "Why must we approach this with such fatalism?"

"Because," said Muller, surprising everyone by speaking up, "hope of survival will breed terror within us over the prospect of dying. Men who have no hope of life are fearless in the face of death."

"Thank you, Randolf," said Legrasse with quiet gratitude. Releasing Leigh from the fierce hold of his gaze, the inspector said, "we're about to face things, the very sight of which can freeze a man in his tracks, whose gaze alone can pitch the human mind forward into the darkest madness. We can afford none of the usual human luxuries—no compassion, no ethics, no feelings whatsoever. When we reach our destination, we must kill everything in our way, everything in sight. We must not stop, we must not think. We must only react."

No one replied. One by one, those around the pitifully small fire entered their tents and tried to sleep. None of them found much success.

* *** *

The crossing of the plateau was a nightmarish struggle. The glacier was broad and treacherous—a vast expanse of slick death for which Legrasse and his party were vastly unprepared. As the group struggled through the arduous trek, they applauded their enemies in the choosing of the site for their stronghold. Throughout the journey progress was hampered not only by the instability of the slippery ice field, but also by the blinding sunlight reflected a thousand times over from every angle. Indeed, if their guides had not packed them all pairs of handmade snow goggles, they would never have been able to complete the crossing.

They were simply-made, but sophisticatedly designed things. Carved alternately of wood, bone and even from antler, they were contoured to fit the face snugly so that no light could reach the eyes except through their narrow slits. Their hollowed out insides were even smoked black to eliminate the chance of internal reflection. Professor Webb had seen such devices in his travels often enough, but the others marveled over their design for quite some time. Eventually, though, an appreciative silence set in and the grueling trip across the glacier continued.

Long before that journey could be completed, however, the group spotted something that brought their assault to a momentary standstill. Late in the afternoon of their second day, one of the Sherpas informed Legrasse through Professor Webb that he and his companion would be leaving. When pressed for an explanation, the man pointed forward, repeating that he would go no further.

While Galvez broke out his spy-glass to search the cliff wall ahead, Legrasse continued to speak to their guides through Webb.

The man and his partner, the Sherpa explained patiently, had been willing to guide the Americans to the vicinity of the Tsang Plateau. Now that it was in sight, however, neither of them having any desire to die, they would be returning to the edge of the glacier immediately. There they would wait one week. If the inspector and his party did not return by then, they would forfeit the second half of their pay and descent to the base camp where they left their fellows. They would wait there one additional week before returning to Nepal, on the off chance some of the party might survive.

"'Survive?'" responded Legrasse. The inspector knew what the man meant, but asked anyway, "and what does he mean by that?"

Webb posed the question, then translated the answer.

"He asks that you not pretend to not know where you are going, John. Shall I tell him that you've suddenly remembered?"

Legrasse eyed the professor and then the Sherpa. Stepping forward, he took the grizzled Mongolian's gloved hand in his own and shook it soundly. Staring the man in the eye, he said, "You've done an excellent job, my friend. You and your fellows are brave men all. I want you to know that if, in three days time, the sun rises again, that it will be no accident, and that you will be as responsible as any for that happy moment."

Webb took several minutes to translate the inspector's words. When he finished, the Sherpa stood up straight, stretching his short, bent body to its fullest. Opening his jacket, he pulled forth a stone disc—an amulet made of a light green jade shot through with veins of silver. Carved into the flat surface on both sides was a pattern consisting of three concentric circles. Each of the circles was surrounded by a never-ending string of characters, delicate figures carved into the rock and then inlaid with the same silver running through the jade. Instinctively knowing he was being given something the man believed to be of great power, Legrasse slipped the amulet's silver chain over his head, tucking the whole affair inside his coat.

"Inform our friend," he told Webb, "that I am greatly touched by his generosity, and honored by his contribution to our cause. Tell him that if it is at all possible, I shall see he gets this back."

The professor delivered the message. The Sherpa smiled, then responded, causing Webb to grin warmly.

"What did he say—doesn't he want it back?"

"Our friend says that if we succeed in returning, he will no longer need it."

Legrasse smiled broad and wide. Shaking hands with the Sherpa once more, he watched the man join his partner and begin their journey back to the glacier's edge. Afterward he turned to Galvez, asking what he might have found. The officer handed the inspector his eye glass, pointing him in the right direction. Legrasse scanned the horizon for only a few seconds before spotting what obviously had to be their objective.

Some three miles across the ice there stood a passageway carved into the side of the cliff. It stood large and ominous, a black maw offering no clue as to what lay beyond its threshold. The wall to both sides and above it was ornately carved—hundreds of sculptures of hideous creatures intertangled one atop the other stretched in all directions. There was no reason or logic to the sprawling bas-relief. The artists had simply worked where they wanted for as long as they wished, following some utterly alien design sense, meandering off across the cliff wall in wildly twisting loops, stopping wherever they cared to halt.

Still too far away to make out much in the way of specific details, Legrasse returned his companion's spy glass and told the others they needed to get moving once more. As they resumed their cautious march, Galvez asked, "Don't you find it odd that door is at the right level?"

"What do you mean, Joseph?"

"This glacier—it covered this area a million years ago, correct? And yet that doorway looks to be at just the right level. I know this thing's been melting slowly over the centuries, but still, isn't this all a little too convenient?"

Agreeing with his former lieutenant, Legrasse requested Galvez return the spy glass for a moment. Studying the doorway once more, the inspector began moving the magnifier steadily along the horizon, scrutinizing the cliff wall in all directions. After a while, he nodded to himself, handing the glass back to his friend.

"No mystery, Joseph," he said. "Look far to the left and then the right."

Galvez did as Legrasse instructed. After a long while, suddenly everything became clear to him. Quietly, he collapsed his spy glass and returned it to its case. Spotting the inspector staring at him, he nodded his head with a nervous twitch. When Muller voiced what everyone in the party was wondering, Legrasse stretched out his arm and pointed.

"Do you see in the far distance—to both sides—how the ice slopes upward, as if this section of the glacier were a crescent valley of some   sort ..."

Angela's hands automatically made the sign of the cross. Forcing herself not to stutter, she gazed in horror out over the hundreds of thousands of tons of missing ice and said, "You mean ... it was melted clear?"

"Apparently so, sweet lady."

One by one the various members of the party gathered up their packs and bed rolls and started forward once more. At that point there simply was nothing else left to do.

* * * * *

Night had come, but the group did not stop. Close to the horrid entrance, they kept moving onward in hopes of reaching its possible shelter during the night. There was some small hope of utilizing the element of surprise as well, but such was an emotion born of desperation. Legrasse harbored no illusions over being able to catch the cultists unawares. The mere men amongst them, these could be tricked. But, those agents of the beyond in their thrall, such things he knew could not be surprised.

And even if they could, he thought, *there are still the Bla'raff ... well, probe all you want you monsters. We still have some secrets.*

And then, a terrible shriek pierced the star-pricked blackness all around. As Legrasse and his people stumbled blindly, a score of terrible, unfathomable shapes descended upon them. Long and twisted they were, serpentine lengths held aloft by the aide of black rubbery wings of singularly monstrous dimensions. The horrible creatures fell on the group, one or two of them attacking each member of the party as needed. In mere seconds, all had been captured, wrapped around by the great viperous creature's tails, or held fast in their foul, clawed appendages.

None of the party had time to grab their weapons, to even think, before they were hoisted aloft by the hunting horrors. The creatures shook their captives violently, knocking any objects they might be holding from their hands, tearing their backpacks away from their bodies. In seconds they were not only all aloft, but being borne forward at terrible speed. The creatures moved in single file, bearing their captives toward the great black hole in the ice wall beyond. In moments they were passing through it, one after another, those trapped within their grasp helpless to resist.

Legrasse ceased his struggles the moment he was flown through the doorway. Instantly the inspector began taking mental notes of where they were, mapping their surroundings for future reference. Considering their theory of how the doorway had been uncovered, he was not surprised to find the temperature within the cavern extremely higher than that outside. Nor was he surprised at what he saw all about him.

As they descended through the great length of the tunnel a harsh luminescence given off by a series of massive, uncut crystals embedded in the walls lit the way. They came in a variety of colors, all of them somber unto the point of being unhealthy—cancerous. What they illuminated, however, was far more suggestive of that same condition.

As Legrasse and his fellows were moved through the passageway, they saw that the walls and floor and ceiling were adorned with a cruel mosaic, one both elaborate and psychotic in design. All about the sickly glowing crystals, covering every free inch, lie a pattern depicting a mad jumble of images, one growing into the other, none of it designed with any plan inspired by human mind. Worse yet, the materials used were all human bones.

Skulls, hands and feet had been reduced to their component parts and used accordingly. Encrusted with stringy ribbons of a slowly pulsating, purplish moss, the bone-work stood as a chill road sign of what must be awaiting the group. The captives had little time to speculate upon their immediate fates, however. After only a few seconds the party arrived at their destination.

Coming into a large central chamber, the hunting horrors hovered for a moment over a complex stone pattern set in the center of the room's vast floor. Surrounding the design were five poles, tall, strong things, each with a set of manacles hanging from their apex. After only a brief glance about the dimly lit chamber, Legrasse and the others were jerked abruptly sideways and held above a deep pit off to one side. Then, they were suddenly released one by one to fall into the dark circle below. As the captives fell, the flying monsters departed through a tunnel leading off through the ceiling the instant their task was completed.

In the pit, Legrasse untangled himself from Muller who had been dropped atop him. Making his way to his feet, he willed himself to ignore the pain of his bruises.

"You, up there," he shouted, letting the full force of his anger bubble to the surface. "Show yourselves!"

Padded footsteps were heard in immediate response. After a few moments, the chamber above began to glow with spots of light all coming from different directions. From somewhere above, an unusual voice called to the captives.

"Please excuse us, Inspector—we're a trifle busy at the moment."

Everyone in the pit stopped what they were doing, frozen by the voice. It was familiar to them all, though some element within it kept any from knowing why. A cold thing it was, frozen with a slowness that chilled the listeners, as if its words were not created by human design, but rather were things filtered to them from an open grave.

"You had us worried, Inspector. It wasn't at all certain you would arrive on time."

"What do you mean?" snapped Galvez abruptly, irritated by his inability to identify the voice from above. Keep it talking, he told himself, saying aloud, "You didn't know we were coming."

"Of course we did, Joseph. We've known everything from the very beginning. How could we not? After all, we're the ones that extended the invitation to this moment of glorious fulfillment."

Listening closely to the words coming from above, Professor Webb whispered to Legrasse, "I don't think that's one person's voice. I believe we're hearing two voices speaking in tandem."

"Explain yourself," demanded the inspector of the speakers, nodding to Webb as he did so.

"Really, Inspector, if we must play games … you have been a thorn in the eye of our vision whenever it has been aimed at this puny sphere. With the stars having reached their final zenith, it was decided that no further chances would be taken with you. The Bla'raff were dispatched to infect you weeks ago."

"So I am the one carrying a Bla'raff?" asked Legrasse.

"It was soon apparent to us that you could block the Bla'raff's sendings from us, but your companions … well, seeing is believing."

And, as the dead voice intoned the enigmatic phrase, suddenly there came a sextet of sparking explosions, thick, purplish light roiled out of not only Legrasse, but Muller, Angela, Galvez, Webb and Louis as well. The twinkling displays blasted upward with vicious speed, disappearing up and over the edge of the pit. Those who had been infected with the Bla'raff staggered from the sudden extractions, most barely able to keep their feet, some falling to the hard-packed earthen floor.

"As if such chances would be tolerated any longer concerning yourself, Inspector. No," the voice answered, "our respect for you has grown according to your propensity for thwarting us. We used our pets to guide your every step toward us."

"All of us?" asked the inspector with no little concern.

"All but the magician," answered the intertwined voices. "His trinkets made him to risky. Nor the fat one."

207

"Clutts?"

"Yes, by the time he joined you, we had believed your crew settled upon. He was another of your surprises. But, circumstance eliminated him for us. Not that we were worried about one insignificant human."

"Why not?" asked Leigh with confusion. "As you yourself said, the Inspector has had more success stopping your entry to this plane than any living mortal in all of history. Why would you bring him here?"

"Retribution," sneered the hollow voice. "Too many times has he stood in our way. Thus, it was decided the easiest way to neutralize him would be to allow him to believe he was in command. Rather than thwart him, we encouraged, removed barriers. The poles here above, the altars upon which you shall be sacrificed so that R'lyeh may rise once more, so that great Cthulhu may awaken and begin his never-ending reign anew, needed to be fed. How glorious to feed them with our most persistent enemy!"

"I counted five poles," called out Webb. Also puzzled by the familiarity of the mysterious voice, he tried to help the others keep it talking by asking, "but there are seven of us, and more that five made this journey. If you indeed invited us, why did you invite so many?"

"Like Sunday dinner, Professor," answered the hollow voice. "You always make more than you need to ensure against embarrassment. But you are correct. There are now too many of you."

A strange trilling noise was heard then, followed by a clattering shuffle scraping along the bony floor above as if in response. As the group looked upward, two crested, cylindrical heads poked their way over the edge above. Then suddenly, a pair of creatures one could only describe as armored worms, both covered with a stiff fringe, launched themselves downward. Dropping with a frightening aim, they burst through the chests of Webb and Louis, killing them instantly. Blood splattered everywhere as the terrible grotesqueries continued on out through their victims' backs, driving into the floor and disappearing as quickly as they came.

The rest of the group stood momentarily frozen in horror, staring at the bodies of their companions as they folded in upon themselves and crumpled to the floor. Shaking with anger, Legrasse raised his balled first to the ceiling and bellowed.

"Show yourself, you cowardly bastard!"

A pair of figures came to the edge of the pit and stared down at the captives below. Between them the two possessed only three eyes, for the one had a good third of its head scooped away. It did not matter, however. The trio of glazed eyes actually saw no one for they were but puppets being manipulated by some other intelligence. Nonetheless, the reanimated corpses of Joel Carrinelle and Ernesto Nardi answered Legrasse in their toneless harmony.

"Really, Inspector, calm yourself. The end will be here soon enough, and you will have finally played your destined role in the return of great Cthulhu."

And then, the figures turned and walked back to rejoin the Tcho-Tcho cultists preparing for the final sacrifice, the faraway force controlling them confident that the bothersome Inspector Legrasse had been dealt with once and for all.

X.

Half an hour later, the five survivors huddled together off to one side of the pit in which they had been imprisoned. Legrasse looked at the meager pile of objects on the ground at his feet, his mouth drawn into a tight line.

"So, that's it, then?"

"Looks like it," answered Galvez.

The group had gone through all their pockets, looking for anything that might help them escape their fate and possibly reverse the tables on their captors. They had, of course, gone through Louis and Webb's clothing as well. The survivors regretted their ransacking of the dead, but they striped the bodies and turned the corpses' pockets inside out nonetheless. As ammunition for a major assault, what they found was not much.

Between all of them, they found they were in possession of only two pistols, with rounds enough for but some two score shots. Three knives did they have between them, as well as one of Leigh's star stones. After that, their find was reduced to a quantity of coins, several watches, two lighters, Galvez's spy glass, some handkerchiefs and a few rings. Taking the pistols one in each hand, Legrasse distributed one each to Galvez and Muller.

"No arguments, lads," he said. "Divide the ammunition between you. Be quick about it."

Handing the star stone to Leigh, he passed one of their knives to the apprentice as well, handing the second to Angela while keeping the last for himself. At the same time he instructed Muller and Galvez to return to the pile of clothing left over from the search of their friends.

"Find some appropriate sections of cloth or leather for making a few saps," he said. "Get their belt buckles, belts, too, their boot heels, as well. We'll need the weight." While the officers busied themselves, the inspector turned his attention to Leigh. "Did you note the transfer point when we were brought inside?"

"I believe so," answered the apprentice.

"You've mentioned this before," said Angela. "What is it?"

"When the cultists cast their spell to raise R'lyeh, the energy created by the ceremony has to be sent to the site where it is needed. In the distant past, through a combination of magic and other-worldly science, portals were opened at various sites around the Earth which can be used to transport cargo or passengers from one to another instantaneously. When the proper words are spoken, one can move to any other of these spots at will, even to those set on other planets."

Angela simply stared at Leigh, her mind reeling as it tried to process the information it had just been given. At the same time, Muller and Galvez returned from their further looting of the dead's belongings. Legrasse inspected the segments of cloth chosen for the saps. Nodding in approval, he worked with the officers on their desperate project and, after a few minutes time, they had transformed their remaining booty into a trio of highly effective bludgeons. Taking one for himself, he told Galvez and Muller to keep the others. Then, as armed as they were ever going to be, the inspector asked Leigh to explain what would come next.

"As best I can predict," the apprentice said, "the cultists should begin their ceremony close to three o'clock in the morning—the moment of greatest darkness. Once the portal to R'lyeh has been opened, they will chain us to the surrounding poles. We will be tortured, our fear used to anchor the portal so that Cthulhu can return to this world."

"Wrong tense, kid," whispered Galvez. "Sounds to me like they're opening their damn doorway now!"

"*Ph'nglui mglw'nafh Cthulhu R'lyeh wgah'nagl fhtagn.*"

"In his house in R'lyeh," translated Legrasse automatically, his intestines going cold, fingers clenching into fists, "dead Cthulhu waits a dreaming."

"Good," said Galvez, smacking his sap against the palm of his hand. "Let's do something about keeping him that way."

Instantly the five survivors moved toward the edge of the pit, heading for a spot Galvez had noted earlier. Working together much like circus acrobats, the quintet struggled to boost each other up the near sheer sides of the rock wall. Legrasse took Angela's hand, helping her up to the first level of handholds. As his fingers closed around hers, their eyes met, a thousand questions flashing between them. For only a moment, they fell into each other's minds, electricity running from their hands to each other's brains and back again.

"*Ph'nglui fhtagn. Ph'nglui fhtagn. Guemglui fh'gah. Guemglui fh'gah. Cthulhu gib gib conna. Gib gib conna.*"

An ache crushed Legrasse's heart, squeezing his sides until the air within his lungs went hot. He wanted to kiss the woman so close, to crush her to him, could feel the fear and desire mingled in her touch. Instead he ground his teeth together and pushed her upward, clambering alongside and past his love to take the lead in their assault. At the same time a horrid shrieking crashed over the cultist's mournful chanting. Far in the background, it was a sound shrill and mindless, one that grew and faded in eerie rhythm with the Tcho-Tcho's clacking prayers.

"*Ph'nglui mglw'nafh Cthulhu R'lyeh wgah'nagl fhtagn.*"

Halfway up the side of the pit, Legrasse bent low, straining not to lose his handhold. Extending his free arm to its fullest, he grasped Leigh's outreaching hand and pulled him close.

"Can you tell how much time we have left?" he whispered.

"Two, three minutes," answered the apprentice quietly. "In a few more choruses the portal should begin to form. They'll want us directly after that."

"*Cthulhu, hecti gargah, aggli wgah'nagl. Cthulhu hecti, Cthulhu hecti. Wgah'nagl bid hecti.*"

Shifting his weight, ready to move upward again, the inspector asked, "How will we know when our time is up?"

A blinding purplish light, infused with streaking rivers of what might have been green and yellow bubbles, burst over the edge of the pit like syrup, flowing slowly, falling where it might.

"That's it," answered Leigh. "Time's up."

"*Ph'nglui mglw'nafh Cthulhu R'lyeh wgah'nagl fhtagn. Ph'nglui mglw'nafh Cthulhu R'lyeh wgah'nagl fhtagn.*"

With a Homeric effort, Legrasse pulled himself up over the edge of the pit from a fingertip handhold alone. Staring around, he saw scores of dwarf-like people, a deformed race possessed of twisted, stunted limbs and large, bulbous eyes. Their noses were flat, their nostrils wide and vibrating. The half-human creatures were kneeling in rows around the central mosaic, prostate before a shimmering disc hanging in the air over the transferal point. The disc was not a solid thing as the word was understood by Legrasse and his party. More it was an absence of reality, a boil of shining color that seemed to be sliding into the world from some beyond out of sync with anything the inspector could imagine.

Ignore the light, he told himself sternly. Turn away, get your job done—do your duty!

Turning back to the edge, Legrasse reached down as far as he could, grabbing Leigh's hand once more. Dragging him upward, he pulled the apprentice over the lip, immediately reaching back for Muller. And, while the inspector and Muller struggled to bring Angela and Galvez to the surface, Leigh drew out his star stone and began a chanting of his own.

"Get the sacrifices."

His partial understanding of the Tcho-Tcho tongue gave Legrasse the gist of the order given the cultists by the thing speaking through Carrinelle and Nardi. Pointing toward a section of wall that looked defensible, Legrasse told the others, "This is our moment, let's make the most of it."

As the five moved across the chamber, a great cry went up from the Tcho-Tchos sent to the pit to prepare the sacrifices. Muller took a dead aim, sending one of his precious bullets through the head of the cultist in the lead. Galvez followed suit, dropping another of the half-breed monstrosities.

"No!" screamed Nardi and Carrinelle in monotone tandem. "Take them, kill them! Kill them!"

Muller and Galvez continued to lay down a cool pattern of covering fire, each shot deliberate and calculated. Falling back on their old training, Galvez allowed Muller to empty his weapon first, then covered him while he reloaded. The men went about their killing with fearful professionalism, dropping some thirty of the cultists with but thirty-two shots. Not all those hit were slain, but they were out of the melee, which was good enough as far as the officers were concerned. Suddenly, however, the twin-voiced thing called back his minions. As Legrasse and the others hid behind their wall, searching desperately for some way to turn things in their favor, a new chanting went up from the remaining Tcho-Tchos.

"What're those heathen bastards up to now?"

"It's a summoning, Mr. Muller," answered Leigh. "They're calling something down to send against us."

"What?"

"I don't know ... I can't quite make out the ... something about 'that which protects Cthulhu's tomb' ... oh my God ..."

"What?" asked Legrasse again. "What is it?"

"They're calling down a Shoggoth."

"Can you do nothing?" asked Galvez, ready to grasp at any straws available.

"No. Not without ... we lost all our equipment—my books, my elixirs and powders ..."

Across the way, an acrid hissing filled the center of the room. In the middle of a great black cloud, a long, gelatinous shape began to form.

"What about your star sign necklace?" asked Angela.

"No good," answered Leigh in a frenzy. "Not by itself, it's not enough. If only ... *wait!*" The others jumped slightly at the young man's sudden shout. "Inspector, do you still have the amulet the Sherpa gave you?"

Not waiting for a reply, Leigh tore away at Legrasse's coat and shirt, digging down through the layers until his fingers brushed the jade disc. Ripping it away from the inspector's body, he shouted, "The Circles of Thaol! Yes!"

Across the chamber, the great black mass began to make its way toward the survivors. Stepping out from behind the wall, the apprentice held the two mystic symbols up, praying he could remember the necessary hand movements required for the incantation he was about to recite.

> *"Ya na kadishtu nilgh'ri stell-bsna Nyogtha;*
> *K'yarnak phlegesthor l'ebumna syha'h n'ghft.*
> *Ya hai kadishtu ep r'luh-eeh Nyogtha eeh,*
> *S'uhn-ngh athg li'hee orr'e syha'h."*

And, with the Vach-Viraj completed, suddenly the Shoggoth was stopped in its tracks. The massive, pulsating beast strained and bellowed, blowing acid-frosted steam through the great oozing vents covering its sides. But, no matter how hard it struggled, it could not free itself from the bind placed upon it.

"Now," shouted Legrasse. "We have to make the transference now!"

"I can't," answered Leigh in a desperate voice. "If I change my pose the Shoggoth will be freed. I have to stay here."

"The transference," asked Angela. "Isn't that what we're supposed to be stopping?"

"No," answered Legrasse. "Our own transference. I couldn't tell you anything before for fear of alerting our enemies through their Bla'raff spies."

Across the chamber, the twin-voiced horror raged in disbelief. Its frustration growing boundless, it called out to its minions, whipping them into a frenzy. From all about the hollow mountain, more of the Tcho-Tcho streamed forth, knives and bludgeons in hand. Leaping up and down, the leader massed them for a new assault.

"J. R.," said Galvez. "Randy's got a full cylinder. I'm down to two plugs. From the looks of things, that's about eighty bullets too few. You got any bright notions—this would be the time to share them."

Legrasse looked around the chamber, the fire and hope beginning to drain out of him. Everything had gone wrong. He had thought he had been clever, when in fact it had been he and his companions that had been used and manipulated all along. He stared at the circle of transference. Not quite forty yards away. If only they could reach it. If only—

Across the chamber, the reanimated corpses raised their arms in tandem. With a scream, the Tcho-Tcho charged.

"I thought I had a plan," Legrasse said simply, pulling his knife. "I guess ..."

And then, the inspector's words were cut off by a thunder of explosions from above. Eight of the cultists were thrown to the floor as a barrage of lead pellets tore through their bodies, splattering the floor with blood.

"Clutts!" screamed Legrasse.

Again and again the fat man fired, raining shotgun shells and machine gun fire down on the Tcho-Tcho. Laughing, pointing upward at the lone figure blasting away from the cavern's tunnel entrance, Galvez cried;

"You decoyed him!"

"Had to make you all think he was dead. Only way to fool the damn Bla'raffs. Told him to drop out when we got near the top and then follow along—just in case something happened to us."

"A good idea, chief," said Muller. "Maybe we shouldn't waste it."

Across the cavern, the Tcho-Tcho's had recovered from the surprise of Clutts' attack. Their forces divided, two columns rushed their targets anew.

Exhaustion tore at them all, nonetheless Legrasse readied his sap and knife, saying,

"Leigh, you hold the monster, I'll do the transference. All right, let's do it. Let's send them to Hell!"

A wave of cultists rushed their position. No longer worried about covering each other, Galvez and Muller stepped out first, blasting away the last of their ammunition. Then, the Tcho-Tcho were upon them. Knives flashed and clubs cracked. Muller hurled his empty weapon straight-arm into a cultist's face, tearing away one of the creature's eyes. Taught to handle a blade by her father at an early age, Angela danced between the Tcho-Tchos, slashing and stabbing, sending a half dozen to the ground with mortal wounds.

In the meantime, Legrasse kept only one eye on their enemy, his attention more aimed at finding a way to reach the transference point. Finally, the inspector saw the opening for which he was looking. Stepping over a fallen Tcho-Tcho, he readied himself for a run at the transfer site. But, just as he began to bring his leg forward over the body, the cultist reached up and grabbed onto him, holding him in place. Legrasse stomped on the man, but it was too late. Instantly he was surrounded by a quartet of cultists. The closest, a long and ugly blade to the ready, slashed forward, a perfect thrust aimed directly for the inspector's chest. A blur of motion appeared between the two men, and suddenly, the sword tore through Angela Buttacavala.

For a split second, time stopped around the two enemies. At first, neither knew what had happened. But then, as everything hung frozen about them, they saw the action replayed across their minds. Seeing the mortal blow about to be launched, Angela had acted without thought. As then did Legrasse.

With a roar torn from a time before written language or spoken words, the inspector reached out around the dying woman and grabbed up her murderer. Lifting the dwarf above his head, he hurled the creature across the chamber with unbelievable force, sending him into the depths of the still immobilized Shoggoth. As the half-breed began to dissolve on contact with the pulsating thing, Legrasse pulled the blade from his love's body and turned it on the remaining cultists. Hewing them without style or design, he waded into their midst, spilling their blood with mad abandon. Flecks of thick spittle slobbering from his mouth, he cut and hacked man after man, the carnage of his assault bloody beyond description.

And then, stepping to Leigh's side, he grabbed up the apprentice and with the last of his strength, hurled him across the chamber into the transfer point. Instantly the Shoggoth began to move forward. Legrasse fell to his knees, utter exhaustion slamming him against the horrid bone floor. Next to him he noticed Muller's body, its lifeless eyes staring at the ceiling. The Tcho-Tcho retreated as the Shoggoth slithered forward toward Legrasse and Galvez.

Inside the transfer point, Leigh struggled painfully to his feet. Fear and doubt clawing at him, still he forced himself erect. Then, raising his arms over his head, he pulled the energy of transference to himself and disappeared, only to be replaced by—

"Zarnak."

Legrasse hissed the single word with his waning strength. Bolts of mystic green energy boiled out of the doctor's hands, burning great holes in the Shoggoth's sides. Noticing that a number of the Tcho-Tcho had reached Clutts' position, the mystic sent a flash of emerald fire in their direction as well, searing the flesh from the cultists' bodies. Their target slumped to the ground in an awkward heap, but their was no time to attend him.

While Zarnak tore through the cultists, however, Legrasse managed to fumble his way to Angela's side. Finding her still breathing, blood leaking from her nostrils, trickling from her mouth, he cradled her in his arms.

"Why," he cried, great tears washing down from his heavy eyes. "Why?"

"I was told," the woman croaked painfully, "that we could afford none of the ... usual human luxuries—no compassion, no ethics, no *feelings* whatsoever."

Legrasse sobbed at the sound of his own words repeated to him, his mind breaking down in a chaotic jumble.

"We had a world to save, my love," she whispered. "My good, sweet John ..."

And then, her lips went cold, and the life was drained from her. How long Legrasse knelt holding her body, he did not know. Nor did he care. When finally a rough shaking of his shoulders snapped him back to reality, he found Zarnak and Galvez standing before him, Galvez holding up a terribly battered Clutts.

"We're all there is J. R.," said Galvez.

"We've routed the Tcho-Tcho," said the doctor. "But it's not over yet. R'lyeh has risen. Cthulhu is afoot."

"How?" croaked Legrasse. "There was no sacrifice."

"Your blood may not have been spilled, but plenty of other people's was. Think you such niceties matter to a god? Without the proper words, he's been slowed down, but he's here, awake and on the move. We've got to destroy the transfer point. Now!"

"How?" asked Legrasse weakly, the strength gone from him, his resolve evaporated.

"I brought the explosives through with me as planned. Your fellow here," Zarnak said, indicating Clutts, "has volunteered to stay behind and set them off."

"I'm finished, Legrasse," muttered the bloody Texan. "It don't matter. Nothin' ... nothin' for me back home."

"Nor me, either," answered the inspector. Rising to his feet, he grabbed hold of Clutts saying, "Not now."

And then, Legrasse dragged the fat man stumbling toward the transfer point. Throwing himself forward with all his remaining strength, the inspector pulled them both into the dimensional rift. Then, suspended in between a near infinite number of possibilities, Legrasse told himself—

Anything, anything can be done. As Leigh reached Castro's mind, so will I find my way into yours.

What? thought Clutts. What're you doin'?

With sudden fury, Legrasse forced his way into the Texan's self, shoving the fat man's consciousness aside with ruthless savagery. With nowhere else to go, Clutts' battered mind fled to the safety of the inspector's brain.

"There," muttered Legrasse. "Complete."

The two men stumbled out of the transfer point, both dazed and terribly weakened. Pushing his old body forward with Clutts' hands, Legrasse ordered;

"Take him! Go—do it. Now!"

Thousands of miles away, the waters of the Indian Ocean churned around the still settling obscenity of R'lyeh. Across the dripping mass's charnel shore, a titanic Thing slavered along, pursuing two helpless human forms.

In Tsang, Zarnak stared at Clutts' body. Not fooled by so clumsy a trick, he told Legrasse, "There is no time for this. What we must do must be done now."

"Then do it," came the inspector's simple response.

"I, I can't let you ... I don't deserve ..."

Legrasse moved Clutts' arm with his mind, holding the Texan's finger up in a silencing gesture.

"No, Mr. Clutts," said the inspector. "You have more than made up for your crime of passion. Go—live." Then, turning to Zarnak, he said, "Take them. Before it's too late."

The doctor nodded.

Off the coast of R'lyeh, great Cthulhu slid greasily into the water, heading toward the just turning yacht, *Alert*. Its engine set for full speed, a mighty eddying and foaming filled the noisome brine as the pursuing jelly rose above the unclean froth all about it.

In Tsang, Zarnak disappeared into the pulsating shimmer of the transfer point along with Galvez and the body of Legrasse. Carrying

Angela to where the doctor had left the explosives, the inspector used Clutts' over-sized hands to set the corpse gently down next to the main crate. Breaking open his sap, he salvaged the lighter from its center. In a matter of seconds he confirmed that all of the explosives had been wired together.

Far away, a horrid squid-like head broke the water, a terrible trio of eyes looking out over the world it would claim. Hundreds of feelers followed, rising above the tide, all of them different lengths and thicknesses, all of the writhing independently from each other.

Knelling next to Angela's body, Legrasse flipped open his lighter.

In the *Alert's* wheelhouse, a Norwegian named Johansen laughed with a lunatic's trill. His arms tight as poured steel, he held the wheel firm, plunging the yacht straight on toward the madness so fast approaching.

Legrasse bent low, warm lips touching cold as the smell of burning powder filled the air.

Then, a bursting—the slushing nastiness of a cloven sunfish, a mountain top torn asunder, the stench of a thousand opened graves, one last life extinguished in the never-ending battle, and slowly, the black Cyclopean towers began to slide back beneath the waves once more.

And thus did great Cthulhu returned to his brief nap, knowing all too well that there can be no death for that which can eternal lie.

ALSO AVAILABLE FROM MYTHOS BOOKS

WALTER C. DEBILL, JR.

THE BLACK SUTRA

Nineteen tales of terrors from prehistory
encroaching on the modern world
from Walter C. DeBill, Jr.

$20

THE LOVECRAFT CHRONICLES

PETER CANNON

From Peter Cannon, author of *Pulptime,*
Scream for Jeeves, and *Forever Azathoth and Other Horrors*
comes three new tales, alternate histories of the Old Gent.

$15

The Taint of Lovecraft

by Stanley C. Sargent
Robert M. Price, Editor

DH

The second collection from the author of *Ancient Exhumations,*
Stanley C. Sargent, with wonderful illustrations and
featuring his novella, *Nyarlatophis, a Fable of Ancient Egypt.*

$20

UNHOLY DIMENSIONS

JEFFREY THOMAS

Twenty-seven excursions into the Lovecraft Mythos
from the imagination of Jeffrey Thomas, author of
the highly acclaimed *Punktown* and Terror *Incognita*.
$20

Printed in the United States
32754LVS00005B/77